BOUND

HIGHGATE PREPARATORY ACADEMY
BOOK TWO

ROSA LEE

DIRTY LITTLE PUBLISHERS LTD

Copyright © 2024 by Rosa Lee

All rights reserved.

No part of this book may be reproduced in any form or by any electronic or mechanical means, including information storage and retrieval systems, without written permission from the author, except for the use of brief quotations in a book review.

Cover design provided by Jodilock Designs

BLURB

"I do."

Two words that taste bittersweet, their meaning conflicting within me. They roll off my tongue, tasting both right and wrong, as if the hand that gives also seeks to take away, uncaring and unapologetic.

Can I truly have it all? Can I keep them, these pieces of my heart?

Shakespeare knew true love's path is anything but smooth, especially when it collides with an unknown past, while our own demons threaten to consume us.

Questions multiply, each answer giving rise to more as history, that unpredictable force, repeats itself, and we are mere passengers on this wild ride.

Bound, the second book in the Highgate Preparatory Academy series, an electrifying contemporary romance where choices need not be made and our courageous heroine finds solace in multiple lovers. Swords clash, both figuratively and literally. If your heart yearns for broken, tantalisingly handsome men who thrive in darkness, a fierce young woman unafraid to wield colourful language, and intimate encounters that ignite your desires—each chapter ablaze with temptation—then Bound awaits.

***Warning: 18+ This book is a fast burn #whychoose romance so our leading lady won't have to choose and will end up with more than one lover. Please be aware that this is a dark contemporary romance with graphic scenes that some readers may find upsetting or triggering, so please read the author's note at the beginning. You will need to read Captured, Highgate Preparatory Academy Book 1 first. ***

Disclaimer: please note. Rosa Lee cannot be held responsible for the destruction of any panties, knickers, or underwear of any kind. She recommends that you take adequate precautions before reading Bound to avoid any sticky situations.

This book is dedicated to all the people who make grey sweatpants. I salute you.

Rosa Lee
Xxx

"Love to faults is always blind, always is to joy inclined. Lawless, winged, and unconfined, and breaks all chains from every mind."

— WILLIAM SHAKESPEARE

I love books with playlists and I listen to my compiled playlist as I'm writing. I've even based some scenes solely around one track, let me know if you guess which ones! And you'll see a lot of the music mentioned in the book itself.

Listen to the full playlist on Spotify HERE

Pillowtalk - Zayn
I want To - Rosenfeld
Hard to Love - Lee Brice
Sexual Healing - Azee
Bom Bidi Bom - Nick Jones, Nicki Minaj
Candyman - Christina Aguileria
I Feel Like I'm Drowning - Two Feet
Twisted - Two Feet
Slow Hands Acoustic - Niall Horan
Afterlife - Hailee Steinfeld
Bad Drugs - King Kavalier, CrisLee
Opus 38 - Dustin O'Halloran
I Love You - Jurrivh
Too Sad To Cry - Sasha Alex Sloan
Better - Khalid
Night Drive - HENRY
Birthday Sex - Jeremih

The Boy is Mine - Liv Lovelle
Carry You - Ruelle, Fleurie
Bad Child - Tones And I
Renegade (Slowed + Reverb) - Aaryan Shah
Sacrifice - Black Atla;;, Jessie Reyez
Him & I - G-Eazy, Halsey
A Thousand Years - The Piano Guys
Earned It Solo Piano - Stephan Moccio
If We Never Met - John K, Kelsea Ballerini
Die A Happy Man - Thomas Rhett
Unconditional - Aaron Smith
Young And Beautiful - Lana Del Ray
Steady Now - Nilu
Love is a Bitch - Two Feet
If You Let Me - Sinéad Harnett, GRADES
White Lies - Bolshiee
Church - Chase Atlantic
Nothin but a Monster - Ari Hicks
Earned It - The Weekend
Fuck You - Lily Allen

FOREWORD

Dear Reader,

Firstly, thank you so much for taking a chance on me and reading *Bound*. I hope you enjoy it!

Also, as you may already know that I am British and so *Bound* is written in a mix of British and American English. This has been done on purpose, to reflect the different characters and their cultures, so some words will be spelled differently throughout depending on who's speaking or thinking! If you see some unfamiliar words, know that they are there intentionally and I hope you enjoy discovering new phrases!

As mentioned in the blurb, *Bound* is a dark romance. There are many subjects explored that some readers may find disturbing.

For a full list of triggers please visit www.rosaleeauthor.com/trigger-warnings

Also a small word of caution. My books have a lot of BDSM vibes in them, and if they inspire you to dive into that kinky world, please do your research and educate yourself before trying out anything new for the first time. Take care my little smut bunnies!

CHAPTER ONE

LILLY

What was Mum doing in that picture? And why was it hanging in Loki's dad's office of all places?

The drive to the private airstrip is quiet, both myself and Loki lost in our thoughts as the scenery flashes past our window.

"Hey, Pretty Girl," Loki's familiar drawl washes over me like a gentle breeze, bringing me back to the present. "Penny for your thoughts?" he asks in a terrible British accent, and a groaning giggle escapes me as he takes my hand in his warm one, squeezing it. As always, butterflies dance in my stomach at his touch, my body heating at his nearness.

I stare into his beautiful emerald eyes, and although there's laughter there, there is also a genuine concern for my well-being, and it makes me love him that much more.

"I can't stop thinking about that picture, Loki," I confess, desperate for him to give me answers that I know he doesn't have, but I can't help voicing my worries anyway. "Why was she with all of your mothers? What was she doing at that Black Knight gala?"

He sighs, rubbing his fingers over my knuckles, soothing me with his gentle caress as he scoots closer. We're riding in style, in a black limousine with glasses of bubbling champagne sitting in door holders, and the soft sounds of *Sacrifice* by Black Atlas and Jessie Reyez, coming over the speakers.

"I don't know, Lilly. But Adrian went to Highgate, and you said he had friends here, so perhaps it was something to do with that?" He ends on a question, and although I wish otherwise, I know that he only knows as much as I do. I can feel a headache beginning to form behind my eyes, and I lower my head, rubbing my temple with my free hand.

I don't know why it's bothering me so much. It just doesn't feel right. Mum never told me that she spent any time here, even to visit Adrian. But, then again, she didn't tell me about Adrian either, so what the fuck do I know? A flash of anger towards her flares within me, my jaw clenching with the effort it takes not to lash out.

I'm unnerved by all the secrets, the lies. I didn't even know I had an uncle for fuck's sake! And when I think back on it, she told me nothing about her past, where she came from. About her family, *my* family. I had a right to know.

"Hey, where'd you go, baby?" Loki whispers as his other hand comes to my face, his fingers turning my head up and towards him so that I'm looking at his face once again. My fingers fall away from my temple, landing in my lap. His eyes soften at whatever he sees in mine. "Don't be pissed at her, Pretty Girl. I'm sure she had a good reason for not telling you about her past," he assures me gently.

"How do you know that?" I question, not even surprised anymore that he can read me so easily. For all of his carefree attitude, he's incredibly empathetic, especially where I'm concerned.

"Because she raised you, and I know that you would do anything to protect the ones that you love," he tells me, his fingers caressing the side of my face and causing my breath to hitch. One second, I am looking at the sweetest, most understandable man alive, and the next, a decidedly devious gleam enters his eyes.

"Loki..." I start to scold when he leans in, his luscious lips hovering over mine until I can taste him on my next inhale. And boy, do I take a deep breath of him, breathing in his taste of naughty deeds, and passionate kisses at sunset.

"What you need, Pretty Girl, is a distraction," he informs me, his mouth caressing mine in the barest of touches that sends tingles skittering all over my body, my nipples pebbling in my bra. I'm reminded of Halloween night, in the back of Jax's truck, my nerve endings stirring at the memory.

"Loki..." And I truly mean it to be another reprimand, but it comes out as a moan when the hand that is holding mine moves to my inner thigh, bringing both our fingers up to dance at the edge of my knicker line under the pinafore dress I foolishly chose to wear today. Talk about easy fucking access.

"Shhh..." he murmurs against my lips. "Stop thinking, and just feel, Lilly," he orders me in a husky tone.

"The driver, Loki," I manage to choke out as he brings our fingers underneath the silk, running them along my slit, which admittedly is already slick with arousal. A groan slips out of my lips, try as I might to hold it back, I can't. Not with him.

"Can't hear or see us, baby," he tells me, and I glance over to see that the blacked out divider is up. A second later, his hand leaves my jaw, and the music turns up, *PILLOWTALK* by Zayn blares over the speakers. "Now, spread those pretty thighs for me."

I whimper as I obey, helpless to resist. His breath hisses out between his teeth at the same time mine does when our fingers dip inside my inner lips and find me fucking soaked.

"Shit, Pretty Girl," he groans, slipping both of our middle fingers inside me, moving them in tandem, and rubbing at the rough spot inside that makes me squirm.

All thoughts fly out of my head as pure delicious pleasure ripples through me, my juices sliding down both our hands.

"Loki..." I moan, knowing that I sound like a broken record, but giving no shits as he picks up the pace. Zings of electricity shoot through me as we finger fuck my pussy in earnest, the wet sounds almost as loud as my moans, which are rivalling Zayn right now.

"That's it, come all over our fingers, baby. I want you to coat both our fucking hands with how hot I make you," he whispers huskily in my ear, then moves down to start sucking and nibbling my neck.

"Fuck!" I exclaim, the nails of my other hand digging into my palm as the crest crashes over me, dragging me with it, and obeying him to the letter as I cover both our hands in my liquid release.

"Fuck me. I need to be in you now, Pretty Girl," he groans, removing our hands and pushing me down so that I'm lying on the plush leather seat with him kneeling in between my spread thighs.

Looking down at me with hooded eyes, he unbuttons his jeans, his thick, pierced, rock-hard cock springing free unencumbered by any underwear, as is his preference. Taking out a condom packet from his back pocket—*this man is always prepared to fuck. Well, when he's fully awake that is*—he opens it, taking the rubber out and rolling it over his hard member. Her Vagisty clenches at the sight, desperate to have him fill us. *We agree on that, at least!*

He looks back up at me, a devilish smirk on his beautiful full lips as he grabs the leg that is pressed up against the seat, and places it over his shoulder, doing the same to the other one, making the skirt of my pinafore dress bunch around my waist.

Loki leans down so that I am basically folded in half—*yay for yoga!*—he moves the silk of my knickers aside, lining up his tip with my opening. He looks back up, captivating me with eyes full of emerald fire, as he slides torturously slowly inside me, making us both groan aloud with intense pleasure.

"Fucking hell, Pretty Girl," he groans, his hands coming up on either side of my face. "You feel so fucking good." Thrust. "Every." Thrust. "Damn." Thrust. "Time."

He moans, beginning to move in and out of me with a rhythmic undulation of his hips, lowering down onto his forearms, his lips hovering over mine. The deeper angle makes me gasp, my hands grasping his biceps as wave upon wave of sublime pleasure rolls over me. If fucking was an Olympic sport, Loki would win the gold every time.

I'm so wet that there's no resistance as he starts to thrust harder, driving into me, the sounds of our fucking competing with our moans and gasps.

"Loki...Fuck, Loki. I'm going to come," I rasp as I feel the burn of another orgasm start in my core. Loki moves his head, his lips next to my ear.

"That's it. Come all over my dick, baby," he growls out, pounding harder, and then biting my neck seconds later, triggering another release. Stars flash across my eyes, my body tightening around him as I self-combust with a husky yell, uncaring at this point if the driver hears us. He follows me into oblivion moments later, groaning out his own climax, buried to the hilt inside me.

He lets my legs down, not letting his cock slip out, placing gentle kisses on my neck, throat, and lips. We lie like that, rumpled and spent, for what feels like hours, but in reality can only be twenty minutes at most, until the car begins to slow down. Loki rolls up and out of me, kneeling and staring down at me, his expression one of pure male satisfaction.

"I must look like a hot fucking mess!" I laugh out, still feeling a little boneless, and not really that worried about my freshly fucked appearance.

"You look fucking hot, Pretty Girl," he says licking his lips. "I would fuck you again right now if we didn't have places to be."

Leaning back and opening one of the many compartments the limo has in its interior, he grabs out a warm damp cloth—*don't even ask why they have those in here, ignorance is bliss, my friends*—and reaches down between my legs, wiping it along my still sensitive folds. My breath hisses out at the contact, which only makes him chuckle. *Bastard.*

"We've arrived, sir," a male voice says over the speakers.

"Thanks, Tom," Loki replies, but there's a shit eating grin on his face as he holds my glower. It takes me a second to realise that he didn't move from his position kneeling above me. My eyes widen and he chuckles. "Whoops. Looks like I forgot to turn off the two-way speaker."

Fucking exhibitionist donkeycock ballbag!

I'm still grumbling at the wanker as we get out of the car once we've straightened our clothes, which just makes him laugh openly at me. Tom, our driver, holds the door open and the blush on his cheeks is nothing compared to mine, which feel like glowing red beacons. He's handsome for an older guy, his blond hair peppered with grey, as is the scruff covering his jaw, and bright blue eyes. Apparently, he's been a driver for Black Knight Corporation since the beginning, before even the guys were born.

"Thanks again, Tom." Loki chuckles like a cockgobbler, but I see him slip some folded bills into Tom's hand as he shakes it—*hopefully not with the fingers that were inside me!*

"No problem, sir," Tom replies in his gravelly voice. "I hope you have a nice trip, sir, miss," he tells us without looking at me, then closes the car door and heads to the boot to grab our bags.

"You're a shitstain, you know that?" I tell the naughty redhead next to me, looking up into his mischievous green eyes. He grins in response, no shits given, proving my words correct.

"You're late," I hear a smooth, low voice say, my head whipping round towards the sound as my heart flutters in my chest, like a bird trying to escape its cage.

My gaze drinks in the dark angel as he stalks towards us, from his custom-made shiny black shoes to his tailored black suit, complete with waistcoat and tie, with all that glorious ink peeking through at his neck and on the back of his hands. My whole body tingles as I take him in, as if for the first time, then in a sudden decisive moment, I rush towards him, throwing myself into his arms. He catches me, just like I know he always will, and pulls me into a tight embrace, engulfing me in his spicy ginger scent as he lifts me off my feet for a moment.

I breathe him in like he's my oxygen, sagging into him with weak knees as I wrap them around his waist.

"Hello, Princess," he says gruffly, and I tilt my face to look up into those swirling grey eyes of his, the hint of a soft smile on his plump lips.

His whole body relaxes around me, and I feel him take a deep inhale, as if it's the first proper breath he's taken in weeks.

"Hello, Ash," I whisper, swallowing, my throat tight with emotion. I've missed him, and the others, so fucking much.

I can't bear to be parted from them again. It feels as though pieces of me have been taken away, and I won't be whole until I get them back. We are all irrevocably bound, so intrinsic to one another that we can never be truly separated, and any physical distance hurts.

He leans his face down, his lips hovering over mine for an agonising second before he closes the distance, my feet settling back on the tarmac. One of his hands comes up to palm my cheek, tilting my head back further as he deepens his kiss, his tongue demanding entry. Ash tastes like moonless nights, and exquisite sin, like the darkest chocolate that at first is bitter, and only sweetens the longer you hold it on your tongue.

My own hands grip his lapels, uncaring if I crease them all to buggery, just needing him closer. Deeper.

A growl sounds in his throat when I nip his tongue, and he pulls away, sucking my bottom lip before he releases me from his thrall.

"You smell like sex, Lilly Darling," he tells me gruffly, his words falling over my lips and making me quiver. "You have two minutes to get on that plane, or I'm adding to the scent right here on the runway."

I take in a sharp breath, my thighs clenching as I pull back, looking into the swirling vortex of his eyes, seeing only primal need and truth there. He really will claim me like an animal for all to see if

I don't get a wriggle on. Her Vagisty practically drools at the idea, as if we weren't just satisfied twice. Yes, twice.

Greedy bitch!

"Hello, Lilly," I hear Kai's melodic voice sound behind Ash, and I tear my gaze away from Ash's to meet comforting honey brown eyes, although there's an edge of something in them that hasn't been there before.

"Kai!" I squeal, ripping out of Ash's grip, a snarl leaving his lips as I launch myself at Kai.

Luckily, he catches me too, folding me in a hug, nestling his face into my hair, and breathing me in deeply. My arms wrap around him, pulling him close so that no space is between us. We hold each other for a few moments, his scent of fresh woodland after the rain surrounding me, until the need to feel his lips against mine becomes overwhelming.

He must feel it the same time as I do, for his lips are suddenly on mine in a blistering kiss, full of desperation and white hot need. I meet him stroke for stroke, groaning when he grabs a fistful of my hair and tugs sharply.

Kissing Kai is like coming home, a taste of peaceful serenity coating my tongue, his domination grounding me.

We break away at the sound of a cough behind us, both of us panting and unable to look away from one another.

"We should get on board," Ash tells us, and even though I know he's not being an arsehole, Kai actually growls at him. "We can resume this once we're in the air," Ash snaps in response.

Well, looks like the alphas have come out to play.

Kai wraps his arm around my shoulders and leads me towards the stairs that lead up to the door of the plane. He helps me up them, my heels clattering against the metal.

Stepping inside, my steps falter, and I gasp, my eyes going wide.

Jesus fucking Christ on a cracker!

This place looks nothing like a plane on the inside. There's not a straight line to be seen, with curved seating leading to a curved bar against the front of the plane. There's a door to one side that I assume leads to the captain's cabin. I turn my head to look in the other direction, and see that there's a partial wall in the middle, with cut out panels that have what looks like bubbles floating in tanks set into them. Everything is in soft grey and turquoise, and there is a light fixture that looks like a constellation in the ceiling. The small windows are all running along the sides of the plane, letting in winter sunshine and making everything glow.

"Come on, Pretty Girl," Loki says as he brushes past me, grabbing my hand and pulling me away from Kai. *See, shithead behaviour right there.* "Let's give you the grand tour."

He leads me towards the bubble wall, and I see that there are wooden panels on either side, jutting out of the plane's interior sides. They're set back so that when you look head-on, it looks like a solid wall, and what's behind is not immediately obvious. We walk through the gap, and I stop dead in my tracks.

Before me is a full size super king bed. Complete with crisp white bedding and turquoise scatter cushions.

"This is the most important part of the tour," Loki whispers in my ear from behind, having taken advantage of my stupor to press himself to my back, pulling me to his chest. I see the others come up either side of us in my peripheral vision, their footsteps silent on the thickly carpeted floor.

I shiver as Loki licks up the edge of my ear, undoing the zip on the side of my dress. Ash steps in front of me, my eyes landing on his silver hungry ones, my breath stilling in my lungs at the intensity. He reaches up with long fingers, loosening the buckles of my shoulder straps and pushing them down my arms. Loki pushes the dress the rest of the way off, letting it fall to my heeled feet. Leaving me in my T-shirt, silk knickers, stockings and heels.

I look down as I feel hands running up my stockinged legs to see Kai on his knees, the others having successfully preoccupied me up until this point. I'm momentarily distracted when hands grasp my T-shirt and start pulling it upwards, my arms lifting as they pull it over my head. I feel the tug of my damp silk knickers and look back down again to see Kai pulling them down my legs, helping to guide my still heeled clad feet out of them.

There's a breath of cold air against my back, then the sounds of *Feel It* by Michael Morrone starts to play over speakers. Seconds later, Loki's warmth is back, his hands sending cascades of shudders flying across my skin, his fingers tickling up my sides until they reach my bra line. Moving to the back, he easily unhooks it, Ash helping to guide the straps down my arms, looking directly into my eyes.

I feel like I'm on fire, having their hands on me all at the same time, building something within me that's desperate for release.

"We're ready for takeoff, sir," a female voice sounds from the other side of the bubble wall behind us. I freeze, my heart thudding as if I've been caught doing something naughty, appalled that I didn't even hear her approach.

Well, if the shoe fits, Lilly...

"Excellent, Alisha. See that we're not disturbed," Ash tells her, not taking his stare from mine.

"S–shouldn't we, like, buckle up or something?" I ask, a full body shiver taking over me as Ash's fingers graze the side of my breast at the same time that Kai's tickle my inner thigh and Loki's pushes my hair to one side, his lips teasing my neck. A moan escapes my lips, my own fingers flexing at my sides with the exquisite sensations rolling over me.

Ash smirks as I feel the plane begin to move.

"Rules are made to be broken, Princess."

Loki's hands come to steady my hips, gripping tightly as the plane begins to tilt upwards, my heart beating wildly in my chest at the thought of not following the rules. *Shit, I'm sure it's the law.* His mouth fastens onto the base of my neck, and I moan again loudly when he starts to suck, no doubt leaving a hickey, all thoughts of seat belts literally flying from my mind. A hot tongue runs along my slit, Kai's mouth sealing over my clit and mimicking Loki's sucking. My knees buckle, and I would have fallen if Loki didn't have such a tight grip on me.

"S–shit..." I gasp, my palms alighting on Kai's head, gripping his soft hair in my fingers and pulling him closer. A soft, satisfied grunt feathers over my cunt, making me tingle even more.

"Open your eyes, Princess," Ash commands, the plane tilting further, but I almost don't notice the movement, lost as I am to what Loki and Kai's mouths are doing to me.

I do as he directs, seeing him bring up his thumb and placing it against my lips.

"Suck," he orders, pushing the digit into my mouth. "It'll help stop your ears popping," he tells me, a devilish grin on his face that turns heated as I suck his thumb deeper, swirling my tongue around it.

He brings my own thumb up to his lips, kissing the tip before taking it into his mouth and copying my movements.

Fucking hell.

Shockwaves of electric pleasure zing from my neck, clit, and thumb until I feel like I'm a ball of energy, pulsing and sparking, ready to electrocute everyone on this damn aircraft. As the plane starts to even out, Kai chooses that moment to push two fingers inside me, crooking them to rub against my G-spot.

I cry out, letting go of Ash's thumb as I fracture into a thousand pieces, liquid rushing out of my lower lips, which Kai drinks up like it's the finest wine. My free hand grasps Ash's forearm, my nails digging into his suit clad forearms as I come all over his friend's face.

I stand there, shuddering and twitching, my eyes closed, whilst I come down from the Heavens.

"Good girl," Ash huskily whispers, having let my thumb drop from his mouth. I crack my eyes when he steps away, and see him take off his tie. "Hands out, Princess."

"W–what?" I question, still lost in my orgasm high, my voice coming out a little rough.

A sharp tap lands across my pussy, making me gasp in pain and pleasure, my thighs instinctively clenching. I look down, and Kai is resting back on his heels, a hard look in his eyes, his hand hovering over my dripping cunt.

Sir is in the room, I see.

"You were not given permission to speak or question our orders," he tells me sharply, his voice threaded through with heated disapproval. "Now, apologise to Ash, and do as he says."

I look back up into Ash's smug face, waiting until his eyes narrow, knowing that he loves the brat in me. I think I may push it today.

"Make me," I challenge, raising a brow and tilting my head, my own smirk tugging my lips up.

CHAPTER TWO

LILLY

Ash's nostrils flare, but excitement lights a fire in his eyes as he roughly grabs my wrists, bringing them in front of me lightning fast, and tying them together with his tie in one of his signature complicated knots. It's so quick that I don't have time to argue, let alone stop him. Okay, who am I kidding? I don't exactly try to stop him either.

Yanking me so hard that I stumble in my heels, he sits on the end of the bed and pulls me down so that I'm lying across his knees, my bare arse in the air, my bound hands hanging down in front of me. His suit trousers are of the finest quality fabric, but even so, they chafe my sensitised nipples as I squirm against his hold.

My face heats with a mixture of anger and lust as he strokes and caresses my backside.

"Naughty, disobedient princesses are taught their manners when they forget them," he tells me, his voice a husky growl, threaded with arousal that sends a shudder running through my body, ending at my pulsing mound. "And how to follow orders."

His hand leaves my rear, and I look to the side to see Kai and Loki standing there, hunger written across their faces, their eyes devouring my submissive position. Both boys have tented trousers, their hands held rigidly at their sides, fists clenched.

Loki uncurls one fist, taking his phone out of his pocket, his eyes lowering as his fingers fly over the screen. *Do I Wanna Know?* by the Arctic Monkeys comes over the speakers, the beat resounding in the pit of my stomach.

Suddenly, a loud crack sounds in the room, and I gasp at the sharp pain that spreads across my lower left cheek. I squirm in Ash's lap, my nails digging into my palms as desire starts to replace the anger within me, although not fully.

Another hit lands on the right globe, and this time, I almost rise to meet it, relishing in the pleasure-pain that it gives me. A third punishing smack makes my arse cheeks burn, and I moan, hanging my head, heady acceptance flooding my veins as I give myself over to the punishment.

I'm panting, my heart racing in time to the beat of the song as Ash continues his assault on my arse, his palm landing time and time again until my buttocks are burning and throbbing, and my cheeks are wet with tears.

His hand stills, after more hits than I could count, resting on my hot smarting backside.

"Ready to apologise, Princess?" he asks in a rasping voice. He's breathing hard, and the evidence of his arousal is pressing against my waist. I'd be lying if I said that it didn't make me even wetter, moisture dripping between my thighs.

I hope it stains his trousers.

Guess he didn't quite beat the brat out of me. But then again, that's our game. He enjoys the challenge as much as I do.

"I–I'm sorry, sir," I gasp out, my voice croaky.

"Good girl," he replies, eliciting a hiss from my lips as he caresses my tender behind. "I'm glad to see that you've learnt your lesson well, Princess. Loki, Kai," he says gruffly, and the snick of a drawer opening soon follows after his words.

"You took that so beautifully, Lilly," I hear Kai say in my ear, a touch of awe in his tone. He brushes my sweaty hair aside, and I raise my head slightly to look at him. "Drink, my darling," he instructs caringly, holding a glass of iced water with a metal straw in it. He brings the straw to my lips, and I sigh as the cold water hits my mouth. I hadn't realised how thirsty I was.

"You're such a good girl, Princess," Ash praises. "I'm just going to put some Arnica gel on you, then you can have your treat, okay?" he asks.

"Yes, sir," I whisper once Kai takes the glass away, placing a brief kiss on my lips and brushing the tears from my cheeks away with a cloth napkin. I hiss when the cool gel hits my overheated skin, sighing as Ash rubs it in, the throbbing immediately dulling.

"You look so beautiful, Pretty Girl," Loki tells me, and I turn my head to see him ravenously staring at Ash's hand, which has stilled on my arse, his erection straining against his jeans.

"All done, Princess," Ash informs me, with one last caress. "Now, get your feet under you, and we'll help you up.

I awkwardly obey, managing to get to my feet with their help, and swaying slightly with my hands still tied in front of me. I'm standing before Ash, who's sitting with his knees wide, a small space between us.

"What's my treat?" I ask him, and a jet black brow lifts, even as he smirks. "Sir."

His grin turns feline as he gets up, shrugging his jacket off, then starts to unbutton his cufflinks, diamonds glinting in them of course, all while looking me in the eye. I can't resist looking down as he exposes his forearms, and my breath hitches at the sight of his inked flesh against the crisp white shirt. *Why are guys' forearms so fucking sexy?*

"The boys will show our appreciation at the same time, Princess. You can handle them, can't you?" he questions me, a twinkle in his grey eyes. I'm reminded of the time in Loki's house, by the pool, when I told him that I could handle them all.

"Yes, sir," I say, willing to tone the brat down to get what I'm hoping he's offering. Kai and Loki inside me at the same time. For a second I wonder why not Ash too, he's yet to join in a threesome, yet I know he enjoys watching and ordering us around. Although this will be Kai's first multiplayer—*snort*—event too...

"Such a beautiful, good, Pretty Girl," Loki murmurs behind me, and I take my eyes off Ash, my thoughts distracted, to see that he and Kai are both stripping.

My breath comes in a sharp inhale as I look my fill. The sight of them, their glorious bodies coming onto display. These guys, my guys, are so stunningly gorgeous it hurts. And I still can't believe that they're all mine. I lick my lips as sweet anticipation trickles through my centre.

"*Our* beautiful, good girl," Kai whispers, stepping up to me, naked and hard. He cups my face in his palms, leans in, and presses his lips to mine in a gentle, worshipping kind of kiss that leaves my toes tingling.

I give in to him freely, opening up fully as I'm caged in his embrace, my hands trapped between us. He breaks the kiss, rubbing his nose against mine in such a sweet gesture, that a lump forms in my throat.

"I'm so glad to be with you again, Lilly," he reverently confesses against my lips.

"Me too, Kai," I choke out.

"Get on the bed, Princess," I hear Ash say from across the room after a moment. My head snaps in his direction; he's lounging on a white leather swivel chair, facing the bed. *All the better to direct us, I guess.* Though, a pang runs through me at the thought that he won't be joining in.

Kai lets his hands drop away, and I turn to see that Loki is lying naked on the bed, propped up on his elbows, his dick hard and already rubbered up lying against his firm abs, the piercing glinting in the light.

"Come ride me, Pretty Girl," Loki says with a lopsided grin, folding his hands behind his head. "And leave your heels on."

I huff a laugh, Loki really has a thing for fucking me in heels. I mean, these are gorgeous glitter mermaid rainbow shoes, so I can't blame him.

Swaying over to the bottom of the bed, my butt is still smarting but the rush of arousal that floods my body is helping to mask the ache, alongside the soothing gel. I crawl up the bed on my knees, my hands held in front of me, making me a little wobbly as I position myself so that my thighs are on either side of his hips.

"God, I love it when you're on top, baby," Loki groans, one of his hands coming to my hip, the other holding his erect cock up, helping guide me down onto his shaft.

We both moan when my opening is flush with his pelvis, his dick buried deep inside me and feeling fan-fucking-tastic. He was right earlier; it feels incredible every damn time!

"Jesus fucking Christ," Loki hisses out when I start to move my hips, both of his hands now on my hip bones, his fingers gripping me tightly, indenting my soft flesh.

The song changes to *I Want To*, by Rosenfield, and I gyrate my hips to the rhythm, rising up and sinking down, riding him like he commanded, my tied hands resting on his tight abs for balance. The pleasure is exquisite, almost unbearably so, combining with my throbbing rear to send sweet tendrils of pleasure-pain skittering across my whole body.

The bed dips behind me, and my movements falter. Turning my head, I look over my shoulder to see Kai kneeling on the end, lubing up his hard pierced dick, and my breath stutters, my pussy clenching around Loki, leaving him groaning.

"Bend forward, Princess, and let Kai fuck that pretty asshole of yours," Ash orders gruffly, and I obey without question, Loki helping me as my bound hands make it tricky.

I'm desperate to feel Kai's fully pierced member inside me along with Loki's. My hardened nipples brush Loki's chest, sending a shiver over my skin, adding to the hypersensitivity that I'm feeling. Loki's hands move to the globes of my arse, and I gasp sharply as he grabs them none too gently and spreads them wide for Kai.

"Shhhh," he hushes in my ear when I squirm against him, my arms above his head as I simultaneously try to escape the biting sting, and push into it. "I just need to open you up nice and wide for Kai's hard dick."

A gasp escapes my lips at his words, a sharp inhale leaving me as I feel a cold dollop of lube run down my crack, followed by a deep moan when Kai's thumb starts rubbing it around my puckered hole.

"Kai!" I hiss when he pushes the digit in, feeling a delicious fullness as he starts to pump it in and out of me.

Shudders rack my body as the heady sensation sweeps through me, and I can't help rocking and clenching around Loki, causing deep groans to leave his plush lips.

"Kai, please," I beg, needing more. I need him inside me too.

He's obviously in a forgiving mood, ignoring my lack of addressing him as 'sir,' because he pulls his thumb out and replaces it with the tip of his hard length. I look under one arm to see his knees on either side of Loki's thigh as he presses forward.

"That's it, Lilly. Relax for me, darling," he coos as he pushes in, the piercings on the underside of his cock eliciting desperate animalistic noises from my throat.

"Fuck, dude," Loki moans as Kai keeps thrusting forward until his hips are flush with my arse cheeks. "I can see the appeal of all that metal."

I'm shaking and panting like a fucking dog at how full I now feel. Having the two of them, both with piercings in their dicks, is overwhelming to say the least. Kai gives me no chance to adjust as he starts pounding hard into my arse, Loki following from underneath, until they are both fucking me so hard, with alternating thrusts, that the slaps of our bodies can be heard over the music.

"Oh god, oh god, oh god..." I moan loudly, uncaring if the fucking pilot can hear me, as wave upon wave of pleasure rips though my entire body.

Suddenly, Kai leans forward, grabbing my bound wrists and pulling me sharply. He brings them above my head, holding them so my elbows are bent and my hands are behind my head. My back is arched almost uncomfortably as he continues his hard, frantic thrusts.

"Fuck, Kai," I cry out, just as Loki, clearly feeling left out, starts to rub and pinch my clit, making me fucking squirm. "Loki..." I pant, feeling the delicious burn of another orgasm building in my core.

"That's it, Pretty Girl. Come all over us," Loki orders, and I'm helpless to disobey when his other hand leaves my hips and slaps my breasts hard, the sound as loud as the noise of our pelvises rocking together.

I scream as I tumble into Wonderland, flashes of bright light blinding me as I climax all over them. My body goes boneless, the guys using me for their own pleasure, seeking their own release, which they achieve one after the other, growling as they come.

After a few minutes of tranquil oblivion, there's a tug at my wrists; Kai loosening the tie. My hands fall into my lap, unable to hold them up, I'm that fucked out.

I whimper when Kai pulls out, feeling his cum seep out of my back hole and slide down my arse crack, shuddering and causing Loki to groan below me when my inner walls clench around him.

"Let's get cleaned up, sweetheart," Kai offers, holding his hand out for me to take.

I grasp it, getting up on shaking legs. He pulls me to him, his arms wrapping round my waist, and my own settling round his neck. Lowering his lips, he kisses me affectionately, setting my body tingling all over again.

"I love you, Lilly Darling," he whispers on an exhale, and a smile tugs at my lips.

"I love you, Kai Matthews," I tell him back, my fingers playing with the hair at the back of his neck, warmth suffusing my whole body at his words.

Sighing in contentment, he turns, keeping one arm round me as he leads me to the side of the bed. What I thought was wood panelling to either side, turns out to be more partial walls, and there's a full on shower room behind the bedroom, complete with a large shower, sink with vanity, and full length mirror on the back of the wall that the bed rests against.

"There is a toilet behind that door," he tells me, letting me go and walking over to the shower, opening the glass door and turning it on.

I head to the loo, taking care of business, then step out to find him already in the shower alongside Loki. I stand there, dumbstruck, watching as they soap themselves up under the spray. *Too fucking hot! How's a girl meant to function?*

"You gonna keep staring like a pervert, Pretty Girl, or are you hopping in?" Loki teases with a smirk.

I roll my eyes at him, walk towards the shower and join them, closing my eyes and letting the hot water run over my body and relax my muscles. Soapy hands caress the front of my body, washing me, and a sigh falls from my lips at the soothing touch.

"Can I ask you guys a question?" I say, my eyes still closed as it's the only way I'll feel brave enough to ask. A second pair of hands joins the first, washing my back. My nipples pebble under their ministrations.

"You just did, baby," Loki tells me. *Shithead.*

"Fuck off, Loki," I sass back, cracking my eyes to glare at him, then closing them again.

"Ask your question, Lilly," Kai offers over my shoulder. I take a deep breath.

"Would you two, ever, you know, be up for some...sword crossing. Outside of my body that is."

Both sets of hands still, and I hold my breath, desperate to see their faces but a little afraid too.

"Open your eyes, Pretty Girl," Loki commands gently, and I do as he says. His smile is gentle, but also lascivious at the same time. "Would that turn you on? To see me with Kai's cock up my ass? Or mine in his mouth?"

My breath stutters, my eyes widening at the mental image that gives me.

He chuckles. "I guess that gives me your answer," he says, his hand tightening its grip on my waist. "You up for a bit of experimentation, bro?" he asks Kai over my shoulder, and I turn my head to look back at him.

Kai's eyes are serious, considering. There's darkness in their depths that's not all heat. It makes my brows dip in worry.

"Kai? It's okay if you're not, truly," I assure him, turning to face him fully and stroking my arm down his.

"I'm not sure about anal, but maybe other stuff. I think I'd like to be top, though," he tells us honestly, looking between Loki and I.

"We can work with that, can't we, Pretty Girl?" Loki states, his hand dipping in between my still tender arse cheeks. "I'm up for your dick in my chocolate starfish."

"Loki!" I chastise, my nose wrinkling as my head whips round.

"What? Would you prefer my ham flower? Or maybe the Hershey highway? The brown puckered eye?"

Tears of laughter are streaming down my face, even as I cringe, and I look to Kai, finding him in a similar state, the darkness of moments ago gone, as he laughs at his friend.

"I can't even with you, Loki," I tell him in between gasps as I step out of the shower and reach for a towel.

"What about Gary?" he asks, and even he can't hold back the chuckles.

And now, I'm officially dead.

CHAPTER THREE

LILLY

Once I've gotten over the fact that Loki just called his arsehole Gary—*fucking snort*—I get dressed in some navy lacy French knickers, soft colourful harem pants, and a dark red vest top sans bra. Luckily for me, Tom brought in my hand luggage whilst we were otherwise—*ahem*—occupied, and I'd packed some comfy flight clothes knowing that we'll be in the air for over eighteen hours.

I walk out of the bedroom to find Ash lounging on one of the curved sofa type seats, a drink, whisky on the rocks by the look of it, in his hand.

"Better, Princess?" he asks with an indulgent smile, and I sit right next to him, snuggling under his arm, and feeling all kinds of languid from my many orgasms.

"So much better," I tell him, sighing and wrapping my arm around his chest. He has also changed into something more casual; soft grey linen trousers, a white linen shirt, sleeves rolled to the elbow, and black flip-flops that showcase his beautiful inked feet. "I missed you, Vanderbilt."

He pulls me in closer, his arm around my shoulders, and I take in a deep inhale of that spicy scent that is all Ash.

"I missed you too, Princess," he whispers, placing a gentle kiss on the top of my head.

"You didn't..." I start, trying to tread carefully with what I'm about to say. "That is, I didn't get any texts from you?"

I feel him stiffen ever so slightly underneath me, but as I make a move to sit up so that I can look into his eyes, he holds me tighter to him.

"Rubber duck was not needed," he tells me in a low voice, and I exhale a long breath at his words, grateful that he didn't feel the need to cut himself whilst back at home.

Just then, what I assume is Alisha, walks over in stiletto heels and a navy flight attendant uniform. She's an attractive blonde with a perfect hourglass figure, sparkling blue eyes, and plush lips. Someone who looked like her would have intimidated me previously, leaving me feeling inadequate. But not so much anymore. She's carrying a tray of drinks, ice clinking in the glasses, looking at us with a broad smile and not spilling a single drop.

"Here you are, Mr. Vanderbilt," she says, setting the drinks aside on a low table in front of us, and giving me a quick glance.

"Thank you, Alisha," Ash replies. "May I introduce Lilly Darling," he says, not moving his arm, clearly staking his claim.

"Pleased to meet you, Ms. Darling," she says, her American accent husky as she gives me a quick smile, a slight blush stealing over her cheeks.

"You too, Alisha," I respond, feeling my own face heat with embarrassment.

"Will that be everything, sir?" she asks, turning to face Ash, being the consummate professional that she is, and not acknowledging the DP that went on earlier, which she clearly heard.

"Just dinner in about an hour, please," Ash replies in a business-like tone, and I get a flash of the man he is becoming, a leader of a multibillion dollar corporation.

"Of course," she says and walks away.

I groan, slapping my palm to my forehead once she closes the door to presumably the cockpit. Ash just chuckles, the muff tickler.

We hear Loki and Kai laughing as they walk in, Loki's gaze zeroing in on me snuggled next to Ash, and then the drinks.

"Perfect. Fucking always makes me thirsty," he claims, reaching over and grabbing his bourbon whilst passing me a fruity looking cocktail. *Yum!*

Kai grabs his wine glass, which is filled with clear liquid.

"What's that you're drinking, Kai?" I ask, curious.

"It's Yaegaki Mu, a junmai daiginjo sake," he tells me as he takes a seat opposite us, next to Loki. He takes a small sip, savouring the flavour and heaving a contented sigh as he swallows.

"I thought sake was served warm?" I enquire, taking a sip of my own drink, the tart raspberry bursting on my tongue as I watch him swirl the liquid round in the glass.

"This is a premium quality sake, and it's best to serve it chilled like a white wine. Regular sake is served warm to uncover the flavours in less complex brews."

Learn something new every day!

"So, are there any pharmacies where we land?" Loki interrupts, and I choke a little on a sip of my raspberry cocktail. Fuck, I'd forgotten all about that, what with the picture of Mum, and the sex.

"Why?" Ash questions, his voice containing a hint of warning that makes me sit up a little.

Loki's face flushes, one of his hands rubbing the back of his neck.

"I need to get Lilly the morning after pill," he admits, almost cringing.

Before I can even blink, Ash is launching himself across the small table, and I hear the thud of a fist hitting flesh followed by a groan of pain.

"Ash! What the fuck!" I shout, leaping up, setting my drink on a side table to rush over to Loki, who looks like he didn't even defend himself.

As I reach him, Loki makes another grunting sound as Kai's fist connects with his ribs.

"Kai!" I scold, seeing Kai pull his fist back and pick up his glass, taking a large sip. His face is set in a scowl, glaring at Loki.

"When did this happen? Why the fuck didn't you wrap up?" Ash practically roars in Loki's face, his chest heaving and his hands clenched into fists at his sides. Loki just sits there, looking ashamed, his lip starting to swell and bleed. I sit down next to him, turning to glare at Ash.

"Hey, it's not just his fault. It takes two to tango, cunt whiskers," I snark at Ash, and his lips twitch slightly at the insult, although he's clearly still pissed as all hell, his cheeks flushed and his nostrils flaring.

"It was Christmas morning and I fucked up. I'm sorry, okay?" Loki tells them, his hand running through his hair and not looking at me.

"Hey, it'll be fine, Loki. We'll grab a pill, and it'll all be gravy," I try to assure him, placing my palm gently on his cheek, and turning his head to face me. I wince at his split lip, grabbing one of the napkins that Alisha left to dab at the blood trickling from it.

"Well, by the time we get to Bali, that'll be over forty-eight hours. The morning after pill becomes less effective the longer you wait, going down to around fifty-eight percent chance of success," he tells us, his fingers dancing over the screen of his phone.

Ash growls and looks like he's about to hit Loki again.

"Fucking cool it, Vanderbilt," I tell him firmly, narrowing my eyes. "It'll be fine. Chances are I'm not in that part of my cycle anyway."

"Where are you in your cycle, Lilly?" Kai asks with no hesitation, looking up at me.

"Fuck's sake, Kai! I don't know." I can feel the blush returning to my cheeks, which is ridiculous given that he was in my arsehole less than an hour ago. *Fucking stupid patriarchial society making women feel embarrassed about periods.* "It can be a bit random, and I don't really check, so..." I trail off.

"Well, I've got someone meeting us when we land with the pill, so let's hope it works," he says gently, then turns to glare at Loki.

Desperate for a subject change before it turns violent again, I blurt the first thing that comes into my head. "So, there was a photo of my mum, with all of yours in Loki's dad's office."

Really?! That's what you choose to go with? FML.

"What?" Ash yells, grabbing my hand and pulling me away from Loki, dragging me back to the sofa opposite like some cave dwelling Neanderthal. Or, like Loki can't be trusted not to try and impregnate me. *Sigh.*

"Yeah, Lilly's mom was standing with all of ours, at some Black Knight Gala or some shit," Loki tells him, taking a sip from his glass which he somehow managed to keep from spilling when Ash punched him.

He pulls his phone from his pocket, scrolling a bit, and then leans over to hand it to Ash. On the screen is the picture. Mum's dressed up in a midnight blue beaded evening dress, holding a champagne flute and smiling for the camera, surrounded by four other women, all in similar states like that of my mum.

My gaze flits back to my mum, who looks so young but no less beautiful than when I knew her. As I stare at the photograph, I can't help feeling that although she looks happy and is smiling, there was something that was not quite right. Maybe it was because of the tightness around her eyes, and the death grip she has on the glass in her hand.

"Did she ever mention Highgate, Princess?" Ash asks me, handing the phone back to Loki, then pulling me in close again and tucking me under his arm.

"No," I reply, frowning. "But she didn't tell me about my uncle either, so..." I trail off, still feeling hurt at the things that she withheld from me, a painful tightness in my throat.

"Your uncle came to Highgate, didn't he, Lilly?" Kai inquires, rubbing his chin as he looks at me.

"Yes, he did."

"So, maybe she was just visiting him?" Loki suggests, taking another sip of his drink and wincing when it hits his split lip. "He was in our parent's class, wasn't he?"

"I think so, although I don't think he's ever mentioned them, or anything really," I tell them, pursing my lips in thought.

"Well, it's probably that then," Ash says, not sounding convinced at all, and when I look up at him, his own brows are dipped, and he's sharing a look with the others.

"What?" I question, sitting up so that I can see him fully, his arm dropping from around my shoulders. "You think that it doesn't quite add up?"

"I just don't trust my dad, or any of the board, as far as I could throw them," Ash tells me, reaching out to brush some hair out of my face. "And your safety and well-being are my top priority. *Our* top priority."

He leans in and places a gentle kiss on my lips, leaving me feeling all fuzzy and tingling whilst helping to lessen the unease that I was starting to feel. It doesn't disappear completely, though, and I can't help wondering what else my mother has kept from me.

The rest of the journey is pretty uneventful. We have some dinner; steak cooked medium rare, small buttered potatoes, and a colourful salad. Don't ask me how we got this on a plane, apparently, it's what you get for being rich bastards.

After dinner, I take a long nap with Ash once he's made me explode several times on his tongue and fingers. I fall asleep, exhausted before I can return the favour.

We land some hours later, although because of the time difference, it's only eight in the evening, which is all kinds of mindfuckery. Feeling slightly discombobulated, we exit the jet to find a car waiting for us on the tarmac. It's another black limousine with a smartly dressed Balinese guy, who looks about our age, waiting by the open door.

"Good evening, sirs, miss. Welcome back," he greets us, his speech slightly accented as he puts his hands in a prayer position and gives us a shallow bow, then straightens up. All the guys follow suit, bowing, so I do the same. "Your package is in the back, Master Matthews."

"Thank you, Nengah," Kai responds with a smile, indicating with a hand that I get in first.

I smile at Nengah, then climb in the back. The boys follow me in, and soon we're on our way. Kai hands me a paper bag, and I open it to find a box. Opening that, I find a single white tablet inside. The morning after pill. My heart does a little flip, which is stupid because there is nothing to worry about either way. He hands me a bottle of water.

"Thanks." I smile tightly at him, aware of three pairs of eyes on me as I pop the pill on my tongue and take a mouthful of water, swallowing it down. "So, when do we see Jax?" I ask them, wanting to move on from that shitstorm.

"We're headed to the port now, and from there we'll take the yacht to Cempedak Island, which should take just over an hour," Ash informs me, looking down at his phone briefly. *Of course they have a fucking yacht.*

The car journey feels like it whizzes by, and takes an age at the same time. I'm so excited to see Jax, to have all my boys together with me again. It feels so wrong to be apart from any of them. Anxious butterflies flutter around my stomach. I'm worried about how we'll find him. What state he'll be in, and how he's coping with his withdrawal. I know there will be side effects from the withdrawal, that he may be suffering from all sorts of things, but I'm desperate to see that he's okay. That's he's still my He-Man.

By the time we reach the port, I'm practically vibrating, much to the irritation of Ash.

"Bouncing in your seat won't get you there any faster, Princess," he comments, looking at me with slightly narrowed eyes, his tone surly and sounding a tad jealous as he waits for Nengah to open the door.

"Don't be a dick just because you've got blue balls, Ash," Loki teases, earning a whack in the chest from the Ice Knight himself.

"I can sort those out for you on the boat, if you like?" I offer, my voice dropping huskily without conscious thought, and his frown lessens slightly. That is, until Loki opens his mouth again as we exit the car.

"That's the rub of it. No sexual intercourse for the man, for six to eight weeks, right *Lucifer*?" Loki tells us like the shit stirrer he is, a wide grin on his face. That earns him a punch to his gut this time.

"What? Why?" I ask, looking at Ash and frowning. He raises his brows, and then it dawns on me. "The dare!" I hiss, my eyes widening as we walk towards the docked boat, which is fucking huge.

"A Vanderbilt never reneges on a dare or bet," he tells me casually, not making eye contact, and acting like he's not talking about a dick piercing as we board the yacht. Nengah and some other guys bring our luggage behind us.

I'm momentarily distracted from that revelation by the sheer beauty of the craft we've just stepped onto. It's all sleek lines and polished light wood and has several levels, or I guess decks. On the side, in scrolling script is the name *The Princess Lilly* and my heart stutters to see it. *Did they name a boat after me?* There's soft lighting everywhere, and as I look around, I find all three boys looking at me intently.

"Do you like it, Pretty Girl?" Loki asks, his uncertainty completely adorable. He bites the edge of his lip and shuffles his feet on the wooden deck.

"Did you buy a fuck off massive boat and name it after me?" I ask, slightly aghast. Obviously, Her Vagisty preens at the show of adoration.

"We've had the yacht for a while, but decided to rename her after you," Kai tells me in his lovely melodic voice, and I can feel myself turning into girl goop. I've missed the sound so much over the past couple of weeks.

"Thank you," I tell them, deciding to embrace the romantic gesture for what it is, and not letting my ideas over the unfairness of wealth get in the way. "I mean it. This is one of the most romantic things anyone has ever done for me."

I notice a smartly dressed older man, in a crisp white uniform, waiting on one side of the deck to greet us.

"Welcome aboard, Mr. Vanderbilt, Mr. Matthews, Mr. Thorn," he says in cultured tones, with a wide smile. "Nice to have you back with us."

"Thank you, Wayan," Ash replies. "May I present Lilly Darling. Lilly, this is Captain Wayan."

"Ah, the name change makes sense now. A pleasure, Miss," Wayan says, inclining his head in my direction, his grin getting even broader. Then he turns back to Ash. "We're just loading up, and then we'll be ready to set sail. If you'll excuse me, Ketut here will see that you are settled." He indicates with a hand towards another smartly uniformed man, younger this time. Then Captain Wayan turns and walks off.

"This way please, sirs, miss," he tells us, holding his arm out, and the boys seem to know where we're going as they stride ahead into the interior.

I follow behind, gaping at the plush decor. We are led down some floating wooden stairs to a huge seating area with cream leather sofas and armchairs surrounding coffee tables. At the far end is a huge dining table next to semi-circular French doors that open onto another deck.

"Some drinks, please, Ketut," Kai orders. "I'll take my usual.

Lilly?" he asks me, looking at me as I stand at the base of the stairs, trying and failing not to show how out of my depth I am.

"Um, just some iced tea, please, if you have any?" I ask, feeling overwhelmed.

"Of course, peach or lemon?" Ketut responds with a polite professional smile.

"Lemon, please."

He takes the others' orders, then leaves to get our drinks, and some snacks Loki asked for.

"Come sit, Pretty Girl," Loki orders, grabbing my hand and dragging me over to the sofas. He sits down, then pulls me into his lap, the others joining us seconds later.

"So, can I see?" I ask Ash with a raised eyebrow as soon as we're settled.

"He won't even tell us what he got," Kai tells me, a slight smile on his face.

"Good things come to good girls, Princess," Ash says with a sexy as sin smirk on his face.

"I am a good girl," I whine, pouting to see if that works. He just shakes his head.

"Well, keep being good, and I might show you." I stick my tongue out at him, and he narrows his eyes. "Brat," he says under his breath, although there's a heat turning the silver molten, and a tilt to his lips that tells me he loves my brattish attitude.

Ketut comes over with our drinks and snacks; all kinds of yummy things from sweet potato fries, to golden crispy calamari, and nutty satay chicken. We spend the next few minutes talking and catching up with what we've all been up to in the two weeks that we've been apart.

Kai remains pretty quiet throughout our conversation, a pensive frown on his face as he stares into his wine glass, full of what I assume is sake. I get up from Loki's lap, walk around the low table and reach out to Kai. As my fingers brush the side of his face, he flinches so hard that his drink sloshes down the side of the glass, dripping over his hand. Lightning quick, his hand shoots out, grabbing my wrist in a bruising grip that sets my heart racing.

His eyes are wild, and he looks into my panicked gaze, his own clearing as confusion crosses his features.

"Fuck, Lilly! Are you okay? You scared me," Kai exclaims, abruptly letting my wrist go, and reaching over to grab a napkin whilst setting his glass onto the table. I can't help rubbing at the bruised skin, and his eyes dart down, tightening in the corners when he sees what I'm doing. "I'm so sorry, darling."

"What the fuck, Kai?!" Loki snarls, coming to stand next to me, taking my hand in his grip, and inspecting the joint. I wince when he moves it a certain way, and he growls.

"Kai, I'm so sorry," I rush out, a little breathless from the adrenaline rush. "You looked sad, and I wanted to, I don't know, give you a hug," I tell him, still standing and shrugging my shoulders.

His own droop, and look of desolation flits across his eyes, making tears spring unbidden to my own, before he looks down to the napkin in his hands, his fingers slowly shredding it. Ordinarily, I'd go to him, but his reaction to my touch just then has left me reeling.

What the fuck happened in the past two weeks?

"Shit, I'm sorry if I scared you," he says gruffly, dropping the shredded napkin and clawing through his hair.

I shake my head in disbelief.

"You have nothing to apologise for, Kai," I say, trying to assure him, but he doesn't bother to look at me. "Kai, you're scaring me now. What happened?" I murmur, swallowing thickly.

Ash and Loki have gone quiet, Loki still grasping my arm and taking a step closer as if he doesn't trust his friend, but I don't pay him any attention. I've only got eyes for the man who looks so broken before me.

He sighs again, and when he looks up at me, his eyes are a maelstrom of swirling emotion, it's hard to pinpoint them all. There's an aching sadness, anger, and his lip curls up a little as if in self-loathing.

"Nothing, darling," he tells me after a deep breath. "I just hate going back *home*," he spits the word as if it's poison on his tongue.

I know that he's not telling me the whole truth, that there's more going on here. My heart pounds with the knowledge.

"I've got some work to do," he tells us in a monotone voice, before getting up, and walking off into the depths of the yacht.

Something is terribly wrong.

KAI

Fuck!

The flash of pain in Lilly's hazel eyes haunts and excites me in equal measure. That's how I know I'm broken, beyond repair. The fact that inflicting pain on her gives me a semi, even when we're not in a sexual situation, when she's not enjoying it tells me all I need to know about how fucked up I truly am.

How can she ever love someone as terrible as me?

I stalk off, heart pounding and limbs shaking. I don't see my surroundings as I try to outrun the demons that always rear their heads after I've been home for any length of time.

Home, what a fucking joke. It's not been a home since the night my parents were placed into the ground when I was ten years old.

Sounds from the past try to push their way to the surface; the muffled cries of a child, the comforting touch that turned unwelcome.

I shake my head, my hands reaching up to cover my ears, as I begin to pick up my pace, coming to an abrupt halt at the railings surrounding the deck. Looking down, the churn of the dark water below soothes my erratic thoughts, hypnotizing me and calling to me like a siren song.

Briefly, I wonder what it would be like to let the waves take me into their watery embrace, thoughts of sinking to the depths swirling in my mind.

Would the sea be cold, or warm? Would it hurt? Or would it be a blessed relief from this torture, this crippling shame that I've lived with since that night?

I come to with a ragged gasping breath, my knuckles white on the top rail, and my upper body leaning precariously over the edge.

Taking another deep inhale, I can feel the salty spray hit my face and burn my lungs. I can't let him win.

I'm not fucking stupid. I've done my research. I know that keeping this secret, even from my best friends, my brothers, isn't healthy. But how can I tell them the darkest shame of my life? I know that the part of me that believes it was my fault, that I deserved it, that I must have wanted it, is full of shit. That I shouldn't feel so worthless.

But knowing something in theory, and believing it are two very different things.

My head drops into my hands, suddenly feeling far too heavy to hold up.

I can feel myself unravelling at the edges, the darkness threatening to overtake for good.

And there's not a damn thing I can do to stop it.

CHAPTER FOUR

LILLY

We don't see Kai for the rest of the journey, and there's an uneasy roiling in my stomach that has nothing to do with the rough motion of the boat. I can see the worry in the others' faces, in the wrinkling of their brows, and the tightening of their muscles.

Although the yacht put down the anchor about twenty minutes ago, the island can only be reached by a smaller craft such as a jet-ski, which is exactly what we shall be using.

"You're with me, Princess," Ash tells me as we step onto the lowest deck. There's an open panel in the side of the yacht, Ketut waiting off to one side, and four jet-skis already bobbing in the water next to us.

Ash passes me a life jacket, as Loki strolls past us, grumbling about not being quick enough.

"Thanks, but where are yours?" I ask, seeing Loki get off the boat sans life jacket.

"Put on the jacket, Princess," Ash the Ashhole orders me, a smirk firmly in place. I roll my eyes, earning the narrowing of his, but do as he says. I really want to see his dick piercing, so compliant Lilly it is!

Kai comes down the stairs, drawing all eyes to him as he walks past Ash and I with a tight smile, climbs on a jet-ski, waiting for Ketut to unhook it, and then it roars off, carrying him off into the dark night with a spray of salt water.

"Something's not right, Ash," I say, rubbing my arms, feeling cold all of a sudden.

"I know, Princess," he replies, taking one of my hands and squeezing it gently, before leading me to the water. "Fuck, he reminds me a little of Luc before..." he trails off, his shoulders tight and his jaw clenched as he watches Kai disappear into the darkness.

I reach out and cup his cheek with my free hand.

"It won't come to that, Ash. We won't let it," I tell him vehemently, and his jaw eases a fraction at my declaration.

"I hope so, beautiful. I really do," he sighs a great heaving sound, then rolls his shoulders before putting a smile back on his face. "Come on, get on."

He lets go of my hand, stepping away to get onto the jet-ski, then holds his hand out to me. I take it, my pulse racing as I step behind him and sit pressed up against his back, my hands wrapped around his trim waist. It's my first time on a jet-ski and excitement fizzles through my veins.

"The first one there gets Lilly for dessert!" Loki yells, before gunning his engine, and zooming off.

"Fucker!" Ash shouts over the roar, then we're off at breakneck speed. I grip tighter as my heart leaps, and my stomach flip-flops as we race in the dark, the stars and moon our only light.

"Are you sure that this is safe?!" I shout, leaning closer so that Ash can hear me. My fingers instinctively curl tighter into his linen shirt, uncaring if I leave it all crumpled.

I feel him chuckle, his back vibrating against my front as he just guns the engine more, making us go faster, and a squeal leaves my lips. I'd be lying if I said it wasn't exhilarating as hell. My whole body feels alight with nervous excited energy, my heart thrashing in my chest as we speed through the night.

Within minutes, we are pulling up beside a wooden pier, Loki leaning against one of the tall wooden posts, arms crossed over his chest, and a smug as fuck grin on his face. I look around, noting with a frown that Kai is nowhere to be seen.

There are several posts, torches on every other one lighting up the way along the boards. They lead right up to a huge bush, standing at least ten feet into the air, with an archway carved into it. Peeking above the bush, is the outline of a peaked thatched roof, which must be the villa and as with most things of theirs it looks fucking huge. *Snort.*

Ash kills the engine, then grumbles as Loki takes the rope he throws, and helps guide the ski, tying it off. Loki then reaches out his hand, pulling me up and into his arms in a single smooth move.

Helping me out of the jacket, he pulls me close, and then leans in, whispering into my ear, "I'll claim my prize once Jax has said hello." He bites my lobe, sending shivers rippling across my body, like the trails we left in the water with our jet-skis.

"Lilly," a voice deep as the waters that surround us says, and my head whips round to see Jax strolling down the jetty. My eyes drink him in for a second, noting that he's trying to test my sanity by wearing loose grey sweatshorts, and nothing else, which is obvious by the tantalising outline of his huge cock.

I tear out of Loki's arms with a half sob, half laugh, and run to Jax, throwing myself at him. Luckily he catches me, wrapping his huge arms round me, although he does stumble back a step, which makes me begin to pull back in concern.

"Shit, Jax, I'm..." Before I can finish my sentence, one of his big hands comes up between us and grasps my throat, using his grip to pull me in for a searing kiss.

He forces his tongue into my mouth straight away, leaving me no option but to open up to him and let him plunder my mouth. I gladly give him full access, loving the taste of his kiss after all this time without him, the intense worry, making the wait extra fraught. He tastes like the safest place in the world, like being wrapped up after being out in the cold.

My hands claw at his biceps, trying to get even closer, and his grip on my throat tightens just enough to let me know that he's in charge of this reunion.

Warmth pools in my centre, dampening my knickers as my whole body feels alight, even though there is a slight chill in the night-time air that pebbles my skin. I want to, no, *need* to feel him everywhere, and I let out a frustrated moan at the clothes that separate us.

His hardness presses into my lower stomach, letting me know that he's on the same page, and when he grinds his dick into me, I break the kiss with a gasp.

"Jax, fuck. I need you, Jax. So bad," I pant, feeling wild in my desire.

He leans back with a smirk, and I notice the tiredness in his eyes, even though they're sparkling with lust as well. I almost hesitate, but his other hand leaves my waist to snake round the front of me, dipping into my harems, and under the waistband of my underwear.

A rumbling growl sounds in his throat as he makes contact with my slick folds, his pupils going wide when more juices flow out of me at his simple touch. I'm so wound up, so fucking needy for him, that I'm almost climaxing from his fingers alone.

"Jax..." I plead, my hips moving and seeking more. I hear groans behind me, looking up to see Ash and Loki, their eyes blazing heat.

My attention returns back to Jax when he pinches my clit, a sharp cry leaving my lips at the addition of pain. I'm like a bitch in heat, needing to reassert our bond and mark him, having him mark me in return. My nails rake lightly down his arms, his whole body shivering as they leave red trails in their wake. I can't help the purr that sounds in my own throat as my eyes follow the lines.

A deep chuckle tumbles from his kiss-swollen lips, his fingers continuing their dance around my nub and along my slit, but never going deeper, leaving me desperately wanting.

"I wanna hear you beg, Baby Girl. Beg for my fingers, for my cock," he orders gruffly, still teasing me, and denying me what I desperately need.

"Jax, please. Please give me your fingers. I need your cock so deep inside me that I can't fucking breathe," I rasp, looking him straight in the eyes. His smile turns positively feral, but he doesn't relent, still tantalising me until I feel like crying.

"Loki," he rumbles. "Condom."

"Why the fuck do you all assume I have them on me at all times?" Loki asks in exasperation, but when I turn to look at him with a—*are you serious?*—look, he's pulling a foil packet from his chino shorts pocket. He walks towards us, then holds the condom out to Jax.

"Take it, Baby Girl," Jax commands me, his tone telling me that if I want what he's not currently giving, I best follow orders.

"Yes, sir," I say, a touch of snark in my tone as I do as he says. I just can't help myself, clearly.

His eyes narrow and his nostrils flare.

"For that, you'll get one clit orgasm, but no prep for my, what do you call it?" he asks, looking all kinds of smug. "Oh, that's right, my *monster cock*."

I swallow hard, but I can feel wetness seep from me at the threat, even though given my experience with that cunt, Robert, I know how fucked up it is to get turned on by consensual non-consent. Although, the keyword here is consensual.

"Oh, you like the idea of me forcing my cock inside your tight pussy, do you, baby?" he questions huskily, and I whimper.

He's still not giving me what I'm craving, and as he's maintaining eye contact, he sees every glimmer of frustration that crosses my face. Fuck, at this stage, he'll brush my clit and I'll fucking come all over him. I nod my head.

"I want to hear you say it, beautiful."

"Yes," I murmur, my mouth dry.

"Good girl. Put the condom on my dick, Baby Girl," he tells me, licking his lips.

It takes me a couple of tries to open the packet, my hands are trembling that much. Finally, I take the rubber out, and after checking it's the right way up, I look down between us to Jax's massive erection, straining against his shorts. There's a spot of dampness on the fabric, right over the top of his cock, which I know is precum, and if Jax didn't have such a tight hold of my throat, I'd drop to my knees and lick the salty drops that are bound to be smeared all over his tip.

I lick my own lips at the thought, earning dark chuckles from all three boys, Ash behind me and Loki in front.

"Don't worry, baby. Plenty of time for me to choke you with my cock later," Jax assures me as I lift the waistband of his shorts up and over his hard length, leaving them to drop to the floor.

Taking his solid member into my hand, I relish the silky soft feel as I wrap my fingers around him, the tips not touching because he's just that big, and pump up and down a couple of times. I moan at the same time he does. *God, I've missed this cock!*

"Keep that up and I won't make it inside you. Baby Girl," Jax rasps, his hand flexing on my throat, tightening so I can no longer move my head.

Although tempted to torture him a little more, I want to feel him push his way inside me, so I stop playing and roll the condom on. He's breathing pretty hard, and before I can ask if he's okay, Loki, the wind-up merchant, pipes up.

"Sure you're fit enough, big guy? I can always take over for you if you're struggling. We all know blue balls over here ain't of any use."

I hear two low growls simultaneously, and I look up to give Loki a *cut it the fuck out* look.

"Eyes on me, Lilly," Jax tells me. My attention snaps back to him, at the same time his finger picks up speed, circling ever faster but avoiding my nub until I'm a squirming, panting mess.

"Jax..." I plead in desperation, begging with my eyes for him to let me come.

Without any warning whatsoever, he presses down hard and gets exactly what he ordered moments ago. I fucking shatter with a cry, soaking his fingers, my knickers, and I suspect my harems, as the mind-blowing orgasm sweeps over me, making the stars overhead shine brighter.

Before I can come down from the heavens, Jax lets go of my throat and is tugging my harems and knickers off, helping me to step out of them and my flip-flops, my legs trembling. With a strength that is reassuring given his withdrawal, he picks me up, his huge hands under my thighs, my arms instinctively wrapping around his thick neck, my legs round his waist. He walks us to one of the huge wooden posts, slamming my back against it with a jarring thud.

I barely have time to take an inhale when he's nudging my entrance with his bulbous tip. He lets out a hissing growl, pushing forward and I can feel my pussy walls stretching almost painfully to accommodate him. Due to the lack of prep, there's a sharp sting as he keeps surging, and I gasp and squirm in his arms, my legs clenching around his waist.

"Stay still, woman," he snarls as he goes deeper, and my fucking eyes roll when finally, he bottoms out.

"Fuck, Jax," I moan low, my body relishing the fullness that only he can give. It's almost too much when he's fully seated inside me, I swear he touches my cervix, but I love it.

"Jesus, I've missed being inside you, Baby Girl," he confesses, his voice raspy like sandpaper as he starts to withdraw, mindful of my comfort even though he threatened force.

"Show me, Jax," I urge, grabbing his man bun in my fist and yanking, looking directly into the swirling depths of his blue eyes that flicker in the light from the torches. "Show me how much you've missed my cunt."

His answer is a growl, and he thrusts hard, filling me up and making me scream with the hint of pain and the overwhelming pleasure that follows. My arse is still throbbing from Ash's attention earlier, the rough wood chafing the marks that he left, and just adding to the delicious sensations that are running all over my body.

True to my request, Jax shows me how much he's missed my pussy. With every powerful thrust and animalistic sound that leaves his lips, he tells me that I am his, and he is mine. I take all that he has to give me, feeling him deep inside me, rubbing and massaging my inner walls, until the wonderful burn of an orgasm builds in my core.

"Jax..." I gasp, my hands letting go of his hair, nails digging into the back of his neck.

"I got you, baby," he rumbles out.

Without missing a single thrust, he leans in and bites down so hard on my neck, I know that he's broken the skin. I throw my head back, hitting it on the post as my climax tears through me with the force of a riptide, my mouth open in a soundless scream. My whole body shudders and convulses, my pussy clenching and fluttering around Jax's huge member, gripping him so tightly that I'm surprised he can continue.

But he does, not letting up, and sucking my neck so that my orgasm keeps rippling over me, almost becoming too much. Finally, after a few long minutes, he thrusts deeper than he has done so far, a whimper leaving my lips just as a roar leaves him, and he stills.

We stay connected, panting and trying to come back to the pier, the Indonesian night wrapping around us in a comforting embrace, the sound of the waves lulling us into a trance-like state.

I feel a cool drop on my overheated skin, landing on my shoulder. For a moment, I panic, thinking that Jax is crying for some reason, but then another lands on my knee, and another on my head, until all of a sudden the heavens open, and rain pelts down on us.

A joyous laugh tumbles out of me, my head still tipped back and my eyes closed, letting the rain cool me and wash over my body. Jax nuzzles my neck, a spike of pain flaring where he bit me.

"We should probably get inside, Baby Girl," he raspingly says into my ear, and I shiver at the sound combined with the feel of cool rain.

He pulls out, helping me down and stabilising me on unsteady legs. Looking down, I can see he's still pretty hard, the condom filled with his cum, slightly dangling off the tip. I smile as my idea from earlier pops back into my mind.

As Jax reaches down, I grab his wrist, halting his movement. He looks up at me in confusion, then a heat enters his lust filled eyes as I sink down onto my knees before him. Carefully, I take the rubber off, holding it upright, then roll my eyes back up and watch him as I lick his dick clean. He twitches like he wants to pull away, but instead, he wraps his hand in my hair.

I finish with a final lick to the tip, noticing that he's almost fully hard again. Then, keeping eye contact, I bring the condom up to my lips and tip it so that his cum flows into my mouth. His eyes widen, nostrils flaring, and the hand in my hair tightens, as I lower my hand, opening my mouth so that he can see the salty liquid on my tongue before I close my lips and swallow.

I hear two groans next to me.

"Did you just..." Loki trails off, and I look over to see him with his dick out, his own cum glistening on the tip.

"We should get in from the rain," I hear Ash order, his voice husky, but sounding pissed off.

"Just because you've got frozen blue balls, Vanderbilt," Loki grumbles, putting his dick away.

"Or it could be because Lilly is shivering and her lips look blue," Ash deadpans, stepping up to me and holding out his hand. I can't help but notice the boner he's sporting, poor man.

His words set the guys in motion, Jax's hand falling from my hair as he pulls up his shorts. He reaches down, grabbing my knickers and harems, then frowning when he realises how wet they already are. Ash helps me up, having taken off his shirt and wraps me in it. It reaches to just below my arse so I'm somewhat covered, and he tucks me under his arm, all of us tramping down the jetty towards the entrance to the villa whilst the tropical rain pours down on us.

JAX

I pull the sleeping beauty closer to me, wrapping myself around her soft, naked body and taking a deep inhale of everything that is Lilly as I listen to the rain that still pours outside the open window. My body starts loosening up as her smell settles into my soul after the past two weeks of hell.

I breathe a sigh of relief that Lilly and the guys weren't here to see the more serious withdrawal symptoms. An image of lying on the floor, curled up into a ball crying with the pain in my joints and muscles flashes across my mind, my arms pulling her even closer as I bury my face in her ginger scented hair—*fucking Ash.*

The symptoms have eased, the only reason that I agreed to seeing everyone, although as tonight seems to be proving so far, the insomnia is still going fucking strong. I've been swinging between being wide awake to sleeping for what's felt like days. And the mood swings have been off the charts.

Part of the other reason for seeing the guys, especially Lilly, is my hope that it'll help to stave off the depression that's been looming over me the past few days. I can already feel Lilly's magic working, weaving over me like a spell of protection. Ash was right when he called her a pixie, and I am willing to surrender myself to her fae powers.

"Jax..." she moans sleepily, and it's so damn sexy that I can feel my dick stirring against her ass. At least reduced libido is one symptom I'm not suffering from. "I can practically hear the cogs in your mind whirling."

"Sorry, Baby Girl," I mumble in her ear, loving the way her back arches into me. "Can't sleep," I tell her with a sigh.

She turns around so that she's facing me, her face outlined in the soft light that's filtering in from the hall. God, she's so fucking beautiful. It blows my mind that she's even in my bed, let alone that she loves me. I am the luckiest fucker alive, even if it's not felt like it the past few weeks.

"You look tired, love," she says, a cute as fuck frown creasing her brow. I swear my heart skips a beat when she calls me that. I want to hear it on her lips for the rest of my life.

Her hand comes up to cup my face, and my breath stills gazing into her hazel eyes, seeing the love shining in them. Before Lilly, no one had ever touched me with affection, not that I can remember anyway. Maybe my mom used to, but my sperm donor soon beat that out of her, telling her it would make me soft.

Suddenly, an idea springs to mind, and my skin gets itchy with the need to be outside with my girl.

"Will you come with me, baby?" I ask her softly, watching every thought that crosses her stunning face. "I want to show you something."

"Of course," she says with a smile. "I'd go anywhere with you, Jax."

The truth of her words hits me square in the chest, the trust that she's placed in me makes me feel as though I'm ten feet tall. I give her one last squeeze, placing a quick kiss on her lips, then get up and help her out of bed, grabbing some clean sweatshorts and pulling them on whilst she dresses in a tank and tiny shorts that have me rethinking my plans.

I grab my phone, then pull her out of the room and head towards the front door. The lodge is quiet, everyone else having gone to bed long ago and giving me some alone time with her.

She gives me a quizzical look as I lead her to the door, opening it, the sound of the hammering rain filling the quiet space.

"Jax!" she hisses through her teeth, and I pull her out into the downpour. "What the fuck are you doing?" she asks, laughing as I tug her faster, heading for the pier.

A chuckle of pure happiness rolls out of me as we walk along the wooden boards, and I stop in the middle, turning to face her. Her usually bouncy brunette hair is plastered to her head until she resembles a drowned cat, but she's never looked more beautiful to me. I probably look similar given that she pulled my hair out of its tie earlier.

"One of the few positive things that my shitstain of a sperm donor insisted on growing up, was that I had to keep in touch with my Southern roots," I tell her, scrolling through my phone until I find the song I'm after. Thank fuck for waterproof iPhones.

There's that cute frown line again as she looks at me, the beginning of *Hard To Love* by Lee Brice starting to play. Walking over to one of the posts, I place the device down, then stroll back to her, stopping a step away.

"Dance with me?" I ask, my heart drumming for some inexplicable reason. I've never shown anyone this; not even the guys know my love for country swing dancing.

She beams, water cascading down her face as she steps towards me, taking my outstretched hand. We begin to move, slowly at first with a two step, but she quickly picks up the steps, following my lead. She sways her hips like a pro, unsurprisingly, a delighted giggle falling from her lips when I back slide into a pivot and spin her, in front and behind me.

I basically dip her like Prince fucking Charming, and her laughter fills my ears as I bring her back up, stealing a quick kiss. Beaming back at her, I keep leading us, twirling her around me, swinging my hips in time to the beat, the rain falling around us as we dance.

We get lost in our own world, partners in perfect synchronicity until all too soon the song starts to come to a close. I finish the dance, dipping her several times, then pulling her close and slow dancing, our hips pressed tightly together.

As the song ends, I capture her lips with my own, kissing her until I'm lightheaded and we break away, gasping.

"Jesus, Jax," she pants, her pupils blown and chest heaving, her nipples hard and pressed against the thin fabric of her tank."How did I not know you could dance like that?"

I shrug, smiling like a loon at her.

"It was my escape growing up," I confess, my voice low as if worried we'll be overheard. "Something my father encouraged that I loved doing."

I suddenly feel shy, exposed, in a way that I've never let myself be before and I look out towards the sea, the rain obscuring my view. I feel her hand on my face, bringing me to look back at her.

"It was an escape for me too. Dancing," she tells me when I give her a questioning look, a soft, gentle smile on her face. "We all need at least one thing that we love doing, Jax. It's nothing to be ashamed of."

I can't help myself, I lean down and kiss her fiercely again. *Could this girl get any more fucking perfect?*

Bending down a little more, I pick her up under her thighs, which wrap around my hips, not breaking our kiss as I start to stride back to the lodge.

"Phone!" she gasps, breaking our kiss with a laugh.

Turning back around, I walk to the post, letting Lilly grab my phone, and then turn us back, walking up the pier with her tight in my arms.

"Looks like I've made you all wet again, Baby Girl," I say, trying and failing to hold in the smirk.

"Jax Griffiths," she laugh-scolds. "Was that a dirty joke coming out of those lips of yours?"

"Sure sounded like one," I tease, releasing one hand to swat her hard on the ass for being a brat.

She squeals, laughing as I jog the rest of the way up the pier, back to the shelter of our island home.

"I love you, Jax," she tells me, giving me all kinds of chills as we reach the door.

"I love you, Lilly," I reply, the words coming easier than breathing as I open the door, walking through and kicking it shut behind me.

And I spend the rest of the night showing her just how much she means to me.

CHAPTER FIVE

LILLY

I wake up with a delicious ache between my thighs and a warm lemon scented body wrapped round my naked back. There's also something hard and unyielding, poking into my arse, and a throaty chuckle escapes me.

"God, I missed waking up next to you, Baby Girl," Jax rumbles in the sexiest voice known to man, all gruff and husky from sleep. His arms tighten round me, pulling me against him even more, and he nuzzles into my neck as his hand starts drifting south.

Just as I'm about to reply, though he's already turning my mind into mush with his touch, the door flies open and with a sense of déjà vu, Loki strolls in. Jax groans, pausing in his attentions.

"The fuck you want?" he growls at the angel faced intruder, who smirks in return.

"Merry belated Christmas!" Loki shouts, darting to the bed and grabbing my hand, yanking me away from Jax who snarls like a wolf and lunges to grab my other hand, missing by a hair. "Need to be quicker next time, *He-Man!*" Loki cries triumphantly, pulling me out of the bed.

"Hey! I am not a fucking dog toy!" I scold as Loki pulls me close, grabbing a handful of my arse as his lips descend onto mine.

I get lost in his kiss, drowning in all things Loki. My hands rub up and down his bare chest, teasing his nipple bar with my fingertips, eliciting a deep moan from his throat.

"Much as I would love to take this further…" he murmurs against my lips. "Ash and Kai want to give you their presents."

"Presents?!" I screech, pulling away and starting to walk towards the door. "Why the fuck didn't you start with that?"

"Um, Baby Girl?" Jax questions, so I stop and turn back, brow raised. "Not that I'm complaining, but you may want to put some clothes on, otherwise I don't think it'll be just gifts that are exchanged."

"Fair point, well made." I nod seriously, looking down at my naked, slightly flushed body. Turning back into the room, I head over to my bags, which are on a stylised carved wooden chair.

I do a quick pit sniff, decide I'm not too fruity given that Jax and I had a shower when we got in last night. I hear manly chuckles behind me.

"What?" I ask, my forehead creased as I turn to face them, one hand on my popped out hip.

"Need me to sniff your pussy to make sure that's okay too?" Loki asks, trying and failing to keep a straight face. Jax outright barks a laugh, and then, I kid you not, they fucking high five like children.

"Fuck off, Loki," I tell him, sticking my tongue out, then smirking as a diabolical idea comes to mind.

Reaching my other hand down, I use a finger to swipe between my folds. Both boys go deathly silent as I bring the finger up to my lips, darting my tongue out and licking the digit before sucking it into my mouth. My own flavour bursts on my tastebuds, musky, but not unclean.

"I'm all good, ta," I tell them, turning back to my bag, and pulling out some underwear and clothes for the day. I go for red lace—*obviously, given the festive theme*—and a light cotton rainbow sundress with a full circle skirt.

Before I can so much as take hold of my knickers, strong hands spin me round, throw me over a huge shoulder, and then deposit me on the bed with a bounce and a squeak.

"Jax..." I warn, and he smirks down at me, getting to his knees on the bed. His smile grows wider as Loki joins us. "Ash and Kai will be mad..."

"Don't worry, Pretty Girl. I'm sure you'll enjoy their punishments," Loki tells me seconds before they descend on me like lions on a kill.

Suffice to say, we are late, and all need a shower after all.

Once we're clean and dressed, we walk into the living room area, where I get to appreciate the guy's island villa that it's daytime. It's stunning. The far wall is floor-to-ceiling glass doors, revealing a stunning view over the water. There's a swimming pool set into the deck with one of those disappearing edges so that it looks like you are swimming out to sea. We're on a higher level, so the view goes on for miles, with small specks in the distance that I assume are other islands.

The room is all light wood, carved in an Indonesian style. There are brightly coloured textiles everywhere, making my inner creative very happy, and comfy looking light grey sofas, with throws and blankets, again in bright colours, thrown over the backs and sides.

On one side is a wooden open style kitchen, with wooden countertops and all the modern conveniences one could wish for. To the left of the glass doors is a beautiful carved wooden table and dining chairs, enough to seat eight people comfortably, and let them enjoy the view whilst dining.

"Merry Christmas, Lilly," I hear Kai's melodic voice, and I look to the side to see him approaching me.

He has dark circles under his eyes, his hair in its usual disarray, and my eyebrows draw together with concern.

"Merry Christmas, Kai," I say back, a catch in my throat as he stops in front of me, holding a thin, long deep red box in his hands.

"I'm—" he starts.

"Kai—" I say at the same time, then we both chuckle ruefully. "You go first," I offer, desperate to reach out to him, to wrap myself around him, but a little nervous given his reaction last night on the boat.

"Lilly, darling, I'm so sorry about last night. I—" he cuts himself off, one hand running through his hair and mussing it more as he sighs. "Going back home...it brings up bad memories for me. It takes me to a dark place, and well, I guess I was still there, even though I was with you."

He looks up at me, his eyes full of torment, and I know that I'm not getting the full story. I know that things were bad with his uncle, his training horrific and brutal. I'm starting to think that it is worse than we all thought, and my stomach churns at the idea of him suffering even more at the hands of that evil man.

"Kai, there's nothing to apologise for. You can't help instincts, love," I tell him, not able to help taking a step forward, my hand reaching out to cup his cheek automatically. I pause in the movement, and he huffs, closing the distance.

The relief that floods my body when my palm makes contact is so strong that tears sting my eyes. I blink them away, seeing his whole body relax as he steps closer, our bodies flush. A deep exhale comes rushing out of me. I can feel his warmth through our clothes, and my soul sings as his hand alights on my own cheek, his thumb rubbing it.

"Fuck, Lilly," he whispers, leaning in further until his lips hover over mine. I can taste his breath, a mixture of mint and the green tea he favours, and I breathe him in until he's once again a part of my very being. "Don't give up on me," he pleads, and his words make the breath catch in my lungs.

"I will never give up on you, Kai. On any of you," I assure him, my own fingers moving into his hair and gripping tightly, pulling him closer until I no longer know whose breath is whose. "We are bound together, you and I, Kai. And nothing in this world, or the next will be able to keep us apart."

His lips slam down on mine, swallowing my moan as he kisses me with such desperation I can barely keep up. It's as if I am all that lies between him and the darkness, a darkness that is threatening to overwhelm him completely.

He breaks away panting, his eyes a little wild. Clearing his throat, he holds out the box in trembling hands.

"This is from all of us," he tells me, a slight tremble in his voice.

I take it, a small smile on my lips, my heart still thudding from our kiss. Looking down, I see it's wine red velvet, beautifully soft under my fingertips, and tied with a black ribbon in a bow. I pull one of the ends, the knot unravelling, and the ribbon falls free. Opening the box, I gasp as a platinum silver charm bracelet winks back at me. It's already got several silver charms, which I take to represent the guys and me; a lily, a sugar skull for Ash, a koi for Kai, an angel for Loki, and a Norse style wolf for Jax. There's also some more; a silver Big Ben to show my birth city, a fairy to represent my favourite Shakespeare play, and a silver American flag for my senior year.

I swallow hard, the lump in my throat making it hard to say anything.

"Do you like it, Princess?" Ash asks, his low voice sending a shiver across my skin like the caress of a night-time breeze. I look up with a watery gaze seeing that the others are all standing in front of me, all four of them waiting to hear my answer.

"I love it, thank you," I manage to whisper out, kissing Kai on the cheek, then stepping to Ash and Jax, doing the same. Loki, my wonderful Loki, breaks the serious moment by polishing his cheek and presenting it to me, making all of us laugh.

"Can I give you guys your gifts?" I ask, excited anticipation running through me as we all go to sit down on the sofas, picking up drinks from the side tables as we pass. They're all soft drinks or juice, as Jax's doctor said to lay off alcohol for a bit too, just to clean out his entire system, and make sure that he doesn't slip from one addiction to another.

"I thought you'd never ask, Pretty Girl!" Loki exclaims, his arms along the back of one of the sofas.

I get up, walk over to the palm tree that has been decorated like a Christmas tree including twinkling lights, and grab the four black gift bags, bringing them over and handing one to each of the guys. They are specific, so I wrote gift tags to make sure they each got the right one—*See! Not just a pretty face!*

They all look up, and when I nod in encouragement, they tear into them, and for a split second, I wonder if they've ever received a real gift before. One with no expectations or strings attached. The thought makes me frown until I hear Loki roar with laughter as he pulls out a bright pink fluffy bunny onesie.

A grin splits my lips as Jax holds up a huge Incredible Hulk onesie, his lip twitching. Kai takes out a stormtrooper one, a boyish grin on his handsome face, and all traces of darkness gone for the moment. Finally, Ash takes out a red devil one, and they all look at me with adorable confusion.

"Are we going dogging?" Loki asks, and all eyes swing to him.

"What the fuck is 'dogging,' dude?" Jax grumbles, throwing a cushion at him, which Loki dodges like a wanker.

"'Dogging is a British English euphemism for engaging in sexual acts in a public or semi-public place, or watching others doing so,'" Kai interjects, reading off his tablet.

"For fuck's sake, Loki!" I exclaim, my jaw dropping at his suggestion. "How did you even come to that...No, we're not going dogging, Jesus. Just keep going."

They do as I say, pulling out the large black boxes, and I watch as they each open them up and take the top layer of black tissue paper out.

"Fuck yeah!" Loki shouts, pulling out the paintball gun, aiming at Ash, and pulling the trigger. *What a cuntcake!*

Ash just raises a black brow, not even flinching as nothing happens. Loki looks down, pouting at the gun.

"You need to get the ammo at the centre, fucking imbecile," Ash says, rolling his eyes and setting his bag and box aside on the floor.

He gets up, all leisurely insouciance, and stalks towards me. He's wearing some grey linen trousers without a shirt, and all of his inked up muscles are on display, distracting me to no end.

"Thank you, Princess," he says once he reaches me, stepping close and pressing a light kiss against my lips.

"How long until you're healed again?" I ask against his lips, his kiss setting a fire in my core. Having to wait for him is like the most delicious torture I've ever been through.

He chuckles, the sound seeming to vibrate right down to my clit, and a moan escapes my lips, passing into his.

"Another five weeks, maybe four. I'm a fast healer."

I let out a shaky breath as he pulls away, stepping behind me to the palm-Christmas tree. The others have all gotten up, and they too thank me, pressing kisses on my lips and making me feel so loved up it's almost sickening.

"We each got you some other presents too, Princess," Ash tells me as Loki takes my hand and leads me to take a seat on the sofa once more. From there, I spend the next forty-five minutes being absolutely spoiled rotten.

Kai gives me a book of American poetry, plus a huge bag of Bordelle lingerie; basques, harnesses, bras, bodies and thongs. I squeal, throwing myself in his arms, scraps of lace and straps flying everywhere.

Loki presents me with five—*yes, fucking five!*—Irregular Choice shoe boxes, all new arrivals including yellow Shirley Bass rainbows, rainbow dinosaur Nick of Time's, and red Full House boots with gold stitching that reads 'Queen of my own destiny.' He also gets a shriek and a full tackle hug.

Jax gives me a gold pair of boxing gloves with matching wraps. The gloves have 'Baby Girl' written across the wrists, and Jax tells me that training starts when we get back. I'm a little more careful with his praise, sitting in his lap and kissing him when he growls that he's not, and I quote, 'a fucking pussy invalid.' He also gives me several sets of silk cami and shorts PJs with a knowing smirk and a comment that they should see me through the next term. *Ballbag.*

Then, finally, Ash kneels in front of me, a medium-sized black velvet square box in his hands.

"If I didn't know you better, *Ice Knight*, I'd say you have a flair for the dramatic," I tease him, earning a small tilt of his lips as he opens the box so that I can see the gold collar and matching cuffs nestled in red silk inside. There's a chain that links the cuffs, although they look like they can be separate too.

"Something to look forward to," he tells me with a devilish grin that sends shivers cascading down my spine and causes my nipples to harden.

By the time we're done, it's lunchtime, and although it's not a full Christmas dinner—it's way too hot and all of us, bar Jax, are suffering from jet lag—there is a wonderful buffet laid out on the table for us by Mama Dewi as they call her. She's an older Balinese lady, with a face as wrinkled as a walnut, and a wicked dirty laugh.

She lives with her family on the next island over, and the guys give her several gifts and kiss her weathered cheeks before she leaves. Ash tells me that she has been taking care of the Vanderbilts since he was in nappies, so when Julian let her go some years back, Ash employed her. Apparently, Julian owns a different island—*fucking rich peple*—but Cempadek belongs to all the guys outright.

Loki helps her down to the pier where a grandson is waiting with a boat to take her home for the day. When he returns, we all sit round the table and begin to tuck into the feast that she left for us.

Obviously, I show my appreciation for her cooking by way of

moans and groans about how fucking awesome the food is, earning heated looks from the guys. Deciding to tone it down, otherwise I'll never get to finish my meal, I turn to Jax who's sitting next to me.

"How's it all going, Jax?" I ask, looking him over and seeing that he's not digging in like the rest of us, but is pushing his food around his plate which is unlike him. I worry my lower lip, a move which has Jax reaching out and tugging it from under my teeth.

"I'm okay, Baby Girl. Just not as hungry as I usually am at the moment, I guess," he tells us, his thumb still brushing over my bottom lip. "Loss of appetite is normal. And I've been sleeping a lot. Again, all normal, so nothing to worry about."

I still can't help looking him over, in his loose sweatshorts and tank top. Is he looking slimmer? Maybe he's not eating enough, and he does look really tired...

"Lilly," he growls out, and the sound of my name in his deep voice is enough to shock me out of my spiralling thoughts. "Come here," he tells me, scooting his chair out a little and patting his thigh, which still looks huge, to my relief.

I get up, grab my plate, and sit down on his lap, wiggling until I'm comfortable. His big palm comes to rest on my waist, and the tension flows out of my body at his touch. I'm completely lost to all these guys, dependent on them like I've never been before. A part of me knows it's dangerous, especially given their families and the violent nature of their lives. But it's too late now, we complete each other in a way that few ever get to experience, and if the sudden horrific death of my mum has shown me anything, it's that life is too short not to take every blessing, every piece of love and hold on to it fast.

Taking a piece of satay chicken in my fingers, I twist in Jax's lap until I'm facing him, holding up the morsel to his lips.

"Eat," I command in a firm tone. He raises a brow, one side of his lips tilting in that almost smile of his, but does as I ask and opens his mouth, letting me slip the chicken in. "Good boy," I tell him with a smirk of my own.

His fingers tighten on my waist, his other hand coming to rest on the apex of my thigh, over my dress. He applies a little pressure, enough to make my eyes widen and my breath catch. I can see by the gleam in his blue eyes that he's letting me know who's the boss here.

"Kai, any luck on finding out more about that picture?" Ash asks, interrupting our stare-off.

"What picture?" Jax enquires, turning his head to look at Ash, his forehead wrinkled.

"There's a picture of Lilly's mom in Chad's study, with all of our moms at a Black Knight Corp gala," Ash tells him, that look of unease back in his eyes.

"What? Why?" Jax asks, looking up at me.

"I don't know, she never mentioned even coming to America," I say, placing another bite into his mouth. "Let alone having any connection to your company." And yes, I'm still a little pissed at being so out of the loop where she's concerned.

"So, interestingly, I managed to get the guest list from that gala," Kai informs us, pausing to reach over and grab his iPad, bringing up a list of names. "Your uncle is on there Lilly, Adrian Ramsey, but his plus one is someone called Violet Rochester. No mention of a Laura Darling on the list at all."

I can feel my eyebrows drawing together, my stomach fluttering, as he looks up at me.

"So I did some digging into Violet, and it turns out she and your uncle were engaged, and then she disappeared completely, about nineteen years ago. Never to be found again."

"What?" I murmur, my whole body suddenly feeling overheated, and sweat trickles down my spine, even though we have the air con on.

"That must be the heartbreak the newspaper articles were talking about when we looked up Ramsey," Loki adds, and my head whips in his direction.

"I'm sorry, what? You looked into my uncle?" I ask, my tone a little caustic and my body stiff. Loki rubs a hand across the back of his neck, looking away as his cheeks flush.

"Hey, Baby Girl, it's okay. Take some deep breaths, baby," Jax says in a soothing tone, his palm leaving my waist to rub comforting circles on my back.

His words make me realise that I am indeed panting, so I do as he suggests and close my eyes, taking some deep, long inhales and exhales until I feel better.

"I'm just so confused," I tell them when I open my eyes again, my gaze immediately finding Ash's grey ones. His eyes are hard, brows dipped, but there's a softness there that I know is for me. "Your parents don't seem the sort not to have everyone's names on the list. And it seems so strange that Violet disappeared around the time my mum was pregnant with me." My head is swirling, and I can feel a headache coming on, the food lying all but forgotten in front of me.

I feel Jax's hands alight on my tense shoulders, rubbing and kneading them until I'm relaxing and trying to hold back moans at how good it feels.

"We'll work it all out, Princess," Ash tells me, his tone resolved, letting me know that he's taking this seriously. "Trust us."

CHAPTER SIX

LILLY

After lunch, Loki suggested we go down to the beach, so we spend the rest of the day on the golden sand or in the beautiful turquoise waters, relaxing and listening to music, because of course, Loki has a playlist. He told me that you need a playlist for every occasion; from torture to chilling on the beach. I mean, he's not wrong.

Although this time of year in Bali and the surrounding islands is often quite wet, the rain holds off, and the temperature is balmy and the perfect amount of heat. I can feel my troubles and worries melt away as the sun warms my skin, and the sea breeze kisses my body.

Kai is still a little distant, yet I can see him trying to act normal, to hide the darkness that has surrounded him since that night on the boat. But even though he is a part of our group, sitting on a colourful outdoor rug on the warm golden sand, he's lost in his own mind, gazing out over the water. His face is a blank mask of indifference, his eyes intense, staring at the horizon. It's frightening to see him so…closed off. I'm sure the others notice. I see Ash looking Kai's way as much as I am, a frown marring his brow.

"We'll get to the bottom of it, Ash," I tell him, reaching out for his hand as he sits next to me.

"If anyone can, it's you," he replies, squeezing gently as he wraps his inked fingers around mine. His faith in me is warming, and I can only hope that it's not misplaced.

He looks mouthwateringly good, positively edible, in just some loose black swimming trunks and his ink covered skin. Her Vagisty is going all kinds of crazy, the horny bitch!

As I look at Kai once more, a wicked, bratty idea comes to mind, which will hopefully lighten the mood a little and chase some of that darkness from Kai's eyes. A flutter of nervous anticipation alights in my stomach; *what if he rejects me?* I brush it aside. I'll take the risk if there is even a small chance that it'll help him.

Letting go of Ash's hand, I get up, going over to the bluetooth speaker and Loki's phone, scrolling until I find the song I'm after. The beginning of *Sexual Healing* by Azee starts to play, the slow sensual beat washing over us like the caress of the waves on the shore.

Ash's grey lust filled eyes are fixed on me, and I glance over to see Loki and Jax who are in the water. They look up, pausing their game of catch—*I know, boys, eh?*—watching to see what I'm up to. Turning, I fix my stare on Kai, who's still looking out at the sea, his arms draped on his bent knees, and I walk towards him, coming to stand in front of him as he sits in his koi fish print swim shorts.

Finally, he looks up, his honey eyes dark, and gives me a small smile that makes my heart ache, and butterflies flutter in my stomach all at once. It's such a beautiful, lost, sad kind of smile that I have to hold in the cry that wants to escape my soul.

Keeping eye contact, I reach behind me, undoing the string securing my cherry print bikini top. Moving up to my neck, I do the same to that tie, letting the fabric drop between us on the rug. I reach for the strings at my waist next, undoing them one at a time until I'm standing before him, our toes touching, fully naked, and the sun licking every inch of my body.

I close my eyes briefly as a fragrant breeze teases my nipples, hardening them to tight nubs, and pebbling bumps all over my skin.

"I will risk sand in Her Vagisty, Kai, if that's what it takes to make you smile," I inform him, my lips lifted in a smirk. I open my eyes as a husky laugh falls out of his own lips, transforming his face into something worthy of the gods. "There he is," I say, my voice a rusty whisper, full of swirling emotion.

"Lilly, I'm sorry..." he starts to say, frowning, but trailing off as I get to my knees, one thigh on either side of his lap, my bare pussy hovering over his crotch.

His hands come up, caressing my thighs in a touch that leaves me shivering and aching, his eyes lowered as he watches his hands. Pausing at my arse, his fingertips dig into the flesh until I gasp, desperate for more despite the lingering sting from Ash's punishment yesterday.

"Please don't apologise, love," I tell him in a slightly breathy voice, and a bright smile lifts his lips at the endearment. "Talk when you're ready, but until then, use me as you need to."

My own hands embrace either side of his face, tilting it upwards so that our eyes meet, and we're gazing into each other's souls. I let him see all the love I have for him, hoping that he knows it's unconditional, and won't change regardless of what is going on in his head.

"You are too good for me, Lilly Darling," he murmurs, his own voice catching as his eyes glisten slightly, and my heart bleeds for him.

"No," I murmur back, leaning down so that the next part is said against his lips. I want him to take my words inside of himself, to taste their truth. "I am just right for you, as you are for me."

He pauses, his hands tightening even more on my lower cheeks before he closes the distance between our lips. The kiss starts out slow, a tentative exploration of each other, a rediscovery. I let him take charge, opening myself up to him as our tongues tangle and caress. Soon our embrace becomes heated, the sun above us eclipsed by our passion for each other, as we devour one another.

Kai pulls me tighter to him, my core lining up with his hardness. A groan leaves both our throats at the contact, and we start to move in unison, seeking more of that delicious friction. I shamelessly grind down on him, unable to help myself as Kai uses his firm grip on my arse to guide my core, so that it rubs up and down his shorts covered shaft. It feels as though the sun has somehow come down from the heavens, and is now in the centre of me, burning me up from the inside, making me desperate for more of Kai.

"Kai, love, sir...please," I moan when Kai's lips leave mine to trail a blaze of fire down my neck.

His head dips, capturing one of my hardened nubs into his warm mouth, teasing it with his tongue. My hands pull his head closer, trying to show him what I want, what I need. He pops off immediately, looking up at me with hard, hot lust in his eyes.

"Ash," he says, voice soft yet commanding. "Hold Lilly's hands behind her back."

His stare doesn't waver from mine, and I feel Ash's hot skin press up behind me, my breath shuddering out of me at the touch. I was so wrapped up in Kai that I didn't even hear my dark knight's approach. His smooth palms glide down my arms from behind, leaving a cascade of shivers in their wake. Placing a soft kiss on my bare shoulder, he grasps my wrists, then brings my arms behind me, holding both in one hand.

I whimper as he slowly, torturously, smooths the other hand around to cup one of my breasts, squeezing hard enough to turn the whimper into a gasp. Kai gruffly chuckles, then lowers his head once more. I watch as his tongue darts out, teasing my nipple again, his teeth occasionally grazing the sensitive nub.

His hands leave my hips, and I watch as he pulls the waistband of his shorts down, freeing his beautiful, fully erect cock. It stands straight up, and a moan escapes my lips at the sight of his piercings glinting in the sun. Bringing his hands up to guide my hips once again, he closes the distance between our bodies so that I'm grinding on the underside of his hard length, his metal adding a layer of sensation that's driving me wild. Ribbed for her pleasure as they say!

I rest my head back on Ash's shoulder with a deep breathy sigh, and Ash uses the access to pepper kisses and nibbles along the column of my neck. A sharp pain makes me jolt, and I look down to see Kai using his teeth to pull my nipple taut. He lets it go, then begins on the other side, Ash holding both my breasts out like an offering, massaging the one that Kai has just released.

I can feel the familiar burn of an orgasm begin in my core, and I start to move faster, desperately chasing the elusive pinnacle. But I need more.

"Please..." I murmur, my head once again on Ash's shoulder, my arms still trapped behind me in his strong grip. My eyes are closed, the rays of the sun making even the darkness bright.

Ash ceases his assault on my neck and breast, clearly waiting for Kai's instruction. Kai pauses, leaving us in stillness, me panting and exquisitely aching.

I crack my eyes, just catching Kai's nod, and a thread of excitement sizzles through me as Ash's hand leaves my aching globe, making its way slowly down the front of my body.

"Are you going to come on my fingers with just a touch like you did so prettily for Jax last night?" he asks me in a husky whisper.

"Yes...Ash..." I beg, almost crying with need as Kai resumes the movement of my hips, building me up again so that I'm on the edge of the precipice, looking down, but needing a push.

"When Kai says you can, Princess," he tells me, and I part moan, part cry with the need for release.

I open my eyes and look down at Kai to see he's leaned back a little, his eyes focusing on the way my pussy is rubbing up and down against him. There's precum glistening on his lower stomach, and my mouth waters for a taste.

Kai picks up the pace, rubbing me along his length furiously, sending jolts of sharp pleasure up from my core, his body at the perfect angle. I can't tear my eyes away from the sight of us, with Ash's tattooed fingers waiting to one side but not obstructing our view.

"Now," Kai growls out, and I watch as Ash's fingers finally make contact and pinch my clit hard.

That's all I see as the world detonates around me, my eyes closing with the force of my climax, my fingernails digging into my palms behind me as wave upon wave of intense pleasure rolls over me. My cunt clenches around empty air as I come, my release definitely soaking the front of Kai's shorts, which are pooled beneath me.

I hear his guttural moan moments later, his body going rigid underneath me, and I look down with a satisfied smile to see that he has climaxed too, ropes of glossy cum covering his stomach, my pussy, and Ash's fingers.

"I don't blame him, Princess," Ash whispers in my ear, nipping my lobe as he pushes his own hard-on into my arse crack.

"Fuck, Ash," I gasp, pushing back but stopping when he takes a sharp breath.

"Trust me, Princess. If I wasn't still sore, I'd fucking destroy this pretty ass and cunt right now," he tells me, pulling back a little. His words cause a full body shiver to whisper over me.

Finally, he lets go of my hands, and I roll my shoulders back, enjoying the tingling feeling of being unbound. I grab Ash's hand, the one covered in Kai's cum, and bringing it to my lips, I suck each finger, then lick anywhere that still has the salty liquid on it. Both men give a low moan, and I look down to see a satisfied heat in Kai's amber eyes.

I give him a cheeky grin, then push gently on his shoulders so that he lies back on the rug. Bending over, and shuffling down on my knees, I force Ash to back up until my face is hovering over Kai's cum covered stomach and crotch. With long sure strokes, I lick his seed off, loving the burst of salt on my tongue.

A soft warm tongue runs up my slit, an animalistic groan falling from my lips as Ash begins cleaning me with his own tongue. I'm still so sensitive, and the idea that Ash is also tasting Kai on my cunt is so arousing that it doesn't take long for him to build me up again until I'm quivering and shaking, and on the brink of a second climax.

Kai's abs tense, and I roll my eyes up to see his hooded gaze staring down at me as I squirm and gasp. His hands come up into my hair, gripping it between his fingers and forcing me to look at him as I get closer and closer to release.

Suddenly, Ash's lips seal around my clit, sucking hard and then biting down, and with a cry, I explode once more, my whole body flushing hot then cold. My arms give way, and I collapse on top of Kai, his fingers releasing their grip. I'm panting and sweaty, my heart pounding as I lay my head on his damp stomach and relearn how to breathe.

I hear Ash's deep rueful chuckle behind me. "Never thought I'd taste your cum, bro. It's not that bad."

Kai's stomach moves with his own gruff laugh, and I lift my head to look up at him through heavy lids. There's a wonderful sated look on his face, a smile gracing his lips as he looks down at me.

"I love you, Lilly Darling," he murmurs, and the heat from the sun's rays on my skin are nothing compared to how his words make me feel.

Delicious warmth floods my body, and I know that he'll be okay. We've not lost him, and hopefully, he'll feel comfortable enough to share whatever it is that's bothering him soon.

"I love you, Kai Matthews," I tell him back. "More than I knew was possible."

We spend the next few days in utter bliss, playing and lounging on the beach, or in the crystal clear sea. We eat delicious food made by Mama Dewi until we're fit to burst, and we make love as if there'll be no tomorrow. Well, apart from Ash who, although drives me wild with his fingers and tongue, won't even tell me what his piercing is, let alone show me. I don't hold it against him too much, seeing as he's currently healing, but still, it's a dick move, pun intended.

I know that it's not all about sex, but it's part of our bond, it's how we heal and work through things. And I don't care if people say it's not healthy, screw them. Seriously, sex is a completely natural way to express your feelings for someone and to connect in the most primal way. Not to mention, orgasms are great for your health and wellbeing so...yeah. I'll be carrying on, thank you very much.

I'm awoken in the middle of the night by the vibrating of my phone on the bedside table. Grumbling, I try to ignore it, but it starts up almost immediately again.

Untangling myself from the angel on one side of me, and the viking on the other, I scramble out of bed to grab the offending device, intending to hurl it out the window. Looking down at the flashing screen, I see it's a British number, from London, I think.

My brows draw down as I contemplate for a moment who would be calling me from the U.K. with a number that I don't know, but coming up blank, I decide to answer. If it's a cold-call, they can pay the fucking extortionate overseas call rate.

"Hello?" I ask, voice low and croaky, sitting down on the edge of the bed.

"Is that a Miss Lilly Darling?" a well spoken British male voice asks.

"Y–yes, I'm Lilly Darling. Who are you?" I query, sitting up straighter on the side of the bed, and blinking more sleep away whilst rubbing my eyes with my free hand.

I feel the rustle of bedsheets behind me, then a warmth presses against my back, and the comforting smell of vanilla washes over me. Leaning back into the embrace, Loki's arms come around my naked body, and I tune back into what the man on the phone is saying, just in time to hear his reply.

"Firstly, can you please confirm your date of birth, and the address that you were living at until January of last year?" he enquires, and because I'm still half asleep, I give him the information.

"Thank goodness. You are one hard young lady to get hold of, Miss Darling," he says with a rueful and relieved sounding chuckle. "I'm Richard Payne, from Payne & Sons Solicitors, in London."

Confusion wraps around me like a foggy blanket. *Why have solicitors in London been trying to get ahold of me?*

"Oh...I wasn't aware of any solicitors trying to get ahold of me?" I say aloud, wondering why my uncle has never mentioned it. *Perhaps he doesn't know?*

"Well, we've been trying to reach you since January of last year, but with no forwarding address, it's been quite a challenge. Especially as your mother was most insistent that only you were to know that we were even looking for you."

"My mother?" I question, my brows lowering even further and my heart rate picking up. Loki pulls me closer so that my entire back is touching his front, as if he can sense that I need comfort.

The bed dips next to me, and my hand is taken into a huge one. I look up to see Jax sitting next to me, a look of confusion over his face too. Both guys don't say anything, just lend me their strength and support, letting me know that they're here if I need them.

"Yes, I'm calling about her will, as you are the sole beneficiary."

I feel a wind rushing in my ears, and my hand tightens in Jax's grip. Taking a deep shaking breath, the room comes back into focus.

"My mother's will?" I ask, my voice quivering. Loki's arms around me tighten, and Jax starts rubbing my knuckles in a soothing motion.

"Yes, her last will and testament. Would you be able to come to the office in London? We really need to verify your identity, and talk this through in person," he asks. "I'm free tomorrow, anytime if that's convenient?"

"Ummm...I'm not sure, I'm in Bali, but maybe..." I trail off, not quite knowing what to say, and looking to Jax. "Can you hold on a second, please?"

"Of course, Miss Darling," he replies.

Bringing the phone away from my ear and looking down, I press the mute button on the screen.

"What is it, Baby Girl?" Jax questions when I look back up at him. He's all washed out in shades of grey, the tattoos on his arm standing out in stark contrast in the predawn light.

"A guy claiming to be a solicitor in London," I tell him and Loki, who snuggles even closer to my back. "He says my mum left a will, and he wants to see me tomorrow to talk through it." My mouth feels dry saying the words, my tongue darting out to lick my lips. My head is spinning with all the possibilities, with even more secrets that she must have kept. *Why could no one else know about this?*

"Hey," Loki says gently from behind me, bringing his face round so that he's looking directly at me in the dim light. "If you need to go to London, we can go to London."

"Really?" The sense of relief that floods through me at his words is palpable. My whole body sags into his embrace, which tightens further.

"Absolutely, baby," Jax replies, squeezing my hand reassuringly, and I turn to give him a small relieved smile.

Bringing my phone back up, I take it off mute and bring it up to my ear.

"Mr Payne?" I enquire.

"I'm still here, Miss Darling," he responds kindly.

"Can I give you a call when we land? I'm not sure when that will be, what with the time difference and the flight, but maybe we can arrange a time to meet then?"

"That sounds like a grand plan, Miss Darling. I shall ping over my personal mobile, and this is the office number. Just drop me a line, and provided it's not after midnight, I shall answer."

"Thank you, Mr Payne," I say, feeling lighter now that we have a plan.

"You are most welcome, Miss Darling. I shall speak to you soon. Goodbye."

"Goodbye," I return, ending the call.

I sit staring at the screen for a moment, my head swirling with the phone call, and what it all means.

"Let's go wake the others," Loki suggests, kissing my cheek. "One step at a time, Pretty Girl."

I nod. "One step at a time."

CHAPTER SEVEN

ASH

We step out of the plane to drizzle and grey skies. *Ah, England in the winter, nothing quite like it.* Especially after leaving the tropical climes of Bali.

But I promised myself that I would be everything that Lilly needed, and she needed to come to London, so here we are, on a private airstrip just outside of the metropolis, freezing our nuts off.

Pulling our coats tighter around us—*thank fuck we brought them when we left Colorado*—we hurry over to a black Mercedes V Class, our private transfer provided by Claridge's Hotel. We could have stayed at the London home, but it belongs to my shitstain father, and I try to avoid anything to do with that waste of life. I also like showing off for Lilly, stupid I know. But what's the point of wealth, if you can't experience the luxuries of life? Or share it with those that you care about?

Our driver is standing there in the rain, holding the door open for us as we approach. No umbrella poor fucker.

"Thanks," I say as we climb in, the others getting in behind me.

Loki and Jax are quicker than me and manage to sit on either side of Lilly, facing myself and Kai. *Bastards*. This sharing thing definitely can be a challenge at times. It takes getting used to, although, it's easier because it's them, my best friends in the whole world.

We all buckle in and are driving off toward the motorway within minutes.

"Breakfast at Claridge's first, then Paynes," I tell Lilly, glancing down to see her wringing her hands in her lap.

The boys take one hand each, intertwining their fingers with hers, and she visibly relaxes at the contact. I feel a spark of sharp jealousy, wishing it were me sitting next to her. Holding her hand. Comforting her. But then the sticky feeling passes as I see the way her shoulders relax a little at their touch.

The voice of my cunt of a father tells me I'm letting her make me soft. But as with most things he says, I ignore it.

My eyes land back on the road, noticing the traffic building up as we get closer to the city. *Fucking rush hour*.

Eventually, we make it to Claridge's, which isn't far from our home in Mayfair. The car drops us off outside the red brick facade of the hotel, the flags looking bedraggled in the rain. The Head Concierge, Martin, comes out to open the car door and direct the bellboys towards our luggage in the trunk.

"Welcome back, Mr. Vanderbilt," the older man greets me as I exit the car, holding an umbrella up so that I don't get wet from the rain that is falling harder now.

"Thank you," I reply as he hands it to me.

"Mr. Matthews, good to see you again," he says as Kai emerges, handing him an umbrella too. Kai nods in return, and a pang of worry shoots through me for him. He's been unusually quiet since Christmas, and I bet his fucking uncle is to blame. "Mr. Thorn, a pleasure as always," the man smiles wide at Loki, giving him an umbrella too.

Martin goes to help Lilly out, but I step back towards the door, cutting him off and holding out my hand for her to take. She grasps it and a fissure of electricity shoots through me at the touch, as she places one heeled foot onto the wet pavement. She's wearing the new boots Loki bought her, and she looks hot as hell in them.

I pull her towards me so that she's under my umbrella, and even though I can see that she's nervous by the tightness of her eyes, she still gives me a smile so warm, that it makes it feel as though we are still on the beach in Cempedak.

I can't help but lean in and place a kiss on those luscious lips of hers, sucking gently on her lower lip and swallowing the gasp that escapes. I release her before things can get heated, or more heated, between us.

"You must be Miss Darling," Martin says warmly. "Welcome to Claridge's."

"Thank you," Lilly replies, looking up at the art deco frontage with slightly wide eyes, that sparkle and gleam even in the dull winter light.

"Mr. Griffiths, welcome back," I hear the man say as I tuck Lilly's hand into the crook of my arm and lead her towards the glass doors.

A pair of smartly dressed doormen open the doors at our approach, nodding in welcome. As we step through, I hear Lilly sigh as warmth envelops us, and I look down, unable to stop myself from taking in her every reaction to the elegance that surrounds her.

Her troubles are clearly forgotten as she gawps at the entryway with her lips parted, and eyes widening further, wonder written across her face. She's fucking mesmerizing, and it's all I can do not to sweep her up and run to our suite.

"This is…this is incredible," she whispers, looking around at the black and white tiled floor, the white columns, and shaped mirrors that are all around us.

Lilly has this ability to make you see things as if for the first time, and I feel a stirring, a lightness in my chest as I take in the entrance. It really is the pinnacle of refined elegance. I can't wait until she sees our suite.

"Your bags will be taken to your rooms, Mr. Vanderbilt," Martin informs me, having caught up to us. "Would you like to freshen up first, or head straight to breakfast?"

"Breakfast!" Lilly interjects before I can say anything.

It comes out a little loud, unintentionally so, if her blush is any indicator. I chuckle at her slight outburst, earning a small glare from her, which only makes me smile wider.

"Breakfast first it is then, Miss," he says with an indulgent smile. This girl has some magic power over men, I swear. We all become her slaves, fulfilling her every whim, just for a smile in return. "If you'd care to follow me to The Foyer, your table awaits." He indicates with one arm down the hall.

We follow him, Lilly's hand still clutching my elbow like we're in *The Great Gatsby* or some shit. I place my hand over the top of hers, loving the contact of skin on skin. *Just three, maybe four more weeks*, I say to myself, then we can have all of our skin touching. It can't come fucking soon enough, any longer and I think my balls will legitimately explode.

Loki and Jax are shooting some shit behind me, and I can see Lilly smile as she glances over her shoulder at them. Kai is still pretty quiet, walking at the back of our group, and my brows droop to see him still so withdrawn.

I feel Lilly squeeze my arm, and I look down to see her soft smile.

"He'll talk to us when he's ready, Ash," she reassures me, and I squeeze her hand back in gratitude, looking ahead once again. She really is too good for the likes of us, taking time to reassure me, even though I know that she's stressed about seeing Payne.

I hear her intake of breath as we step through the doors into The Foyer. Like the entrance hall, it's all cream walls and mirrors, only with silver and sage accents instead of black.

"Your table, sirs, miss," Martin says, leading us to a table in the corner that's a little more private than the others, as it's set back into an alcove.

It's the one we usually like to sit at, and I must remember to leave him a good tip for remembering again. He gets one of the servers to take our coats, then he pulls out Lilly's chair, waiting for her to lower down before starting to push it back in.

We all take our seats, the servers bringing us a selection of breakfast foods. Pancakes, fruit platters, and even what they call a full English, which consists of sausages, bacon, eggs, mushrooms, and tomatoes. It's all delicious, although Lilly mostly picks at her plate, which is very unlike her.

I can see the others glancing at her, worried frowns on their faces.

"I– Do you think we could get there early?" she suddenly asks, looking up from her mostly untouched plate. "I just...really want to get this over with, you know?" She looks at me, and I smile gently while nodding.

"Sure, Princess," I reply, getting up and holding my hand out for her to take.

She grasps it, a grateful smile on her own lips as she stands up. The others stand as well, and Martin rushes over, his face creased with concern.

"Is the breakfast not to your liking, Mr. Vanderbilt?" he asks.

"Oh, I'm sorry, it's my fault," Lilly rushes in, drawing his eyes to her. "You see, I've a very important appointment that I'd just like to get to, and I'm too nervous to eat. It really looks amazing," she assures him, and my love for this girl, this angel, increases at the pains she takes to make sure Martin doesn't think that he, or his team, has done anything wrong.

"I quite understand, Miss Darling," he tells her with a fatherly smile, his eyes soft as he looks at her. *You and me both, dude.* "I'll get them to put some in containers for you to take with you in case you feel peckish later."

"That would be wonderful, thank you," she replies, darting forward and kissing his cheek.

The poor man blushes scarlet, clearing his throat as he indicates for a member of the serving staff to take some of the food for wrapping, and instructing another to bring back our coats. If she hadn't caught him before, she certainly has now as he turns to her with stars in his fucking eyes.

"I'll get them to bring the car around," he tells us, still looking at Lilly. "This way to reception, and it'll be along in a jiffy."

He turns on his highly polished heel, and we follow behind, Lilly still holding my hand.

"A bit old for your harem, Pretty Girl," Loki murmurs from Lilly's other side as we head down the hall. I growl like an animal at him, which just makes the shithead laugh that roaring laugh of his.

"Shut up, Loki." Lilly sighs, playfully whacking him in the chest with her free hand. Again, he just laughs, taking that hand and placing a kiss onto the back of it. *Fucking smooth kiss ass.*

We arrive in the entrance hall once more, one of the doormen coming over to let us know that the car is waiting out front. The server comes over, handing us our coats. Martin guides us to the glass doors, telling us that our food is already in the car.

We step out into the drizzle once more, umbrellas ready for us and being held by a bellboy each. A quick few steps to the waiting vehicle, and we're once again inside the Merc. This time, I make sure to sit next to Lilly, much to the annoyance of Jax who grumbles as Loki takes her other side.

Buckling up, we're driving off in a matter of minutes, Lilly's hand still firmly in my grasp. I sent Martin our itinerary before we landed, so the driver heads towards Buckingham Palace. Victoria Chambers, where Payne & Sons is located.

Looking across at Lilly, I can see she's worrying her lip between her teeth, so I reach over and pull it out.

"Only one of us gets to bite that lip, Princess," I tell her, my voice firm.

It may make me an asshole, I mean more of an asshole, but I feel the need to control her. Especially when she's doing something that may hurt her at all. Her pain is all mine. And I guess, the others' too.

She gives me a small glare, which reassures me that she's not too anxious, and I can see the temptation to bite it again, just to test me, written all over her face. I arch a brow at her, and it seems she accepts my challenge, as I knew she would, because her bottom lip starts to disappear into her mouth again, all while holding my gaze.

Glad that my distraction is working, I swoop down, my hand grabbing a fistful of her hair as I capture her bottom lip in my own teeth, biting hard enough to bruise, but not break the skin. I swallow her gasp as my mouth closes over hers, my tongue forcing entry inside, to tangle and stroke hers.

She leans into my kiss, her body relaxing as my tongue coaxes hers.

"We're here, sirs, miss," the driver informs us as we come to a stop.

I release her mouth, loving the fact that her pupils are blown with lust, and her chest is heaving. Her lip has the beginnings of a purple bruise, and I want to fucking growl in appreciation at seeing my mark on her. *Yep, I'm fucked.*

"Let's go, Princess," I order gruffly, a smirk on my face as I let go of her hair and open the car door before the driver can.

I give her my hand again, helping her out onto the sidewalk. Thankfully, it's no longer raining, and we look up at the row of white buildings before us. I look back down at her to see her straighten her shoulders and taking in a deep breath as the others come around us. My chest swells with pride. *That's my beautiful, brave girl.*

"Let's go." She nods, taking a step towards the building with a brass plaque that reads *Payne & Sons, Solicitors*.

She lets go of my hand, stepping forward, and as we all follow behind, I'm reminded that although we may be Knights, she's our Queen, and we will follow her wherever she leads.

CHAPTER EIGHT

LILLY

I walk up to the navy panelled front door, pressing the brass bell, my muscles quivering with a nervous rolling in my stomach. All my senses are heightened; I can hear a faint birdsong above the sounds of traffic, smell the mixture of dirt and wet leaves from the damp pavement.

It's strange being back here in London. Feeling this mixture of homecoming, yet a little like a stranger at the same time. Like this is no longer my home at all.

"Paynes and Sons," a female voice crackles over the intercom.

"Hi, um, Lilly, um, Darling here, to see Richard Payne," I stutter back, cursing my nerves. A warm hand lands on the small of my back, Ash's ginger scent washing over me and instantly calming me.

"Ah, come in, Miss Darling," she replies, the door buzzing, and I push it, stepping away from Ash's comfort and missing his touch immediately.

We walk into a brightly lit reception area, a Georgian window on the same wall that the outside door is situated, letting in some winter daylight. There's a crystal chandelier hanging down from the incredibly high ceiling, and a dark wooden desk sits at the base of a curving staircase. Behind it is an attractive older woman, with a neat blonde bob streaked with grey, looking at the screen of an iMac.

She looks up at our approach and smiles widely at us, not faltering when her eyes flick to the guys behind me.

"Good morning, Miss Darling, and guests," she says. "Mr Payne is expecting you and will be down shortly. Can I check your documents, please?" she asks, and I hand over my passport. She takes it, looks at the back page, then nods. "Please take a seat if you wish." She indicates a plush Chesterfield sofa in teal velvet, that's opposite her desk.

"Thank you," I murmur back, feeling nauseous, and wishing that I had eaten breakfast back at the hotel. We walk over to the sofa, but I can't sit down, nervous energy making me too jittery.

"Hey, Pretty Girl," Loki murmurs gently, taking one of my hands in his and stopping me from picking at my corduroy pinafore dress. I chose the mustard with a bee print, in the hope that it would make me feel cheerful. It's not working. "It'll be okay, promise," he assures me as I look into his beautiful green eyes that are sparkling as the weak sunlight hits them.

Just having him, all of them, near is helping to ease some of the tension inside of me. This whole thing has bought up feelings about my mother's death that I thought I'd dealt with. Foolish really, to think that the trauma would just disappear.

I nod, not knowing what to say, but stepping into him until I can rest my head on his strong chest, my arms wrapping around him and his own coming to pull me into a tight hug. Closing my eyes, I take a deep inhale, breathing him in, and being surrounded by Loki's familiar vanilla scent calms me further, until the nausea abates.

"Good morning, Miss Darling," a cultured man's voice calls out, and I open my eyes to see an older gentleman reaching the bottom of the stairs, a broad smile on his face.

He's of a slight build, and to be honest, he doesn't have many defining features, he'd be quite unmemorable. I recognise his voice from our phone call yesterday though, or maybe it was the day before with the time difference? Fucked if I know.

I take a step back, but keep hold of Loki's hand, and give Mr Payne a small smile.

"Good morning, Mr Payne."

"Richard, please," he replies, stepping towards me but keeping a respectful distance. "I'm so glad you could make it."

"Me too, although, I'm still a little confused and frankly in shock," I tell him honestly.

"Of course, that is to be expected. If you follow me, we shall get down to business and keep you in suspense no longer," he says kindly, stepping to one side and sweeping his arm towards the stairs he just came from.

He starts forward, and Ash immediately steps up next to him, striking up a seemingly casual conversation.

"So, Richard, being a solicitor is a bit of a change from police work," Ash says, and Mr Payne's, Richard's, steps falter slightly, although his smile doesn't drop.

"I'm flattered that you took the time to look into my background, Mr Vanderbilt," he replies, heading up the stairs.

I just stare at the exchange, not surprised that Ash looked into him, but I am impressed that Richard knows who Ash is given that I didn't mention it in any of our communications.

Ash nods. "I like to protect my interests, Richard. I'm sure you understand."

I bristle at being referred to as an 'interest,' and Loki must notice as he leans in to whisper into my ear.

"Don't worry, Pretty Girl. You can punish him later when we make him watch you ride my cock." I shiver at his words, whilst also being appalled that he just said that here, in the offices of what looks like a pretty high-end solicitor. *Fucking piss artist!*

Deciding that the only reaction that comment deserves is an eye roll, I look around to see several panelled wooden doors lining a carpeted corridor. We head towards the first one, and I catch a glimpse of his name on a brass plaque before Richard opens the door and ushers us in.

A large dark wood desk sits in front of double windows, the same multipaned ones as downstairs, with a view of St James' Park filling them. The whole office is not quite what I expect, with box files stacked everywhere haphazardly, and the chaos makes me like Richard more.

"Now, before we begin, Miss Darling," Richard says, closing the door softly behind him and coming around to sit behind the desk. He gestures to the two leather chairs in front of it, so I sit down, Ash beating Loki to the other chair. Loki stays beside me, and I can sense Jax and Kai flanking me, creating a wall of protective comfort at my back. "I need to check that you are happy for these boys to be present too?"

"Absolutely," I say with no hint of hesitation in my voice. That is one thing about today that I am certain of, their presence.

"Excellent. So, as I briefly mentioned in my phone call, your mother entrusted Payne and Sons with her last will and testament."

At his words, my breath hitches, and I feel Loki's hand come down onto my shoulder, squeezing gently and lending me strength. My hand comes up to grasp his, our fingers intertwining.

"Yes," I manage, my voice a little raspy. He nods, then looks down at a sheaf of papers.

"I shall read it now for you.

"Last Will and Testament of Laura Darling

I, Laura Darling, presently of Newland House, England, hereby revoke all former testamentary dispositions made by me, and declare this to be my last will."

I can't help the way my body tremors at hearing those words, knowing that my mother most likely sat in this chair and filled this out.

He continues reading some legal shit that I don't understand at all. He then goes on to list my mother's estate, and a lump fills my throat at the mention of a small sum of money, and our flat, which I'm pretty sure I am going to sell because I can't bear the idea of living there or even going back there.

"I also bequeath Lilly Darling the bonds and shares that I own pertaining to Black Knight Corporation in their entirety."

The entire world stops spinning, the universe holding its breath as those words sink in.

"I'm sorry, what?" I squeak. Richard looks up from the document at my interruption.

"I beg your pardon?" he asks, an open, if slightly confused look on his face.

"You said bonds and shares in Black Knight Corporation?" I reply, feeling Loki's hand gripping my shoulder tightly, his body stock-still.

"Yes, that's right," he says, shuffling the papers on the desk and bringing out one to read. "The bonds each give you an annual yield of one hundred and fifty thousand dollars, currently just over one hundred and twelve thousand pounds, plus an additional one hundred and fifty thousand upon their maturity, in eighteen months time. The shares make you the majority stakeholder, or shareholder, in the company."

My eyes widen at this causal impartation of information, my chest tingling and a sense of lightheadedness coming over me as I take in what he has just said.

What the ever-loving fuck is going on?

"I guess this helps to explain the photo," Loki says with a rueful chuckle, and my head whips up to look at him.

"What do you mean?" I ask, brows furrowed.

"Well, your mom was obviously a shareholder from the start, so it makes sense that she was at the gala," he reasons, and I just shake my head at how crazy this all is.

I turn to look at Ash, who has deep frown lines marring his brow as he looks at the papers on Richard's desk.

"Did you know?" I ask him, a flash of unease spiking through me. "Is this why your dad is so interested in me?"

His own head turns to look at me, his eyes hard.

"No, I didn't fucking know, Princess," he replies, his tone scathing and cutting like the steel of his eyes. I take a sharp breath in at his words. "And I have no fucking idea why my dad is interested in you. Although, this would help to explain it." He says the last part almost to himself as he looks at Loki standing next to me, then the others behind me.

"Ahem," I hear Richard clear his throat in front of me, so I turn in my seat to face him once more. "Your mother had the forethought to register everything in your name, so there's no sticking point there," he tells me reassuringly.

"Oh, okay," I mumble back, my head spinning still from the majority shareholder bomb.

I own a fucking company! And not just any company, either. The guys' company.

"Now, that concludes the reading of your mother's Will. Here are the documents that outline everything that we've discussed, including bank account details, how many bonds you have, etcetera," he says, handing me a manilla folder, which I take, my movements on autopilot. "I can see that you're a little surprised by what you've heard today, so can I suggest you take a few days to let it all sink in, and then if you have any questions or need of my services, just make an appointment with Sammi downstairs?"

"Y–yes, that sounds good," I stammer out, getting up and clutching the folder to my chest with slightly trembling hands. "T–thank you, Mr Payne, uh, Richard."

"You are most welcome, Miss Darling," he smiles kindly at me, getting up and coming round to open the door for us. The guys each shake his hand as we leave, but I can't seem to make my hands let go of the folder to do the same, so I just smile and leave the room.

We walk down the stairs silently, Loki holding my elbow, providing a steadying grip as we descend. Reaching the bottom, we make our way across the foyer, leaving the building. I take a huge lungful of the damp London air once we're outside, feeling like it's the first time I've taken a proper breath in hours.

"You realise what this means, right?" Loki says as we wait for the car, and I look up at him to see an achingly familiar gleam in his eye.

"What's that?" Jax asks, and his low voice sends the usual delicious shivers over my body, like the caress of a warm breeze in the heat of summer.

"We're officially fucking the boss," Loki quips back, barking out his sexy laugh at his own joke.

I can't help it, my face splits into a wide grin that soon turns into a full belly laugh until tears stream down my face. Before I realise it, I'm sobbing, tasting salt as tears drip down my cheeks. Someone gently takes the folder from my grasp, then I'm surrounded by my guys in a group embrace that is so full of love and support, the tears flow faster until it feels as though there are none left.

"It wasn't that bad of a joke," Loki says as I lift my face, his thumbs brushing the remnants of my tears away. I shake my head, unable to speak just yet, although I do manage a watery smile.

"Let's get you back, Lilly," Kai murmurs from my side, and I startle a little at hearing his lovely melodic voice. He's been pretty much silent thus far. I turn to face him, Loki's hands falling away to be replaced with Kai's as he cups my face, bringing his forehead to mine. "It'll be okay, my darling," he whispers, placing a gentle kiss on my lips. "Promise."

CHAPTER NINE

LILLY

As we step towards the idling car that has been waiting for us, I hear an achingly familiar voice call my name.

"Lilly!"

My stomach drops. You know, like when you are at the top of a rollercoaster and start to descend? It's like that but about a million times worse, like my heart skips a beat and the world stops spinning for a moment. I turn around in what feels like slow motion.

"Lexi?" I whisper as the gorgeous brunette woman comes towards me, wearing killer heels and a tan Burberry mac that showcases her curves to perfection.

My eyes flit to the hulking man coming up behind her, and my breath stills as I take in his huge form, tattoos pecking out of his shirt around his wrists and neck. He could definitely give Ash a run for his money in terms of the amount of ink that covers his skin. I'm speechless, not able to say anything as they reach our little group. *What the fuck are they doing here?*

"Lilly. My little Lilly Bear," Lexi croaks, voice full of emotion as tears fill her green eyes. They're not emerald like Loki's, but more of a spring green like newly sprouted leaves covered in dew. "Oh, Lilly love, I've missed you so much."

She goes to close the distance between us, but a blond Viking steps in her way, completely blocking her from my view.

"Who the fuck are you," I hear Jax rumble as the others close ranks, until all I can see is a wall of muscled backs.

I mean, the view is fucking awesome, but, yeah, I need to see what's going on in front of them as well.

"Guys, it's okay. I know them," I assure them, trying to push between Loki and Jax but not getting very far. "Fucking move!" I hiss out in frustration, ready to start shit if they keep ignoring me. I feel a desperation to make sure that they're really here begin to stir in my chest, my pulse pulsing in my ears.

They move aside slightly, leaving just enough of a gap for me to squeeze through. Fuckers. As I step through, I see Ryan squaring up to Jax, both practically snarling and vibrating with the need to let their beasts loose. I roll my eyes.

"Can you guys do the whole my muscles are bigger than yours shit later please?" I huff, stepping in between the fucking giants, causing Ryan to back up a step.

Jax brings a hand to my waist, pulling me closer to his body until his heat feels like it seeps into me, regardless of our clothes and outside coats. It's really bloody distracting, but I manage to keep Her Vagisty under control to deal with the matter at hand. *Ho-bag!*

Ryan's gaze flicks down to Jax's hand, then over the other boys, all of whom look a little scary with scowls on their faces. It's pretty adorable, and I have to rein in the smile that wants to spread on my face. Turning back to look at Lexi and Ryan, the almost smile drops as I wonder what they're doing here, and how they knew I'd be here.

"Damn, girl! You got yourself one of those reverse harems that you were always reading about, huh?" Lexi laughs, taking in all the guys with a glittering twinkle in her eyes.

It helps break the whirlwind of thoughts swirling in my mind, whilst also causing me to blush scarlet. She always knew what was going on with me, so I'm not surprised that she guessed correctly what is between me and the boys.

Her eyes come back to rest on me, and the soft look of pure love that shines in them makes tears spring to my own.

"Oh, darling," she says, her own eyes filling up as she holds out her arms to me.

I don't think about the fact that I haven't heard from them in almost a year. I just tear out of Jax's grip and throw myself at the woman who was as close to me as my own mother. Her arms wrap tightly around me, surrounding me in her floral perfume and love as she holds me close. Tears track down my face, dripping onto her mac and darkening the fabric. My own arms band around her, holding on for dear life.

I feel Ryan step up behind me, and his own arms come around both of us, adding his scent of sandalwood that feels so much like home that even more tears fall. I soak in their embrace for several moments, letting the comfort wash over me and soak into my bones.

Finally deciding that I need some answers, and need to explain to the guys what the hell is going on, I straighten up, untangle myself and take a small step away. Immediately, Jax is at my back again, pulling me against him, and I draw from his strength to ask what has been silently eating away at me for almost a year.

"Why did you disappear?" I ask, swallowing the lump that is still in my throat. Ryan's brow dips, his jaw clenching.

"We didn't disappear, little one," he tells me in his gruff voice. His chestnut hair is peppered with grey, more than when I last saw him a year ago, and his jaw is covered in a light stubble that really suits him.

"I haven't heard from you in almost a year! What the fuck else do you call it?" Anger washes over me in a wave at his words, the feelings of rejection and abandonment roaring to the surface.

"Lilly lovely, he's right. We've been trying desperately to get ahold of you, but seem to be blocked at every turn," Lexi rushes in, stepping towards me and taking hold of one of my hands. "We tried everything. All the socials, email, and even sending bloody letters! But we never heard a dicky bird," she tells me, her eyes pleading and her East London roots showing with the use of Cockney slang.

"I–I don't understand..." I trail off, looking between her and Ryan whilst being held by Jax with the others on either side of us.

"It's the truth, little one," Ryan assures me, his hazel eyes boring into mine. "We didn't even get invited to the funeral, so we couldn't talk to you then." His jaw works like his teeth are clenched tight, a shimmer of tears in his own eyes that he tries to blink away.

"W–what?" My breath whooshes out of me, and I suddenly feel lightheaded, leaning into Jax more who tightens his grip.

I never got to go to her funeral. I was too drugged up, basically under sedation for several weeks after Mum's death. Whenever I was awake, I would be an absolute mess. Screaming, rocking, and unable to cope. My uncle said that anytime the funeral was mentioned, I would fly into a mindless rage, and they'd have to sedate me yet again. I have very little memories of that time, more a feeling of pain and terror, but then, I guess that's what trauma and heavy drugs will do to you.

Although I wasn't able to attend, I'd assumed that Lexi and Ryan would have been there.

Before I can even formulate a response, Ash steps in.

"Can I suggest that we take this indoors somewhere? Before it starts raining again. This seems like a conversation to have in private."

"Y–yes, that's a good idea," I stammer out, seeing the concern in Lexi's and Ryan's eyes, their gazes pained as they look at me. "We're staying in Claridge's, can you meet us there?"

"Of course, Lilly Bear," Lexi replies, squeezing my hand. "We'll be right behind you."

I watch as they walk away until Jax takes a step back, and turns me back around to face the car, his huge hands on my upper arms.

"Come on, Baby Girl. Let's get in the car, and you can have some breakfast," he softly suggests, letting go and grasping my hand in his warm one. I follow him, my mind a maelstrom of emotions and thoughts.

We settle inside the plush interior, the luxury lost on me as Jax buckles my seatbelt, and Ash opens one of the food containers that he got from somewhere. It's full of fruit and those small caramel Stroopwafels, and although it feels as though my stomach is churning, when he brings a waffle to my lips in silent command, I take a bite. My appetite returns full force as the sweet flavour hits my tongue, and before I know it, I've finished them and the fruit, leaving the container empty.

I must have eaten quickly, because we pull to a stop outside the hotel as I swallow my last mouthful.

"Good girl," Ash praises, using his thumb to wipe a crumb from the corner of my mouth. "Right, before we go in, can you tell us who Lexi and Ryan are?" he asks, and I'm shocked to realise that I didn't even introduce them. I take a deep breath.

"Lexi was Mum's best friend, she worked at Grey's too," I tell them, looking at Kai who gives me a small smile that warms me more than the heating in the vehicle. He's putting his stuff aside to help me deal with mine, and my chest feels like it's going to burst, my heart so full as I look at him and then the others. "Ryan was Mum's long-term boyfriend, practically a father to me although she never made it official for some reason."

Ash nods, Kai obviously filled him in on our conversation by the lake last term, then the door opens and he's stepping out, holding out a hand for me to take like a gallant Knight.

I look around to see Lexi and Ryan walking up to us, tentative smiles on their faces as they take in the hotel. Like Mum, Lexi earnt well, but this is next-level shit.

I step away from Ash, taking hold of Lexi's hand and her face lights up with a brilliant smile, the very reason why she had the best tips at Grey's. It feels so comforting to be holding her hand, and we walk like that, following Ash and Jax with Kai, Loki, and Ryan coming up behind us.

Once inside, Martin, who was there to greet us, takes us over to the Art Deco style lift, ushering us inside. He leaves us to it, only after Ash assures him that we know where we're going several times. Apparently, The Prince Alexander suite is their usual, and they've stayed here quite often before.

We take the lift up to the third floor, the male uniformed lift attendant making sure we get where we need to be, because heaven forbid we press the damn button ourselves.

Our personal butler, Edwards—*I know, what the ever-loving fuck has my life become?*—greets us as the gold lift doors open. He's of middle age, dressed in a smart dove grey uniform with white gloves.

"Good morning, Mr Vanderbilt, Mr Matthews, Mr Thorn, Mr Griffiths, and Miss Darling," he says politely as we step out of the lift onto the carpeted hallway floor. "This way, please." He indicates with an outstretched arm, and we follow after him to the end of the corridor where he opens white wooden double doors. "We've added a slightly larger table to seat five, as per your request, Mr Vanderbilt," he tells Ash as he ushers us through into an entrance hall.

Yep, you heard me right. Our suite has an entrance hall, complete with black, white, and grey marble tiled flooring, a crystal chandelier, and mirrors reflecting the space making it feel light and airy.

"Thank you, Edwards," Ash replies, and his American accent is stark against the butler's upper class British one. "Can we have a light buffet lunch sent up, please, enough for us and our guests."

"Of course, sir," Edwards bows his head, opening one of the doors and revealing the living room space before holding his arm out to take our coats. Once he has them all, including Lexi's and Ryan's, he hangs them up on an antique coat stand, then turns away to presumably fulfil Ash's request.

My steps falter, alongside Lexi's, as we take in the room before us. We seem to be in a corner of the hotel, because there are floor-to-ceiling windows draped in white gauze, and framed with duck egg blue watered silk curtains on two sides. Coordinating silk cushions are scattered on the navy blue velvet sofas, walnut side tables situated next to them. Other silk upholstered chairs are dotted around the room, and there's a small dining table, plus a fucking baby grand piano. To top it all off, there's another crystal chandelier. *Jesus.*

It's not quite Buckingham Palace, but it wouldn't be out of place in a stately home.

"Drinks?" Ash queries, snapping me out of my room-fest.

"Whiskey, single malt," Ryan says gruffly, and I arch a brow at him. "Please."

Loki chuckles, obviously remembering all the times I pulled him up on poor manners.

"Lexi?" Ash asks, and I think it takes her a little by surprise as she jumps.

"Same, please..." she replies, raising her perfect eyebrows at him.

"Asher Vanderbilt," he says, heading over to what looks like a drinks cabinet. *He's such a cuntwaffle sometimes!*

"You can call him Ash," I tell her, earning a raised brow from the devil himself, although he doesn't say anything further as he turns and starts preparing drinks.

I pull Lex towards one of the sofas, heaving a sigh of relief as I sit down in the soft cloud-like seat.

Loki and Jax come to sit opposite us on the other sofa, taking up the whole fucking thing. *Bloody massive bastards.*

"Loki Thorn," my fallen angel announces, leaning forward. "And this hulking piece of real estate," here he pauses to wink at me, and although I roll my eyes, my face heats fifty shades of crimson, "is Jax Griffiths."

Jax just nods at Lex, then at Ryan who grabs his drink off Ash and comes to stand behind me. Ash brings me over a fruit juice mocktail, and I'm touched that he somehow knew I wanted to keep a clear head for this.

"Thanks," I say, and his grey eyes soften ever so slightly, his lips twitching in response.

Kai hands Jax an orange juice, which makes Jax rumble something that no doubt was rude under his breath, and passes Loki a bourbon. He sits down on one of the cream silk chairs with a wine glass of clear liquid, which I'm guessing to be sake.

"Kai Matthews," he tells Lex and Ryan, giving them a small smile.

Finally, Ash returns with what I think is whiskey for himself, and sits on my other side, even though there is a vacant chair to my left.

I take a sip of my drink, loving the burst of pineapple and coconut on my tongue.

"So," I begin, taking a deep breath and setting my drink down on the walnut coffee table in front of me, and turning to face Lex with Ryan in my peripheral vision. "How did you know where I'd be this morning?" I ask, as it's been bothering me since I first saw them.

"Sammi told us," Lex replies breezily. "She used to work at Grey's, remember?"

And suddenly it hits me, my eyes widening. I knew I recognised Richard's receptionist.

"Shit! I thought I'd seen her before," I exclaim, inwardly rolling my eyes at the fact that I didn't guess who she was.

"Wait, Payne's receptionist told you we were there?" Ash cuts in darkly. His warm hand comes to rest on my neck, his fingers lightly playing with that sensitive spot between my neck and shoulder, sending tingles racing across my skin straight to my now pebbled nipples. *Twatwaffle.*

"Please don't be cross, Ash," Lexi begs, her eyes flitting over my shoulder before coming back to rest on me. "We've been so desperate, and she knew that. I know she probably shouldn't have told us, but I can assure you she didn't tell anyone else. She's one of us."

Ash just hums in response behind me, so I decide to try and focus on something else.

"Why weren't you at Mum's funeral?" I ask, feeling a chill as I look at her. There's a sharp pain on my hand, and I bring my finger up to see that I must have been picking at my cuticles, my index finger is bleeding around the nail bed.

Lexi tuts, grasping my hand and inspecting my finger. She reaches into her trouser pocket, pulling out a tissue to wrap around it, all while keeping my hand in hers.

"We didn't know," she tells me sadly, her eyes glistening and making the green colour shine like grass after it's rained.

"The first we knew was when we finally managed to get hold of Adrian's secretary who told us that it had already happened and was a quiet, family only affair," Ryan cuts in, his voice rough. I glance at him to see his jaw is tightly clenched, his fist gripping his glass.

"I don't understand," I tell them, my confused gaze fliting between the two of them, then settling on my hand in Lexi's. "I wasn't there either," I admit softly, a tear escaping my eye, and slowly making its way down my cheek, my throat thick. "I was too...fucked up, sedated for three weeks, and by the time I was compos mentis, it was weeks later."

It's the one thing, apart from the argument I had with her, that I am ashamed of. I was too lost in my grief to attend my own mother's funeral. But to know that she may have been...alone. *Why would Adrian do that?*

I feel Ash shift closer to me, his warmth caressing my back as his hand moves to rub soothing circles on my upper back.

"Oh, Lilly Bear," Lex murmurs, squeezing my hand. "Don't blame yourself, love, it's not your fault. Any of it." More tears drip into my lap at her words, yet I know that what she is saying is true, and a small part of me is beginning to let go of the blame. "Do you, do you know where she's buried?" Lex asks gently, and my head snaps up, my heartbeat thrashing in my ears.

"I–I, n–no," I stutter, realising that I truly have no idea where she is, or what happened to her after the funeral. Nausea fills my stomach, my fingers going cold.

"Highgate Cemetery," Kai tells the room in his melodic voice, my head turning in his direction as I let out a huge breath, my muscles going weak. I catch his eye, giving him a wobbly smile, which he returns, pushing his glasses up his nose. I've never been more thankful for his research skills.

"How do you know that?" Ryan asks suspiciously, and I turn my head back to look at him with a slight glare. He's staring at Kai, eyes narrowed.

"Cool your heels, Ry," Lex scoffs. "If Lilly trusts these boys, then so do we. End of."

Ryan grumbles, but backs down, looking at me again a little sheepishly.

"Did Sami tell you that Richard was reading Mum's will to me today?" I ask her, and her eyes go wide, mouth falling open a little.

"No, she gave us no details. Just said that you were going to be there, and what time," Lex replies.

"Did you know Mum had stocks, shares, and bonds in Black Knight Corporation?" I question, suddenly desperate to know more about this part of my mum's life. Lexi's arched brows dip.

"Isn't that the big company who used to bring clients into Grey's?" she turns to Ryan and enquires. He also frowns.

"Yeah. And come to think of it, Laura was never there when they came…I don't think, apart from maybe once…" he responds in an uncertain tone.

I look round at the guys, but if their furrowed brows are any indication, they are just as confused as we are.

"I wonder if that Mr Black guy would know more…" Lex muses aloud, and I catch Kai sitting up straighter, leaning forward.

"Did you say, Mr Black?" he quizzes her, his tone urgent. Jax and Loki sit forward in their seats too.

"Yeah, he's a regular," Lex tells him, then looks at me. "He was your mum's biggest fan," she says, flashing a small smile. "Why?" she asks, looking back at Kai.

None of the boys say anything, just exchange glances. I let go of Lex's hand, turning so that I'm facing Ash, knowing that the others will follow his lead.

"What's going on, Ash?" I ask firmly. He darts a look to Ryan and Lex, and I can't help but roll my eyes at him. "I trust them as much as I trust you. They were at my birth for fuck's sake!"

He waits a beat, then sighs, taking a sip of his drink.

"Well, apart from apparently you, a Mr Black is the second largest shareholder of Black Knight Corp."

CHAPTER TEN

LILLY

After that bombshell, which poses more questions than answers, we all eat a light but delicious lunch of finger sandwiches, more fruit, and some divine mini cakes.

The boys leave Lexi, Ryan, and myself to catch up, sitting on the sofas as we sit round the small table. I tell them all about Highgate, about the crazy amount of schoolwork, and the beautiful Colorado scenery. Lexi almost chokes when I tell her in hushed tones the story of Ash's party, when I danced for the guys using all the moves she taught me—obviously omitting being tag teamed afterwards by Loki and Jax whilst Ash watched.

She makes me promise to have a girl's night whilst I'm here, and I just know she's going to ask me all about the guys, because she's always been a dirty bitch!

As they're getting their coats on, Lex suddenly turns, a huge smile on her gorgeous face.

"What are you doing tonight?" she questions, practically bouncing on her toes.

"Um, I don't think we have any plans..." I start, but she interrupts with a squeal.

"Yay! It's the Grey's New Year's Eve party, you must come!"

"Wait, it's New Year's Eve?" I ask, my head spinning as I try to work out what day it is. She rolls her eyes at me.

"You always were clueless, Lilly Bear!" she laughs, pulling me in for a hug. "I'll tell Grey to reserve you a table. You remember *Bom Bidi Bom* and *Candyman*, right?" she whispers in my ear, and it suddenly dawns on me what she's saying.

A grin takes over my face, which she returns with a wink as she pulls away, and leans back in to kiss my cheek. "Let's show those boys what you can really do, huh?" she murmurs.

LOKI

We find ourselves standing in the entrance hall of one of the most exclusive gentlemen's clubs in London. The walls are painted a soft grey, with matching velvet drapes, and black and white tiled flooring.

A thrill runs through me at being here. I mean, it's fucking Grey's! This is where deals that change the course of the world are made, all whilst sipping the finest alcohol, and watching the most gorgeous girls dance, although the latter no longer interests me now that I have the most beautiful woman in my bed nightly. In all our dealings and preparations to take over our roles at Black Knight, we've never been invited inside Grey's until tonight.

"Welcome, and Happy New Year," a stunningly attractive redhead greets us, beaming but not overly familiar. "Let me show you to your table, Lilly will join you shortly," she tells us, leading the way to a dark wooden staircase and down to a basement level.

The lighting down here is more typical of what I would expect from a strip joint, albeit a high-class one, being dark and moody, with clearly expensive furnishings, a clean woodsy smell and twinkling lights on the ceiling that I think are in the patterns of star constellations. The redhead leads us to a set up in the corner that has dark grey semi-transparent drapes surrounding it, a large circular table in the center, and is surrounded by deep red leather chairs. There are steps that lead up to the table, and I notice that each of the tables are set up the same, all with identical drapes to create a more intimate feel. I like it and my heart beats faster with anticipation of the unknown.

She takes our drinks order, leaving us to seat ourselves. I look around as we take our seats and grin, excited to see what Lilly thinks of our attire. Being an exclusive joint, Grey's demands high standards from its guests, so we are all wearing black tie outfits, as is the expectation here, and look fine as fuck.

Lilly left this afternoon, not long after Lexi and Ryan, as she said she needed to prepare for tonight. Whatever the fuck that meant. Our drinks are brought to us, and I peer around, fingers tingling with the night to come, whatever it entails.

"Where the fuck is Lilly?" Jax growls out, sipping his soda like it did him wrong. I can't help chuckling at him, earning a glare which only makes me laugh harder. "Fuck off," he grumbles, but the corner of his lips lift ever so slightly.

We appear to be the last people to arrive because we've not long sat down when suddenly the lights go out, plunging us into complete darkness. My heart starts racing again as the familiar opening beat of *Bom Bidi Bom* by Nick Jonas starts to sound over the speakers. Spotlights appear in front of the tables, one by one, illuminating girls wearing a variety of black lingerie, standing there clicking their fingers in time to the beat. A wicked smile comes across my lips as I get an idea of where Lilly might be. The naughty minx.

The light in front of our table goes on, and I swear I stop breathing, my heart pausing in its thumping rhythm. *Holy fuck.*

Lilly stands in front of us, wearing...well, fuck me. My eyes peruse her body slowly, giving me the best kind of torture as I take her in.

She has a jeweled halter bra of sorts on, the jewels swirling around her gorgeous fucking tits, with a small part, just over her nipples, covered with black cloth. There are ropes of sparkling crystals dangling down from her bra to her hips, and I bite my knuckles at what lies there. A jeweled belt lies low on her luscious hips, so fucking low that I'm not sure how the fuck it's staying up. The sparkling gems swirl, creating a heart type shape right over her pussy, where black silk, that is almost fucking transparent, flows to the ground, scooping down so that her bitable thighs are exposed, and presumably just covering her ass in the back. More ropes of jewels hang from the belt, decorating the outside of her thighs.

I manage to tear my eyes away for a brief second to glance around at the guys. They are all in a similar state to me, devouring her like she's a meal and we are starving men.

My gaze flits back to her as she ascends the steps, the curtains coming to close behind her of their own accord, creating a magical world where only she exists. The beat changes and she begins to dance for us.

Jesus fucking Christ.

The way she moves her body hypnotizes us, like a snake luring its prey. We are her willing fucking sacrifices, eyes following her every move as she dips and turns, running her hands all over her delectable body. I'm hard as a fucking rock right now, almost ready to blow my fucking load watching this goddess perform for us, and only us.

It suddenly feels very warm even though I can feel the breeze of the air conditioning against my neck, and I pull at my shirt collar, knowing that it's no good, it's the fire inside me that burns for this woman that's raising my temperature.

She catches my eye, giving me the sexiest fucking grin, and a groan slips from my lips when she moves her leg and her skirt splits, revealing a creamy inner thigh. Ash hisses a breath to my right, and I can hear Jax's growl over the music to my other side.

She turns around, giving me a view of her silk-clad ass as she winds down to the tabletop, going on her knees then spinning round, facing me and moving her body the way she does when she's riding my fucking cock. Instinctively, my hand goes to my crotch, rubbing my hardness to try and get some relief from this inferno inside of me.

Suddenly, hazel eyes have caught mine, darting down and becoming hooded when she sees what I'm doing. Licking her lips, a wicked, naughty smirk comes over her plump lips, and I just know that what she has in mind may get me in trouble. *Fuck it!*

Her eyes come back up, and she mouths, *"I dare you,"* at me. She fucking knows I can't resist a dare, so holding her hazel eyes with my own, I lower my zipper. She looks down, still moving her body, kneeling on the table. A gasp leaves her lips, that I want so desperately wrapped around my cock, when my dick springs free. I lean back to make sure she has a good view as I spit into my hand, grabbing it in my slicked palm. *Shit, that feels good.*

Pumping my fist a few times, I can't help but close my eyes at the rush of pleasure that skitters up my spine. My lids jerk open when I feel something brush my tip softly, to see Lilly leaning over me, her fingers outstretched. She catches my eye.

"Stand up," she orders, and although I raise my brow, I'm not objectionable to being ordered around in the bedroom. Or well, exclusive strip club.

I do as she says, glancing around to see that with the drapes, you can barely see what's happening at the tables. All thoughts are cut off when smooth lips give me what I want, wrapping around the tip of my aching cock.

"Fuck...yes..." I hiss, my hand coming up to tangle in her hair, grabbing a fistful and using it to push down slightly.

She follows my lead, taking me all the way to the back of her throat and holding me there, swallowing around my length until my legs fucking twitch. Looking down, I watch as she starts to pull back, taking a breath before sinking down again.

I look up at the others, seeing that they all have their dicks in their hands, stroking to the same rhythm that Lilly is sucking. Even Ash has his out, and I finally get to see what metal he got. Fuck, he doesn't do things by halves! I catch his hooded gaze, smirking, and he puts his finger to his lips, clearly asking me to keep my mouth shut.

Before I can think of a smartass remark, Lilly does something with her tongue that she knows drives me fucking wild, and I snap my hips forward, burying deep inside her throat.

"Jesus, Pretty Girl," I exclaim in a whisper-growl, drawing my hips back so that she can breathe before snapping them forward again. I repeat the move until I'm fucking her mouth, and she relaxes, letting me use her.

Shooting stars of pleasure light up my whole fucking body until I feel the familiar burn of my orgasm fast approaching. The possibility of being caught any moment, in one of the most exclusive clubs in the world, has me climaxing so fucking hard I swear I black out.

Ropes of cum coat the back of her throat, and I pull out so that it covers her tongue and fills her mouth too. She looks up at me, eyes watering with her makeup smudged. But to me she's never looked more beautiful, especially when she opens her mouth to show me my own cum before closing her lips and swallowing it down.

The guys groan around us, and I see Ash quickly put his dick away before Lilly turns her head in his direction. Her chest heaves as she looks at him, and her eyes narrow when he holds his cupped hand out.

"Drink, Princess," he smirks, his voice a little breathless.

I swear my dick starts to get hard again when she crawls towards him, grabbing his hand and bringing it to her lips. Not taking her eyes off him, she starts lapping at the cum in his palm like a cat with fucking cream, only stopping when it's all clean, his palm glistening.

"Good girl. Now the others," Ash commands, stroking the side of her face tenderly.

My breathing quickens as she does his bidding, turning to go over to Kai who holds out his jizz filled palm to her. She drinks that, then moves on to Jax where she does the same thing one more time. Even I hear his growl of approval as she licks his big palm with sure strokes of her pink tongue.

She finishes with one final lick, and I regret not putting my dick away sooner as he's pretty much hard again. But I guess I can't spend the whole night with him out. Shame.

I Feel Like I'm Drowning by Two Feet comes over the speakers just as Lilly straightens up and the drapes around our table begin to slowly open.

"That's my cue," she tells us, giving me a cheeky wink, then walking down the steps, scurrying off across the polished floor towards a door that Ryan is guarding. He gives us a nod.

"What the fuck is she up to now?" Ash muses aloud, his eyes narrowed on the door that our brunette pixie vanished through.

A devilish smirk lifts my lips, my own eyes going back to the door as I remember the feeling of her plump lips wrapped around my cock, which twitches at the visual.

"Whatever it is," I start, grabbing my drink and leaning back in my seat, "you know it'll be good," I tell him. "And besides, you can punish her later, brother."

LILLY

My mouth still tingles from the pounding that Loki gave it earlier, my throat a little sore and my pussy damp and fluttering, Her Vagisty demanding satisfaction.

"Did they enjoy *Bom*?" Lexi asks, leaning over and helping me to pin the army-style navy blue garrison cap into my forties styled hair.

My lips twitch, and that's all the answer she needs. She chuckles that throaty laugh of hers, and I get up, surveying my costume in the full-length mirror for the next dance. I'm looking damn fine if I say so myself!

A navy and cream striped bra, which gives me awesome cleavage, with red sequin trim; high waisted navy shorts, with gold buttons that end just along my arse cheek line, with red sequin suspenders; black fishnet tights, and red sequin heels complete the look. My makeup is on point with cherry red lips and sharp cat eye eyeliner.

"Your mum would have been so proud of the stunning young woman you've become, Lilly Bear," Lexi tells me as she comes up behind me, wrapping her arms around my waist. Tears sting my eyes at her words, my heart beating double time.

"Do you think so?" I ask, a slight wobble in my voice as I catch her eye in the mirror.

"I know so, gorgeous," she assures me, straightening up. "And I think, for what it's worth, that she would approve of your harem," she adds with a wink.

"Lexi!" I scold, my cheeks flushing as she just smirks at me. "Thanks for convincing Grey about tonight," I say in a more serious tone. "I know he doesn't usually let underage girls perform."

"No worries, darling. You're practically part of the furniture here, and he, like the rest of us, was just so relieved to have finally found you," she replies, dropping an air kiss on my cheek then sauntering off in her own red sequin heels.

My mind takes me back to entering the club earlier this afternoon, the squeals and tears from the girls, and the way that Grey's eyes glistened slightly as he looked me over. He's a man of few words, and when he does speak, people tend to listen, so when he said "Welcome home, Lilly," I got so choked up I could barely breathe.

Lexi's right, I basically grew up at Grey's; apparently, I used to nap the best in a corner during rehearsals with the music turned up full volume. These people are my family, and I'm ashamed that I forgot that fact for a time.

"Time to go, girls!" Justin, who's been at Grey's for-fucking-ever shouts, clapping his hands and breaking into my thoughts.

We all start to exit the doors, down the performers' staircase to the basement, and I can just hear the faint sound of the current song coming to an end as I reach the bottom step. Nervous butterflies flutter in my stomach as the door opens into darkness, and I bounce on my toes in anticipation of what the boys will think when the lights go up.

They looked utterly drool worthy in their tuxes, so much so that it was hard to remember my steps when I danced for them earlier. I don't have any more time for thoughts of my hot as fuck guys, as the opening bars of Christina Aguilera's *Candyman* starts playing, the lights go up, and I run to my table, along with the others, in order to get there on time to start the dance.

I can't keep the wide smile off my face as I step up onto the table and see my guys' faces. Loki's jaw is hanging open, Jax is biting his lip in the most distracting way, Ash is rubbing his jaw, his eyes molten, and Kai's eyes are full of fire as he takes me in from my cap to my heels.

It's a quick paced dance, a mix of sensual burlesque moves, pausing in provocative positions, and lindy hop, with some good old sexy dancing thrown in. The true beauty of this number is that we dance in unison, some moves even in perfect synchronicity following on from one another, and as the curtains around the table are open, I see the other girls all dancing with me.

I'm not sure the Knights notice though, their eyes glued to my body as I dance in time to the beat. The look in each jewelled orb is positively feral, like wolves that have spotted their next meal, and my heart starts racing from more than just the dancing. We come to the part of the dance that's floor, or table work, our legs in the air opening and closing in time to the music.

As the number begins to draw to a close, I keep Ash's eye, unable to look away as I perform the closing moves. I can't help the smirk that lifts my cherry lips when he reaches down to adjust himself. I'm still pissed that I clearly missed seeing his dick earlier, and the mystery piercing. And I bet Loki won't tell me later! *Jizzfucker!*

My chest is heaving when the song finishes, leaving me in a

classic pin-up pose; standing with my knees bent, arse out, and hands on my thighs. I vaguely register the applause around us, watching as Ash slowly brings his hands together, keeping eye contact.

Our stare off is interrupted by two of the serving girls bringing over what looks like chocolate fondue. I look back to Ash, registering his devilish smile as they set it down.

"Thank you," he says to them, and they bow their heads in return.

The curtains that surround us start to whisper closed, encasing us in our own world again. I look over to Loki, seeing a look of delighted puzzlement on his face that probably matches my own.

"What's going on?" I question, locking eyes with Ash as he reaches over to grab a strawberry.

"Lie down, back on the table, Princess," he orders, and his hard voice lets me know that I best obey. Of course, my inner brat decides to make an appearance, unable to help herself.

"Why?" I query. His nostrils flare, but a delighted gleam enters his steel eyes. I hear Kai growl behind me, just as *Twisted* by Two Feet starts to play.

"For that, you don't get to come until the stroke of midnight," Ash informs me casually, taking off his jacket.

My gaze is focused on his hands as he achingly, slowly undoes each silver cufflink, setting them on the table. Then, he rolls the sleeves of his shirt up his forearms and to his elbows, showcasing his beautifully inked arms, leaving me breathless and my cunt dripping. I swallow hard at the arm porn show he's giving me, hearing his low chuckle.

"Now. On. Your. Fucking. Back," he orders, all traces of humour gone, and my gaze snaps up to see his grey orbs are hard and unblinking, his jet black brows lowered over them, screaming that he's the hunter and I'm the prey.

Unable to keep standing, even if I wanted to, I sink shakily to my knees, careful to avoid the desert that surrounds me. Sitting back, I finally lie down, looking up at the dark ceiling that resembles the night sky, with glittering crystals and twinkling lights.

Kai's face comes into view, and I notice that he too is without a jacket, his sleeves rolled up. The top two buttons of his shirt are undone as well, and his bow tie is missing.

"See," he whispers seductively as he leans further forward. "You can be a good girl." He pulls back, bringing his hands up, and I notice that he is holding his undone bow tie in them. "Lift your head up, darling."

This time I do as ordered straight away. I wouldn't put it past them to withhold orgasms all night. He wraps the cloth around my eyes, plunging me into darkness, only the slight glitter of light appearing along the edges of my blindfold. My head jerks slightly as he knots it to one side so that the knot isn't pressing on the back of my head when I lower it back down.

"Arms up, Baby Girl," I hear Jax rumble, and my head turns towards his low voice, again doing as I'm told without a fuss.

My heart rate picks up, my breathing coming in short pants as I feel my wrists being bound, presumably with his own bow tie. My thighs rub together, desperate to ease the ache that is building in my core, soaking through my thong and shorts.

"Naughty, Lilly," Loki croons, grabbing my foot, and bringing my leg up, placing a gentle kiss on my inner ankle that sends shivers skittering across my skin. The move effectively stops me from even attempting to ease the throbbing between my legs, and I whimper.

"Oh, Princess," Ash tsks, and my head turns to look down, but obviously with the blindfold, I can't see what he's doing. "You've got forty-five minutes until midnight yet," he chuckles like the cunt-muffin that he is. "Loki, take her shorts off, expose her pretty pink pussy."

My breath hitches at his words, a flash of nervous anticipation flooding through me. I mean, I know I just gave Loki head, and there aren't any more dances planned for me to take part in, but someone could interrupt us at any moment. The thought of getting caught has a rush of liquid seeping out of my cunt.

What I assume are Loki's hands brush the bare skin at my waist, my skin tingling at the touch.

"Lift your hips, Pretty Girl," he orders once he's undone the side zip, and I obey.

Slowly, he pulls them down my legs, managing to get them over my heels without taking the shoes off. I swear that boy has as much of a shoe fetish as I do!

He'll have to take them off to take the tights off... I start to muse but the fucker just has to prove me wrong. With a tearing sound, that I hope the music covers, he rips open the crotch of my fishnets.

"Don't you fucking dare!" I hiss, but it's too late as I feel the crotch of my knickers rip, Loki snapping the thong.

Before I can curse him out, I hear a growl, then feel a wet tongue lick my damp folds from opening to clit, and my hips buck off the table as a deep moan leaves my lips. The action causes more liquid to seep out of my lower lips, earning another Loki growl.

"She's fucking soaked," he groans, and I can feel cool air as he blows on my overheated sex.

"Such a pretty pink pussy," Ash coos in appreciation. "Now, there's some melted chocolate up there that I'm sure Kai will enjoy," he tells me, and a fine tremble begins in my limbs at the idea of the burning hot chocolate dripping on my body. "But I prefer my strawberries with cream, don't you, Loki?" he asks.

I whimper as I feel the cool round fruit being dipped into my dripping cunt, just as someone moves the cups of my bra aside, exposing my pebbled nipples to the air. Ash hums in approval from near my feet, just as my left nipple is tweaked hard, and I cry out.

"What's your safe word, Lilly?" Kai asks, his voice gruff and full of desire.

"Red," I whimper back just as I feel a hot tongue slide through my folds again, not sure if it's Ash or Loki.

"Good," he replies, seconds before I feel the burn of the molten chocolate hit my sensitive nipple.

I gasp, which turns into a moan as a mouth seals over the bud, a tongue swirling over the sensitive flesh, then sucking the chocolate off. Another burn on my other nipple leaves me panting, a cool strawberry dipping into my cunt at the same time.

I lose all sense of time as I'm consumed, lost in the sensations of hot tongues, cool fruit, and burning chocolate until I'm quivering so close to the edge I can feel myself beginning to fall off.

"Not yet, Princess," Ash's husky voice growls out, and I cry out in alarm as all of them stop, leaving me untouched until my thrashing heart starts to slow.

Then, they begin the sweet torture once more, building me up only to stop as soon as I near climax. They repeat this process several times over, swapping places, until I'm a sweaty, sticky mess, aching and pleading for release.

After what feels like a lifetime, the music quietens, and a countdown begins.

"Ten!" voices from outside our bubble shout.

"Ten seconds, Princess," Ash whispers in my ear, and I jump thinking he was at the other end of the table. He pinches my nipple, tugging it until I groan.

"Nine!"

I can feel myself edging closer as a hot mouth covers my other nipple and a tongue dips inside me.

"Eight!"

My whole body starts to tingle, from my toes to my teeth in sweet anticipation of the release to come.

"Seven!"

"Not yet, Pretty Girl," Loki cautions, his musician's fingers teasing my side as he peppers my neck with gentle kisses. He must have swapped places too.

"Six!"

God, I'm so fucking close, my entire body trembling with the need to come.

"Five!"

"Are you going to squirt for us, Princess?" Ash's husky voice asks in my ear. *Fucking hell.*

"Four!"

Ten seconds have never felt so fucking long!

"Three!"

"Almost there, darling," Kai's melodic voice sounds from the bottom of the table, his fingers teasing my clit. "You're doing so well, beautiful."

"Two!"

"I want you to come all over my face, Baby Girl. On the one," Jax orders, his husky voice and naughty words bringing me so close I can taste freedom.

"One!"

Thick fingers slam into me as four mouths descend on my body at the same time.

I.

Fucking.

Shatter.

My whole body lights up, only being held down by strong hands as I explode like the fireworks that are no doubt covering the sky in multicoloured lights at this very moment. Wave upon wave of intense pleasure crashes through me, and I obey Jax's command coming all over his face as my liquid release gushes out of me.

Happy fucking New Year.

CHAPTER ELEVEN

LILLY

We spend the next couple of days enjoying the sights of London, doing the whole tourist thing. We take an open-top bus, something I've never done before even though I grew up here. Lexi and Ryan join us every day, and it's wonderful to have them back in my life again, as if they were never out of it.

Ryan is still a little unsure of the guys, casting suspicious looks their way every so often until one day, Jax and him start talking and discover that they both spent time in South Africa training. Although I'm not sure what that means for either of them. I know that it can't be good if Black Knight was involved, which they would have been given that Jax mentions it as part of his training. It hurts my soul that they went through that, especially Jax. I can see a newfound respect in Ryan's eyes after that, and I'm glad that they've found some common ground.

We have two days left, and I wake up in an empty bed, wondering where Loki and Jax, who spent the night exploring my body in the most mind-shattering ways, are. Coming out of the bedroom, dressed in just Loki's T-shirt, I sleepily stumble into the living room area to find a wonderful breakfast laid out for me, and all four guys sitting round the small dining table with *Slow Hands* by Niall Horan playing softly in the background. They all stop talking when I enter, looking up at me as I walk towards them, their eyes drinking me in and causing a blush to spread across my cheeks.

"Morning, Princess," Ash greets me, getting up and pulling out the chair in between his and Kai's for me.

He kisses my cheek sweetly when I reach him, then motions for me to take a seat, pushing the chair in as I lower myself down. He resumes his seat, and it's then that I notice they're all still looking at me intently. I can't help narrowing my eyes at them.

"What's going on?" I ask, raising a brow as I watch Kai begin to fill up a plate with pancakes, fruit, greek yoghurt, and then drizzling it all with syrup.

"We thought, Pretty Girl, that you might like a girls' day with Lexi, so we organised a spa day in town with lunch and champagne," Loki tells me, pouring me a large glass of fruit juice, most likely tropical, as he knows that's my favourite.

"Oh," I respond, my lips lifting at the thoughtfulness of these men. "That sounds wonderful, thank you," I tell them, accepting the plate from Kai and the glass from Loki.

I take my knife and fork, cutting some pancake and piling on some strawberries and yoghurt, and bring my fork to my lips just as Ash speaks.

"And then tomorrow, we're visiting your mom's grave, Princess."

His tone is gentle, but even so, my hand freezes, my appetite vanishing. I've been avoiding the subject, knowing that I have to face it soon, but unable to bring myself to even think about it, about going there.

With measured control, I lower my fork down, the food uneaten on it. Looking up and round at the guys, they've all paused in their eating, and are looking back at me with varying degrees of love and concern etched on their faces. Taking a deep breath, I turn to face Ash.

"Okay," I say with a nod.

His hand comes up, his warm, dry palm cupping my face in a gesture so loving and sweet that the tears I've been trying to hold back spring to my eyes, and a lump forms in my throat.

"Good girl," he says softly. "Now, eat your breakfast, and drink your juice."

Part of me knows that I should probably bristle at his dominating ways. That my inner feminist should be burning her bra and screaming 'down with the patriarchy!' But I just feel a sense of relief at following his orders, at not having to decide anything. There's something so freeing about relinquishing control to another person. Ash knows that I need to eat, even if I don't feel like it, so he's not saying it just to be a controlling dick. He's just taking care of me in the only way that he knows how

Before I can pick up my fork again, Kai's slender fingers grasp the silver handle and bring the morsel to my lips. His honey eyes capture mine sans glasses, encouraging me to open up, which I do, letting him place the fork on my tongue. I take the food off with my teeth as he pulls the fork out, a smile lifting his lips as I begin to chew, the sweetness of the fruit and syrup bursting on my tongue and making me realise how hungry I am.

"Mmmm...thanks," I mutter, swallowing it down and reaching for my juice.

I take a big gulp, smiling when the tropical flavour fills my mouth. I can feel my forehead crease as I see that darkness is still there in his amber depths. I hate that it looks a lot like pain and inner turmoil. Reaching out, I take his hand, twining my fingers with his, marvelling for a second that although he's slighter than the others, his hand is still bigger than mine.

"I love you so much, Kai Matthews," I whisper to him, catching his gaze so that he can see the truth of my words.

Afterlife by Hailee Steinfeld starts playing softly in the background, and his hand tightens around mine, his breath leaving his chest on a shaky exhale.

"I wish I deserved it," he murmurs back, his demons rising to the surface so clearly I can almost see them gazing back at me, eyes full of self-loathing.

My heart drops at his words at the same time that a fire lights inside of me, determined to make him believe that he is worthy, regardless of what happened to him to cause this doubt.

Getting up out of my chair, I let go of his hand and manage to squeeze myself onto his lap without knocking anything off the table —*go me!* His hands immediately go to my bare thighs, the touch sending a shiver running through me that goes straight to my core. Placing my hands on his cheeks, I run them up the sides of his face and into his hair, gently tugging until he's looking up into my eyes again. His pupils are blown, a mix of lust and self-deprivation swirling in his eyes.

"You are worth everything, my love," I tell him fiercely, feeling his fingers digging into my thighs as I speak. "Every drop of love, every-fucking-thing. You are mine, Kai, as I am yours, and nothing on this earth will change that. Understand?" I'm practically snarling at him, my grip tight as I force him to feel my truth. I'm so fucking angry at a world that would make this incredible man feel undeserving.

A small growl sounds in his throat when my fingers pull his hair more, the sound making a rush of wetness leave my pussy that's pressed up against his rapidly hardening dick. I can't help but grind against him, inwardly cursing the silky material of his pyjama trousers that acts as a barrier.

Abruptly, I let go of his hair and reaching down, I pull Loki's T-shirt off my body, dropping it to the ground next to us.

"Now, show me you deserve me by taking what you want," I command him, knowing that it'll make his dominant side sit up and take notice, and hopefully help to draw him out of this pit of self-despair.

A breath hisses out of him as he takes in the sight of my naked, flushed body. My nipples peak even more when his hungry eyes alight on them, and one of his hands leaves my thigh, pinching the nub between his thumb and forefinger hard enough that I cry out as another rush of wetness coats my inner thighs.

The sound must be his undoing as in the next second, my feet crash to the floor as he stands up, his chair falling on the wood with a thwack. I'm spun around and pushed down, my breasts squashed into his plate of food, the sweet smell of crushed fruit and syrup filling my nose. I hear other items crash to the floor seconds before a hand cracks across my arse so hard that I scream, my cunt clenching on nothing but air as my fingertips claw at the wooden tabletop.

"Dude," I hear Loki say, his tone uncertain just before a second punishing hit lands, causing another shriek to leave my lips.

"I'm okay," I rasp out, my heart pounding in my chest. I trust Kai, even now. He won't hurt me, not ever.

Kai growls at Loki, low and loud in return, and this time a moan leaves me, my hands grasping at the tabletop on either side of my head. It's such a fucking sexy sound that I can't help but squirm, seeking relief for the desperate ache that has built so suddenly in my core.

"Do. Not. Move," Kai rumbles behind me in a voice so unlike his own that I immediately obey.

I hear the rustle of foil, then suddenly my legs are being kicked apart wider seconds before I feel the tip of him nudging at my entrance. An animalistic keen sounds in my throat as he pushes inside me, forcing his way into my tight channel with no preparation, his metal hitting me in all the right places. A hand wraps around my messy bun, pulling me up sharply, my palms supporting my weight as I finally look round me, both of us moaning when he bottoms out.

All three guys are now standing, watching us with a mixture of lust and worry, yet their sweats are tented. I meet each of their stares, giving them a small smile to show that I'm okay. My heart rate picks up because even though I trust Kai completely, this is uncharted territory for us.

His monsters are riding him hard, and I've laid down a challenge that he's unable to resist. However, I'd be lying if I said that the fear is not turning me all the way on, and if the grunt behind me is any indication, Kai can feel my pussy clenching around him in excitement.

Kai presses us forward, taking something from the table that I'm unable to see due to his tight grip on my hair.

"Kai!" Ash exclaims, stepping forward with his eyes wide just as I feel cool metal pressed against the top of one of my breasts.

"Tell him your safe word, darling," Kai purrs in my ear, his breath hissing as my inner walls tighten round him.

"Red," I whisper, holding Ash's worried gaze. I've an idea of what Kai might be doing, and if I'm correct, I can totally understand why it may be triggering for Ash. "I'm okay, Ash. Truly."

He gives a brief nod, but I can see his hand shake as it sweeps through his hair, even as his gaze fills with lust, his inner Dom enjoying watching me in fear. Kai chooses that moment to use his grip to tip my head down so that I can see that my guess was correct. He's holding a small fruit knife with a wooden handle, and a wicked sharp, slightly curved blade, the tip indenting my flesh just above my areola, but not cutting it. Not yet.

Even though I knew it was there, seeing the blade pressed against my skin causes my heart to start drumming in my chest even more, something that Kai must feel as he thrusts forward, burying himself even deeper inside me, which feels fucking amazing.

"See how fucked up I am, Lilly love," he growls in my ear, nuzzling the side of my neck with his nose, a gasp falling from my lips as I shudder. "Your fear turns me on like nothing else, and I want to hear you scream in pain as I'm buried deep inside you. I want to see your blood running red when I'm using you like you're nothing but a hole."

"Kai..." I moan, my voice low, letting him know how much his words are affecting me in all the right ways, which is probably the complete opposite of what he thinks they would do. "Please."

His grip on my hair turns punishing, pulling until tears sting my eyes. The room wavers, and although I know the others are there, everything else fades away apart from me and the broken man behind me, holding a knife against my soft skin.

Bad Drugs by King Kavalier, ChrisLee begins to sound in the room, and I gasp as a sharp pain stings my right breast. I'm still at an angle that I can look down and see a bead of red well at the knife point. Fascinated, I watch as it drips down the globe of flesh, trailing a path towards my cleavage. A hiss of pain falls from my lips, my fingers flexing as he draws the blade down, creating a shallow cut, and more drops of blood drip down over my pale flesh.

Jesus fucking christ. Who knew Diesel Viper had it right all along?

The fear, mixed in with the pain, and having his thick, pierced cock inside me is a heady combination, leaving me gasping as the familiar burn of an orgasm begins to build in my centre.

"Fuck, Kai," I groan, as he takes the knife away, the acidic fruit juices coating my skin stinging the cut, and just adding to the myriad of sensations that are assaulting my senses.

Suddenly, I hear the clatter of the knife against the table as he withdraws, leaving me bereft. For a moment I worry that he's going to leave me unsatisfied, covered in fruit, yoghurt, and my own blood, but before the thought can settle, he twirls me round, picks me up under my thighs, roughly lifting me onto the tabletop. Giving me no time to adjust to my new seated position, he pushes my chest roughly, my back landing amongst the spilled breakfast as he forces me down.

He snarls, leaning over me to lick and lap at the cut, the sharp pain from his tongue leaving me squirming and desperate for more, my fingers trying to find purchase on the smooth wood I'm lying on.

"Sir," I plead, hoping that he won't leave me unfulfilled for long.

His head snaps up, and I'd laugh because the tip of his nose and his chin are covered in a mix of squashed fruit and yoghurt, but the sight of my blood on his lips stops me, as does the feral look in his eyes. He bares his teeth, which are also tinged red, in a smile that sends shivers running all over me as fire races through my veins.

Straightening up, he reaches over for the knife once more, picking it up as he stands between my open thighs. I watch transfixed, my heart racing, as he brings it to my inner thigh, gasping sharply as he makes three shallow cuts in quick succession. With a wicked smile on his lush lips, he places the knife carefully down beside my hip on the table, then brings his hand back to my leg. Wiping his finger along the cuts, the sting intense, he gathers my blood on his fingertip, seemingly hypnotised by the drops of glistening ruby.

His eyes flick up to mine, the amber almost entirely swallowed up by black, before they look back down, and with barely a touch, his finger alights on my cunt, rubbing my own blood on my clit.

I'm so wound up with the pain, fear, and the taboo nature of what he's doing, that one brief touch is enough to detonate an earth-shattering orgasm that rips through me, my liquid release gushing out of me as I yell his name.

I crack my lids just in time to see Kai kneel down, eye level with my still pulsing pussy. Before I can even think about coming down from the heavens, his hot warm tongue licks my clit in a firm hard stroke.

"Fuck! Shit! Fuckity shit!" I whimper, as he licks me again, and again, and again, until I'm squirming, whining, and panting, not sure if I'm trying to escape or get closer as wave upon wave of pleasure rolls over me.

Suddenly, he stops and I yelp like a kicked puppy.

"Hold fucking still!" he bellows in a rough voice, making me jump, the remaining crockery on the table rattling. My heart feels like it's pounding hard enough to escape the confines of my chest, a slight tremble in my limbs.

"Kai!" Ash snaps behind us, and I hear Jax's growl sound in warning.

"I'm okay, Ash," I say, not taking my wide eyed stare off Kai.

My eyes meet his, dark and drowning as he gets up, my gaze darting down to see his beautiful cock rock-fucking-solid, and begging to be buried deep inside me once more. I look back up to see his chin glistening, and a dangerous smirk on his lips.

"You still deserve me, my love," I pant, watching as his eyes widen and nostrils flare.

With a roar that leaves me quivering and snatching my arms onto my chest, he sweeps his hand across the tabletop to my right, sending dishes of food crashing to the floor. He repeats the move on the other side before stopping to look down at me, his chest heaving, hands and arms covered in breakfast foods.

I lie there, the slight shivering of my body the only outward sign of the effect his behaviour is having on me. And part of that is pure, unadulterated lust. This uncontrolled wild side of his is turning me on. A lot.

With a snarl, he grabs my thighs, spreading them even wider to the point of pain, and I gasp. A malevolent grin takes over his lips, and he catches my hand, wrapping it around my leg, and then doing the same with the other until I'm holding myself completely open for him.

The next thing I know, he's grabbing his dick, lining it up with my soaked entrance before he slams inside of me, hard and fast. An animalistic groan leaves his lips as a scream of pleasure-pain leaves mine, then he starts pounding into me, using me like I'm a hole to be filled, just as he promised. I know I'll be aching later, but I currently have no more fucks to give because it feels so damn good, my whole body lights up with pleasure that has an edge of exquisite pain.

I look up to see his face creased in a frown, his hands holding my hips in a bruising grip as he thrusts harder and harder, impaling me on his cock, the sound of our bodies, moans, and grunts louder than the music in the background.

Sparks ignite in my core, my climax rushing towards its peak with the force of two atoms colliding until I'm screaming his name, uncaring if the whole fucking hotel hears, my nails digging into my thighs as I come. Stars burst, and new galaxies are formed as my orgasm tears me apart, leaving me utterly spent.

Moments later, I hear the roar of a thousand lions as Kai finds his own release, jerking inside of me, then collapsing on top of me, his weight a welcome heaviness.

We lie there, panting and breathless as the world rights itself around us. Slowly, I begin to hear the sound of someone clapping. Opening my eyes, I look to the side to see Loki standing there, his rapidly softening dick hanging out. Clearly he enjoyed the show. His emerald eyes are alight with sated satisfaction, as well as the usual shit stirring mischief.

"Bra-fucking-vo, my friend!" he shouts. "Nice to finally see you let go, dude," he adds, continuing to clap until Jax steps into view, and cuffs him on the back of his head.

"That was...a little fucked up," Jax tells Kai, a feral grin on his face, and he, too, obviously liked what he saw, especially if his flushed cheeks and post orgasm glow are anything to go by. "But so fucking hot."

Kai lifts his face off my chest, a huff of laughter escaping as he turns to look at me.

"Are you okay?" he asks, concern filling his honey eyes as he lifts himself off me even more, looking down to the cut on my breast, a flash of predatory satisfaction gleaming in his eyes.

"I'm peachy," I reply, still breathless and my voice all kinds of husky. "Are you?"

"I—" he starts, biting his bottom lip adorably. "I do feel better," he tells me, a blush staining his cheeks as he stands up, holding out his hand for me to take.

I can't help but chuckle softly, then wince as I sit up, Kai noticing the move and frowning. Her Vagisty, for once, is quiet, probably hiding after the pounding we just got.

"Good," I say, using his help to stand. I wobble, and he catches me, bending down to pick me up bridal style. "I can walk," I tell him, although that may be bullshit if my still quivering legs are any indicator.

"I know," he says softly, nuzzling my cheek. "But I need to take care of you," he whispers in my ear, giving me all the warm and fuzzies as he turns and walks off towards the main bedroom.

I look over his shoulder to see the others starting to clean the mess up. Catching Ash's eyes, I raise a brow, hoping he knows I'm asking if he's okay. Placing a hand on Kai's pec, I halt his movement so that Ash can come towards us. My dark Knight, my big daddy Dom—*fucking snort*—cups my face with his warm palm, looking deep into my eyes as Kai stands there holding me close.

"You okay, Princess?" he asks, his voice rough. There's a fine tremor in his hand against my face, and a spark of worry tinged with guilt alights in my stomach. With Ash's history of self-harm, that must have been all kinds of triggering for him.

"Yes," I murmur back, rubbing my cheek into his hand. "I'm sorry if that was triggering for you, love," I tell him, loving the way his breath hitches at the term of endearment.

"Shit, dude, I didn't fucking think," Kai says, obviously upset if he's cursing so much.

"It's cool," Ash replies, looking up at Kai briefly. His steel grey gaze comes back to mine, swirling with love, and lust, and a hundred other things. "Maybe, in the future, we keep the knife and blood play to a minimum when I'm around?"

"Sure," I reply at the same time as Kai does, also agreeing.

Ash gives me a soft smile before he leans down to place a gentle kiss on my lips, then goes back to clearing the mess of shattered plates and squashed food. I'm seriously impressed that they're actually bothering to clean. Being the rich bastards that they are, I had expected them to just call for one of the maids to come and deal with it.

Carrying me back into the main bedroom, Kai walks over to the en suite, switching the light on as we pass. He takes us to the enormous shower, setting me carefully down onto the chaise that's next to it as he turns it on, waiting a few moments for the water to warm up.

I watch as his back muscles bunch and cord as he goes about his tasks. Turning to face me, he stops, going to push his glasses up his nose then realising that he's not wearing any.

"I love you, Kai," I say with a smile as he leans down to help me up. He pauses, his hand coming to cup my jaw.

"I love you, Lilly," he whispers gazing into my eyes with such intensity it's a wonder the world doesn't stop spinning.

Then he proceeds to make good on his promise, taking care of me thoroughly and showing me that he is a man of more than just words.

If only he would believe mine.

CHAPTER TWELVE

LILLY

We take a long, gloriously hot shower, where Kai washes me from top to toe until I'm squeaky clean all over, using my new favourite ginger shampoo and conditioner to wash my hair. Wrapping me in a huge white fluffy towel that he prewarmed on the heated towel rail, he grabs a medical first aid kit Ash brought in whilst we were showering. Lifting me up, he places me on the sink countertop, setting to work wiping my cuts with antiseptic and covering them with gauze, bandages and tape.

"You are amazing, Lilly," he tells me softly, placing the last bit of tape on my inner thigh to hold the gauze in place. "I don't know why I thought I could scare you off with my darkness," he adds, looking up at me, his eyes holding equal measure of wonder, awe, and pain. "The light you have in you shines so brightly, is so strong, that you can take any amount of darkness, and burn it away. People often mistake goodness as a weakness, but you are stronger than all of us, my darling. We would truly be lost without you."

I don't realise that I'm crying until I taste salt on my lips, his thumb coming up to wipe my tears away as he leans in closer, his hand then moving up into my wet hair, his fingers tangling in the brunette strands.

"You are my light, Lilly. My soul. Everything that I am, or ever will be, is yours and yours alone. And when we take our final breaths on this earth, our souls will remain bound, travelling the winds together for all eternity."

"Oh, Kai," I say in a broken whisper against his lips as he presses them to mine in a kiss so tender and sweet that the stars sigh.

"I promise that I will tell you everything soon. I just need some time," he murmurs, pulling away and looking into my eyes once more, his hand still in my hair.

"Take all the time you need, my love," I tell him, his eyes closing and a beatific smile comes over his features at my words. "I'm not going anywhere."

I lean in, placing my head on his damp chest and wrapping my arms round him in a tight hug, sighing in pure bliss and contentment when he returns the embrace. We stay that way until Loki pops his head past the door, an indulgent and relieved smile on his lips as he looks at us.

"Time to get ready, Pretty Girl," he tells me. "Your carriage awaits!"

I can't help giggling when he waggles his eyebrows in that goofy way of his before disappearing again. Kai helps me off the counter, holding my hand as he leads me to the bedroom, exiting wearing only a towel to go to his room and get dressed.

On the bed I find black lacy underwear, a navy cropped T-shirt, and some new mustard yellow Run and Fly dungarees with a bee print. There's a piece of the hotel notepaper with Ash's elegant scrawl over it.

Wear these today

I can't help beaming down at the note in my hand, loving the sweet yet commanding gesture. He knew I was eyeing these very dungs up. I do as he says, pairing them with the yellow and rainbow Irregular Choice Shirly Bass shoes that Loki bought me for Christmas. I walk back into the main living room area to, once again, find all the guys waiting for me, and my gaze immediately connects with Ash's grey one, the corner of his lips lifting to see me wearing what he laid out for me.

He walks towards me, stepping so close that I'm completely consumed by his spicy ginger scent. Leaning down, he takes a deep inhale, a low rumbling sigh escaping his lips.

"I fucking love that you use my shampoo," he says so that only I can hear as his hand finds the bare skin on my side that the crop top leaves exposed.

Tingles and goosebumps spread from his touch as he glides his hand upwards, a hissing breath leaving him when he discovers that I didn't quite follow his instructions. He groans as his fingers skate across my bare breast, my nipple pebbling as his thumb rubs over it.

"Why do I need underwear for a spa day?" I ask in a saucy whisper, my voice slightly breathless, loving the way he almost splutters when he realises what I'm implying.

"Sorry to cockblock you, Blue Balls," Loki sniggers like a wankstain at Ash's responding growl. He grabs my hand and pulls me out of Ash's grip. "But the car and Lexi are waiting."

I blow Ash a kiss, laughing at the frustrated outrage on his face as Loki leads me to the front doors of the suite. I blow both Jax and Kai kisses as we pass, managing to grab my coat as Loki pulls me out of the door and into the lift.

"That was mean," I mock scold, my eyebrows raised as he pushes me up against the mirrored back wall of the lift, his hand wrapping around the top of my throat, ignoring the poor attendant who stares straight ahead.

He doesn't reply, just closes the distance, covering my body with his as he gives me a bruising kiss that makes me forget where we are, or that we have an audience. He pulls away, leaving my head spinning and my heart racing just as the doors ding open, an evil grin on his face.

"I wanted to make sure you thought about me all day," he says with a smirk, taking my hand once again and leading me out of the lift and across the bright foyer.

"Do you know why Ash was so frustrated this morning?" I ask, a grin to rival his on my own lips.

"Why? His balls about to drop off, they're so blue?"

"Maybe," I start, glad I grabbed my coat, wool scarf, and beanie hat before we left the suite as the biting January temperature hits my exposed face. It may be brilliant sunshine, but it's still winter in England. We stop in front of the open car door, and I turn to face him. "Or maybe it's because I didn't quite follow his instructions about what to wear today and left some bits on the bed."

Giving him a quick peck on his still lips, I climb into the car and shut the door, immediately engulfed in a hug from Lexi.

"Why did Loki look so confused?" she asks, and I chuckle.

About ten minutes later I get an incoming text.

> Angel: ::devil emoji:: You naughty minx! He'll spank you when you get back! Xxx

A laugh leaves my lips even as my thighs clench with the thought of the punishment that awaits me upon my return.

I spend a wonderful day at a high-end spa with Lexi, drinking champagne and being pampered to within an inch of my life. We have full body hot stone massages, pedicures and manicures, mud wraps, facials with the most wonderful smelling products, and spend time in the hot tub and pool.

The car that picks us up takes us to The Hard Rock Cafe, where the guys and Ryan are waiting. We gorge ourselves on burgers, fries, and milkshakes, all whilst listening to nineties rock music, and admiring the memorabilia lining the walls.

Yawning, we head to the car that'll take us back to the hotel, Lexi kissing me goodnight, saying that we will see them tomorrow. I must fall asleep on the way home because the next thing I know I'm being carried into our suite.

Looking up, I give Jax a bleary-eyed smile as he holds me effortlessly, even though he still looks pretty tired himself. He sets me down gently on the bed, helping me to strip off, and then we crawl under the covers, Loki joining us a moment later.

I fall back asleep surrounded by warmth and love, feeling so safe sandwiched between two of my guys, like nothing can ever touch me as long as they are near.

I wake up, unsure at first what woke me, then hear the hint of a piano melody caressing my skin being played somewhere nearby. Gently extracting myself from the sleeping men in my bed, I pad naked across the plush carpeted floor and out the door, heading towards the main living area and the haunting sound.

My skin tingles, a tentative smile drawing my lips upwards as I gaze at Ash sitting at the instrument, the lid down so to quieten the sound, wearing only light coloured sweats. His tattooed hands are on the keys, his eyes closed as he plays a piece that makes my soul ache. It's utterly beautiful whilst also being desperately sad, and moisture stings my eyes as I watch him shrouded in darkness, the only light in the room coming from a streetlight outside that casts everything in an eerie orange glow.

I remember the story Kai told me, about when they were thirteen or so, and Ash had tried to run away to become a concert pianist, but then his father had found them, and by the sounds of it, punished him severely. I thought he no longer played, that was the impression Kai gave me anyway. But as his fingers effortlessly move over the keys, my heart swells to know that he must have found a way. He wouldn't be this good if he hadn't played all these years.

As the piece draws to a close, he looks up, his hands not faltering even as a banked heat enters his grey orbs when he spots me leaning against the doorframe, naked, watching him.

"It's called *Opus 38*, by Dustin O'Halloran," he explains, his voice gruff as the last note resounds in the still night air. "I learned it after Luc...died."

My feet carry me closer to him without conscious thought, the need to comfort him overwhelming.

"I had no idea that you still played," I whisper, not wanting to disturb this moment, this suspended time we are currently inhabiting.

I come to a stop next to him, my hands reaching out and running through his dark, silky hair, loving the feel of the strands as they move through my fingers.

"It's not something that I can broadcast," he tells me, his own voice quiet. He leans into my touch, resting his head on my stomach, his arms coming around my hips. His breath sends shivers racing across my body, my nipples becoming hard points even though the room is warm. "My father, well, you've met him, does not approve of his son playing a musical instrument. Thinks music is for, and I quote, 'queers and faggots.'" He practically spits the words, clearly disgusted by his father's bigotry. "But fuck him."

I smile at that.

"Yeah, fuck him," I echo, smiling wider and feeling all kinds of warmth inside when a manly chuckle falls against my skin.

Lifting his head, he looks up at me.

"Can I play something for you?" he asks, biting his plush bottom lip as he studies me intently.

"I'd love that," I tell him, heat radiating throughout my body at his soft expression and bright glossy eyes that shine in the darkness.

He smiles in return, his whole body relaxing. I start to turn, intending to sit on a nearby chair, when he stops me, his arms banding tighter. Looking back down, there's a devilish glint in his eyes that I'm more used to seeing on Loki's face.

This is either going to be really good...or really bad. Maybe both?

"Up here, Princess," he orders, leaning back and releasing one of his arms, patting the top of the baby grand piano lovingly.

"What? No!" I exclaim, shaking my head and trying to take a step back.

Of course the wanktrumpet tightens his grip with the arm still around me.

"I don't like to repeat myself, Princess," he tells me sternly, a threat clear in his voice.

"Fine," I grumble, looking at the instrument with a huff. *How the fuck am I meant to get up there?!*

As if reading my mind, Ash scoots back the bench he's sitting on, grabs my waist, and in a single panty melting—*you know, if I had any on*—move, lifts me up, depositing my bare arse on the cool surface of the lid, right on the edge.

"Ash!" I hiss, squirming as Her Vagisty tries to escape the temperature of the lacquered wood.

With just his signature Ash-hole smirk, he sits back down, pulling the bench closer to the keys. Flushing, I suddenly realise that he's in between my legs, getting an eyeful so to speak. I begin to close my thighs when he chuckles in that sexy way of his, making Her Vagisty perk up and twitch. *Greedy bitch.*

Grabbing one ankle, he places my foot on his shoulder, doing the same to the other leg until I am literally spread wide open for him, having to prop myself up with my hands behind me for support so that I can still look down at him.

"Much better," he comments. *Cuntcake.* "I learned this not long after we met you," he confesses softly, looking down at his hands hovering over the keys. "It's called *I Love You*, by Jurrivh."

My breath stills, my heart thudding as my fingertips tingle at his words.

And then he starts to play.

I stop breathing entirely for several moments as the music flows over and through me. I can feel the vibrations of the notes running through my body, making my core ache for this man. This man who feels so much, but hardly ever shows it, has been trained not to show it, but it's all there. And it's the most beautiful thing I've ever experienced.

He doesn't look at me as he plays, his eyes closed, his fingers flying across the instrument in a gentle, loving caress. Taking a large, deep breath, I am grateful that I'm not standing. I don't even think that I could, not with my knees weak and my heart hammering like it is. I'm hyper aware of my entire body; the coolness of the wood that I'm sitting on is warming under my body heat, the notes as they flow through me, letting me feel the music in my very core like never before.

The sounds pour into my ears, teasing moisture to my eyes when I think about what he told me. He learnt this not long after he met me. He's loved me since then, almost from the start.

All too soon, the final notes are sounding in the room, leaving their lingering song in the air like the sweetest perfume. Ash's hands still, his head still bowed and his chest rising and falling with heavy breaths, like this moment was difficult for him.

He's made himself vulnerable in a way that he hasn't done before, and I feel so blessed to have been witness to it.

"Ash," I murmur, my voice raspy with all the love that is desperate to break free, like a caged bird.

"I feel like I've loved you for my whole life, Lilly," he whispers back, his own voice just as choked as mine. "I just needed to find you."

He lifts his head, his eyes shining, and I watch, spellbound, as a single bead of glittering moisture breaks free and glides down his cheek. I move my feet off his shoulders, shuffle-sliding down off the piano and eliciting a jumbled sound as I hit the keys until I'm in his lap, my legs on either side of him. Reaching my hand out, I use my thumb to swipe the tear from his face, bringing it to my lips and tasting his love.

His confession.

His declaration.

A moment later, I feel his hand grab the back of my neck as he pulls me in for a kiss that obliterates a past where we weren't together. A kiss that makes up for all the lost time, for all of the pain that we've been through without one another.

His tongue dominates mine, showing me his love with every stroke, telling me without words his truth. I let him in freely, matching him caress for caress as I repeat back my truth. My love for him. My need for him.

He pulls away, both of us panting. I can feel his hardness directly under my aching pussy, and it takes everything in me not to grind down, to try and seek relief, remembering that he's still healing. His eyes drill into mine, his pupils wide with lust and longing that I know my expression mirrors.

"Fuck it," he rasps out, his voice gruff and lips swollen.

Before I know what's happening, he's lifting me up, his fingers digging into my arse cheeks in a deliciously maddening way. The bench falls to the floor, making a dull thudding noise as it hits the carpet, and he stands, carrying me to the side of the piano.

"Ash, what—" I start, hissing as he none too gently places me back on the lid of the instrument, my arse on the edge of the side. Silencing any further questions that I might have, he slams his lips back onto mine, his hands holding my face captive.

I get lost in his taste; like winter nights, sin, and darkness. But not the kind of darkness that you're afraid of, the kind that protects you and hides you from all harm. He breaks away once more, kissing down my neck, pausing at my breasts to take each nipple into his mouth, his hands cupping and stroking them whilst he sucks and bites the tender globes until I'm a squirming mess. He pushes me down, not pausing in his ravishment so that I'm lying flat on my back, my legs hanging off the edge.

"Ash," I moan, when he goes lower, kissing, licking, and nipping my abdomen. Then lower still, teasing me all around my slit, my cunt fluttering, and Her Vagisty begging for some attention. "Ash," I whine this time, scowling and grabbing his hair in clenched fists when he just does that stupid sexy man chuckle again and carries on with his exquisite torture.

"Impatient tonight, aren't we, Princess," he teases, breathing along my folds, making my breath hitch and my hips buck towards him as I desperately try to bring his head closer with my grip.

He clearly takes pity on me, or can't help himself, because in the next moment, sublime bliss fills my entire being as his warm tongue licks me from opening to clit, and I explode on his tongue, crying out with the force of my release.

Yep, one lick is all it took to make me come. That man can play me just as well as the instrument that I'm lying on, no doubt about that.

I hear a growl of approval, my eyes closed, still riding that orgasm wave, when I hear the rustle of a foil packet, then feel a nudge at my opening. I snap my eyes open and lift my head, only to find him standing between my thighs, pushing his hard dick inside me, his hands holding my thighs open.

My inner walls clench and flutter around him—*that damn dick obsessed butterfly is back*—as I watch him thrust gently, feeling his new piercing massage my passage until he's fully seated inside me. We both groan at the sublime sensation, and I watch, enraptured at the look of pure bliss on his face, his eyes closed as he savours the moment.

"But—" I start, my voice husky as I push up onto my elbows. His eyes open when I speak. "You're not fully healed."

"I'm healed enough, Princess," he informs me in a rough voice, and I study his features to see if there's any pain in his expression, willing to stop this if there is.

He doesn't give me more than a moment, though, a breath, before he pulls almost all the way out, then plunges back in hard. My eyes fucking roll, and I drop back down with a thud and he repeats the move again. And again. And again, until I lose count and all ability to think coherently as he bombards me with his passion, gyrating harder and going deeper.

"Shit, Ash!" I cry out, my nails scraping the smooth surface of the instrument that I'm lying on, uncaring if I scratch it, as electric currents zap and zing across my body with every surge of his, the new metal in his dick adding a layer of sensation that has me seeing stars.

"Christ, Lilly," he hisses through clenched teeth. "I'd forgotten how fucking good your pussy wrapped around my cock feels." His shallow thrusting rubs my G-spot with the piercings on every stroke. "That's it, baby, come for me, come all over my dick," he orders as I start to clench around him, my climax hitting me with the force of a fucking freight train.

He pulls all the way out, causing a squirt of liquid to shoot out of me, covering his lower abs and chest as I scream. I look down just in time to see him pull the condom off, blowing his load all over my stomach and breasts, a deep groan falling from his perfect lips. More moisture leaves me at the sight and knowledge that I'm covered in his hot seed. We've marked each other in the most primal way and I fucking love it.

My eyes catch on glinting silver, and I gasp.

"You got a fucking magic cross!" I exclaim, sitting up to get a better look, uncaring of his cum dripping down my body.

Just beyond the mushroom head of his dick are four small metal balls, creating the impression of a cross with the bars hidden inside.

"How did it feel?" he asks, his voice a touch breathless.

Tearing my eyes away from his new jewellery, I look into his eyes.

"Fucking incredible," I beam at him, and he smiles right back, looking all kinds of pleased with himself.

"Good," he replies, holding out a hand and helping me off the piano. "Now, let's get cleaned up. You've got a big day today and need to get some more sleep." My heart sinks when I remember what we're doing later; visiting Mum's grave. "Hey, it'll be okay. We'll be with you the whole time," he tells me gently, pulling me to him in a tight hug, the warmth of his naked body seeping into mine.

CHAPTER THIRTEEN

LILLY

Blinking my gritty eyes open, I wake to weak morning light, cocooned in a spicy ginger warmth that I snuggle into. Catching movement across from me in the corner of my eye, I'm captivated by honey amber eyes. Kai smiles softly at me from his bed, looking far more awake than how I feel. Yet still, he has bags under his slightly bloodshot eyes and exhaustion coats him like a fog, as if he hasn't slept well in months, years.

I frown as it suddenly occurs to me that we've never slept in the same bed. I've never woken up with Kai wrapped around me, and that bothers me. Is it due to an accident, the others getting in bed with me first? Or has he purposefully pushed me away in that regard?

"Why the frown, darling?" His melodic voice, a little gruff this morning, breaks into my tumultuous thoughts. "Worried about today?" he enquires gently, and my frown deepens, my breath stuttering out of me at the thought of what's to come this morning.

"Yes," I reply in a whisper, my empty stomach rolling. I decide not to press the issue of our lack of bedsharing just yet. I'll wait until he's ready to talk.

He gives me an understanding nod, his head moving on the soft fluffy pillow he's resting it on.

"You're not alone, Lilly," he soothes. "We will be there every step of the way."

I swallow hard, my eyes filling as the arm holding me from behind tightens, pulling me closer to the hot naked body at my back.

"And if it gets too much, just say the word and we're outta there," Ash murmurs in my ear, nuzzling into my hair and sending welcome shivers skipping over my body. "But you need to do this, Princess. Trust me, you need closure."

"I know," I mumble back, gripping his arm tightly as I continue to gaze into Kai's eyes, my breath shuddering out between my lips.

At that moment, the door flies open, and Loki strolls in, completely naked—*obviously*. His emerald eyes find mine, and in the next minute, he leaps onto the bed in front of me, somehow managing to lie down underneath the covers as I'm bounced back into Ash, who gives an oomph sound at the impact.

"Loki!" I cry, a giggle escaping my mouth as he wriggles closer, successfully dispelling the sadness that was building in the room. He smells like vanilla and musky man, a scent that I am addicted to, his hair all mussed from quite clearly having just woken up.

"Dude, what the fuck?" Ash grumbles behind me, shuffling back to make room for the fallen angel that's landed in our bed, which luckily is a double, although it's still a squeeze with these two lumps in it.

"Jax is not a good snuggle bunny," Loki pouts, and it's so adorable, sexy, and ridiculous that I lean forward and plant a kiss on his lush lips. "And his morning wood should be classed as a fucking weapon of mass destruction."

We all snort at that, which turns into full belly chuckles when Jax walks in, proudly sporting said weapon of mass destruction.

"What's so fucking funny?" he asks, his deep voice gruff from sleep as he settles at the end of the bed. "It's like the ass crack of dawn."

I fucking lose it, laughing so hard that my stomach aches, and tears stream down my face.

"I fucking love you all, so much," I choke out, looking around me to see matching grins on all their faces, their expressions soft.

We decide that as we're all awake, arse crack of dawn or not, we might as well get up and get ready. Ordering breakfast, we lounge around in the living room until it arrives. I surprise myself by eating a healthy serving of bacon—*crispy because anything else is just plain wrong and sacrilegious*—toast and poached eggs, all washed down with my favourite tropical juice.

We leisurely eat, talking about everything and nothing. Then Loki and Jax join me for a shower, which helps to kill some time as they coax orgasm after orgasm from my poor abused pussy. *I lie, Her Vagisty fucking loves it!* We take our time getting dressed, using up more time until we're ready to leave.

We're due to meet Lex and Ryan at Highgate Cemetery at ten, so we order a car for twenty-past nine to leave plenty of time to get there. Once we're seated in the car, I look around at my guys, my soulmates. We're fairly colourful, Mum hated black so I decided that we'd be as brightly coloured as possible. The guys, all apart from Loki, struggled a little as they mostly wear dark colours.

Kai found some mustard yellow chinos, which he paired with a red check flannel shirt, a forest green cashmere v-neck jumper, and a matching green bow tie. He epitomises geek chic by topping it off with a green tweed coat and a red cashmere scarf. Jax chose dark grey jeans and a sky blue T-shirt that makes his eyes pop, with a darker blue hoodie and a sports-type wool jacket. Ash has gone for a suit, of course, but in a navy pinstripe instead of black. He paired it with a vibrant Liberty print shirt, no tie, and a navy wool long coat.

He looks like every woman's wet dream, sophisticated yet devilish with his black tattoos peeking out at his neck.

Loki, wonderful, marvellous Loki, somehow without my knowledge, bought himself a pair of black rainbow dinosaur Run & Fly dungarees. He wears them with an emerald green T-shirt, just to prove that his eyes are as good as Jax's, red Converse Chucks, and what looks like a vintage brown sheepskin bomber jacket, complete with tan fluffy wool at the wrists and collar.

I went for my Run and Fly rainbow pinafore, sparkly glitter rainbow heels, and a red wool short coat, with a beautiful Peter Pan collar and ruffles at the wrists. It arrived at the suite this morning, along with a note:

Saw this and thought of you. Wear it today, Little Red.
Ash

I stroke the beautiful soft wool as we make our way through the early morning London traffic, having been driving for about twenty minutes already. I notice my hand shaking moments before Loki's larger warm hand covers mine, intertwining our fingers. His other hand moves my hair over my shoulder, popping an air bud into my ear. The opening of *Steady Now* by Nilu begins to play, the words and gentle swell of the music perfect for calming my nerves.

My hand grips his as we journey on, the lyrics of the song flowing over me, encouraging me to take deep breaths, and know that this is just one moment in my history. It doesn't define me, and it won't be like this forever. The world keeps spinning, new things on the horizon.

The song ends, and I breathe a contented sigh. *Too Sad to Cry*, by Sasha Alex Solan starts to play next, and tears spring to my eyes.

"Shit," Loki hisses under his breath, reaching into his pocket to change the song.

"Leave it, please," I murmur, turning to look at him, his face wavering as the tears spill down my cheeks.

"Pretty Girl," he replies, voice pained, his palm coming up to cup my cheek and bring our foreheads together. "I hurt when you do, baby."

His words make the tears flow faster, and it's a bittersweet relief. I didn't cry for a long time after Mum passed, too terrified to even think about what had happened. Then, that night, when Ash made me recount it all in detail, it was like a dam had been broken inside me as I was able to start my mourning of her.

Now I'm glad to cry, even though it hurts, because it shows that I'm not too scared. We travel the rest of the way like that, Loki holding my face to his, and gently kissing away the steady stream of tears that fall down my cheeks. Jax rubs my back in soothing circles, Ash and Kai leaning forward to take a hand each, surrounding me in their love and support as I quietly cry.

"Hey," Jax says from my other side, his hand stilling in its movements. "We're there, Baby Girl." His voice sounds gruff, and I look over my shoulder, Loki releasing my face, to see his own eyes glistening. "We all hurt when you do," he tells me simply, and I turn, letting go of the others' hands to cup his face in my palms and place a gentle kiss on his lips.

Ash and Kai get out first, then Loki, leaving just Jax and I in the car. My heart rate picks up as the moment draws closer, the moment when I will have to face what happened.

"I'm scared, Jax," I whisper, pulling back and looking at him with wide eyes, my hands moving to grasp his own.

"I know, Baby Girl," he responds, a frown drawing his brows together. "But we're all here for you, and we're not going anywhere. Nothing bad will happen to you," he assures me.

His words calm me a little, enough that I can take a deep inhale and nod. He flashes me a minute smile. "That's my girl," he praises, keeping hold of my hand as he gets out, then helping me to exit the car.

I see Lexi and Ryan, holding a bunch of flowers each, waiting near the ornate black cast iron gates to the beautiful cemetery.

"Hey, Lilly Bear," Lex greets me softly, and I let go of Jax to give her a hug, then do the same with Ryan. His jaw is clenched tightly, and deep lines are etched on his forehead.

"You doing okay, big guy?" I ask him, my own brows dipping in concern for him. Mum's death wasn't just hard on me. Ryan was practically her husband in all but name. They loved each other deeply.

He gives me a tight smile in response. "I'll be fine, little one," he reassures me, giving my hand a brief squeeze.

"Shall we?" Ash asks, and I notice that each of the guys holds a huge bouquet filled with different coloured lilies, Mum's favourites. A lump forms in my throat as I step towards Ash's outstretched hand.

"How did you know they were her favourites?" I ask, my voice a little wobbly.

He gives me one of his Ash-hole looks, raising an eyebrow. Right, I am named after her favourite flower after all. He kisses the top of my head, then leads the way through the gates and along the winding paths of the cemetery.

We're surrounded on all sides by gravestones, monuments, and beautiful statues, with bare trees dotted here and there. We've lucked out on the weather again today; it's chilly but sunny. Turning off down a more narrow path, we come to a stop underneath an oak sapling with a simply carved headstone in front of it.

Laura Darling
Beloved mother and sister
18th September 1980 - 21st February 2025

The ground surrounding the grave looks freshly cleared, only a few dead leaves litter the space, with nothing but neatly clipped turf covering the site. Glancing around, frowning, I see that the surrounding graves are not as well kept as Mum's.

"We came here yesterday to tidy it up a little." Ash's ginger scent washes over me as he leans down to speak. "Apparently, wild violets grow here in the spring," he tells me.

I squeeze his hand in silent thanks, letting go when he passes me his bunch of flowers. They're simply tied with natural string, no cellophane, and I step forward to place them on the grass, a tremor in my hands.

"Hi, Mum," I whisper, tears springing to my eyes again as they trace the simple lettering carved into her headstone.

And then it hits me. I'll never be able to tell her about the guys, about how wonderful they are, and the fact that they're helping me to heal. She'll never meet any children I may have one day, never hold her grandchildren in her arms and sing them lullabies like she did to me as a child. We'll never dance to awful eighties pop songs on the radio, never make another Christmas cake together. I'll never be able to tell her how sorry I am about that stupid argument. Never tell her how much I love her.

I don't realise that I've collapsed, my nails digging into the turf, sobbing as my heart breaks for all the things I'll never get to do with her again until strong arms wrap around me, lifting me and turning me round so that I can bury my face into a ginger scented cashmere covered chest.

I fist the soft material, tears tracking down my cheeks and soaking into his no doubt stupidly expensive coat. He just holds me, his arms banded tightly around me, keeping my pieces together whilst I fall apart under the winter sun.

Some moments later, I lift my tearstained face towards the sky, closing my eyes and letting the sun dry my cheeks. Taking what feels like the biggest breath I've taken all year, I look back down and find Ash's steel eyes on my own.

"Thank you," I whisper, my voice cracking slightly.

"Of course," he says back.

Looking to the side, I'm met by Jax's piercing blue gaze. I give him a watery smile.

"Thank you, Jax," I tell him, wetting my dry lips.

"Always, Baby Girl," he replies gruffly.

I turn to the other side to find Loki studying me.

"Thank you, Loki."

"No need, my heart," he says, reaching out to stroke my slightly damp cheeks. "I'd do so much more without even a thought," he adds, fresh moisture stinging my eyes at his heartfelt words.

I turn my head to find Kai's honey amber eyes watching me with such love it steals my breath for a moment.

"I told you, darling," he says, stepping closer to my back until I can't see him as he's right behind me, his scent of fresh woods after the rain mixing with Ash's. "Everything I am, or ever will be, is yours," he whispers in my ear, placing a soft kiss on my neck that sends tingles racing over me, despite my sadness.

I stay surrounded by my guys, my warriors, my Knights, for several minutes, breathing them in under the winter sun, the sounds of birds chirping in the background.

Inhaling deeply, they give me the strength to look round, remembering that Lex and Ryan are here too. I find Lexi's green eyes, not far from where I stand, swimming with tears as she looks at me surrounded by my guys.

"Your mum would have been so happy to see you with them, Lilly Bear," she tells me in a choked voice.

Fresh tears well in my own eyes at that. Kai steps back and to one side, and I turn in Ash's arms so that I'm facing Lex and Ryan.

"For what it's worth," Ryan begins, stepping closer to us, glancing at each of the guys in turn. "You have my approval and blessing. They are good guys, little one." He gives the guys a sharp nod, which they return. *Men.*

Kai takes a step forward, looking at me as he takes a piece of paper out of his pocket.

"I have a poem that I'd like to read, if that's okay with you, Lilly?" he asks, and I give him a wobbly smile.

"I'd love that," I say, my heart swelling.

He turns to face the grave, but still so that I can see him in profile and begins to read.

> *"'Do not stand at my grave and weep.*
> *I am not there. I do not sleep.*
> *I am a thousand winds that blow.*
> *I am the diamond glints on snow.*
> *I am the sunlight on ripened grain.*
> *I am the gentle autumn rain.*
> *When you awaken in the morning's hush*
> *I am the swift uplifting rush*
> *Of quiet birds in circled flight.*
> *I am the soft stars that shine at night.*
> *Do not stand at my grave and cry;*
> *I am not there. I did not die.'"*

He turns to look at me once again, his features soft as he takes in my tearstained face.

"It's called *A Thousand Winds*, by Mary Elizabeth Frye," he tells me.

"It's beautiful and perfect," I whisper, reaching out to take his hand, bringing it up to my lips and placing a kiss on his knuckles.

Looking back up, I glance round at the people who I love, and who love me in return without condition. It feels as though my heart swells to twice its size, threatening to burst from my chest as I drink them in, the winter sunshine wrapping its chill around us but unable to touch us.

Stepping forward, I walk to Mum's grave, kneeling down to place my hand on the headstone.

"I'm going to be alright, Mum," I tell her, my eyes welling up once more. "They'll look after me."

Closing my eyes, I stay there for a few moments, hearing the breeze rustling in the trees, the birds chirping around us, the sunshine warming my face as the world keeps spinning.

Standing up, I take one last breath, gazing down at the stone.

"Bye, Mum," I whisper, then turn around to face the others, focusing on my guys. "Let's go home."

They all break out into blinding smiles, obviously realising that I don't mean the hotel, but back to Colorado. Back to Highgate Prep.

Although, they do say that home is where the heart is. And my heart is standing before me, kept safe in the bodies of four beautiful men.

CHAPTER FOURTEEN

LILLY

We arrive back late, stepping off the plane into the crisp winter Colorado mountain air, the stars shining brightly above us, our breath coming out in puffs of steam. Luckily, there are a couple of days before the new term, or semester starts because my body is all kinds of fucked-up from the three different time zones.

I sleep for a solid fourteen hours, my Viking on one side, my fallen angel on the other, and wake up groggy, but feeling less exhausted as afternoon sunshine filters around the edges of the curtains in Loki's dorm room. Stretching, I notice that the bed is empty either side of me, Jax and Loki clearly having left some time ago if the cold sheets are any indication.

Getting up, I grab a navy blue T-shirt from the floor, Loki's vanilla scent all over it as I take a whiff before throwing it on, and heading out of the room and down the stairs towards the bathroom. My brows draw together in a frown as I register how quiet it is, and looking around, I can see that the guys aren't down here.

I take care of business, flushing and washing my hands before coming back out and looking around again. Spotting a piece of paper on the kitchen island, I make my way over and grab it.

> *Got called away to a Black Knight Corp. meeting, be back this evening.*
> *Your breakfast is in the fridge, make sure you eat it all up and drink your juice, Princess.*

An empty feeling lies in the pit of my stomach as I read the note, my appetite gone as thoughts race across my mind. *What Knight meeting? Did they only just find out about it? What if they have to...hurt someone?*

Closing my eyes, I take a deep, calming breath, although nausea still swirls in my stomach at the thought of them being forced to do awful things at the hands of those that are meant to care for and protect them. They'll tell me what happened when they get back. I can't do anything to change things now anyway, so I might as well try and distract myself until they get home.

I decide to follow Ash's instructions and have something to eat, opening the fridge to find a yummy bowl of Greek yoghurt, and a glass of juice on the shelf. Fresh granola flapjacks and syrup are waiting for me on the counter, with another note next to them.

> *I made your favorite, chocolate chip*

Oh, Kai, you wonderful human!

Tucking in, I moan at the buttery oat-y taste, the flapjacks still warm from the oven. Finishing up, I put my bowl and glass in the dishwasher, and go to take a shower, then head back upstairs to get dressed.

Suddenly, I crave fresh air and looking out the window, although it's a little cloudy, it's not raining. A walk around campus sounds perfect to help blow these cobwebs away, and just what the doctor ordered.

Twenty minutes later, I'm heading out of the front doors of the Academy, wrapped up in my wool coat, hat, and scarf, with super cute mittens on my hands, and wearing my favourite Run and Fly rainbow dungarees. Taking a deep inhale, a smile lifts my lips as the frigid air hits my lungs. This is exactly what I needed.

Rounding the corner of the building, my lips drop into a frown when I hear girlish jeering and laughing up ahead. Narrowing my eyes, I come round a large topiary bush to find Amber Cuntmuffin—*surprise, surprise*—and her two fanny flap sidekicks surrounding a girl I've not seen before.

I can't see much of her, as they have her completely surrounded, but what I can tell from the ugly twists of their faces is that whatever they are saying isn't nice. Frowning harder, I approach them and catch Amber sneering at the poor girl, who looks close to tears.

"Why don't you go back to the gutter that you came from, charity case."

What the ever-loving fuck is wrong with this cumdumpster?!

"You know," I start, having stepped up right behind her. She whirls round, eyes bulging unattractively when she sees that we're almost face to face. "Just because you have a cunt, doesn't mean you need to act like one all the time." I smile sweetly at her, tilting my head to the side in a fake gesture of innocence.

"Oh look, here comes the other English bitch." Her lip curls back as she practically snarls at me. "She's the school whore, so you guys should get along just fine, Trash," she says, looking over her shoulder at the new girl, spitting out the insult and making the other girl flinch. Her name-calling just washes over me, and I smirk at her. "Let's go, Bianca, Tina." Ah, so those are their names. I guess I couldn't call them fanny flap one and two forever. *Snort.*

Amber takes a step away from me, her clones on either side of her. I swear they used to have different hair colours, but they're all varying shades of blonde now.

"Yeah, we wouldn't want to catch something," sneers Fanny, I mean, Tina. Or maybe Bianca. Fuck if I know, they all look the bloody same.

"What, like a personality?" I ask with a smile, earning more sneers from all three of them. "Run along, Fanny, your master is calling." *Whoops, guess Fanny it is!*

She vibrates with fury, like a little bunny boiler ready to explode. I can't help the chuckle that escapes at the visuals of bunny fluff flying everywhere when she detonates. Fanny aka Tina takes a step forward, but Amber lays a hand on her arm.

"She's not worth it, Tina," she growls out, then looks at me with a smug smile that makes my heartbeat thump in my chest uncomfortably. "She'll be put back in her place soon." Then, with perfectly executed hair flips, they turn on their heels and walk off.

"Well, that was ominous," a soft British accented voice says next to me, and I startle, having forgotten all about the new girl.

"Ah, don't mind Cuntmuffin. She's just sore because I'm with the guys that she wants," I tell her, finally able to take her in.

She's a petite blonde, barely reaching my shoulder, and I'm not exactly tall at five-six. Her pale blonde hair sits close to her head in tight curls, and with her sparkling blue eyes, all big and round like a bushbaby, she definitely looks like she belongs in the forest behind us. She's wearing jeans, Doc Martens, and a massive green puffer jacket with fake fur round the hood that practically drowns her. She smiles mischievously at the nickname I have for Amber, holding out her hand, the gesture drawing my lips up.

"Willow Anderson," she states as I grasp her tiny hand in mine, shaking it. She really is like a fairy.

"Lilly Darling, pleased to meet you, Willow," I reply. We let go of each others' hands with a chuckle, and I can see that she's eyeing me up as much as I did her. "Out with it," I say with a laugh, turning and indicating with my hand that we walk together.

"You said 'guys' that you're with, like there's more than one..." she trails off, a cute as fuck blush stealing over her cheeks as she looks at me from under her lashes. I can feel an answering heat in my own face, but I'm not ashamed of my unconventional relationship.

"That's right, I have four guys, who are all best friends, that I'm seeing," I tell her, watching as her eyes widen slightly, but her steps don't falter, and instead, she tips her head to the side a little, a slow smile building on her face.

"My brother and his best friends are inseparable. I can't imagine them ever being apart," she says, looking up at me with a twinkle in her eyes. "I might have to drop some hints about Iris when I speak to them next."

"Iris?" I question, loving how this girl's mind works, similar to my own in that we carry on conversations that we're having in our head out loud.

"Iris Montgomery sponsored me to come here after... Well, after some shit happened back home," she informs me, looking away, her hands twitching by her sides.

"And where's home?" I ask, seeing that a swift subject change is in order.

"World's End Estate, Chelsea, in London. You?" Another slow smile tilts her lips upwards.

"Islington, then Wiltshire with my uncle after some shit happened," I beam at her, and her grin grows wider. "And Iris sponsored you to come here?"

"Yeah, well, she persuaded her dad to pay for a sponsorship for me. I just...needed to get out, you know?" She looks at me then, and I can see pain so similar to my own swimming in her deep blue eyes. Although, my heartache is less now than it was when I first arrived.

"Yeah, I know," I reply softly, and we continue to walk a little ways in comfortable silence.

"So," she begins, that mischievous look back in her baby blues. "Wanna tell me all about your four guys? I'm gonna have to live vicariously through you. My brother and his friends, the fuckers, scared off any prospective boyfriends I may have had before I even got to say hello." She chuckles in a frustrated way, her blue eyes taking on a haunted look for just a second, but then she blinks and it's gone.

My heart aches for her, knowing that feeling so well. The feeling of being so overwhelmed with your trauma that you daren't even think about it. I can only hope that she'll be able to talk about what happened one day and start to move on.

"Well," I say, knowing that right now she needs a distraction, "there's Loki, Jax, Kai, and, of course, Ash."

"Oh shit!" she exclaims, stopping us and grabbing hold of my arm. "You're seeing the Black Knights?!" She's practically bouncing with excitement.

"You've been here, what? Five minutes? And you know about them already?" I shake my head.

"Girl, they're the hottest guys here. Not to mention the richest and the most dangerous." She fans herself ridiculously, and I laugh out loud at her antics. "Tell me, are they as incredible in bed as the rumours suggest?"

I like this girl, we are kindred spirits. Not afraid to get straight down to the nitty-gritty of a situation and all the good stuff. She is my spirit animal.

"Better," I say, a salacious grin pulling my lips up. She squeals, scaring some birds in the nearby trees who take flight, and we both chuckle.

"I knew it! Tell me everything," she demands, and a blush steals over my cheeks again thinking over all of mine and the guys' intimate times together.

"I could tell you, but then I'd have to kill you," I answer, faking a sigh. "But I will tell you how we met."

I spend the rest of the afternoon walking with my new fairy friend, talking about everything under the sun. I invite her back to our dorm, and we get pizza delivered from the kitchens, eating the cheesy goodness whilst she regales me with tales of her own misspent youth.

It's the perfect distraction, and although I get twinges of worry,

I'm also full of happiness at having met Willow. I can't wait for the guys to meet her.

LOKI

Worry swirls around us like a dark storm cloud as we step inside our dorm. Fatigue washes over me as I take my Chucks off, trying to be quiet so as not to wake the sleeping beauty upstairs, who is hopefully in my bed, waiting for me.

A need for her crashes over me with the force of a sledgehammer, and before I know it, my feet are carrying me towards the stairs.

"Loki," Ash quietly calls out as I reach the bottom step. I turn to look at him, seeing the unease in his eyes reflecting my own. He won't sleep tonight. "They're up to something. Stay sharp."

I nod, seeing Kai and Jax head for the drinks cabinet. I can't blame the big guy for going against the doctor's orders after a visit with our folks. BL—*before Lilly*—I would have joined them. Now, I just want to lose myself in her softness. In her. Ash is right, the cunts at Black Knight are up to something, inviting us all for a Knight dinner this Friday, instructing us to bring Lilly. I just hope that they don't know how important she is to us, otherwise, they really will have us by the balls.

I look up to find that I'm in front of my door, my hand on the brass knob and no recollection of how I got here. Turning it slowly, all thoughts of my parents, the company, and anything that is not Lilly Darling fly out of my mind as the hall light casts a soft glow on Lilly's sleeping form.

She's on her back, the sheets tangled around her waist, her glorious naked tits left exposed. I stand and watch her like a total fucking creeper for several moments, following all of her delicious curves with my gaze.

Deciding that I can't stand not touching her for a second longer, I walk in, leaving the door open as usual. Those fuckers downstairs can enjoy her cries when I'm balls deep inside of her. Stripping, I place one foot in front of the other, careful to be silent as I approach the bed. *Guess my training is good for more than just sneaking up on my marks.*

I take a condom out of my jeans pocket before taking them off, and slowly roll the rubber on my already hard dick. I also grab my phone, scrolling until I find the song that I've been obsessing over for the past few days. Setting the volume on low, I connect it to my sound system, but don't hit play just yet.

With my heart beating fast in anticipation of what I'm about to do, I gather saliva in my mouth, before quietly spitting in my palm. Watching Lilly sleep, I bring my hand down, wrapping it around my hard cock and spreading my spit over the surface. My eyes roll as I repeat this twice more, pleasure exploding along my length as I make sure I'm nicely lubed up for my girl.

I reach over and carefully pull back the comforter, exposing her beautiful pussy to me. My breath hitches as she gives a gentle moan, shifting her legs, then settling back down. I pull the covers right off her, happy to see that her thighs are parted enough that I can get between them.

Flicking my eyes up to her face, I watch her features as I climb onto the bed, gently pushing her legs wider apart until I can see her glistening cunt, open and ready for me. My dick twitches at the sight and a part of me wants to dive in between them with my tongue and teeth, making her scream my name. But the need to be surrounded by her, her body gripping mine, is too overwhelming to ignore. Lowering myself down, I move so that my tip is notched at her entrance. Fuck, I know that this is wrong. Forcing myself inside her whilst she sleeps. That doesn't stop me from surging forward though, grunting as her unprepared walls clamp around me. I quickly hit play on my phone, dropping it beside us just as she wakes with a gasp.

"Shit, Loki!" she rasps out, ending on a moan as I keep moving, thrusting until her body accepts mine and I'm fully seated inside her.

"Shhh, baby," I murmur, my voice strained with how fucking good it feels to be inside her, lightning tickling my nerves as her inner walls grip me exactly as I hoped they would.

Pausing, which is sweet agony, I wait until Khalid starts singing *Better*, and then sing along, crooning in her ear as I begin to move, our bodies flush together. It takes everything in me to keep my voice steady as I thrust inside her wet heat, her walls already fluttering around my cock.

"Loki," she moans when I hit that sweet spot inside her over and over again. Her nails rake down my arms, back, and ass, and I fucking love the edge of pain just as much as she does.

"You love it when I force my way inside you, don't you, naughty girl," I say, grabbing her wrists and bringing them up over her head, pinning them to the mattress.

She moans, a rush of wetness coating my dick as I pick up the pace, starting to fuck her hard, just the way she likes.

"Yes! Fuck, yes, Loki!"

I knew she would love it. She likes it as rough as we can give, and I'm more than happy to oblige. Transferring both her wrists to one of my hands, I move the other to wrap around her neck, like Jax often does. As soon as I start constricting her airway, her pussy walls clamp down so hard I almost shoot my load then and there.

"Uh ah, Pretty Girl. You don't come until I tell you to, understood?" I question through gritted teeth, stopping completely and gazing down at her. Her cheeks are flushed, her nipples peaked as they press against me. *Fuck, I'm not gonna last long at this rate.*

"Please..." she whispers, opening her eyes and looking into mine, begging me to allow her release.

"Soon, my heart," I reply, capturing her soft lips with mine and kissing her deeply. She tastes like every hope I've ever had, every good thing, and all the happy days rolled into one.

Unable to help myself, I begin to move once more, starting off slowly again.

"Keep your hands there, baby," I order, letting go of her wrists. Using my free hand, the other still wrapped around her slender neck, I hook her leg over my arm, and we both fucking groan at the new, deeper angle.

"Harder, please, Loki," she asks, her eyes closed, a look of pained bliss on her face as I fulfill her request.

I begin pounding harder, faster, until I'm impaling her on my cock. Letting go of her throat, I move to grab her other leg, and go up on my knees to get an even deeper angle. *Fuck.*

I feel like my entire body is on fire, my teeth clenched so tightly I'm surprised they don't crack as I fight my release. Feeling my balls draw up, I know that I can't hold it back anymore.

"Come now, baby," I growl out, pulling out of her completely. I watch enraptured as she squirts all over me and herself, her release even reaching her shoulders. She cries out in ecstasy, her whole body going rigid as her legs shake in my grip and her hands claw at the mattress. *Jesus, that is so fucking hot.*

Releasing her thighs, I whip the condom off, pumping my cock in my fist until I, too, explode, seeing stars as I cover her pussy, stomach, and breasts with my climax. I stay kneeling, panting, watching our combined essences cover her glorious body. *It's enough to make any man hard and ready for round fucking two!*

She opens her eyes, a lazy smile on her lips as she glances at me with a look that sets my heart racing all over again. Her whole body practically glows in the darkness, highlighted by the light coming in from the hall.

"I love you so fucking much, Loki Thorn," she whispers, her voice husky and satisfied.

"I love you, Lilly Darling," I reply huskily, leaning down to capture her lips again, tingling all over at the contact of our bodies, not giving a fuck about getting my cum all over me. "Now, let's go downstairs, and you can show the guys how pretty you look covered in my cum," I tell her, nipping her lip then getting up and holding a hand out.

"Fucking wankstain," she chuckles, rolling her eyes at me, but taking my hand anyway.

Wrapping my arm around her, I pull her close, kissing her hair and savoring the just fucked smell that is all Lilly. The first moment I caught it wafting off of her, like spring after the darkest of winters, I knew she would be our fresh start. Our new beginning.

Shit, I would make a fortune if I could bottle that scent, but she's all ours, only we are allowed to cover ourselves in her bounty. And we don't share with anyone else; they can all live in despair for all I care. As long as she's by our side, in our beds, the rest of the world can fuck off.

CHAPTER FIFTEEN

LILLY

The next morning, Loki and I head downstairs to find the others sitting round the table, eating breakfast. I sit down to a plate of pancakes, crispy bacon, and eggs, all drizzled with syrup, with a glass of fresh orange juice and ice.

I look up to catch Kai's amber stare.

"Thank you. For this, and the granola bars yesterday," I tell him, a feeling of lightness descending over me. I love that they take care of me.

I know that in this day and age of feminism and equality between the sexes, it's not necessarily the most popular view, but there's something about being cared for by a man, or in my case four men, that feels right. Like it's meant to be this way. And anyway, we look after each other, just in different ways.

"It's my pleasure, darling," he replies with an upturned face, his beautiful smile lifting my spirits further. There is still that darkness in the depths of his eyes, like something is eating away at him from the inside. A fissure of worry skitters through me.

"I'm sorry we weren't here yesterday, Princess," Ash says to my left, and I turn to face him, my heart beginning to race as I suddenly remember why they were gone.

"What happened? Did you have to..." I trail off, swallowing hard, unable to finish my sentence. Ash grimaces, pausing with his coffee cup partway to his plush lips.

"No, just usual training stuff, and a meeting afterwards," he tells me, and I just know that there's more to it. I want to know what the meeting was about, but I want to find out about their training first.

"What does your training entail?" I ask hesitantly, watching him intently. His face starts to shut down, then he sighs, closing his eyes and setting his cup down.

"Well," he starts, opening his lids and locking me in his steel gaze. His brow is wrinkled, his hands clasped on the table, his cheeks tight with the force of his clenched jaw. This isn't easy for him, and my heart aches for this strong man who's seen such horrors. "There's the usual self-defence and offence training," he tells me.

"Basically, we learn how to beat the shit out of people," Loki interrupts, Ash snapping his head towards the redhead and snarling. "Don't fucking sugarcoat it, man. Just tell her, she can handle it," Loki argues, looking my way with a small smile as he says the last part.

"Hey," I say gently, resting my hand on Ash's arm which is vibrating with tension. He turns to look at me, his eyes pained. "I will not think any less of you, my love. Or any of you," I tell them, looking at each one in turn. "I love you. It's a forever kind of thing," I joke, loving the stunning smile that graces Ash's lips once I look back at him.

"Loki's right, we learn to beat people up. As you know already, we extract information from them and often have to get physical. So we practice to prepare, and *they* like for us to keep up with our skills," he practically spits out. "We also have different roles that we train specifically for. Loki specializes in stealth and espionage, blending into different situations seamlessly."

I can't help my snort at that, Loki being subtle is not something I'd imagine him capable of. He looks at me, with one auburn brow raised as if to remind me of exactly how stealthy he was last night, and my cheeks heat with the memory of waking up with him pushing his way inside me.

"Jax trained in South Africa, learning how to patch people up in appalling conditions, so that he can better..." Ash pauses here and swallows.

"Torture people," Jax simply states, his low voice sending shivers across my skin as always, although not just the usual lust filled ones. I look to see his blue eyes are hard, no doubt remembering all the pain that he's doled out over the years.

I reach across and grasp his huge hand, giving it a squeeze. His eyes brighten, a small tilt of his lips letting me know that he received the message of acceptance and love I was trying to give. I don't blame any of them for what they've been forced to do, forced by the very people who should have been protecting them.

"Kai specialises in tech, as you know," Ash carries on, and I study Kai, who gives me a tight smile. "He's trained in online warfare, hacking, and pretty much any way to take someone down, ruin a life or business, all from the comfort of home." I give Kai a reassuring smile, and he nods in return. But his deeds clearly trouble him too as I see his jaw is clenched and hands are nervously picking at the food on his plate.

"And you?" I ask, turning back to Ash. His jaw is steel, rock-solid, his stare faraway, avoiding eye contact.

"As our leader, Ash has to make hard, impossible decisions, and they test his commitment regularly," Loki once again interjects, his voice full of pain for his friend, and Ash's eyes go dark, his brow furrowed.

"Like what?" I whisper, my mouth going dry as my grip tightens on Ash's arm.

"Like whether someone lives or dies," Ash tells me, voice lacking any emotion, his eyes empty and staring just over my head, like he's recalling all of those lives he's been forced to take.

Tears sting my eyes as I let go of his arm, and use both hands to guide his attention back to me. His grey eyes find mine, and they are haunted, full of ghosts that no eighteen year old should have following them around.

"I'm so sorry, my love," I murmur, feeling moisture spill down my cheeks. His whole face softens, his own hand reaching up to wipe away my tears with his long pianist fingers.

"Don't cry, Princess. Please. I can't bear to see you cry over me," he pleads huskily, leaning down and placing our foreheads together.

"I told you, you are worth every tear of mine, Asher Vanderbilt. You all are. My tears are not mine anymore but yours, as the rest of me is yours."

He takes a sharp inhale, his large chest rising, and I know that it will take time and persistence for him, for all of them, to believe that they are worthy of my love. I will tell them a thousand times a day if that's what it takes. Closing the distance, I place a gentle kiss on his lips, tasting the salt of my tears mingled with the coffee that lingers on his. He kisses me back, his whole body relaxing as he seeks entry with his tongue. I willingly give it, loving the taste of him in my mouth as we explore each other, like discovering a new place just off a well known path.

He ends the kiss with one last sweet peck on my lips, pulling away and looking more at peace than he did before.

"I love you so much, Lilly," he confesses, staring into my eyes with such intensity, I know that I should be scared. But I'm not. I meant what I said. We are a forever type of thing. "Now eat up, otherwise, we'll be late for our first day back."

I begin to cut into my pancakes, heaping my fork with eggs and bacon too, and moaning when I place the food in my mouth. *Fucking yum!*

We finish breakfast in a comfortable silence, although I do catch the others giving Ash funny looks every so often. After the fifth time, where Jax actually elbows Ash in the side, I turn to face the man in question.

"Out with it, Lucifer," I tell him, his lips quirking at the nickname. He sighs, setting his own cutlery down.

"At the meeting last night, Julian told us that we're having dinner this Friday with all the Black Knight families," he tells me, peering at me. He rubs the back of his neck whilst biting his lip in a way that would be very distracting if I didn't suddenly feel butterflies take flight in my stomach. "And we've been told to bring you."

"W–what?" I ask, my stomach dropping. "W–why?" I look at the others, but they all have matching looks of worry on their faces.

"We don't know, Pretty Girl," Loki answers, taking hold of my suddenly cold hand. "But we will be there, and I promise we won't leave you alone, not even for a moment," he tells me vehemently, rubbing his fingers across my knuckles.

"Do they...do they know about the bonds and shares?" I question, turning to Ash. His brow is once again deeply furrowed. Poor guy will have terrible frown lines soon if this keeps up.

"I'm not sure how they can, although that thought did occur to us, too," he muses. "I looked at the papers. Laura was, and now you are, silent investors. Completely anonymous."

"But I wouldn't put it past them to have found out," Kai states, his melodic voice full of concern.

"Maybe it's just dinner, you know?" I say, feeling unconvinced. "I mean, Julian seems to have a bit of a...thing for me, right?" My nose wrinkles remembering his inappropriate looks and touches.

Ash's upper lip peels back.

"I hope that you're right, Princess," he says, looking round at the others before settling back on me.

But as chills spread over my skin in the warm room, I can't help the feeling that I'm wrong.

The first day back in class flies by, and before I know it, it's lunchtime. Willow shared my last class, Interior Design, so we head to the dining hall together. I open the wooden doors, hearing a gasp next to me as Willow takes in the beautiful, light-filled space with a slack-jawed expression.

"We're not in Kansas anymore," I say with a chuckle, thinking back to the first time I stepped foot in here, and the awe I felt seeing it.

"We are definitely not in World's End, that's for sure." She ruefully laughs as we make our way to a table next to one of the floor-to-ceiling windows.

"Did you not come here for breakfast?" I ask as we take our seats, Willow facing the door, whilst I choose one looking out at the breathtaking view of the mountains and forest.

"I was too nervous to eat," she admits, looking a little lost as a waiter, Gerald, comes over.

"Good afternoon, Miss Darling, Miss Anderson," he greets us, Willow's eyes going wider than even I thought possible.

"Hello, Gerald," I reply, beaming at him. "Have a good Christmas and New Year?"

"Yes, thank you. And yourself?" he politely enquires. I decide against telling him that I went to Bali to see one of my boyfriends who's recovering from steroid abuse, discovered that I'm rich in my own right, have stocks and shares in a company of dubious intentions, and visited my mother's grave for the first time.

"Lovely, thank you," I say instead.

"Do you ladies know what you want today?" he asks, looking from me to Willow.

"Ummm..." she starts, looking all kinds of flustered as her cheeks heat up.

"I'll take the steak, chunky fries, and side salad please, and a glass of full-fat coke with ice," I tell him. My intention was to have a salad, but I'm suddenly craving meat. *Snort. Not that kind of meat. Although...*

"Of course. And you, Miss Anderson?" he questions Willow, who looks like a rabbit in headlights.

"Uh, I'll take the same," she quickly replies, breathing out a relieved sigh.

"I'll put the order in and bring your drinks back shortly," he tells us with a smile. I grin back, I like the old man. Not like that butler, fucking Crow. Speaking of, I haven't seen him around for a while.

"What kind of school canteen is this?" Willow hisses at me, interrupting my thoughts, and I laugh at her.

"I know, right. The day's menu choices are on your iPad. Or you can just order what the fuck you like, and they'll make it for you," I inform her with a roll of my eyes. *Rich pricks.*

"Jesus," she murmurs, going still as the whole place goes quiet. Her eyes widen again, and it really is adorable.

I turn round, a huge smile lifting my lips as my Knights walk in looking all kinds of dark and dangerous. My core twinges at the sight of them. They spot me and head towards our table. Having spent the past few weeks with them, I'd forgotten just how imposing they can be.

Ash in his usual pristine black suit, tie, and smoothly styled jet hair, his eyes the colour of steel. Jax dressed head to toe in black, his bulging muscles threatening to rip his T-shirt in a Hulk moment. His lips twitch ever so slightly when his sparkling blue eyes meet mine, and I savour that almost smile that's meant for me alone. Kai is the epitome of geek chic in green chinos, a chequered shirt, navy bow tie, and a mustard cardigan. He looks so damn hot I can feel my temperature rise just watching him. Loki struts in like a fucking peacock, his auburn hair artfully disheveled, his low slung jeans hugging his toned legs, his white T-shirt sculpted to his torso in the most mouth-watering way. Today his shirt has a drawing of an eye in black ink, an anatomical heart in red, and an etching of a cockerel.

A delighted laugh tumbles from my lips as my hands cover my mouth, and his face lights up with an arrogant as fuck smirk. When they finally reach our table, he swoops down, capturing my lips in a bruising kiss that leaves me breathless and tingling.

"I missed you, Pretty Girl," he says, his lush lips turning down in a pout as he sits in the seat next to me and pulls my chair closer to his.

Jax sits on my other side, scooting his chair closer, then leans in and tangles his hand in the hair on the back of my head. Using his grip, he turns my head until I'm facing him, then proceeds to decimate my lips with his velvety ones. Her Vagisty is panting like a bitch in heat by the time he pulls away, and my heart races seeing the look of wild hunger in his blue eyes.

"I missed you, too, Baby Girl," he rumbles against my lips as he pulls away, his own lips lifting as he sees my dazed look.

"Shit, girl! That was hot!" Willow blurts out, and all eyes turn to her, Ash and Kai having sat down too, making her squirm in her seat.

"Who the fuck are you?" Jax growls, letting go of my hair and levelling her with his piercing stare. She swallows audibly.

"Hey!" I scold, whacking his pec with the back of my hand. *Fuck! When will I ever learn that their muscles are hard as fucking rock?* "That's Willow. She's my new bestie, so play nice."

Bad bitch that she is, she holds her hand out, waiting for Jax to shake it. To his credit, he does and doesn't pull a dick move like squeezing too hard either. *Brownie points, Jax.*

"Jax Griffiths," he introduces himself, letting go of her hand with a small nod.

"Nice to meet you, Jax," she replies politely, holding her hand out to Loki next, then Kai, who both introduce themselves. Finally, it's Ash's turn.

"Asher Vanderbilt," he states, shaking her outstretched hand. His voice is cold, but not unfriendly. "Your brother is Hunter Anderson, co-leader of The Shadows crew, based in the World's End Estate, Chelsea. And Iris Montgomery convinced her father to sponsor your senior year here."

I look at him with wide eyes, almost as round as Willow's.

"That's right," she says, her voice a little shaky. "How did you know all of that?" she questions, suspicion laced in her tone.

"I make it a point to know things, especially if they involve my girlfriend," he tells her, and my heart does a little pitty-pat at the term. Stupid really, given all that we've gone through.

"Good to know," Willow murmurs, just as Gerald comes back with our drinks.

He takes the guys' orders, then heads off again, leaving us in a slightly strained silence.

"Fuck's sake," I huff out, turning to Willow and ignoring the brooding arseholes around me. "How was your first morning?"

She proceeds to tell me all about it, and before long Loki joins in, with the odd word from Ash and Kai. Jax remains quiet, but that's no surprise given his usual engagement level with strangers being zero. Our food arrives, and we all eat, continuing to chat. I invite Willow back to our dorm for dinner later, both of us silencing any arguments by offering to make shepherd's pie for the guys.

I'd call that a successful introduction.

After all, they didn't threaten to kill her.

CHAPTER SIXTEEN

LILLY

The rest of the week is over in a flash, and before I know it, it's Friday, and I'm getting ready for dinner at the Vanderbilt's mansion. I've chosen an original nineteen-thirties bias cut gown in wine coloured velvet. It has a high scoop neckline, and is strapless, with a silk waist tie and a short train. The pièce de résistance is the back, which is completely open, the fabric gaping on either side of the opening to give tantalising glimpses of my sides as I move.

I've put my hair up, wisps teasing around my face and neck, and my makeup is all smokey eyes and dark red lips. And of course, my feet are in Irregular Choice heels, emerald green sequin ones with a matching bow on the toes.

"Jesus, Pretty Girl," Loki rasps, and I look up from applying the finishing touches to my face to see him devouring me with his stare, leaning in the open doorway of his room. Luckily, the fabric is fairly thick so it hides my pebbling nipples, and I watch him in the mirror with bated breath as he stalks towards me, a predator's gleam in his eyes.

When he's behind me, he reaches out and runs a single finger down my spine. I can't hide the full body shiver that races across my skin at his touch.

"Fuck, if we didn't have somewhere to be..." he trails off, swallowing and biting his lip as his other hand goes to his crotch, adjusting himself, the outline of his dick clear through his dress trousers.

He's looking fucking edible himself in black trousers and a matching jacket, with a crisp white shirt and black bow tie. My whole body is suffused with heat, my nerve endings tingling as I stare at his reflection. I watch as he brings his hand up to my face, and lean into his touch when his finger brushes me from temple to jaw, leaving a blazing trail behind.

"You keep eye fucking me like that, Pretty Girl, and I won't be held responsible for my actions," he whispers in my ear, his voice low and sinful, his breath tickling my skin and stirring the hair around my face.

"Loki..." I whine, my whole body alight, my skin suddenly feeling too tight to contain the fire that is burning inside me.

"Time to go!" Jax calls from downstairs, breaking the tension that's threatening to drown Loki and I.

Loki heaves an enormous sigh. "Come on. Let's get this shitshow over with."

The fire suddenly goes out, his words effectively dousing the flames and leaving me feeling nauseous. I turn with my own sigh, and he grasps my hand in his warm one, looking down as my charm bracelet tinkles. A beautiful smile tugs at his lips as he leads me out of the door, grabbing my clutch like a true gent, and down the stairs.

"Ash and Kai went ahead..." Jax starts, trailing off as he spots us. "Fuck."

I can't help but chuckle at his awestruck look, his eyes like blue flames as he takes me in. I'm sure mine are just as heated as his, my stare devouring him. He, like Loki, is also in a tux and bow tie, and damn, does it look fucking incredible on him. His hair is tied up in the usual sexy as fuck man bun, his beard neatly trimmed. Her Vagisty is practically weeping at this point, begging me to take them both back upstairs and get lost in their arms.

"It gets better, bro," Loki tells him, a sexy yet pained smile on his face. *Same, Loki, same.*

He takes a step away from me, holding our hands up, encouraging me to do a slow twirl. A satisfied smile tilts my lips when I hear Jax curse behind me.

"Fuck," Jax repeats, and I turn back to see him rubbing a huge hand over his face. "We best leave now before I change my mind, Baby Girl, and take you back upstairs."

My breath hitches at the promise in his eyes, sweet anticipation making my core ache, mixing with nervous butterflies taking flight in my stomach as we leave the safety of our dorm, and head towards the lion's den.

We walk out of the front doors to be greeted by a valet holding out Jax's truck keys to him, the truck idling on the drive in front of us.

"Shotgun!" I cry, quickly making my way to the front passenger side and sticking out my tongue at Loki, who pouts back.

We all get in and buckle up, the butterflies flapping their wings furiously and increasing my heart rate. I don't know why I'm so nervous. Perhaps because the boys are? Or maybe it's just instincts. Whatever it is, I need to calm down before I explode. What I need is a distraction. Luckily for me, I've a hulking Viking who's sporting a semi sitting next to me in the driver's seat.

"How far until we get there?" I ask, an idea forming in my mind as we start to drive off. I grab Jax's phone, which is wirelessly hooked up to the speakers and scroll, selecting *Night Drive* by HENRY and hitting play, putting the phone back on the magnetic charging port.

"About fifteen, maybe twenty minutes," Jax says, eyes flicking to me, driving through the ornate gates. "Why do you have that look on your face, Baby Girl?" he asks as he focuses back on the road, his brow furrowed.

"What look?" I say innocently, unbuckling my seatbelt.

"What are you doing, Pretty Girl?" I hear Loki question from the back, but my attention is all for the big guy next to me. Leaning over, trying to avoid the gearstick, I open his suit jacket, popping open the button on the waistband of his trousers.

"Baby Girl..." Jax warns in a growl, which I ignore as I carefully undo the zipper, my breath coming in a sharp gasp as we take a bend at high speed.

"Eyes on the road, big guy," I tease with an evil smile.

"Shit," Jax gasps as his huge, beautiful erect cock springs free.

Commando in all situations, huh? I muse as I wrap my hand around it, barely able to get my fingers to meet, it's just that big. I pump his silky length up and down, making Jax moan low and deep, and the car lurches as his foot presses a little too hard on the accelerator.

"Jesus Christ!" Loki hisses from the back, and I glance over into the backseat to see the glint of his pierced dick, which he has out and palmed. "You are something else, Pretty Girl," he moans, pumping his own fist up and down in time with my movements, his eyes locked on my hand wrapped around Jax. I whimper at the sight, my pussy fluttering as I take both these beautiful men in.

"Fuck. That feels so good, Baby Girl," Jax moans, and I can see he's struggling to keep his lids open and on the road, his hands clenching on the steering wheel, his knuckles white.

Taking my other hand, I start to gently massage his balls, every so often hitting that sweet spot just behind them. As I stroke and tease his member, I can feel him getting impossibly harder in my hand, his balls getting tighter and starting to draw upwards.

"Fuck, Lilly," he growls, his husky voice making my thighs clench. "I'm gonna come!" he gruffly shouts, and that's when I lower my head, taking his tip into my mouth and sucking hard whilst my fist keeps a tight grip, pumping harder and faster.

Hot salty cum shoots into my mouth, coating my tongue as he orgasms with a roar, and the car jerks to the side. I swallow every mouthful, loving how I can affect this strong man so much that he loses control.

Seconds later, I hear Loki gasp out his own release with a curse. Sitting up, there's a satisfied smirk on my face when I notice the lipstick marks on Jax's cock.

"Jesus, Baby Girl." His voice is a husky rumble, deeper than usual, which I didn't think was possible. I just beam back, almost preening at his tone of sated disbelief as I tuck him back into his trousers, lipstick marks and all. Grabbing my clutch, I drop down the sun visor, using the mirror to fix my lipstick.

"Hey, Pretty Girl, grab the wipes from the glovebox for me, please?" Loki asks from the back. "I didn't have that naughty mouth to catch my load."

My cheeks flush as my thighs clench together with the thought of wrapping my lips around Loki's cock, using my tongue to play with his piercing. *I swear I'm in a permanent state of horniness whenever I'm around any of these boys!*

I take a deep shuddering breath, grab the packet of wipes, and reach back to hand them to him. Loki keeps my stare for a moment more before taking them and cleaning himself up. He looks up again as he leans forward, his thumb wiping the side of my mouth, then he brings the digit to his own mouth, sucking off the drop of Jax's cum that sits on the tip.

My heart fucking stops, my stare locked on his mouth as he slowly withdraws his thumb, the heat in his emerald orbs sparking and flickering like a flame.

"Not bad," he whispers, a sexy as fuck smile on his plush lips. Fire roars around my body, consuming me with lust and creating an ache so intense I feel like I may pass out from need. "Touch yourself, baby. I know that you need to. Ease that pressure," he commands me, and I whimper, my breath stilling in my chest.

"Loki! Fuck, dude, I'm hard again," Jax grumbles, kickstarting my breathing once more.

But my hands move of their own volition, reaching for my hem and drawing my skirt up my legs, the soft velvet making my whole body tingle as it slides up my skin. Loki's now sitting so far forward, he's in between the front seats, staring down as I inch the garment up my thighs. Lifting my arse, I make sure to pool my skirt around me so that I'm not sitting on it. Wouldn't want a wet patch.

"Good girl," Loki croons as I expose my black lacy thong, moving it aside to show him my glistening pussy lips. I hear a manly gasp as he takes in my bare cunt. "You've been busy," Loki comments in appreciation. I had a full Hollywood wax after class, driving into town with Willow.

"Wha–" Jax cuts off, swearing as he looks down and sees the view Loki has.

"Keep driving, *big boy*," Loki teases, earning a snarl in return, to which he just chuckles.

Love Is a Bitch by Two Feet comes over the speaker, the beat heightening my senses, as my hand drifts down of its own accord, to swipe between my slick folds. A low moan falls from my lips as pleasure bursts across my closed eyelids, my head falling back to hit the headrest with a dull thud.

"Such a good fucking girl," Loki praises as Jax groans beside me, my fingers dipping inside my aching pussy and coating themselves in my wetness. "Now tease your cunt, baby."

"Fuuuuck..." I murmur as I go deeper, circling my opening with my middle finger, my lower lips fluttering and desperate to be filled. "Please..."

"Push two fingers in, nice and slow, Pretty Girl," Loki commands, his voice low and full of dark deeds done at night. "And open your fucking eyes."

I obey immediately, my greedy pussy demanding more as I slowly slide two fingers inside myself. My lids lazily stutter as my mouth falls open on a gasp, emerald eyes dark as a raven's feathers staring back at me, full of fire. Movement catches my eye, and I look down to see Loki's hand wrapped around his fully erect cock, gripping it tightly as he moves once again in time with my own hand. Though this time, my fingers are buried in my pulsing cunt.

"Tell me how your pussy feels," Loki demands, and Jax swears, the car speeding up once again as we wind our way down dark mountain roads.

"Wet," I rasp out, breathless with the exquisite pleasure that rolls over me as my fingers start to thrust harder and faster. "So fucking wet."

"Isn't she perfect, Jax?"

"So fucking perfect," Jax grinds out between clenched teeth, and my hooded gaze turns to him to see him once again white-knuckling the steering wheel.

"Loki, please. I'm so close," I say, begging him for release as I turn back to him.

"Add another finger," he orders, his voice harsh as he, too, is close to another climax. I can hear it in the strain of his voice, see it in the way his hand furiously pumps his cock, precum glistening at the tip.

"Shit, yes," I say on a gasp as I do as he says. The sounds my pussy makes, wet and sucking, are obscene, filling the car with the scent of sex. "Loki, yes!" I scream as I fracture into a thousand pieces, my release coating my hand and the leather seat beneath me.

I slump down, my entire body liquified as I ride my orgasm, my fingers slowing, leaving my pussy twitching in the afterglow. I hear Loki grunt, and watch as he catches his climax in his hand, his face blissful.

"Give Jax a taste, baby," Loki commands breathlessly, and I manage to rouse myself to follow this one last order.

Placing my wet fingers against Jax's lips, I sigh as he opens his mouth, his tongue licking my fingers from base to tip, before he takes them into his mouth one at a time, sucking them clean.

"I fucking hate you both," he grumbles once he's finished, fixing his pissed off stare at me then Loki. "We're here, and I've got a raging fucking hard-on."

I giggle, reaching over for the wipes that Loki is holding out and cleaning up, then straightening my dress. My laughter is short-lived, however, when I look past Jax's head, up at the imposing mansion. It's not the grandeur of the building that kills my humour, but the man standing at the top of stone stairs.

In the low light, shadows play across his face until he's nothing but a wraith, a monster, the kind that lives in the darkness and comes out to steal the souls of innocents. I see out of the corner of my eye, both guys turn to look in the direction that I am, but I'm unable to take my glower from that of the man standing there, a demon's smirk on his face.

"Well, there goes my boner," Jax ruefully sighs, and the joke is so unexpected coming from him, that it breaks the spell I'm under, and I turn back to him, my brows raised.

"Jax Griffiths, I love you," I say, leaning over and placing a kiss on his lips, tasting myself on him.

"I love you too, Baby Girl," he mumbles into my mouth, his words flowing into me and giving me strength for the night ahead.

I hear the back door open and shut, then a blast of cold air hits my back as my door is opened. Turning, I see Loki, lined in moonlight and the yellow glow of the outside lights.

"Come, let's go dine with the devil and his minions," he says, his hand outstretched.

Here's hoping we have long enough spoons.

CHAPTER SEVENTEEN

LILLY

The winter chill hits my skin, goosebumps pebbling all over my arms and back as I take Loki's hand, and he leads me up the front steps. They look like marble, grey veins running through them until they have the appearance of bone in the moonlight. When we reach the top, the devil himself is there to greet us, columns of marble on either side of him.

"Welcome to Vanderbilt Manor," Julian welcomes me, all charm and lethal smiles, his hands outstretched to encompass the grand home behind him.

The mansion reaches up so high that I can't see the top and is made from the same bone coloured marble. It stretches either side of us, seeming to disappear into the distance, it's that vast. I can appreciate the beauty in its history, but it's austere, all hard lines and harsh decoration. There's nothing soft and welcoming here.

He walks towards me, stepping right into my personal space, his hand going around my waist as he tries to pull me away from Loki, who keeps a firm grasp of my hand. I shiver, and not from the cold when his thumb traces the bare skin at my back.

"Exquisite, as always, Darling," he whispers against my cheek, placing a soft kiss there that leaves bile in my throat. I don't know if I misheard, or if he purposefully left off the 'Miss,' but I've never disliked my surname before now. He cheapens it, making it sound like an endearment he has not, will not, earn the right to use.

His lips linger on my cheek for a second too long, his hand too, before he steps away and frowns down at Loki's hand, still clutching mine as he steps forward beside me, Jax coming up on my other side. They encase me in their scents, vanilla and citrus, lending me the strength to shake off Julian's inappropriate touch.

"Boys," he says dispassionately, nodding at them both. "Shall we?" Holding out one arm, he indicates that we follow him as he heads inside, a butler closing the door softly behind us.

The grand entrance hall is huge, but dark despite all of the lights, of which there seem to be hundreds. The walls are painted a deep navy, adding to the dark and gloomy feel, and huge portraits of presumably the Vanderbilt ancestors line the walls. The floors are black and white chequered marble, and there's a double staircase, also in marble, leading to the next floor. We pass by several dark wood doors, all closed, and although there must be heating somewhere for the air feels warm, shivers climb up and down my body at the coldness of the interior. There's no life here, only pictures of the long dead.

Julian stops in front of a set of wooden doors, which open from the inside as if by magic, although as we pass through, I see more liveried servants. We enter a vast dining room, panelled in dark wood with more portraits lining the walls and a huge marble fireplace on one wall.

An impossibly long table sits in the middle of the room, lit candelabras along its centre, and sparkling glasses, plates, and silverware in front of each chair. It looks as though we are the last to arrive, as most of the chairs at the far end are full with whom I assume are the guys' parents and members of Black Knight Corporation. Everyone looks up as we enter, and I find myself wanting to shift under their scrutiny. Julian leads us past the empty chairs, stopping in front of the head of the table.

I find Kai sitting ramrod straight next to an older, distinguished looking gentleman, with salt and pepper hair and a very eighties moustache. *Gross.* Kai's honey eyes are dark, and when he meets mine, it takes everything in me not to react. Not to run to him and drag him away, never to return. He has the look of a man who is drowning, desperate for air but unable to reach the surface. My hand tightens on Loki's, and he follows my gaze, a frown drawing his perfect brows together.

"Lilly, may I introduce Stephen Matthews, Kai's uncle," Julian says, and I look to the side, finding eyes similar to Kai's staring back at me. "He stepped up when Kai's parents tragically lost their lives in that fatal car accident, all those years ago."

Stephen nods his head, his eyes devoid of...anything. There's no warmth there, or even dislike. There's nothing, and I feel cold all over. It's like being stared at by a shark who doesn't care if you live or drown in the watery depths.

"A pleasure," he says, his voice a cruel hard thing that sends unwelcome shivers over my skin.

"P–pleased to meet you," I manage to murmur, taking a deep inhale when I feel Jax stroke my free hand, stepping up close behind me.

"Loki, Jax, you know where your seats are. I can show Lilly to hers," Julian says, his tone curt and expression pinched.

Loki reluctantly lets my hand go, my fingers feeling bereft as he leaves me with a look full of worry. He goes to sit next to Kai, a beautiful woman with the same auburn hair tumbling over her shoulders, sitting on Loki's other side. I can see his features reflected in hers, although where Loki is warm and inviting, hers is a cruel beauty, sharp and unforgiving. She must be his mother, and on her other side is a blond man, with the same emerald eyes as Loki. They look me over, undressing me, and his tongue darts out over his lips as if he likes what he sees.

I can't suppress the shudder as Julian introduces us.

"This is Chad and Rebecca Thorn, Loki's parents."

"A pleasure, Miss. Darling," Chad says, his voice low like Loki's but lacking the sensuality of his son's timbre.

"Lovely to finally meet you, Lilly. I can call you Lilly, can't I?" Rebecca says, her voice sugary sweet, but like Snow White's apple, there's poison lurking in the depths.

"Of course, Rebecca," I smile saccharinely back, having to suppress the chuckle at the way she flinches and narrows her eyes when I use her Christian name. "Nice to meet you, Chad," I add, hating the oily feeling that slivers over my skin when he hears his own given name from my lips. *Fucking Chad.*

I look over when I hear a chair scrape on the marble floor, to see Jax sitting next to a tiny blonde woman. She looks up at him with such love and sorrow in her eyes that it takes my breath away. He looks down and gives her an affectionate smile, taking her hand and kissing the back of it sweetly.

"Rafe and Jannet Griffiths, Jax's parents," Julian continues, leaving the top of the table and stepping next to me, taking my elbow. My heart rate kicks up a notch, knowing that I'm in the hands of a predator, but I shake my head when Jax looks ready to get up and knock Julian the fuck out.

"So, you're the cunt leading all our boys around by their dicks?" I hear a gruff voice say, and my head turns sharply to see a guy of similar, if slightly smaller, build to Jax; basically huge and hulk-like, sitting next to Jax. I don't miss Jax's mum flinch at his crude words or Jax's growl.

"That's me," I smile sweetly at him. "You must be the pathetic excuse of a man who beats his wife and child to make up for his micro penis." I hold his gawking glare, even as his face goes an unhealthy shade of purple, and I hear Loki covering up a bark of laughter with a cough.

"Why, you little bitch!" Rafe roars, shooting up from his seat, as if to make his way over to me, but Jax gets to his feet as well.

"Sit the fuck down, *old man*," he snarls, and warmth suffuses my limbs at his defence of me.

I smirk as Rafe does as his son orders, and takes his seat once more.

"You like to keep things interesting I see, naughty girl," Julian chuckles next to my ear, and I literally have to swallow down vomit at his words, chastising me like he's my sugar daddy. *Fucking hell.*

His blasted hand lands back on my bare skin making me jump, and he guides me to an empty chair next to Jannet Griffiths, Ash on my other side.

"And you know me and my wife, Samantha," Julian finishes, pulling out the chair for me as his wife doesn't even look up from studying something on the table.

"Nice to see you again, Samantha," I say, lowering myself in my chair as Julian pushes it in. She looks up, startled.

"Oh, Lilly," she starts, her voice soft and wispy like a puff of smoke. "I didn't know that you were coming."

"I told you, Mom," Ash says from beside me, his hand coming to my thigh and squeezing gently underneath the table.

"Silly me," she says breathlessly, then goes back to staring at her empty plate. She jumps when Julian claps his hands.

"Let's begin!" he calls, and the doors open to reveal servers in smart black tailcoats and white gloves, holding small plates, which must be our starters.

Ash leans in, his ginger scent calming me as it wraps around my body like a warm hug.

"Princess," he murmurs in my ear, the same one his father just spoke into, but the shivers I get this time are all from pleasure.

"'O, she doth teach the torches to burn bright!
It seems she hangs upon the cheek of night

> Like a rich jewel in an Ethiope's ear;
> Beauty too rich for use, for earth too dear!
> So shows a snowy dove trooping with crows,
> As yonder lady o'er her fellows shows.
> The measure done, I'll watch her place of stand,
> And, touching hers, make blessed my rude hand.
> Did my heart love till now? forswear it, sight!
> For I ne'er saw true beauty till this night.'"

My breath catches and my cheeks flush as he quotes Shakespeare at me, his tone hushed, reminding me of the first time he told me he loved me on Halloween.

"Whispering sweet nothings already, eh, boy?!" Chad shouts from across the table, my eyes darting up in time to see him lick his fucking lips again as he looks at me, and effectively dousing all my warm and fuzzies. *Wanker.*

"Chad," Julian snaps out, my head turning to see him with narrowed grey eyes, staring at the other man.

"Apologies, Julian," Chad murmurs, looking quickly down in an act of submission. *What the fuck is going on?*

"Let's eat," Julian announces, his tone light as if he didn't just tell off his business partner and long-term friend.

Ash squeezes my hand before letting go and picking up his cutlery to eat. I look at my plate, noticing a seafood starter, then stare panicked at my cutlery, having no fucking clue which ones to use.

"Outside in, sweetie," a soft voice says to my left, and I turn with a grateful smile as Jannet, Jax's mum, picks up her own smaller set of cutlery from the outside and pointedly looks at mine.

"Thanks," I chuckle, copying her. "I was a little lost."

"It's a small thing in return for the kindness that you've shown my boy," she whispers, her hands shaking, making the fork scrape lightly on the plate. "For helping him to...get clean." She speaks the last part so quietly, if I weren't already leaning in, I would have missed it.

My heart aches for her, tears springing to my eyes. Although I hope I would never be under the thumb of a man, to the point that I let him get my son addicted to drugs, I don't blame her for being unable to stop it. By all accounts, she is the victim of domestic abuse, and you can see it clearly in the way she holds herself, like her very soul is injured.

"I love him," I confess to her, just as quietly as she spoke to me. "I love them all, and would do so much more for them."

"I know," she whispers back. "And they clearly love you in return. I could see it the moment you walked in. For what it's worth, I'm sorry for what is about to come."

My heart throbs at her words, my breathing quickening as visions of a bloodbath fills my mind's eye. Before I can respond, Julian stands up, hitting his wine glass gently with a fork, the tinkling sound halting all speech in the room.

"Before we move onto the main course of the evening, I have a little announcement to make," he says, his face wreathed in smiles as he turns to look at me. Ash's grip on my hand becomes bruising at the same time my brows furrow. "Asher?"

Ash lets go of my hand, turning in his chair to face me as he reaches into his trouser pocket. He's wearing a tux like the others, but I barely register that as my vision zeros in on the small black velvet box that he's holding out in front of him.

"Lilly Darling," he starts, opening the box, and I see the twinkle of a diamond and ruby inside. "Will you make me the happiest of all men, and do me the greatest honour, of becoming my wife?"

CHAPTER EIGHTEEN

LILLY

I stare at the unusual glittering diamond and ruby ring, nestled in deep crimson silk, dumfounded. The sound of a chair crashing to the floor behind me registers, along with a growled curse, but it's as if it's all far away, in some other place.

"Marry you?" I whisper, finally looking up into Ash's face. His steel eyes are swirling, a myriad of emotions running through them, but the overarching one is a plea, begging me to trust him. My brows draw down, my head shaking slightly. "Why?" I ask, but this time I look at Julian. After all, he's the one behind this, the puppetmaster. "Why do you want me to marry Ash?"

He smirks at me, and I want to fucking punch his perfectly straight teeth out of his devil's mouth.

"How was your little trip to London, Darling?" he asks instead, tipping his head to one side like a snake contemplating its prey. I hate that he uses my surname like a term of endearment. Shivers cascade over me as I'm trapped in his predator's leer, and in my peripheral vision, I see Ash stiffen further until he's become the Ice

Knight everyone knows him to be. "You didn't think we wouldn't know about your jaunt, did you?" And then Julian tsks at me like a naughty wayward child, and my blood boils at the fucking audacity of this man. "That somehow, we wouldn't know about those bonds and shares in *our* company your mother had hidden away."

I can feel my face go cold, the blood draining from it, and no doubt leaving me pale and terrified looking. And I am. I'm fucking scared shitless at what this means.

"Now," he starts, stepping out from his space and coming slowly, menacingly, towards me, leering eyes holding mine. "We can't have a slip of a girl like you, who knows nothing about the work that has gone into Black Knight Corporation to make it the great enterprise that it is today, holding us to ransom. At first, I thought that we could just…dispose of you, like we usually do to things that get in our way," A growl sounds behind me—*Jax, no doubt*—but my eyes are full of the crazed grey of Julian's, unable to look away. "But then, everything goes to your uncle, as your next of kin, and that doesn't help us much either."

He steps fully behind me, and my relief at no longer being under his scrutiny is short-lived as his hands come down on my shoulders, gently like a lover's caress, his thumbs stroking the base of my neck. Bile fills my mouth, and it takes everything in me not to throw up all over the glistening silverware.

"Father," Ash grits out, jerking as if he wants to stand up and rip the older man's hands off me. *Please, Ash.*

"I'm not done, boy," Julian snarls, his grip tightening to the point of bruising, and a sharp gasp falls from my painted lips. "Where was I? Ah, yes. I had a better idea, so here is what will happen. You will marry Asher, be the happiest of brides, radiant on your wedding day, etcetera. Ash will become your next of kin, you will name him in your Will so that if anything unfortunate were to happen to you, he will inherit your stocks, shares, and bonds. Of course, you will remain a silent partner." He pauses, going back to caressing my shoulders lovingly, and I can't suppress the shudder that runs through me. "Oh, and they'll be no more whoring yourself out to the other boys. I will not have bastard grandchildren." His fingers dig in again, as if to reinforce his point, but I barely register the pain, my mind a maelstrom. Then I feel his breath against my ear as he leans down and whispers, so only I hear. "Although, if you ever want a real man between those pretty thighs, you only have to ask."

Dizziness washes over me at his words, my nails digging into my palms deep enough to break the skin with a sharp sting. I feel dirty, a sense of violation settling deep within my soul as he straightens up, giving me one last caress before my back is cold once more when he moves away. My eyes are unseeing, staring straight ahead as I think about all that he's just said. I can't see a way out, and panic starts to flutter at the edges of my vision, black dots appearing before me.

Suddenly, I feel a solid weight settle on my thigh, gripping me hard and bringing me back into the room. Slowly my head turns, as if I'm underwater, and I meet Ash's clear grey eyes. There's sorrow there, as well as a fierceness in the tight lines around his eyes that tells me we will get through this. He lets go of my thigh, taking my left hand in his, and bringing it in front of him. I don't look away as I feel him slide the ring onto my finger, the cool metal soon heating up with the contact of my overheated skin. There's a flare of...something, that flashes in his grey orbs. It's very close to possession, and my heart thuds in my chest with the knowledge that I am his now, officially.

"A toast!" Julian cries, his voice jovial and full of merriment, and waiting staff step forward with pre-opened bottles of the finest Dom Pérignon. *They must have known before I did.*

The thought flies through my mind as I continue to stare at Ash, letting his strength flow through me, bolstering my walls until they are solid enough to face these demons. He leans in, keeping his eyes locked with mine until he's no longer able to.

"I will not take them away from you, Princess. I promise," he murmurs in my ear, the same one his father spoke into mere moments ago. But this time, my shoulders droop with relief, moisture stinging my eyes.

"Thank you," I say back, my lips barely moving so as not to alert anyone else of our hushed conversation.

"Anything," he tells me, pulling away just enough so that I can see the vow in his words. "Anything for you, my love."

ASH

I try to reassure her with my eyes, her own hazel ones swimming with a mixture of gratitude and devastation. I can't deny the asshole in me loves the idea of her being my wife. Of owning her, having my family's ring on her finger like countless generations of Vanderbilt women before her. The thought is enough to make me rock-fucking-solid, even with these jackals surrounding us.

But, cunt though I might be, I would never take her away from the others. I couldn't do that to them, to her. She's theirs just as much as she's mine, regardless of what a piece of paper may say.

I look past her to see Jax, hands clenched into fists on the table, his flute of bubbling champagne untouched as he vibrates with anger. Slowly, he turns his head and meets my gaze. *Fuck*. His eyes are full of piercing blue rage, his lips pressed together in a tight line.

Only years of training allow me to hold my ground, no outward sign of the fear that's taken root in my heart. In my soul. He has never, in our entire lives, looked at me like he wants to feel my insides slither between his fingers. And he could, he knows how to make someone's internal organs become external, all while keeping them alive.

I nod my head, the move barely perceptible. But like me, years of rigorous training allows him to see the movement. His brows dip slightly, a note of confusion entering his blue orbs. So I do the only thing that will assure him of my meaning.

The sounds of our parents' celebration and chatting around us fade as I stare into the blue depths of his eyes, and with an infinitesimal movement of my lips, I mouth the one word that will tell him all that he needs to know.

Yours.

His nostrils flare slightly, his shoulders loosening a small amount. He gives me a slight nod back, and I know that he'll give me shit later when we're alone, but at least he understands.

Turning my head, I look across the table to find Loki and Kai watching our exchange. Both have matching looks of rage in their eyes, all directed at me. I can't blame them, I would feel the same if one of them had been chosen. I just got lucky for once in my miserable life, my cursed Vanderbilt blood being good for something at last.

I catch Loki's eye, the emerald blazing as he tries to suppress his anger. People think that he's the least dangerous of us all, all smiles and flirtatious winks. But in some ways, he's the worst of our little group. You don't see the knife coming until it's buried in your chest, all while he smiles at you like you're the best of friends, and your death is a big joke.

His hand grips his dinner knife, and it takes a lot for me to suppress the twitch of my lips at the thought that he wants to stab me, right here and now. Last year, I would have begged him to do it too. Not so much anymore.

Staring into his eyes, just like with Jax, I mouth the word he needs to hear.

Yours.

His grip loosens on the piece of gleaming cutlery, although he doesn't let go of it completely. *Good.*

I meet Kai's narrowed honey scowl, and before I can mouth the same to him, he beats me to it.

Mine.

I nod and see his beast recede into the depths once more. It's always the quiet ones you have to watch out for. They'll dance in your blood, leaving crimson footsteps in the snow just because it looks pretty.

The servers lean in, taking away our starters and replacing them with plates filled with roast meat, golden roast potatoes, buttery vegetables, and lashings of gravy.

"In honor of my soon to be English daughter-in-law, I thought we'd eat a traditional British roast dinner," My father announces, looking at Lilly with far more than fatherly affection in his leer. My hand grasps hers, rubbing her knuckles as I bring it to my thigh and give him a death glare. "Are you pleased, Darling?"

I swear if that cunt uses her last name like that one more fucking time...

I don't realize that I've squeezed her hand tightly until she squeezes back, so I loosen my grip, turning to dip my head in apology at her. She gives me a weak smile that damn near breaks my black heart.

"T–thank you," she whispers, looking quickly down at her left hand, which is still in mine.

I let the sounds of everyone beginning to eat wash over me as I finger the sparkling antique jewel that now sits on her ring finger, the diamonds glinting in the candlelight. It's an antique piece, mid-eighteenth century, and has been in my family since that time. A Burmese ruby and rose cut diamond sit side by side in a heart shape, set in rose gold, with a crown of three smaller diamonds sitting atop them. On the side in enamel is the motto UNIS À JAMAIS which means 'united forever' in French. It suits her delicate hand, and a fissure of certainty runs through me, like she was always meant to wear it.

"Did you know that this ring has been worn by a Vanderbilt woman since the mid-eighteenth century?" I ask her, looking up from our hands to watch her reaction, drinking in every movement of her beautiful face.

"It's stunning," she whispers back, looking at her hand as if it's strange to have the weight of so much history on her finger.

"The story goes that several times great-granddaddy won it from a visiting Russian Tsar in a card game." A rare smile lifts my lips at the memory of my grandmother telling Luc and I the story as children. "Apparently, it belonged to his favorite courtesan, who threw a spectacular tantrum in the middle of the party when he lost it, where, much to the amusement of everyone present, the Tsar threw her over his knee and spanked her until she begged for mercy."

I watch as her eyebrows raise to her hairline, then drop as she sharply looks up at me when it dawns on her what I just said.

"You gave me a whore's ring?" she asks, lifting one eyebrow and giving me a scathing look.

God, she's exquisite when she's angry at me. It takes almost more strength than I have not to give her one of my signature smirks. I lean in, so close that my lips brush her ear as I whisper in them.

"You gonna make me throw you over my knee again, Princess? In front of all these people? Naughty minx." Then I nip her earlobe for good measure, relishing the hiss of breath that leaves her lips.

My smirk is fully in place as I pull away, although it drops slightly when I catch the look of pure unfiltered lust in her eyes. *Fuck, that backfired.* We both swallow hard, but luckily the sound of silverware on glass breaks us from our trance.

"Another toast!" my father cries out, and I turn to see him raise his champagne flute in the air. We all follow suit, waiting for him to speak like good little lapdogs. It makes me feel sick, following him like this. One day soon, just a little longer, and he'll be the one following orders. "To the beautiful Lilly, and my son, Asher. May you have a long and happy life together, a fruitful union..." He pauses here and gives her another lecherous look that makes my hand tighten around my glass to almost breaking point. "And above all else, continue the legacy that is Black Knight Corporation, as your heirs will after you."

Everyone raises their glasses higher, a chorus of "Here, here!" sounding around the table as we all drink the bubbling liquid that costs thousands per bottle, but tastes like nothing but ashes in my mouth.

CHAPTER NINETEEN

LILLY

The rest of dinner—*orchestrated bullshit more like*—flies by, but I don't taste a thing of the delicious-looking meal, too busy trapped in my own head. It's not that I don't want to marry Ash, in fact, the idea fills me with an intense feeling of satisfaction. And there's something almost relieving about belonging to someone officially, body and soul.

But what about the other three pieces of my soul? The other three men that own my body? How can I be happy being the wife of one, and not the others? We are all entwined until there is no separating us, will this change things?

"Ash," Julian says, his voice finally breaking through my turbulent thoughts. "Why don't you take your lovely fiancée back to Highgate? Jax and Kai can go with you." Why not Loki too? I briefly glance at the cuntwaffle but decide not to raise a ruckus since the guys don't seem to be too worried about it.

I hate the way he orders everyone around, tells us all what to do, and expects us to jump and do it. I can see that Ash feels the same, his hands clenched into fists under the table, his eyes full of silver fire. Even so, he gets up, placing his napkin beside our dessert plates, his chocolate brownie untouched like mine.

"Shall we?" he asks in a low voice, holding his hand out for me to take.

I give him a brief smile, hating that I should be ecstatically happy, but am not. Most women are, I believe, when an impossibly beautiful man, who they love, proposes. Taking his hand, I, too, get out of my seat, feeling a gentle touch on my left hand. Turning to look down, I meet piercing blue eyes in a soft, round face.

"Congratulations, Lilly dear," Jannet says softly, giving me a smile full of warmth. "It was wonderful to meet you."

"You too," I whisper, a lump in my throat, squeezing her fingers back briefly before letting them go and turning to face Ash once more.

I hear the others scrape back their chairs, Loki, Kai, and Jax getting to their feet as we walk past, Ash's hand on my bare back a soothing warmth.

"Not you, Loki," Julian's voice cuts across the noise of our departure. "There's something we need to discuss."

Ash tenses up next to me, the hand on my lower back going completely still as we pause and I look back at Julian, then Loki who's jaw clenches.

"Just Loki?" Ash asks his father, whose face darkens.

"I'm not in the habit of repeating myself, boy," Julian replies through gritted teeth, all sense of joviality gone.

Ash simply turns back and urges me to carry on walking, even though I can feel waves of anger radiating off his taut body.

The mansion is a blur as we hurriedly walk through it, my heels clacking on the marble floors. I can't help the sigh of relief that leaves my lips as we step outside, pausing to breathe in the frosty Colorado air, a sigh of relief leaving my lips even though the freezing night air has my teeth chattering within moments.

"Here," I hear Kai say from behind me, and I'm suddenly

engulfed in his woods after the rain scent as his suit jacket falls over my shoulders, still deliciously warm from his body.

"Thanks," I reply gratefully, a shiver of a different kind skittering over my skin as he places a gentle kiss on my cheek.

"Let's go," Ash commands, his tone hard. I know, like the rest of us, he just wants to get out of here as much as I do, plus is more than likely worried about leaving Loki behind. "Jax, I'm driving. Lilly's up front."

"You staking your claim already, *brother*?" Jax snarls, stepping up into Ash's face, glaring down at him. Ash grinds his teeth together so hard I'm surprised that they don't crack.

"That wasn't a request," he growls out. "Give me your damn keys, and get in the fucking truck."

They stare at each other for several moments, huge chests heaving, and a spark of guilt flashes in my chest. I don't want to come between them, to disrupt their bond.

"Hey," I say, stepping closer, placing a hand on Jax's forearm which is vibrating with tension. "Not here. Let's just get back, okay? Then you can go all caveman and throw me over your shoulder." The last part earns a small twitch from Jax's lips, a relieved smile falling from mine.

With a final growl, he tosses the keys at Ash, who deftly catches them, as he walks towards his truck, parked where we left it on the drive. Kai follows, jogging to catch up.

"Come on then, Princess," Ash says with a sigh, taking hold of my hand and leading us towards the vehicle.

A chilly breeze slips through Kai's jacket, and looking up into a starless sky, I can't help the feeling that this is just the start of something that will change us all irrevocably.

LOKI

I sit there, surrounded by these people, monstrous shadows dancing around them in the candlelight, half drunk champagne glasses littering the table. I'm glad the others have left, especially Lilly.

God, how am I going to tell her?

"And if I refuse?" I ask, looking up into the eyes of a wolf, the devil himself, Julian Vanderbilt. He smiles his demon grin, all straight teeth and black lies.

"Then Ash may find himself a widower not long after his wedding day," he casually throws out, eyes hungry for any reaction I show.

However, I've learnt their lessons well, my cool façade not cracking as I stare right back at him. Inside is a different story, my heart rips apart, knowing that with what I must do to keep her safe, I will break her apart, too.

"And anyway, it's not such a bad deal, son," my cuntstain of a dad pipes in, and I turn to glare at him, showing exactly what I think of him. I smirk when he swallows hard. Good. Let him be scared of me.

I don't bother to reply, turning back to the master puppeteer himself, and giving a brief nod, I seal my fate.

Forgive me, Pretty Girl.

LILLY

The next few weeks pass by, tension rife within all of us. When we got back the night after dinner at the Vanderbilt's, Ash, Jax, Kai, and I sat down and talked the whole thing over. Turns out that Ash had found out mere moments before we arrived, Kai, too.

But as Ash pointed out more than once, he had no choice. Julian and the others, bar Jax's mum, are all monsters with pitch-black souls. If Ash had refused to propose, they were going to dispose of me just like Julian had told me at dinner, whispering death threats in my ear like sweet nothings.

Jax relented with a growl, then threw me over his shoulder like the caveman that he is and took delight in making me scream his name over, and over, and over again whilst the Vanderbilt ring sat twinkling on my finger. *Fucking brute.*

Loki didn't join us in the night as he usually does, and hasn't since, although Jax and Ash have been keeping me more than occupied at night. In fact, I've barely seen Loki since the dinner, and a dark premonition fills my stomach. I know there is something going on. I know that it isn't good, and the feeling leaves me sick to my stomach constantly, and off my food with worry.

It doesn't help that Kai is also a little absent and looks exhausted, dark circles ringing his eyes, lines marring his forehead. Seems that his darkness has returned since that night, too.

Things feel like they're spiralling out of control, and I'm helpless to stop it.

It's the day before Valentine's Day, which also happens to be Loki's birthday—*I know, irony knows no bounds*—and I'm walking down the hall with Willow, heading to our yoga class. She's chattering away about some guy she's interested in, and I'm trying to listen, I really am, but sickness swirls in my stomach, making it hard to concentrate. It was so bad this morning that I couldn't face breakfast.

"Lilly?" Willow's sweet voice penetrates my thoughts. "Are you okay?"

I turn to face her, concern in her blue eyes as she takes me in. I'm obviously looking like shit, my face was especially pale in the mirror this morning as I was getting ready for the day.

"I'm just feeling a bit queasy. I have been since dinner at Ash's parents."

She, like everyone, knows about mine and Ash's engagement. However, unlike everyone else, she knows that it was forced by his parents. I gave her some bullshit about them finding out about us being together, so being kind of old-fashioned they expedited things and forced the proposal. I don't think she believed me, but being the beautiful human that she is, she didn't question it.

She doesn't know about the death threats, my standing in Black Knight Corp., or what the guys do. I'm almost certain that she suspects something is up, not wholly believing my excuses for not being over the moon about being engaged to Ash. And given her background, and her brother's involvement in running The Shadows —a notorious postcode gang in West London that even I've heard of —I think she would get it and not be surprised. She's not gone into details, as I haven't with her, but she's seen the darkness that lives in this world. Experienced it firsthand. It's in the haunted look in her blue eyes, and the slight tremble in her hands when she recalls vague stories from the past.

"Lilly, now, don't get pissed, but you've been feeling sick so much recently. Is there any chance you could be pregnant?" she asks, looking at me sideways as we continue to walk.

I stop dead in my tracks, as does she, a sinking niggle in my stomach.

"I can't be. I mean, there was a mess-up at Christmas, but I took the morning after pill a few days later..." I trail off, remembering what Kai had said about how it loses its effectiveness the longer you leave it.

"So there is a possibility?" she hedges, turning to face me full-on, lowering her voice as she quickly glances around. "When was your last period?"

My eyes flitter side to side as I try to recall the last time Aunty Flo came to visit.

"I–I don't think I've had one since before Christmas," I tell her, latching onto blue eyes full of sympathy.

"I'm popping into town later, so I'll grab you a test. Then you'll know for sure either way." She reaches out, taking my suddenly cold hand in hers and giving it a squeeze.

I nod in thanks, swallowing thickly as we continue walking down the hallway.

Shit, what if it's positive? What will I do then? Fuck!

Thoughts tumble in my mind until I feel queasier than ever, swallowing down bile as we approach a group of students standing around outside of the gym building. My eyes roll as I hear Amber Cuntmuffin's nasally voice.

"I think a June wedding would be perfect, don't you?"

I huff a laugh under my breath, pitying the poor fool who'll be shackled to her for the rest of his life. However, as we go past, I stop dead in my tracks for the second time this morning when I catch sight of who's standing next to a beaming Amber, his face bereft of its usual flirty smiles.

"Loki?" I ask, my whole body flashing cold when I meet anguish ridden emerald eyes.

"L–Lilly..." he starts, taking a step forward, but is cut off by cuntface magee herself, who grabs his arm, the crowd before her parting as she drags him towards me.

"Oh, haven't you heard?" she asks, a smug as fuck smile on her face as she holds out her left hand. "Loki and I are engaged."

My whole world shatters, fine tremors wracking my body as I gawp at the garish bauble in the February sunshine.

"Loki?" I ask again, swallowing the lump in my throat, looking up at him. "What's going on?"

His eyes burn with jade fire, but it's soon replaced with a devastating sadness that seeps into my very bones, chilling my soul. His Adam's apple bobs as he swallows hard, his lips moving, but no sound escapes as we stand in awkward silence.

"Aren't you going to congratulate us?" Amber asks, her voice penetrating the haze that's descended over me.

Anger, the likes of which I have never felt before rushes over me in a tidal wave, followed by an intense sickness that rises from my stomach, refusing to be ignored any longer. Without saying a single word, I spin and flee, just making it to the edge of the forest before tossing my bag aside, and falling to my knees, vomiting at the base of a tree.

"Shit! Lilly!" Loki cries and I hear footsteps approaching behind me. A hand alights on my back, rubbing soothing circles. "Fuck, Lilly, I'm so sorry. I should have told you sooner. I was a fucking coward. I have no choice about this, but I shouldn't have let you find out this way."

I finish heaving, acid stinging my throat as I spit on the ground once more.

"Water," I croak out.

Seconds later, a water bottle is pressed into my hand, and I gratefully swill my mouth out, before taking a tentative sip, then another. A tissue is passed to me, too, which I use to wipe my mouth.

My mind still swirls like a tornado with everything that has happened recently, twisting until I want to scream. One thing stands out clearly, though, like a beacon of light. Turning round, careful to avoid the puddle of vomit now behind me, I face Loki, both of us still on our knees. I'm relieved to see that cuntface hasn't followed him out, Willow either.

His brows are drawn together, and there are dark circles under his beautiful eyes, which are full of sadness and anguish.

Cupping his cheek, a move he leans his face into, I hold his gaze. "We will find a way through this, my love." His breath hitches and his eyes fill with moisture when I call him that. It's as if he thought I would have given up on him upon hearing this news. "Our fucking souls are merged, Loki. Nothing can separate them. Not cuntface, not Black Knight Corp., and certainly not Julian fucking Vanderbilt."

His own hand comes up to cup my cheek so that we form an unbreakable circle. "But they'll kill you, Pretty Girl," he whispers, horror entering his gaze as it trails across my face. "If I refuse, you will not live long past your wedding day."

A brief flash of fear lights up inside of me but quickly dissipates when I remember that we are not without power. In fact, we may have more than they do, now that I know about my inheritance.

"So we get them out of the way first," I tell him, fierce determination filling me up and I straighten my back as if preparing for war. "Even if that means permanently removing them from the picture."

His eyes go wide as he registers my meaning. And I do mean it, with all my heart. If we can't remove the rotten core of Black Knight Corp. by legal means, then we will kill them. They've done terrible things, horrific things, without once getting their hands bloody as they force their own flesh and blood to bear the stains of their sins.

And as the saying goes, if you can't beat them...then it's time to get the knives out.

CHAPTER TWENTY

LILLY

It turns out Loki hadn't even told the guys—*stupid ballbag*—and received a few punches when we got back to the dorm after our various gym classes until I managed to calm everyone down with threats of my own brand of violence, i.e. Her Vagisty going on strike.

Grumbling, we all sit on the sofas, a fire roaring in the fireplace, the crackling of burning logs a soothing sound. The soft beat of Sinead Harnett and GRADES singing *If You Let Me* washes over us as we clutch mugs of hot chocolate made by Kai, who used freshly shaved chocolate and warm milk. He usually puts some kind of whiskey in them, but I told him to leave it out of mine, my conversation with Willow playing on my mind. Kai gives me a considering look, but doesn't say anything, doing as I asked. I should tell the guys, but I'm being a coward for now. I'll wait until I take the test tomorrow.

I snuggle up to Loki, loving his vanilla scent mixing with the cocoa scent of my drink. His arm wraps around me, pulling me closer and grabbing my legs until I'm draped across his lap. I decided that she can't have him, I licked him and he's mine now, so she can just fuck right off. Hence the reason he's here with me and not her, and I don't give a fuck if she doesn't like it. Plus, this is his dorm so she can't exactly stop him being here anyway.

"I fucking missed you too much, Pretty Girl," he murmurs, nuzzling the top of my head.

"Well, you've got no one to blame but yourself," I sass back, loving the way his hand tightens on my shoulder and the growl that sounds from his chest. *Got to love an alpha!*

"Right," Ash starts, gaining all of our attention. "Now that, thanks to Lilly, we have a majority share in the company, we need to start putting into place the removal of the current board." His grey eyes are the colour of flint, hard and unyielding, and a fierce sense of satisfaction floods my body at his words. "Kai?" he asks, turning to look at Kai, who unsurprisingly has his tablet in hand.

"The easiest way to do it is to set them up. Frame them with a crime, one so bad that they'll be locked away for a long time, and be forced to step down, giving up any rights, shares, and control of the company," he tells us, his voice hard, eyes unforgiving.

"And the crime?" I ask, having an inkling of where this is going, but needing to hear it from his lips.

"Murder," he replies, with no hesitation. "One of the board must die, the others proven to be the murderers, without doubt or question."

Chills skate across my body, my fingers tingling as they grip my mug, unfeeling of the heat coming from the drink. I look round at the others, matching looks of grim determination on their faces.

"Then we're in agreement?" Ash questions, asking the room. The guys all reply in the affirmative. "Lilly?" He turns to me, his face hard, but not without sympathy, a thoughtful expression on it. "Are you in?"

"Always," I reply, my heart beating a solid rhythm in my chest as the weight of what I've just agreed to settles on my shoulders.

Loki's grip around me tightens as Ash gives me a single nod with a gleam of what looks like pride in his eyes.

"Then it's settled. Any ideas on when? Where?" he asks, and once again, Kai speaks.

"The annual summer fishing trip at Flint Lakes," he says, looking up from his tablet. "It's a male-only trip, no wives or girlfriends," he looks at me apologetically. "So only your dads and my uncle will be there." I can see the others nodding at his words, but an objection rises in my chest.

"I want to be there, to help," I say firmly, sitting up straighter. "They've threatened my life, are forcing me to marry Ash, and have Loki engaged to that fucking cunt. I have a right to get justice, too. Maybe not as much as you all, but still."

"You're so hot when you're being all bloodthirsty, baby," Loki croons in my ear, and despite trying not to, I can't help the grin that takes over my lips.

"We've corrupted you good, haven't we, Baby Girl?" Jax comments next to us, and I turn to beam at him, too.

"Don't worry, Princess," Ash assures me, and I turn my head to look into his steel eyes. "You'll get your pound of flesh." I give him a sharp nod in return, his lips twitching in response. "So for now, we carry on as if nothing is happening. That means, Loki, that you continue with your wedding plans with Amber, keeping your distance from Lilly when out in public."

Loki and I both stiffen at his words, and even though I know Ash is making sense, it still stings like needles scraping along my skin. But then, I think, maybe this is just a new challenge. One I can definitely rise to.

As if by divine intervention, *White Lies* by Bolshiee comes over the speakers, the sensual beat and her haunting voice filling me up, leaving me feeling all kinds of wanton.

Breaking Ash's gaze with a devious smile, I hold my mug up as I swing my legs to straddle Loki's lap, and his hands immediately come to rest on my thighs. He squeezes gently as my knees come either side of his hips, placing my core over his crotch.

"Princess..." Ash starts, his tone stern. "We're not done here."

I just give Loki a suggestive smile, one brow raised, knowing that he'll be up for the challenge, too. His own lips respond with a devilish grin.

"Naughty, Pretty Girl," he murmurs with a chuckle, then licks his lips. I pluck at his T-shirt with my free hand.

"Off," I order, leaning back slightly so that he can comply. He places his mug on the side table, then takes his shirt off in that insanely sexy way guys always do—*what's with that?*

He throws the garment aside, giving me a 'what's next?' look. Taking hold of the spoon in my mug—Kai always tops my hot chocolate with lashings of whipped cream and a spoon to eat it with—I fill it with the still scalding liquid, and holding Loki's stare, begin to drizzle it down his bare chest.

It's hot enough that he hisses, the noise turning into a moan when I follow the path with my tongue, paying special attention to his nipple piercing. His sweats bulge, his hard length begging to be freed. *Patience, Lilly.*

Getting another spoonful, I trickle the drink down his chest once again, then proceed to lap the liquid up like a cat with a bowl of cream. Looking down, there's an obvious stain of precum on his sweats where the tip of his dick is, the outline of his piercing clear underneath the fabric, and I shudder at the sight. I'm faring not much better, my silk sleep shorts already soaked, and Her Vagisty practically shouting to be filled.

Settling back into Loki's lap, I can't help but grind down on his dick, capturing his mouth with mine, our tongues tangling. I can taste the whiskey from his own drink, and for the first time today, my stomach feels calm.

"Fuck, Pretty Girl," Loki rasps out, his fingers grazing my nipple through my silk cami top.

"Allow me," Jax says, taking the mug of chocolate from me, and setting it on a side table on his side.

My nipples start to pebble under Loki's attention, pressing against the silk of the top, zings of pleasure flashing through me. His hands start to trace along the lace hem, dipping underneath it and taking my top with him until he's lifting it up over my head and throwing it aside.

"So fucking beautiful," he rasps out before taking one of my tight buds into his hot mouth, my hips bucking, and his hardness pressing firmly against my silk clad core.

I move against it, creating a delicious friction that begins to drive me wild, and Loki growls, sending delicious vibrations across my breast and straight to my core.

His hands come around to the front of my shorts, and a deep groan sounds in his throat when his fingers find me already dripping.

"Such a good fucking girl, so wet for me already," he says huskily, making another rush of heat flood my aching pussy.

I'm confused for a second when he withdraws his hand, both hands moving to grip the crotch of my shorts, one in front of the other. Suddenly, I get an inkling of what he's about to do.

"Loki, don't you fucking..." I start to say, cutting off at the sound of ripping silk as he tears them in two, opening it up so that I now have two flaps of fabric hanging from my waist, instead of a pair of shorts. He looks up at me with a wolfish grin on his handsome face. "You fucker!" I scold, moaning when two of his fingers enter me.

I forget all about my ire as he moves them in and out of my dripping cunt, and I start to ride his hand, seeking him deeper, faster. One of his hands comes up to my throat, in a very Jax-like possessive move reminding me of the other night, and he squeezes gently.

"Oh shit, Loki!" I scream as I come hard and fast, coating his hand and lap with my release, letting go of everything that is going on, all of the shit that surrounds our lives currently, as I spiral into sheer bliss.

"That's it, baby," he says roughly, "come all over me like a good girl." His dirty talk and still thrusting fingers make me orgasm a second time, seeing fucking stars as I writhe and moan on his lap. Slumping down on top of him, completely spent, I hear his manly chuckle before he whispers in my ear. "We're only just getting started, Pretty Girl," he tells me, his voice giving me shivers at the sensual promise in his words.

He picks me up under my thighs, standing then turning round, all with me wrapped around him like a spider monkey. Encouraging my legs to go down, he then spins me round so that my back is to his front. Pushing down between my shoulders until I'm bent right over with my arms resting along the back of the sofa, he gives me all of half a minute, the crinkling of foil sounding behind me, before I feel him nudging my entrance.

He goes slow, allowing me to feel him inch by torturous inch before he's finally fully seated inside me, both of us groaning at how amazing it feels.

"Shit, baby. You feel so fucking good," he says through gritted teeth as he starts to withdraw before he slams back into me, causing a strangled cry to leave my lips. Picking up the pace, he begins to pound into me, the sound of our flesh slapping together overriding the music, and I can already feel tingles racing all over my body.

I feel a warmth on my face before a hand caresses the side of it.

"Don't forget about us, Baby Girl," I hear Jax growl out as I open my eyes to see him and Kai with their dicks out in their hands, right in front of my face.

Holy shit! Two for the price of one!

Jax is the first to guide his member to my mouth, and I open up, my hand wrapping around the base of him, wanting to taste him so badly, a small keen leaves my lips.

"So desperate to choke on my cock, Baby Girl." He chuckles darkly as I lick the tip, tasting the drop of salty precum.

I greedily take him in, my mouth stretching around his thick length as I look up at his face, loving the deep groan that leaves his beautiful lips. He watches me intensely as I start to bob up and down, sucking and licking him like he's my favourite ice cream. Loki is still thrusting inside me, hard and deep, making me take Jax deeper into my throat, which is not an easy feat given his size.

For a split second, I worry that it'll make me sick again, but my stomach seems to have settled for now, so I go to town, trying to swallow as much of his dick as I can, spit already dribbling down my arm as I pump what can't fit. My eyes water and I gag slightly when he hits the back of my throat, but I carry on, taking him deeper and shivering at his deep groans of satisfaction and pleasure.

I feel Loki wrap my hair around one fist as he pulls me off of Jax's dick with a pop.

"Don't forget Kai, baby. Show his dick the same love you just showed Jax's," he orders, angling my head towards Kai's waiting cock. My cunt flutters around his dick, the note of command in Loki's tone turning me on even more.

I don't have time to hesitate as Kai's hand takes over from Loki, and forces my head down by my hair, pushing his dick into my mouth. I take him in, moaning at the feel of his piercings along the bottom of my lips and mouth. They add a metallic taste to his musk, and I use my tongue to play with them as I sink further. Looking up at him and seeing the searing look in his eyes as he stares down at me, I decide to experiment a little. Bringing my teeth into the mix, I graze them along his length as I bob back up. A hiss leaves his lips, his hand tightening its grip until my eyes water even more with the pain of my hair being pulled, and his hips buck towards me, telling me he liked that. A lot.

I hollow my cheeks and glide down his length and back up using my teeth again, before letting it go. Immediately Jax's hand is in my hair, pulling me towards him, his cock back in my mouth, thrusting deep and hitting the back of my throat once again. I swap between the two of them, learning the differences between them with my lips and tongue as Loki starts to thrust even faster and deeper. One of Loki's hands comes around my front, rubbing my clit, pinching it every so often, and I cry out around Kai's cock in my mouth as his hand cups my jaw hard.

My cries must set him off because the next thing I know, his dick turns rock solid, and he thrusts all the way in, seconds before he pours his hot cum down my throat with a curse. As soon as he's finished, Jax's hand tightens in my hair and pulls me off, replacing Kai's cock with his own and fucking my face in earnest.

I relax my jaw and let him use my mouth like Loki uses my pussy, loving their dominance over me.

"Come for me now, baby," Loki growls out as he coats his thumb in my juices, taking it to my puckered hole and pushing it in.

Jesus, fuck!

I do as he orders, coming so hard that I whiteout, my whole body alight with electric fire. Vaguely, I hear Loki roar behind me, and Jax in front, as they both find release almost simultaneously. I can taste Jax's salty cum in my mouth, and I swallow every damn drop like it's the finest nectar.

I feel utterly boneless and totally blissed out. The boys pull out of me, a final gasp escaping my lips as they do. I slump, draped on the back of the sofa whilst panting when Kai's face comes into view as he crouches down in front of me.

"Such a good girl, my darling," he coos, pushing hair back off my sweaty forehead. "Let's get you all cleaned up." Leaning in, he presses his lips to mine in a kiss that is full of tenderness and love.

"Not quite yet," I hear Ash's deep voice say behind me, and turning my head, I look over my shoulder at him through hooded eyes. He's still sitting on his chair, his suit trousers straining as his fully erect dick pushes against them, his thighs wide.

A small whimper leaves my lips when he raises one hand, crooking his finger at me. Turning round, I get up, and on shaking legs, walk around the coffee table towards him. Stopping in front of him, my chest heaves and my body tingles with the aftereffects of multiple orgasms. Looking down, I stare into fathomless grey eyes, eyes full of fire, lust, and the threat of punishment.

"On your knees," he orders, his face almost blank, yet his eyes churn and swirl. I comply, my legs giving way anyway, landing on the plush rug with a thump. The heat from the fire tickles the right side of my body, a contradiction to my slightly cooler left side, my over sensitised skin pebbling with goosebumps.

"Undo my pants, *fiancée*," is his next decree, his nostrils flaring slightly and letting me know exactly how excited he is. You know, if the massive hard-on he's sporting didn't already give me a clue.

With trembling hands, my fingers fumble with his belt buckle, the metal clinking as I open the clasp. My breathing picks up as I pop the button open at his waist, then carefully unzip him, revealing his black boxer briefs, his rock-solid length pushing against the fabric. His new piercings are outlined, too, four little balls that make my aching mouth water.

I pause, waiting for his next instruction.

"Take me out, and suck me like the good little whore I know you can be," he instructs, and my eyes snap up to his, narrowing when I see his arsehole smirk and raised brow.

Challenge accepted, bellend!

"Oh, one second, Princess," he says, stalling my movements as his hands reach for his belt, pulling it from the loops of his trousers with a rustle as it passes through the fabric. "Kai."

Turning, I see Kai walking over, his navy sweats back in place, his nipple bars twinkling in the firelight. He takes the belt from Ash, a gleam of excitement in his amber eyes.

"When I tell you, whip her with this. She's been a naughty girl, not waiting for us to finish the meeting, so she needs to be taught a lesson on her knees," he tells him, and Kai's fingers tighten on the leather, a short inhale through flared nostrils showing his approval of my punishment. "Look at me, Princess."

I do as Ash orders, looking up at him as my whole body trembles with anticipation. I'm just as excited as they are for this, juices sliding between my thighs at the thought of what's to come.

"You may begin."

I don't move for a fraction longer, pushing his buttons just slightly, waiting for the telltale sign of his brows dropping before lowering my gaze and reaching for his boxers. A sigh leaves my lips when I pull his silky length out, and I can't help rubbing my thumb over the precum on the tip, delighting in the hissing breath that falls from his own lips.

With a smug smile, I lower down, holding him in my palm as I take his head into my mouth and explore the new metal with the tip of my tongue. His deep groan causes heat to flood my core and wetness to fill my pussy, so I do it again, rolling him around my tongue.

"Kai," Ash breathes seconds before I feel a sharp crack along my lower back, making me gasp aloud. A palm reaches down to soothe the hurt, tingles following the move. "Don't stop, Princess," Ash orders, his fist wrapping around my hair as he pushes me down.

I open wide, letting him fill my already abused mouth, then my throat, gagging when he hits the back.

"That's it. Be a good, dirty slut and take me all the way in like you did with Jax and Kai," Ash rasps out, his other hand coming to the back of my head as he forces my head down further.

I can do nothing but relax, trying to calm my panicking heart as he cuts off my air supply with his dick. He groans, and although he has complete control, literally deciding if I breathe again or not, a heady rush of power fills my limbs at being able to bring this man such pleasure that he forgets himself.

"Kai," he grits out, sounding pained, but I barely register it as another hit lands, this time across the back of my waist. I jerk, unable to cry out, but the pain turns to tingling pleasure when a hand strokes down my back, making me arch.

Just as black spots start to fill my vision, Ash lets me up, and I take a gasping breath of sweet air as his dick no longer fills my airways. My eyes are streaming, spit spilling down my chin as my back smarts, but my pussy pulsates, begging for some contact.

"Please," I croak, looking up at Ash as I let go of his cock. I'm begging him for something, anything.

He reaches down, gently caressing my face.

"You're doing so well, little slut," he croons, and I know that I shouldn't, but I shiver at the term. It's fucking hot as hell to be degraded by his words. "You can have a treat. Up on your knees, legs spread," he commands. "And get back on my dick."

I rush to do as he says, pushing up so that instead of sitting back on my heels, my arse is in the air. I shuffle to spread my knees as far apart as I can get them, thanking the powers that be that the rug beneath them is thick and soft. Lowering my head back down, I take his cock in my hand and mouth once more, lavishing it with my tongue and sucking until his hips buck.

"Kai," he grunts out, one hand back in my hair, but letting me take the lead. "Whip her pussy."

I take a sharp inhale through my nose, my heart rate spiking and a mewl sounding in my throat at his words.

Yes! Fuck yes!

No sooner does that thought flit through my mind, than I feel the sharp sting of the leather end of Ash's belt hitting my soaking cunt. I scream around Ash's dick, the jolt of painful pleasure so intense that I almost come from that one hit.

"Another!" Ash demands, taking over and holding my head whilst he thrusts upwards, fucking my throat.

A deep animalistic cry sounds in my throat as the belt lands on my core again, this time, causing liquid to shoot out of me, coating my inner thighs as I shiver.

"Again!" Ash growls, continuing to thrust harder and faster, so much so that I know I'll be sore in the morning.

I don't feel it now as Kai whips my dripping pussy again, and again until I'm a quivering mess, only being held up by Ash's tight grip as his thrusts become disjointed and frantic. Wave upon wave of pleasure rolls through and over me, my nerves tingling almost painfully as my pussy is whipped and my throat fucked.

With a mighty roar, Ash comes, thrusting so hard and deep that I don't even taste his release. I see stars and fireworks all at once as an orgasm hits me full-on with one final whack from Kai.

Moments later, Ash pulls out, and a soft whine leaves my lips as I slump over Ash's thighs, chest heaving and body covered in sweat. Kai places a gentle kiss on my shoulder.

"You are perfection, Lilly," he whispers in my ear before setting the belt down on the arm of the chair.

"Our perfect Princess," Ash murmurs, stroking my hair with languid movements. "Jax, come take care of our girl."

Jax picks me up gently as if I am the most precious piece of china, and takes me to the bathroom, where Loki already has the shower running, and Kai walks in, placing a thick, fluffy towel on the heated towel rail. There's a brief argument about whose soap I'm going to use. I don't bother buying any as I love to smell like one of them every day. They settle on Kai's, I think using a game of rock, paper, scissors to decide, and a minute later, I'm in the shower with Jax washing me, coating my body in Kai's fresh woodsy scent.

The shower wakes me up enough to function slightly, but still, the guys get me out and dry me off. Loki has brought down a new silk PJ set, in navy blue with cream lace, and fluffy bed socks—*I get cold feet, don't judge!* They help me to dress, build up the fire, and we're back to snuggling on the plush sofa, Ash on one side and Kai on the other.

I fall asleep to the sounds of Ash's heartbeat lulling me to sleep, the crackle of the roaring fire my lullaby.

CHAPTER TWENTY-ONE

LILLY

A moan escapes from my lips, my eyelids fluttering lazily open as pleasure unfurls in my core.

"Loki," I breathe, looking down between my parted thighs, and just making out the glint of his auburn hair in the sunlight filtering around the edges of the curtains.

"Shhh," he hushes me, his breath fanning out onto my inner lips, causing a shiver to cascade over me. "You're interrupting my birthday breakfast."

I can feel his smile against my pussy as I groan aloud, grabbing his hair in my fist and bringing his head closer to my dripping centre. Vaguely, I can hear *Birthday Sex* by Jeremih playing in the background, an amused smile drawing my lips up.

He decides that he really is hungry and eats me out with gusto, ruining me with his tongue. His hands pin my hips down as I begin to buck against his face uncontrollably, my moans growing louder and my nails raking his scalp.

"I see Loki's starting to celebrate already," Jax whispers in my ear, his voice all kinds of husky as his hand palms one of my naked breasts, squeezing it and adding a layer of exquisite pain that has me writhing for more. "Care to share, brother?"

"Fine," Loki grumbles, leaving me hanging on the precipice, panting and needy as he pulls away. "On your side, Pretty Girl."

Loki gets to his knees and helps me to turn so my back is to Jax's front, the sound of a condom wrapper being opened behind me, before my leg is pulled over Jax's hip. A long low moan leaves my lips as Jax pushes inside me, stretching my lower lips with a slight burn, but finding no resistance thanks to Loki's ministrations. *I must admit, I'm liking the way he keeps waking me up!*

"Fuck, baby," Jax hisses in my ear, pulling me close by wrapping his hand around my neck from behind. "You take all of me so fucking well."

Then he starts to move, causing fine tremors to wrack through my body at the delicious intrusion. I look up with hooded eyes to see Loki staring at us, his own dick gripped tightly in his fist as he watches Jax's cock disappear inside of me. His eyes flick up and catch mine.

"You up for a birthday sixty-nine, Pretty Girl?" he asks, his wide grin clear in the semi darkness.

"Yes," I murmur, uncaring that my throat is still a little sore from last night and the pounding that Jax and Kai gave it.

Slowly, Loki leans over me, grabbing my lower jaw in his hand, and turning my face so that I'm looking up at the ceiling. The pad of his thumb pulls my lower lip down, encouraging me to open my mouth. Hovering his lips over my now open mouth, I see his jaw working, then a long line of spit leaves his mouth and lands on my tongue. I can taste my own musk, although he won't let me close my mouth, holding it open.

"Don't swallow...yet," he instructs, his voice deep and full of decadent sin. My nipples harden, the pleasure from his naughty action and words adding to that of Jax's huge dick spearing me from behind.

I keep my mouth open, his saliva sitting on my tongue as he gets into position, lying on his side and lining up his hard member with my parted lips. One hand grips the base of him, helping to guide his length in my mouth, the other hand reaches between his legs, grabbing his balls and massaging them as I play with his piercing using my tongue.

"Shit, baby," he groans, pausing as he enjoys the pleasure that I'm clearly giving him. "Best fucking birthday breakfast."

My eyes close as his warm tongue alights on my clit, sparks flying from the connection as Jax keeps up his steady thrusting, the combination of them both making me moan around Loki's length. Loki picks up the pace as Jax does, working so perfectly together as they fuck the living shit out of me.

Suddenly, Jax stills, shudders, then resumes with renewed vigour, pounding into me.

"Dude, what the ever loving fuck?" he groans out, burying his face into my neck and nibbling it, his hand tightening around my throat, not enough to cut off my air supply...yet.

"I didn't want to end up with a black fucking eye from your massive balls," Loki replies, his breath tickling my clit. "Feels good though, huh?" And I can tell he's wearing a shit eating grin.

"Fuck off," Jax grumbles, but he doesn't stop. Whatever Loki is doing to him, fondling Jax's balls by the sound of it, he doesn't seem too bothered by it. In fact, it seems to spur him on, as he starts to fuck me hard, just like I love.

His punishing pace puts me off my rhythm with my birthday blowie, but Loki takes up the slack, fucking my mouth so that all I need to do is open up and give him access.

"Shit, I can feel you in her throat," Jax hisses, his hand tightening as Loki enters my throat, then withdraws. I move my hand from his base, allowing him to thrust his whole length inside.

I can only moan and keen deep in my throat as they fuck both my ends in tandem, somehow finding a matching rhythm. Their thrusts start to grow frantic just as a fire lights in my core, spreading throughout my entire body until I'm blinded by it, screaming around Loki's cock and clamping down around Jax's.

They both give one final, hard thrust, filling me utterly and completely as they find their own climaxes with growls. My whole body turns to jelly as I come down from the highest peak, gasping as Loki pulls out of my mouth, leaving a trail of cum on my tongue.

He flops onto his back, panting, as Jax pulls out from my still pulsing pussy, and falls onto his back too. I let out a raspy breath, my own chest heaving, a film of sweat covering my body.

"Shit, Baby Girl," Jax rumbles, his own breathing laboured.

"Best birthday wake up, ever," Loki chuckles.

I bite my ruby-painted lips, looking in the mirror as I finish putting my hair up in an elegant low bun, leaving some tendrils tickling my shoulders. A sigh leaves my lips as my hand lowers, the last pin in place.

We had a wonderful day in our dorm, celebrating Loki's nineteenth birthday exactly as he asked—; watching nineties films on the sofas, eating junk food, and generally hiding away from everyone and everything. I gave him the retro Chili Peppers T-shirt that I'd ordered, which he put on straight away, looking fucking edible in the faded red cotton.

"Loki will be pleased that you dressed to match his eyes," Ash tells me from the doorway, and I look into the mirror to see him leaning against the frame, dressed in black tie. *God, he's gorgeous.*

He's right, I'm wearing a nineteenth-thirties emerald silk dress that is the exact green of Loki's eyes. The top part is fairly loose, skimming over my bust, with thin silk straps that come up over my shoulders, falling all the way to my waist in the back, leaving my entire back exposed. There's a fitted silk waistband that wraps around me, making my waist appear smaller than it actually is. The skirt flows around me like water when I move, the front slightly higher than the back—which touches the ground.

I watch as Ash stalks into the room, a predatory gleam in his eyes, and I'm reminded of the night Loki did the same. The night that I was forced to get engaged to Ash. I frown at the memory.

"You look too beautiful to be frowning, my love," he whispers once he reaches me, his fingers trailing down my spine. My nipples pebble at the touch, a sigh escaping my lips.

"I hate this," I whisper back, meaning it. I hate the forced situation, the fact that it's tainted something that should be so beautiful. I hate that Loki isn't here, on his birthday, because he's having to escort his fiancée—an engagement that he's also been pushed into—also, to the Valentine's Ball.

"I know," he replies, his own brow marred with a frown. He heaves a sigh. "Time to go, Princess."

I turn to face him, looking up into those unfathomable grey orbs.

"For what it's worth," I begin, gazing deeply into the depths of his eyes, my soul trying to touch his. "A part of me loves the fact that I will be your wife."

I watch as his nostrils flare, a roaring fire blazing in his eyes, his hand alighting on my hip and pulling me closer.

"All of me loves the fact that you will be my wife," he responds huskily, his grip tightening. "Loves that I'll have you in a way they won't." And he takes a deep, pained breath, closing his eyes for a moment. I know he feels the same guilt that I do, the guilt that comes from liking this situation, even though it's been forced upon us.

"You ready, Baby Girl?" Jax calls out, striding into the room and breaking the moment.

I heave a sigh of my own, turning to face him and giving him a weak smile. He, like Ash, is wearing black tie and looks devastating.

"Yes," I reply, shaking myself and taking a step forward. Ash's hand falls from my hip as Jax holds his out for me to take.

"I might as well make the most of it," he tells me as we exit the room.

"What?" I ask, my eyebrows dipping as I turn to look at him briefly as we head down the stairs.

"Once we leave this dorm, we can't touch you, or be overly familiar with you," Kai says, waiting for us at the bottom of the stairs.

"Oh, yeah. I'd forgotten since we spend all of our time here," I reply in a quiet voice, biting my lower lip.

We descend into a weighty silence, no one quite knowing what to say.

"Come on, we may as well get this over with," Ash suddenly says, taking my hand and pulling me to the door. "The sooner we get there, the sooner we can come home."

We follow him, as we always do, squaring our shoulders as if going into battle. I suppose, in a small way, we are. We don't know how much our movements are being watched and reported back, clearly some are if Julian's knowledge of my love life is anything to go by.

Chin up, shoulders back, Lilly.

Let's show them that we're made of sterner stuff than they think.

Like the Halloween party, there are doormen waiting to let us into the ballroom. Unlike the Halloween party, they are dressed in tuxedos with no scary makeup. They open the double wooden doors with a flourish, and I can't help the gasp of breath and my widening eyes.

The room has once again been transformed. Huge bouquets of red roses sit atop white covered tables, red petals strewn across the surface of them, and golden chairs tied with red organza bows seated around them. One wall looks to be entirely covered in red roses, real not fake, and all above the huge buffet table are hanging branches dripping with pink and red flowers and glass globes with flickering candles inside.

"They really do not scrimp on this shit, huh?" I say aloud as we walk down the small set of steps and head towards a table in the front.

"You're only just realising this, Princess?" Ash scoffs, and I scowl at him, earning another chuckle. *Dickbucket!*

He pulls out my chair, pushing it in as I sit down, then calls over one of the ~~waiters~~ waiting staff who's holding a tray of rose champagne. Jax sits down next to me, a huge plate of food in front of him.

"I see your appetite has returned," I tease, a small tilt of his lips causing butterflies to erupt in my stomach.

"Here," Kai says softly, placing a plate in front of me, with a selection of some yummy looking foods.

"Thanks," I say, looking up and catching his gaze. He looks uncomfortable, which isn't unusual for him in these kinds of social situations. I can still see the darkness lurking in the depth of his amber orbs, the tight lines around his eyes giving away the strain that he's currently under. I just wish he was able to share his burden, knowing that it's what he needs. To exorcise his demons. Otherwise, they just fester, eating away at your soul until nothing is left but desperation and the pitch black of loneliness.

A hyena's laugh jerks me from my thoughts, and I clench my jaw when I see Amber the Cuntmuffin leading Loki to the dance floor. I'm staring so intently at them that I don't even know what song is playing, and if looks could kill, she'd be a pile of ashes and fake lashes on the floor.

Loki's whole body is tight when she starts grinding up on him, her skinny arse almost falling out of her dress, it's that short. I'm all for people wearing what they want, freedom of expression and all that, but what she wears is barely more than underwear and just reeks of desperation.

"Princess," Ash warns under his breath, and I take a steadying inhale, trying to relax my tense shoulders.

"Lilly!" I hear Willow call, and turning my head, I see her striding towards me, pulling a guy by his hand.

She looks stunning in a dress the same colour as her eyes, the shape a simple, elegant fitted bodice with a flared skirt that ends just past her knee.

"Hey, Willow. You look beautiful," I tell her, getting up to give her a hug. We've become close over the past few weeks, and it made me realise how much I was missing having a girlfriend.

"So do you!" she exclaims, giving me an appreciative once over as we pull apart. "Oh, this is Ben." She indicates the guy standing behind her.

He's cute, in a kinda All-American way, all thick brown hair and sparkling white teeth.

"Hey," he says, flashing a smile, which dims a little as Ash stands next to me, no doubt scowling. "Ah, h-hi man."

Ash remains silent—fucking rude twatwaffle that he is—until I elbow him in the ribs.

"Hello, Ben," he drawls in that low voice of his, and whilst it makes me shiver, poor Ben visibly swallows. I roll my eyes.

"Don't mind him, Ben. He was hit with the arsehole stick on the way up from Hell," I tell him, watching as his eyes widen, flicker to Ash, then look back at Willow, who's positively shaking with repressed laughter.

"You'll pay for that later, Princess," Ash whispers in my ear, his tone dark.

Oh, I fucking hope so.

"Uh, I-I'll go get some drinks," Ben squeaks out, practically tripping in his haste to get away. Willow sighs.

"Did you have to scare him off?" she asks Ash, hands on her hips as she scowls at him.

"If he was any good, he wouldn't have been scared off," Jax says behind us, and Willow gapes at him.

"Hang on a fuck, you speak?" she exclaims, her hand on her chest and her big eyes even wider with her fake sarcasm.

I hear a bark of Jax's laughter, which really does shock Willow if her 'what the fuck' look is anything to go by. I turn, planning on taking my seat again when I catch sight of Amber pawing at Loki like he's a fucking dog toy.

Oh, I'm gonna cut a bitch.

"Excuse me," I mumble, and without pausing to think through what I am doing, I march over to the DJ and demand the next song. There must be something crazed in my gaze because he nods, his eyes wide and palms held up in a placating gesture.

I set my sights on Amber, still fawning over a stockstill Loki. He catches my gaze as the opening beats of *The Boy is Mine* by Liv Lovelle come over the speakers, and his eyes go wide as I walk right up to them, invading their personal space.

Amber turns round, presumably to see what Loki is staring at, a smug as fuck grin coming over her lips when she sees me standing there. Unfortunately for her, Liv begins to sing, and I mouth along, holding her increasingly narrow gaze as the lyrics start to sink in. I start to dance, gyrating up against her, touching her with dismissive gestures as I successfully manoeuvre myself so that I'm standing in between her and Loki.

I keep her gaze and keep singing along as I start to grind my arse into Loki, his hands coming up instinctively to my waist, even as he leans down to whisper in my ear.

"What are you doing, Pretty Girl?" It ends on a groan as I move my body so that I'm rubbing up against the bulge in his trousers that is now very prominent. "Fuck, you are going to get us in a shit load of trouble, baby," he rasps, pulling me closer, his hands tightening their grip on me.

Amber's face is as red as the roses that surround us as she notes the move, standing there watching as her fiancé basically dry humps me on the dance floor.

"Get your dirty whore hands off of him!" she screeches, taking a menacing step towards me, fake nails ready to claw my eyes out.

"Touch her, and I'll fucking kill you," Loki growls out, continuing to dance with me, his words and the venom of his tone halting Amber in her tracks.

"B-but, you're mine!" she wails, angry tears filling her eyes. "We're engaged!"

"Oh, honey," I reply, my voice sickly sweet as my hand comes up into Loki's hair, pulling his face down into my neck. He places a kiss there, a small moan leaving my smirking lips as the spot tingles. "He will never be yours."

She stamps her foot—legit stamps it like a three year old—then spins on her shiny Louboutins, storming from the room.

"Are you quite finished fucking my fiancée on the dancefloor?" Ash's voice drawls from the side of us, and I turn my head to take in his affected posture of boredom. I'd believe it, too, if it weren't for the way his grey eyes spit with anger.

Whoops.

"Told you, baby," Loki sighs, placing one final kiss on my shoulder before straightening up, but not stepping back.

My eyes narrow, my body flushing hot.

"Fuck Black Knight Corp.," I hiss, loud enough for him to hear but no one else. Both Ash's brows raise at my ire. "And fuck Julian cuntish Vanderbilt."

I spin, slamming my lips on Loki's as my hands tangle in his silky hair. He remains still for a millisecond, clearly in shock, then with a deep, panty melting groan, he kisses me back, pulling me closer with a firm grip on my arse. I vaguely hear gasps from those that surround us, but I've no more fucks to give. Unless, of course, it's with my guys.

Although I long to give into Loki's demanding kiss, I break away, panting and trembling with a heady mix of lust and anger. Turning back, I find Ash still standing there. He looks less angry, a softness to his gaze, even though there's a tightness about his shoulders that tells me he's worried.

Stepping away from Loki, I step into Ash, cupping his face with my palm and bringing him down to my lips. He comes readily, his lips meeting mine in a kiss full of tenderness and understanding. There's definitely another gasp from our audience— *what, are we in some kind of teen movie?*— but like before, it's hardly on my radar as he destroys me with his soul aching kiss. It's sweet and beautiful, like the sun on your face after a long cold winter, and I bask in it.

Reluctantly pulling back, I look past him to see that Kai and Jax have joined us, encircling us in their protection, gazing on with heat in their eyes. I step away from Ash, Jax stepping towards me.

"Fuck Black Knight," he says, his voice fierce, his blue eyes wild and piercing. He grabs me around the waist, pulling me roughly towards him so that I fall into his huge chest.

His lips smash onto mine, his tongue demanding entry like this is a declaration of war. And it is. I will no longer be under Julian's rule. I'll marry Ash because aside from the fact that a part of me really fucking wants to, it makes sense just in case anything does happen to me. I want to make sure that my control over the company goes to them so that they can continue to work towards overthrowing the current regime.

But I will no longer let anyone tell me what I can and can't do. Jax breaks the kiss as abruptly as he started it, proud approval shining in his eyes, and as I turn to face Kai, who has come up behind me, a loud crack lands on my arse, the pain making me gasp alongside the rest of the students who are staring at us with eyes hungry for scandal.

"Lilly, darling," Kai murmurs, holding me captive in his honey gaze as he steps into me, his hands coming up to cup my face tenderly. My own rest on his chest, relishing in the fact that I can feel his thundering heart through the silk of his suit jacket. "You are a Queen, and we are your loyal Knights, ready to go into battle on your behalf, and bathe in the blood of our enemies," he tells me, his eyes boring into mine as he speaks of war like a love declaration.

His full lips lower, pressing onto mine as he holds my face, and my world rocks and tips under his caress. He worships me with his kiss, his tongue tasting like champagne and victory, or a war already won. The rest of the room fades away as we embrace, the music, the decorations, and other students becoming nothing more than a memory as our lips move together.

We part, taking a final breath of each other before separating. I look around at them—my Knights in tarnished armour—and my soul cries with joy at having found our mates. They look fierce, dressed to the nines in their black suits and bow ties, with matching expressions of determination on their breathtakingly handsome faces.

My gaze moves out into the room, seeing many have their phones out, no doubt recording this latest scandal to upload as soon as we leave. I stare into one device, my jaw set and shoulders back.

"The Black Knights are mine," I declare, my war cry carrying out across the suddenly quiet room as one song finishes. "Try to take them away from me at your peril."

My message isn't for the viewers of TikTok, or Instagram, but for Julian Vanderbilt himself. I know that he has eyes everywhere and is watching our every move. I want him to know that he's no longer calling all the shots.

"Let's go," I say to the guys, who continue to surround me as we start to make our way out of the ballroom.

"Lilly!" I hear just as we reach the top of the steps. Willow rushes towards me. "Aside from the fact that that was fucking awesome, even if I'm not sure why it was necessary," she says, and I flush, knowing that there is so much that I can't tell her yet, if ever. "You left your purse at mine yesterday."

I frown, not recalling having even been at hers yesterday, as she hands me a small green silk purse, long and thin. She gives me a look, and like a camera zooming in, it comes back to me. The pregnancy test. Clutching the small bag, feeling the hard edges of the box inside, I throw my arms around her in a tight hug.

"Thank you," I murmur in her ear. She hugs me back just as tight. "What are BFFs for, huh? Good luck, babe."

My heart pounds as I let her go, turning to resume walking out of the doors which open as we approach. Dread swirls in my stomach, alongside fluttering butterflies, my thoughts swirling like a vortex.

Did I just fuck up declaring war on Julian? Will he retaliate? What happens next?

But a single burning question rises above all the others, repeating in my head until it's all that I can think about.

What if I'm pregnant?

CHAPTER TWENTY-TWO

LILLY

"I just need the loo," I say, not even taking off my shoes as I rush into the bathroom.

I can feel their eyes on me as I close the door, but I need to do this alone. I just want to process whatever the result is before telling them. Kicking off my heels, green sequin Irregular Choice, of course, I tear open the purse, finding a digital test inside. Thanking Willow for getting the one that literally tells you if you're pregnant, I open the box, taking the test out of its wrapping.

Now or never, Lilly.

I set the test to one side whilst I hitch the silk of my dress up, tucking the hem into the top so it's completely out of the way—*I know! I am the epitome of ladylike behaviour.*

Grabbing the test, I sit on the loo and do as instructed, peeing on the stick then popping the lid back on. I set it to one side, washing my hands and untucking my dress as I wait.

And wait.

And fucking wait.

Jesus! How long do these things take?!

My breath catches as finally the screen changes.

Pregnant.

Fine tremors wrack my body, and I suddenly feel ice cold. At the same time, a strange surge of blissful elation fills me at the thought of carrying a child. Loki's child. I wonder for a brief second if this is how Mum felt when she found out she was pregnant with me. This bizarre mix of happiness and sheer terror.

Oh god, Loki.

I have to tell him. I look up at my shaky reflection in the mirror, noticing my wide eyes and flushed cheeks.

"You can do this, Lilly Darling," I tell myself, my voice much more confident than I feel.

Grabbing hold of the test, I walk to the door, pausing briefly with my hand on the handle for one final deep breath, before opening it.

The guys are all sitting on the sofas, the fire roaring as they swirl various liquids in glasses. They've taken their jackets off, loosened their ties, and Loki, Jax and Kai all have their shirt sleeves rolled up. I smile at the fact that Ash hasn't, although he has undone the first couple of buttons.

"Everything okay, Pretty Girl?" Loki asks, and my gaze snaps to him. Immediately, he gets up, setting his glass down and coming towards me as if he knows. "What's happened?"

I see the others stiffen behind him, straightening up, but my focus is on the auburn haired angel in front of me.

"I'm pregnant," I whisper, holding out the test for him to see.

His brows dip for a second, looking down at the screen which still shows that one word. I watch him intently, seeing the flush rise on his cheeks as his eyes widen. His gaze comes back up to me, and suddenly, I'm so worried about how he'll react.

"Christmas Day," he says, not as a question but as a statement. I nod, my throat tight, waiting.

"What the fuck is going on?" Ash demands, striding towards us.

"Lilly's pregnant," Loki tells him, not looking in his direction, keeping his gaze on me.

Ash stops like he's just been sucker punched. "What?"

I can see the others come up next to him, shocked expressions on their faces, but my gaze catches on Loki's, waiting for his reaction.

"It's not the end of the world, is it, Loki?" I whisper, pleading with him to anchor me, to tell me that it'll all be okay, regardless of how crazy this is.

"No," he answers, and my shoulders sag, my breath whooshing out of me at his answer. "It's really not the end of the world, Pretty Girl."

He cups my face in his palm, his emerald eyes full of such tender emotion that my own fill with tears.

"I couldn't imagine anyone else I'd rather be in this mess with," he tells me, his own eyes wet as he places a soft kiss on my lips. "Me and you are in real trouble now, Pretty Girl."

Then he drops to his knees, his hands framing my middle as he kisses over my flat stomach.

"Hello, little one."

My eyes close, the tears falling freely as I feel a sudden lightness wash over me. Fingers wipe the tears away, and I open my lids, turning my head to the side to see Jax looking at me, his gaze full of fierce protectiveness and love.

"We'll look after you both," he tells me simply, cupping my face and making more tears fall, my throat aching.

"Nothing will happen to you, I swear," Kai vows from my other side, and an uncomfortable shiver runs through me at his promise. I shake the uneasy feeling off, giving him a watery smile.

Loki stands back up, wiping his eyes, and my heart aches with love for him, for them all.

"Fuck, I'm gonna be a dad," he says, running his hand through his hair.

"Yeah, to my wife's child," I hear Ash snap out, and I look past Loki to see Ash standing there, a face like thunder.

Loki's face blanches. "Shit, that's a cluster fuck."

My attention returns to Ash, who's still standing there, looking lost. Stepping away from the others, still clutching the damn test in my fist, I walk towards him in a swish of silk. Dropping the test onto the side table with a clatter, I step right up to him, my hand coming to cup his jaw.

"Hey," I say softly, his blistering gaze landing on me. There's anger there for sure, but also a blinding terror. "I need you, Asher Vanderbilt. *We* need you," I tell him, taking his hand with my spare one and placing it on my stomach. I swear I almost feel something as his palm strokes me, his fingers twitching. "You will all be fathers to our baby."

"What if I'm no good?" he asks, the terror shining brightly in his eyes. "I don't exactly have a good role model to look up to," he huffs out a self-deprecating laugh that cuts me to the quick.

"You will be an awesome dad, Ash, and our child will love you for it," I say, my voice firm with conviction in that truth.

His eyes close for a moment, his head tipping forward until our foreheads are resting together, his hand still resting over my stomach, warming the area under his palm.

"I love you, Lilly," he says, his voice choked with emotion.

"I love you, Ash," I reply, placing a gentle kiss on his lips.

The others come to us, surrounding me in their loving protection as their hands come to my stomach, until there's not a space left untouched where our baby is growing.

A week goes by, then two, then three, and yet no word from Julian, or any of the other members of the board. I can't even bring myself to think of them as the guys' families, there's no familial love there, nothing that gives them the right to be known as such. The radio silence leaves a sour taste in all our mouths, distracting us from our schoolwork as we wait on tenterhooks for some kind of backlash.

Meanwhile, Kai works on the plan. The murder plan. I hate how right it feels, to be plotting someone's death and the downfall of several others. But this is one thing that they have earnt, and if that makes me a monster, then so be it. I'll embrace the darkness with open arms if it keeps us all safe and stops the abuse that my guys have gone through, and continue to go through.

The weather warms up, signs of spring in the air, although apparently, it's not officially spring until we get snow on the tulips that fill the Academy planters. Something eases in my heart, my breaths coming a little easier as winter starts to wane. It's silly really, bad things can happen at any time, regardless if the birds are chirping and the sun is shining.

We've decided to keep my pregnancy quiet for the moment, I'm only ten weeks or so along anyway, so it's not as if anything shows yet or will for a while. The sickness still plagues me, and reminds me of stories Mum told me of how morning sickness was a load of bollocks when you feel sick all damn day. How right she was.

Kai spends hours in our kitchen making me things to try and tempt me to eat, and he brings me lemon and ginger tea in the mornings which helps to settle my stomach enough for a plain breakfast of peanut butter on toast. He tells me he's stockpiling recipes for when I feel up for more and has researched the best diet during pregnancy to ensure that the baby and I are getting all that we need.

Jax has me on various vitamins and supplements, having done his own research into what I need. He's also planned an entire exercise regime suitable for pregnancy and has added a massage course which includes pre and post natal massage to his studies.

I've had to stop Loki on more than one occasion from buying up the entirety of the Frugi newborn store, an English company online that he found, which specialises in rainbow designs. He holds me close pretty much every night, hardly letting the others get a look in, telling me all the things that he plans to do for our child, the ways in which he'll care for us.

It's enough to make me cry, which I seem to be doing at random points now. Apparently, that's normal.

Ash is the only one that seems a bit reserved, a bit separate from us. I hate it, but I know that he's coming to terms with the situation, with his worry about what lies ahead, and what will happen when Julian decides to get his revenge.

We don't have to wait much longer for the first hit.

We're lounging on the grass outside, in the formal gardens of the Academy, Willow with us, when Jax's phone buzzes. He answers it, his face going deathly pale as his eyes lock onto mine, like a drowning man.

"What?" he growls, chills running down my spine at the danger in his voice. "When?"

I sit up from lying back on Loki, the others and Willow all looking at Jax with alarm. He ends the call, his hand still like the calm before the storm, as he looks at the now dark screen.

"What's going on, Jax?" Ash asks, casting a quick look at Willow, who flushes.

"I've, um, got some homework to catch up on," she says, getting up and giving me a quick peck on my cheek.

"Thanks, lovely," I whisper in her ear, and she just nods with an understanding smile. This girl really is the shizzle.

Jax watches as she walks off, waiting until she's disappeared into the doors of the Academy before he speaks, his voice low and pained.

"Mom's in the hospital," he tells us, and my heart stills, knowing it's not for something routine. "She was beaten half to death last night, supposedly by intruders, who left her for dead while they stole all the valuables."

"No," I whisper, my hand coming to cover my mouth as tears spring into my eyes, making Jax bob and weave in my watery vision.

"It was Dad, I fucking know it was!" he snarls, suddenly standing up and launching his phone at a nearby planter with a roar, shattering the device, and sending little pieces of plastic and glass flying. He turns to us, his eyes wild, and my soul breaks for him. "He's been beating on her for fucking years, always holding back under Julian's orders."

"What?" I ask, horror coming over me and filling me with its icy touch.

"It would look bad for the company if one of the board was found to be a wife beater," Kai spits out, disgust clear in his tone. A fine tremor begins in my muscles, and I wrap my arms around myself, in a bit to warm up my cold limbs.

Just then, my own phone vibrates in the pocket of my dungarees with an incoming message.

I take it out and gaze at the screen, my breath stilling as I read the words on the screen.

Unknown: Do not test me again, daughter darling.

"Oh god," I whisper, dropping my phone like it's just burnt me. I look up into Jax's anguished face, my body temperature rising as nausea swims in my stomach. "I'm so sorry, Jax."

My head drops into my hands as sobs wrack my body. It's all my fault. I was so fucking stupid thinking that I could basically send Julian a middle finger with no repercussions. *Stupid, so fucking stupid.*

"Hey, hey, Baby Girl, look at me," Jax says softly, his big hands cupping my jaw and lifting my head up so that I'm looking into his beautiful blue eyes. "This is not your fault, baby," he assures me, but I'm shaking my head before he's even finished.

"Read the message, Jax! It's all my fault for being a stupid fucking idiot! Your mum is in hospital because of me," I tell him, blinded by my anger and heartache. His eyes harden.

"Don't let him do this to you and fuck with your mind. You're smarter than that."

I want to believe him, so badly, but my stomach churns with guilt at what my reckless actions have caused.

"I'm so sorry, Jax," I whisper, my voice a sad, broken thing, more tears spilling down my cheeks.

"It's not you that owes me an apology, baby," he replies, placing a gentle kiss on my trembling lips. "You didn't order this. You didn't strike the blows."

I might as well have.

I don't say it out loud, but if the sigh that escapes from his lips is anything to go by, and the fact that he knows me better than I know myself sometimes, he sees it in my eyes. My self blame.

"We should go and visit," Ash says from behind us, already up and brushing off his suit. "I take it she's in Mount Vernon?"

Jax nods, letting go of my face and standing up. He looks down, holding his hand out to help me to my feet. My mind races with bloody images, the scene of Mum's murder flashing before my eyes, before I blink it away.

Jax refuses to let go of my hand as we walk to the student car park, throwing the keys to his truck at Ash, who deftly catches them, and opens the driver's side. Jax opens the back, ushering me into the middle, then getting in behind me, Loki on my other side. They buckle me in, my hands too shaky to be able to do it for myself.

"Drink this, Baby Girl," Jax orders, passing me some kind of sports drink. I bring it to my lips on autopilot, making a face at the tart fizzy taste. "Small sips, that's it, good girl," he praises as I continue to take small sips as he ordered.

Loki rubs my other hand, which is feeling a little warmer, and I no longer feel quite so dizzy.

"Thanks," I say, looking up to see Ash's furrowed brow and worried gaze as he looks at me in the rearview mirror.

"You went all pale and cold, Pretty Girl," Loki tells me, bringing my hand to his lips and kissing it. I turn to look at him, noticing that his shoulders are tight as he takes a deep breath.

"I think you went into shock, baby," Jax says, my head turning to look at him. He studies me with a professional eye, and I suddenly have the thought that he'd make an awesome doctor. "But your colour is returning, and you don't feel cold and clammy anymore."

"I'm sorry, Jax. I should be taking care of you after..." My voice trails off, unable to finish my sentence.

"Don't do that, don't blame yourself," he grits out through clenched teeth. "This is not your fault."

Fresh tears sting my eyes at his words. I know he's right, I only stood up for myself. I didn't hurt his mum. But guilt still slivers uncomfortably in the pit of my stomach.

"We're here," Kai says from the front passenger seat, and I look out of the front window to see that we're pulling into a circular drive.

The building that sits behind it doesn't look like any kind of hospital that I've seen before, more like an old style Golden Age mansion. It's all white columns and tall windows, with what looks like beautiful grounds and manicured lawns surrounding it.

We halt to a stop at the front entrance, a smartly dressed valet coming to greet us. Ash tosses him the keys once we get out, coming round to stand in front of me, taking my face in his hands.

"You okay, Princess?" he asks, the muscles in his arms strained as he studies me.

"I'm fine, Ash, just a little shaken," I tell him, feeling even warmer when he leans in and places a gentle kiss on my forehead.

"You went so pale," he murmurs into my hairline, pulling me close until his body is flush with mine. "Shit, I was scared, Princess."

And it's then that I realise that this must be bringing up awful memories for him, too, memories of finding a loved one covered in blood but too damn late to help.

He holds me for a moment, surrounding me with his spicy ginger scent, before pulling back but keeping hold of my hand as we head up the few stone stairs that lead to some imposing glass front doors.

"The hospital has valet parking?" I ask incredulously, stepping through the automatic doors that open with a quiet swish.

"Only the best for the Black Knight families," Loki drawls sarcastically on my other side as we walk on the marble floor towards the reception desk.

The inside feels a lot more like a normal hospital, with modern tech and the residue smell of antiseptic. It still has a glass chandelier, though, just to make sure we all know that this is not a place for the peasants. *Conceited fuckers.*

"Jannet Griffiths," Jax announces in a gruff voice to the young receptionist, who looks up slightly startled before she schools her features and puts on an award winning smile.

"Of course, she is expecting you, Mr. Griffiths," she says brightly, totally at odds with the situation. "Room two-oh-three, up the stairs, through the door, and third on the left."

Jax grunts his thanks, then turns, heading in the direction of the stairs.

"Thank you," I offer as I pass, giving her a smile which she returns tenfold. *That's just fucking creepy.*

"You're most welcome, Miss Darling," she replies, and both myself and Ash stop in our tracks, looking at each other with matching looks of concern, creasing our brows.

"Come on, Princess," Ash says, putting aside that fuckery for another time, as he leads me after the others.

We find the room easily, opening the door to see a huge space, filled with bouquets of flowers, which act as pops of colour in the dim lighting. The curtains are drawn, and as I look over to the bed, to the machines that beep, I can see why.

My breath leaves me in a gasp as tears fill my vision. She, Jax's mum, looks so small and helpless on the bed, her face a myriad of purple and blue, one arm in a plaster cast.

"Mom," Jax says, his voice shattered and broken, like a favourite ornament. He crosses strides to her bedside, picking up her hand that's not in a cast as he lowers to a seat next to her bedside.

Her eyelids flutter, her chest rattling with a deep, painful breath as she slowly turns her head to look at him.

"Jax?" she asks, only able to open her swollen eyes a fraction.

"I'm here, Mom," he says, the heartbreak clear on his face. "The guys and Lilly, too."

"Lilly?" she questions, her voice rough, turning her head to try and find me in the gloom.

"Hi, Mrs. Griffiths," I say softly, letting go of Ash and stepping forward, walking towards her bed. I pick up her cup of water, placing a straw in it before bringing it to her lips for her to drink. Jax gives me a grateful look, his eyes shining.

"Thank you, Lilly dear," she croaks, her voice less raspy than it was before. A lump forms in my throat, hating that she's thanking me when it is partly my fault that she's in this position in the first place.

"Was it him?" Jax bursts out, voice hard and cutting. "Was it Dad?"

An anguished look comes over her face then, and she doesn't take her eyes off me as she replies.

"I'm not as strong as your mother was, Lilly. She was always the bravest of us."

My world spirals, my breath whooshing out of my chest as I look into her familiar piercing blue eyes, and see the truth of her words, even if I can't understand them.

"What?" I whisper, but before she can answer, the door bursts open and a nurse strides in.

"Time for more...oh! I'm so sorry. I didn't realise that you had visitors," she fumbles, flushing as we all stare at her.

"Not to worry, my dear," Jannet Griffiths responds, a kind smile tugging her split lip, making her wince. "I could do with some more pain relief."

Jax leaps up, moving to one side so that the nurse can administer the meds. Before I can step away, Jannet grabs my hand, forcing my gaze back on her.

"You have formidable blood in you, Lilly. Don't let them make you forget it," she says, her voice quiet but intense, giving my hand one final squeeze, before letting it go as she closes her eyes.

I look up into Jax's eyes, finding him looking down at his mother as if seeing her anew. He definitely heard her cryptic remarks, and it's clear that he has no idea what she is talking about.

She's just confirmed that she knew my mum, and by the sounds of it, quite well. What did she mean she was strong, the bravest of them all?

Why does it feel like I'm getting more questions than answers, the more time passes?

And the biggest question of all?

Who was Laura Darling?

CHAPTER TWENTY-THREE

JAX

I sit on the chair next to my mom's bedside, listening to the bleep of the machines and watching the rise and fall of her chest as she breathes. I'm all alone, having sent the others back to Highgate with Lilly, who looked dead on her feet.

I'm gonna fucking kill him, that cuntstain of a father of mine. My lip curls, a sour taste in my mouth as I think of him. I know it was him. I can practically make out that shitty signet ring he wears on his right hand in the bruises on her face.

My fists clench as I catalog her injuries once again, knowing that she won't tell me the truth, and she won't report him. I remember the time that I beat the shit out of him, a grim smile pulling my lips up with the memory of his blood coating my hands for once. Looks like he'll need a little reminder of the lesson that I thought he'd learned that day.

"Be careful, baby." I hear her rasping voice say, and I look up into eyes that reflect my own. Only hers are full of concern and worry. "I know that look, Jax. Nothing good will come from revenge."

I take her hand once more, so much smaller than my own.

"He won't get away with this," I vow, righteous fire filling my black soul until it's ablaze. "He will pay."

"Oh, baby," she whispers, shifting with a small moan, which only adds fuel to the fire of my anger. "And what if Lilly gets caught in the crossfire?"

The fire goes out, cold dread sitting like a heavy weight in my stomach.

"What you said to her earlier, about her mom..." I trail off, seeing her gaze turned pained and knowing that I won't get anything else out of her.

"I shouldn't have said it, but she looked so downtrodden, so broken," she replies, swallowing painfully. I reach for her cup, bringing the straw to her lips so that she can drink. "I can't say any more, Jax. I promised..." she starts, getting restless, and her heart monitor picks up slightly.

"Hey, don't worry, Mom. I won't force you, just rest," I assure her, feeling pleased as she relaxes into the pillows again. Suddenly, I have the overwhelming need to tell her about the baby. She's always loved children, and she desperately needs to smile. Plus, I know that I can trust her, she's clearly good at keeping secrets. "Lilly's pregnant."

Her whole body goes still as she looks at me, joy warring with desperate sadness in her eyes.

"Oh, baby. Is it, I mean, are you..." she trails off, looking away and blushing. I can't help the grin that splits my lips in a rare smile.

"Loki," I say, feeling a twinge of...something, at the fact that it's not my child she's carrying.

"I guess, it doesn't really matter," she surprises me by saying, my mouth hanging open. "I know that you'll all be fathers to that baby, and damn fine ones, too." Her eyes shine as my chest goes tight. "You'll take care of them both, my sweet boy."

"I will," I croak out, clearing my throat which feels tight all of a sudden. A part of me may wish that Lilly's baby was biologically mine, but Mom is right. It doesn't matter if we share the same genetics, that baby belongs to the five of us as we belong to each other.

"Julian has other things planned," Mom says into the weighted silence, the room filling with tension at her words. "I don't know what, but I think he's trying to teach you all a lesson for disobeying him. Be on your guard, son."

My stomach rolls, my heartbeat feeling sluggish as I take in what she's telling me. It seems that Julian's ire is not yet sated.

I just hope we're ready for his next move.

LILLY

Another week passes with Jax's mum still recovering in hospital. He told us of her warning, about Julian's reign of terror being far from over, and to watch our backs. We remain on high alert, tension surrounding us as we wait for his next move.

Jax visits every day after school, somehow managing to keep up with his studies, too. I would be woefully behind if the guys didn't keep on my arse, making me sit down to study, even though some days, I can barely keep my eyes open.

I'm approaching what I think is my twelfth week, sitting in the library with Willow when she leans over to whisper in my ear.

"Have you had your twelve week scan yet?" she asks, jerking me awake after I almost fall asleep in my calculus book.

"Huh?" I ask on a yawn, rubbing my eyes.

"You know, the scan you get at twelve weeks?" she questions me, brows raised.

"Ummm..." I trail off with a cringe, my hands fiddling with my pencil.

"You have seen a midwife, right?" I bite my lip, and her eyes roll so hard I'm surprised they don't get stuck. "Bloody idiots! The lot of you!" she hisses, packing up her stuff, then standing to do mine. "Come on," she orders, grabbing my hand and pulling me to my feet.

"Hey!" I whisper-yell as she drags me from the library, my Converse squeaking on the floor. My feet are just too achy at the moment for my beloved Irregulars, plus none of the guys will let me wear heels because of the baby- *le sigh*.

She manhandles me all the way to my dorm, holding her palm out when we get there.

"Key," she demands, and I can see a fire in her eyes that lets me know she's pissed. I obey, trying to placate her, which doesn't seem to work as she throws the door open once she's unlocked it, pulling me inside before slamming it shut.

"What the fuck?!" Loki exclaims, jumping up from the sofa, Ash and Kai doing the same.

"What the fuck is right, you prick!" Willow snarls, finally letting go of me. I watch wide eyed as she strides towards him, getting all up in his grill. She looks ridiculous, like a tiny fairy up against a giant, but she doesn't let that stop her, poking her finger in his chest. I wince, knowing how much that hurts from past experience. "I don't know what kind of shit is going on with you guys, but you need to get your heads out of your arses and take Lilly to a fucking midwife! She needs tests and a scan to check that the baby is okay. Plus, regular check ups and shit!"

Loki stands there, jaw clenched as his cheeks flush. He heaves a sigh, bringing his hands up to run through his hair. He turns to look at me, his eyes pained.

"Fuck, Lilly, I had no idea," he says, and I shake my head trying to tell him that neither did I.

"Of course, you bloody didn't! You're an eighteen year old guy for Christ's sake!" Will says, throwing her hands up. She turns to Ash, who stands there with a gleam of respect in his eyes as he looks at her. "Get on it, Vanderbilt," she orders.

One perfect black brow arches, his lips twitching with amusement that she probably doesn't spot otherwise she'd be spitting mad again. He reaches into his suit trousers pocket, pulling out his phone and scrolling until he finds what he's looking for. Holding my gaze, he brings the phone up to his ear.

"Dr. Richards? Yes, it's Asher Vanderbilt here," he says, cool as always, holding my gaze as he speaks. "My fiancée needs to see an obstetrician, do you have someone on your team?" He pauses. "Yes, thank you, we are very excited, but needless to say this is news of the utmost confidentiality." He says the last part in a hard tone, almost threateningly, and I wonder if he has something on this doctor that he doesn't want shared. "Tomorrow at ten, perfect. We shall see Dr. Kent then. Thank you."

Ending the call, he bypasses a smug looking Willow to come up to me, hand cupping my jaw.

"I'm sorry I didn't think of this," he whispers, swallowing thickly. "I'd never willingly put you, or the baby, in danger."

"I know, Ash. You weren't to know what I'd need," I tell him, my own hand palming his cheek, but I can see the regret and determination in the hard steel of his eyes.

"But I should know, and I will give you everything you need and more, my love," he whispers back, brushing a light kiss against my lips that gives me all the shivers.

"I'm coming, too," Loki says firmly, and I look to see he's also stepped up to us. "I want to be there, and I don't give a fuck how it looks." Ash just nods, looking over at Kai, who lifts his chin.

"I assume Jax will want to be there as well," he sighs, but not like he minds all that much. "Kai, email administration will you."

"Right," Willow pipes up, and I must admit I'd kinda forgotten that she was here. *Worst friend ever.* "Now that that's sorted, go run my girl a bubble bath, give her something yummy to eat, then an early night."

I love the way she bosses the guys around, and I love that when it comes to me, they all jump and do as she orders, Loki giving me a quick peck before heading into the bathroom, Kai coming over to do the same before heading to the kitchen.

"I'll see you later, babe," she tells me, nudging Ash out of the way so that she can give me a hug. "Let me know how it goes tomorrow, yeah?"

"Hashtag-obvs," I chuckle, squeezing her back tightly. "Thanks, hun."

"Always, boo," she replies, planting another kiss on my cheek before sweeping out of the door. I am coming to love that girl.

"She's growing on me," Ash declares, taking my hand and leading me to the bathroom. I chuckle, moaning as the smell of my favourite lavender, marjoram, and geranium bubble bath fills the air.

Ash kneels down, undoing my Chucks and helping me to slip my feet out of them. I can hear Loki swirling the water around and know that he'll be getting the perfect temperature for me. Ash starts to undress me, helping me out of my berry red Lucy and Yak dungarees, yellow cotton T-shirt, and lacy bra and french knicker set, until I stand before him naked.

"You are so beautiful, Princess," he murmurs, his hand reaching out to trail across my stomach. I swear it flips at his touch, even though I know that there's no way I'll feel anything until at least twenty weeks.

My breath hitches, thinking he'll continue south, but he just takes my hand in his and leads me to the bath, helping me climb into the huge tub. He helps me to get settled, Loki placing a glass of cold water on the side by my head. They both turn, starting to head out of the door.

"'O, wilt thou leave me so unsatisfied?'"

I quote at their backs, and they pause, turning around slowly, a smug grin on Ash's face.

"Did you just quote Shakespeare at me to get you off, Princess?" he asks, amusement clear in his tone, a wide grin pulling up his lush lips. I arch a brow at him, opening my legs in clear invitation.

"Don't have to tell me twice," Loki comments, coming back into the room and walking around the bath, kneeling on the floor. "Want us to take care of all your needs, Pretty Girl?"

"Yes," I reply, my voice breathy with sweet anticipation.

"Yes...what?" he teases, his hand dipping into the water, his fingers grazing my inner thigh and sending shooting stars straight to my core.

"Please," I moan, fingers capturing my jaw and turning my face so that I'm staring into grey eyes instead of emerald.

"Good girl," Ash praises, and my whole body flushes as he dips his head, placing his lips on mine.

His kiss is languid, a slow, torturous teasing of mouth and tongue that soon works me up into a frenzy of need, especially with the combination of Loki's fingers swirling just around my clit but not quite touching it.

"Ash...Loki," I beg, my voice a breathless whine, desperation clawing at my centre. "Please."

"Seeing as you asked so nicely," Loki replies, slamming two fingers inside me, the heel of his hand hitting my clit. My back arches out of the water, my hands grasping the slippery sides of the tub as pleasure explodes across my closed eyelids.

Ash holds my jaw firm in one hand, deepening the kiss, his tongue plunging into my mouth, somehow in time with Loki's fingers. I feel a sharp tug on my exposed nipple, and I cry out into Ash's mouth, but he doesn't release me, swallowing my moans as he destroys me with his mouth.

"That's it, baby," Loki whispers in my ear, voice strained and low as he continues to fuck my pussy with his fingers. "Let us take real good care of you."

My leg lifts, balancing my foot on the side of the tub so Loki can go deeper, hitting that sweet spot over and over again until I'm a writhing mess. Ash's hand slips down from my jaw to the top of my neck, tightening his grip so that I'm struggling to take a full breath as he continues to dominate my mouth.

"Come for us, Pretty Girl," Loki orders, adding a third finger just as Ash pinches my nipple hard.

I scream into Ash's mouth, my pussy clamping down on Loki's fingers as wave upon wave of exquisite pleasure rolls over me, lighting me up from the inside. They don't stop, not until I'm a quivering, twitching mess.

Ash finally releases my mouth with a final gentle kiss, letting go of my nipple at the same time as Loki pulls his fingers out, making me gasp.

"So fucking beautiful, Princess," Ash says, his eyes hooded and making my cunt pulse.

He stands up, his trousers tented in the most mouth watering way. I turn, and Loki does the same, adjusting himself in his grey sweats. He leans down, giving me a peck on my kiss-swollen lips, before straightening up, and walking back around the bath.

I watch, my brows furrowed as they begin to make their way to the open door.

"What about you guys?" I ask, my voice husky, when they start making their way out.

"We're taking care of you, Princess," Ash states, looking at me over his shoulder. "Now, wash up, and come get something to eat. Early night for you tonight."

And with that, they walk out, leaving me very much satisfied.

CHAPTER TWENTY-FOUR

LILLY

I wake up after a gloriously restful sleep, mostly thanks to Ash who insisted I sleep with him to make sure I actually slept, and didn't, well, you know. I do live with four guys after all.

Hashtag-firstworldproblems.
Or, perhaps it should be reverse harem problems?

Either way, I feel much better this morning, especially when a certain ginger scented devil wraps his arms around me and pulls me closer, his morning wood digging into my lower back.

"Good morning, Princess," he rumbles out, his voice fifty shades of husky and making Her Vagisty perk up.

"Good morning, love," I reply, arching into him as he nuzzles my neck, sending shivers of delicious electricity skirting over my body. Naked as always when I'm in one of their beds, I actually should just bin all my pjs at this rate.

"You don't know what it does to me when you call me that, Princess," he growls out, his hand flexing on my stomach, before dipping lower, but not quite low enough, as he teases me.

"Ash, love," I say, squirming and trying to get his hand where I need it to be. He growls again at the term of endearment, thrusting his hard length against my back, making me moan. "Stop being such a cunt tease."

He huffs out a laugh against my neck, more tingles travelling over my skin as his warm breath caresses me. He moves his hand a fraction, then another, and just as he is about to reach the gold at the end of the rainbow - *oh yeah, I just referred to my vajayjay as a pot of motherfucking gold* - the door bursts open with a crash.

"Morning, campers!" Loki declares, strolling in with a swagger and a shit-eating grin. "I hate to stop what looks like a really fun time, but it's nine-fifteen and we have to be there at ten."

Ash groans behind me, the sound a match for my own frustration.

"Fine," Ash practically snarls out, pushing up abruptly and letting all the warm air out of our little cocoon of duvet. Comforter. *Whatever.*

"Don't give me that look, Pretty Girl," Loki admonishes me, still smiling like he's thoroughly pleased at being a cockblocker. And cuntblocker. *Bastard.* "Let's go meet our baby!" he shouts, and a flutter of anticipation alights in my stomach at the realisation that I will be meeting our baby for the first time today.

"Fine," I huff, sitting up, less cross than I was when he first stormed in. "I needed a piss anyway."

"Such a lady," Loki jokes, laughing when I give him the middle finger and follow Ash out of the room.

Jax and Kai are already dressed, waiting in the living room for us, so Ash and I get a wriggle on and somehow manage to get ready in fifteen minutes. As we're heading out of the door, Kai hands me a tupperware and a reusable thermos.

"Breakfast," he tells me with a smile, and my mouth waters at the thought of my ginger, lemon and honey tea, and peanut butter on toast. The same breakfast that I've eaten every morning for several weeks now thanks to Kai.

"You are a godsend, Kai Matthews," I tell him, planting a kiss on his cheek as we leave.

The journey to the obstetrician luckily doesn't take long, and soon we're pulling up to a modern looking wood and glass building, nestled in the forest.

Swallows Birthing Centre is engraved in elegant cursive on a brass plaque next to the glass door, which opens as we approach. We're met by a smartly dressed man, in his mid-forties with dirty blond hair and a square jaw. He's quite handsome for an older guy, if you're into the whole age gap thing. There's a younger looking woman next to him in light pink scrubs.

"Mr. Vanderbilt," he says in a soft, calming voice, a broad smile on his face, and I'm instantly put at ease by his calming tone. "Welcome. And you must be Miss Darling, our mother-to-be. Congratulations."

"Thanks," I reply quietly, a fissure of excitement running through me at his words. It's nice to have someone congratulate me, only the guys and Willow know that I'm pregnant, although we'll have to announce it at some point. I won't be able to hide it forever. *That's future Lilly's problem.*

"Welcome to Swallows. I am Dr. Arnold, and this is Lisa. She'll be your midwife, alongside myself as your OB," he tells us, the woman next to him giving a smile of her own. "Would you like your guests to sit in today, too?" he asks, looking from me to Ash.

"Yes, please," I reply as Ash gives a nod of assent.

"Excellent. If you'd like to follow me, let's have a quick chat about dates etc., then we can get to the scan so you can meet your baby."

My hand finds Ash's, gripping tightly as we walk after the doctor and midwife. Nervous butterflies flutter around in my stomach, threatening to bring my breakfast back up. We are taken into a large bright room with huge glass windows that look out into the forest.

"It's blacked out glass so no one can see inside," Lisa explains kindly, seeing my slight look of alarm.

"Thank goodness," I whisper, clearing my suddenly dry throat as we sit down. Lisa disappears briefly, opening what looks like a fridge on the other side of the room, then walks back over carrying a chilled bottle of water with her.

"Here," she says, handing it to me with another smile.

"Thank you," I say, tearing up a little at the kindness. *Bloody hormones.*

"Would anyone else like anything?" she asks the guys, who all shake their heads, or tell her they are fine.

"Right, just some information gathering first," Dr. Arnold says, looking down at a tablet in his hands. "When was your last period, may I call you Lilly?" he asks, looking up at me.

"Um, sure," I respond, feeling my cheeks flush at the question. "Well, um, as for my least period, I, uh, am not quite sure. But I only had unprotected sex on Christmas Day..." I trail off, my face burning and palms sweaty. Ash reaches over to grasp my hand, rubbing my knuckles soothingly, and I give him a grateful smile.

"Okay, let's work with that for now, and the scan will be able to confirm how far along you are," he replies. He then proceeds to ask me a whole bunch of questions, about myself and my medical history, then my mother's medical history. "Right, I think that's it." He beams at me. "If you could head over to the bed, and just get undressed enough so we can get to your stomach, we can do the scan."

"Okay," I murmur, more nerves flooding my system, my mouth once again dry.

Lisa pulls a curtain round to give me some privacy, and I take the top part of my yellow bee cord dungarees down, lifting up my T-shirt, then hopping up onto the bed.

"Are you ready, Lilly?" Lisa calls softly from the other side of the curtain.

"Yes," I answer, taking a deep breath to calm my thrashing heartbeat.

She opens the curtain, and Dr. Arnold wheels over a big machine with a screen on it, as well as a keypad and a scanner looking thingy.

"You can come over, too," Lisa tells the guys, clearly not sure who to address.

Ash is immediately at my head, Loki next to him, who takes hold of my hand in his warm one. Mine's a little cold, so he rubs it gently. Kai manages to squeeze in next to him, giving me a soft smile, as Jax stands behind them. Being the tallest, he can see over their heads.

"You ready?" Dr. Arnold asks, and all I can do is nod. He sits down on a stool, grabbing a bottle and squeezing some warm gel on my stomach. I watch as he picks up the scanner, rubbing it into the gel and pushing it down into my soft stomach.

Then I hear it.

The whooph-whooph of a heartbeat.

My gaze snaps up to the screen, seeing the unmistakable outline of a baby, white on a black screen.

Fuck.

"Loki," I whisper, gripping his hand tightly as my eyes try to take in every detail, and I am surprised by how much I can see.

"I know, Pretty Girl," he whispers back, his voice choked and cracking slightly. I briefly glance away from the screen to see his glassy eyes watching the screen enraptured.

My gaze flits to Ash, to see a similar expression of wonderment on his face, softening it until I can finally see who he was meant to be, without all the suffering and trauma he's been forced to go through. I next find Jax, looking at the screen with amazement on his face, his usually tight jaw slack even as a fire burns in his eyes. Always our protector. I finally come to rest my gaze on Kai, and he almost breaks me. There's a devastating sadness etched in lines across his face as tears drip down his cheeks. He quickly removes his glasses, swiping under his eyes, and my heart aches for him. Before I can say anything to him, though lord knows what that would be, the doctor speaks.

"All looks good, measurement wise," Dr Arnold states, my head turning back to him. "I'd say you're around the sixteen week mark. Shall we switch to 3D mode?" he asks, and I nod.

A gasp leaves my lips when my baby, *our* baby, suddenly appears on the screen as if it's right in front of us.

"Fuck," Loki breathes, dispelling the tension in the room and making the doctor and midwife chuckle. "Sorry," I hear him apologise, but my gaze is fixated on the screen, watching our baby twitch and turn.

I feel a hand stroke my hair, before lips press a gentle kiss on the top of my head, his ginger scent engulfing me in warm comfort.

"It's our baby, Ash," I whisper, my eyes stinging as I continue to stare at the wriggling baby on screen.

"It's perfect, just like its mother," he murmurs, and a tear escapes my lids, leaving a wet trail down my cheek.

And then it hits me with the force of a mack truck.

I'm going to be a mother.

My breath stills as the thought settles its heavy weight in my very bones.

I am going to be a mother.

A slight panic begins to flutter at the edge of my vision, the idea of being responsible for another being scaring the absolute shit out of me.

"Hey," Ash whispers, gripping my jaw gently and turning my head away from the screen so that I'm gazing into the depths of his grey eyes. "You will be a wonderful mother, Lilly Darling, soon to be Vanderbilt."

He gazes deeply into my eyes, willing me to believe this truth. And although I'm still mildly terrified - *yep, that's a legit phrase and makes complete sense!* - the weight on my chest lessens until I can breathe deeply again. Then the last part of his pretty speech registers.

"Hang on, I never said I was going to change my name," I hiss out, partly outraged at the assumption, partly preening at the idea of being Mrs. Vanderbilt.

"No wife of mine will be anything less, *Darling*," he informs me with his signature Ash-hole smirk. I narrow my eyes at him, deciding not to start an argument, especially when I'm not actually that objectionable to the idea.

"Well, that's us done here. All is normal and expected," Dr Arnold tells me, using a paper towel to wipe off the gel on my stomach. "Would you like some pictures?"

"Yes!" Loki blurts out, and we all chuckle then, an adorable blush covering his cheeks as Jax claps him on the shoulder whilst grinning.

As we exit the building, pictures of our baby safely tucked in pockets, I take hold of Kai's hand, drawing him back from the others who go ahead towards the parking at the rear where the truck is.

"Are you okay?" I ask him, biting my lip as I take in his red eyes and downturned features.

"Yeah...No, shit, I don't know, Lilly. Sorry," he says in an exasperated tone, a hand coming to rub the back of his neck. "It was just seeing that baby, your baby. It's so innocent, so pure, and I guess it just reminded me of all that..."

He looks up to me, his gaze pained and full of guilt all at once. My soul aches for him, and I just want to take his pain away, throwing it to the four winds.

"Hey," I say softly, stopping us and cupping his jaw with my palm. It's slightly rough with stubble, and although it makes me worry that he's not his usual meticulous self, I can't help but like the rough look on him. "First off, it's our baby. All of ours, you included. And secondly," I continue, willing him to believe me, "it's okay to feel sad, resentful, and anything else. All your feelings are valid, Kai. This is a crazy situation, and it's bound to be difficult, and dredge up things from the past. Things that you'd rather forget."

A single tear trails down his cheek, and I use my thumb to wipe it away, even as my own eyes fill.

"You need to let this burden out soon, my love," I whisper, watching as he closes his eyes briefly, tipping his head back, my hand still cupping his cheek.

"I know," he whispers back, his voice broken and bone weary. He tips his head forward again, looking at me with desperation in his eyes. "I'm so fucking scared, Lilly. I've been keeping it in for so long, and I don't know how to let it out."

"Oh, Kai," I choke out, pulling him to me and wrapping my arms around him in a fierce hug. I want to say something, anything, but no words come. Instead, I just hold him close, trying to show him how much I love him.

I just hope that it is enough.

CHAPTER TWENTY-FIVE

LILLY

Several days later we're sitting in our dorm, studying on the sofas. Kai is next to me, tapping away at something uber complicated on his tablet, whilst I try to study for our latest Shakespeare assignment. We're looking at *Macbeth* this term, and it's not exactly a play full of rainbows and sunshine. Ash is on his chair, well, sofa, but he always sits on it, usually alone, and Loki is on the floor, flipping through some textbook. Jax is on the other sofa, his notes spread around him as he looks up something in a huge book, which looks like some kind of medical journal.

My phone buzzes beside me, and I pick it up to see a text. My heart stops as I see who the sender is.

Unknown: Honesty is always the best policy, don't you agree, daughter darling?

My heart pounds painfully in my chest. Does he know about my pregnancy? That we're trying to hide it from him?

An audio message pops up next, my stomach sinking as my

thumb hovers over the play button. Whatever this is, it's not good, not good at all.

My pulse pounds as I hit the play button, my brow furrowing as the distinct sounds of rustling sheets and heavy breathing come over the speakers. I can sense the others still as the sound fills the room, followed by the sound of a young boy crying.

"If you didn't like it so much, Kai, why are you hard?"

My wide gaze snaps up to Kai, who's frozen next to me and deathly pale. Before I can say anything, the man's voice, Kai's uncle if I'm not mistaken, sounds again.

"That feels good, doesn't it?"

"N-no."

A young boy, Kai, sobs.

"Oh my God," I gasp out, my hand covering my mouth as the hideous truth of what I'm hearing registers. Tears sting my eyes, and my hand shakes, but I don't stop the recording, listening to Kai's sobs and laboured breaths, his uncle saying foul things, as he…as he abuses him.

There's a final cry, part pleasure, part pain, before the recording cuts off.

Tears stream down my cheeks as I look up, my whole body trembling.

"Kai?" Ash asks, voice cracking with pain. I turn my gaze to see that he, too, is pale, and looks ready to vomit.

"He stole my first orgasm," I hear Kai say in a voice devoid of all emotion, my head snapping back to him. "I didn't realise that he recorded it, sick bastard."

Then he leaps up, and with a roar like a wounded animal, he launches his tablet at the fireplace. He does the same to the laptop sitting at his side, then the coffee table, lamps, and side tables, until the floor in front of us is littered with debris.

I'm full on shaking now, silent sobs wracking my body as I watch him break, jumping every time he throws something at the wall. The others sit ramrod straight, staring at him with anguish across their faces, their fists clenched, breathing laboured.

Kai stops, like all the life has left him, and chest heaving, he sinks to the floor, unheading of all the shards of glass and pieces of wood that must be cutting into him. I lurch forward, as if to go to him, but Loki stops me, holding me to him as I struggle.

"He's hurting, Loki," I beg, pleading with him to let me go. I still as Kai begins to talk.

"The first time, it was the day that we buried my parents," he begins, looking at his trembling hands. "That night, he came into my room, climbing into bed with me, and—and what I thought was meant to be comfort, turned into something, sick and twisted. I was ten years old." He gives a sharp laugh, and I'm not the only one who flinches at the sound as it cuts into our hearts, leaving us bleeding. "He visited me every night from that night, mostly touching himself, then moving on to touch me. That recording was, I think, the first time I came, his—his hand wrapped around my dick. I was thirteen."

My breath stutters in my chest, horror leaving an acidic taste in my mouth at his words. The boys curse around me, but my eyes are fixed on Kai's bowed head, his limp hands.

"By my fifteenth birthday I was obviously too old for his tastes, probably helped that I'd been training hard, so he could no longer force himself onto me."

He looks up then, straight at me, his eyes those of a broken creature pleading for the pain to stop. My lip trembles, my heart racing as he speaks again.

"But he was right, you know. If I didn't like it, why did I keep getting hard? Why did I come?"

And this time, Loki can't stop me as I tear out of his grasp, uncaring of the pain in my feet as the sharp broken pieces of furniture pierce through my fluffy socks. I drop to my knees in front of him, useless tears coursing down my cheeks as I reach out to touch him, stopping short when I realise that he might not want to be touched.

"Can I touch you, please, my love?" I ask in a shaking voice, thick with sorrow.

"You want to touch me? After hearing that?" he questions, and this time my soul fractures into a thousand tiny pieces, scattering amongst the broken things that lay around us.

"I will always want you, Kai Matthews. Regardless of what some prick paedophile did to you when you were a child." My voice is strong, full of anger at a world that would let this happen. At Julian for obviously knowing about it, but not stopping it. "And as for you wanting it, it was clear as day that you didn't, Kai. That man took what was not freely given, and none of it was your fault, you hear me? None of it."

His lip trembles, tears tracking down his flushed cheeks, his glasses gone. A deep mournful sob falls from his lips, and like a dam breaking, it's followed by another, and another. Throwing my arms around him, I pull his body into mine, his own arms wrapping tightly around my waist as his body shakes with the force of his grief, his head buried in the crook of my neck.

My own vision is blurry as I look up to see Ash on his feet, tears falling down his own cheeks as he gazes at his friend, heartbroken. He comes towards us, wrapping his arms around Kai, who just cries harder. I feel Loki come up behind me, and I look as he kneels, his face wet as he, too, wraps his arms around Kai and me, adding his comfort. I look up as Jax approaches, dropping to his knees in front of us, his jaw working, his eyes brimming with tears. He wraps us all in his huge arms, and we stay that way, holding tightly onto each other, as if we are the only thing stopping the others from floating away.

Eventually, Kai's sobs subside, turning to quiet hiccups, then silence. Lifting his head up, he looks into our faces each in turn, his eyes red and his face tearstained. He looks at Jax last, who takes Kai's face in his huge hands, bringing their foreheads together.

"We will bathe in his blood, brother. You will take what is owed in flesh and blood," he tells Kai fiercely, and the tension leaves Kai's body, a small smile tugging his lips.

Jax's words should chill me. They should fill me with horror and disgust. But they don't. My darkness relishes the idea of hurting the vile monster who stole from one of my soulmates. Who took a child's innocence, and caused such pain and doubt in his heart.

We will all bathe in his blood, paint the walls red with it. And as I look around at the faces of the men I love, body and soul, I see the vow etched there like carving in stone.

Kai's uncle will die.

And we shall be the ones to do it.

We all help to clean up the living room, waving off Kai's apologies. Then I run him a bubble bath, getting in with him at his insistence, and letting him hold me as the warmth of the water surrounds us. After we've gotten out, we eat a simple meal of pasta with herby tomato sauce that Loki and Ash prepare, then I head upstairs with Kai, who takes me to his room.

I realise as I walk in, that I don't think I've ever really been in here before. It's tastefully decorated in burnt umbers, reds, and browns, like leaves in autumn. He has pretty much the same furniture as all the others, with the addition of a large dark wooden cupboard.

He gets dressed for bed in a pair of navy silk pyjama bottoms, leaving his chest bare. I put on my own navy silk nightdress, unintentionally matching him. Looking up at him, I'm suddenly unsure as to what happens next. I've never slept in a bed with Kai. Never stayed the night in his arms.

He looks at me, his brow furrowed, then he sighs, pulling back the covers and climbing into bed.

"Stay with me tonight, Lilly?" he says, the end sounding like a question. I heave a sigh of relief, a smile forming on my lips as I climb into bed next to him, surrounded by his refreshing woods-after-the-rain scent as we settle down, facing one another.

"Can I play you a song?" I ask, remembering a song that I heard recently, which is perfect for all I want to say to him in this moment.

"Sure," he replies, reaching for his phone and handing it to me. I've left mine downstairs. I can't bear to look at it right now, not after that message.

I scroll through Spotify until I find what I'm after, connecting the device to the bluetooth speakers in his room, then hitting play.

Carry You by Ruelle and Fleurie starts to play as we lie there, gazing into each other's souls. My lips move with the lyrics, Kai's hand cupping my face as tears spring in his eyes. My own smart and burn, and soon the pillow beneath us is damp. I keep mouthing the lyrics, telling him that I am here and that he's not alone.

We stay that way, letting the music flow through us, going some way to heal the cuts and gashes that the past few hours have inflicted on our souls and hearts. The song finishes, and we continue to gaze at each other, Kai's hand on my cheek, mine on his bare chest, feeling his heartbeat underneath my fingertips.

My eyes go wide as there's a sudden flutter in my lower stomach.

"What?" Kai asks, his body going stiff as he sits up slightly. I'm about to reply when I feel it again, like butterflies tickling me. A smile tugs my lips up.

"I can feel our baby, Kai," I whisper, my hand leaving his chest, placing it on my stomach where I can feel the movements. I wait for another flutter, and although I feel it on the inside, my hand remains still. "Only inside, but it's moving, Kai."

The smile that lights up his face is so beautiful that angels must weep in the heavens as he practically glows.

"Can I?" he asks, lifting his own hand off my cheek. "I know I won't feel anything."

Taking his hand in mine, I place it directly above where the flutters keep happening. As his palm warms the area up, the flutter happens again, three times in quick succession.

"It knows you're here," I beam, not caring if it's bullshit as the quiver happens once more.

He smiles wide back at me, even though I know he can't feel a damn thing. We fall asleep like that, facing each other, his warm hand covering the life that's growing inside of me, smiles on our faces.

CHAPTER TWENTY-SIX

KAI

For the first time in a long time, longer than I can remember, I sleep soundly, with no night terrors to plague my dreams. Perhaps my sleep these past few months would have been more restful if I'd slept in the same bed as Lilly sooner. But she was haunted by her own night-time demons. I didn't want to add mine as well.

I wake up slowly, beautiful hazel eyes gazing at me, soft with love and acceptance. My heart tightens painfully in my chest, but it's not an unwelcome sensation.

"Good morning, Kai, love," she whispers, a smile teasing those lush lips of hers as she continues to drink me in, as I do her.

"Good morning, darling," I manage to choke out, realising that my hand is still on her stomach, over where her baby grows.

Our baby grows.

That is going to take some getting used to.

But a fierce surge of protectiveness floods my body, settling in my soul as we lie there, my hand flexing on her stomach. I will defend this innocent until my last breath if need be.

"How are you feeling?" she asks, a cute as fuck frown line appearing between her brows as she brings her hand up to cup my face in that way of hers. Shivers run over my body at her touch, as they always do.

I pause before answering, really taking stock of how I'm feeling after everything that happened last night.

"Raw," I reply with complete honesty. "But lighter, now that it's out in the open. Like a weight has been lifted." She gives me a smile so bright, I'm surprised I'm not blinded forever more.

"I'm glad you're not having to carry it alone anymore, my love," she whispers, her voice thick and the shine of tears sparkling in her eyes.

"Me too," I murmur in response, closing my eyes and rubbing my face into her hand with a sigh.

"Kai?" she asks, her voice tentative and a little unsure. I open my eyes to see her biting her lip. My morning wood twitches at the sight.

"Yes, darling?" I reply, my temperature rising as a heat enters her gaze.

"Make love to me. Please?"

Fuck.

This girl. She's something rare. Something precious. And she's asking me to make love to her as if it would be a chore?

Her cheeks heat in that adorable way of hers, and she opens her mouth as if to say something more, but I don't let her. I pounce, loving the small shriek that leaves her lips as I land on top of her, sliding my achingly hard length inside her, the noise she makes turning into a husky moan. There's no resistance, she's already lubricated. It's something I've noticed about her recently, and apparently is quite common in pregnancy. Her legs come up, wrapping around me on instinct.

"Shit…" I rasp out. "You feel incredible without a condom." And she does, her wet heat surrounding me and warming me to my very soul.

"Kai," she moans, her fingers tangling in my hair as she pulls our mouths together. She kisses me like I'm the air that she breathes, and I do the same, trying to inhale everything about her as I begin to move my hips in a slow, teasing rhythm.

My hands take hold of hers, bringing them up above her and pinning them there, our fingers intertwined as I do as she asked me. Make love to her. Normally, I'd want to, crave to, give her some pain, in order to find my own release. But something about this morning is different. I don't need it. Oh, I still undoubtedly will punish her in all kinds of delicious ways, hearing her cries of pain as I'm buried deep inside her.

But today, I just want her cries of pleasure, which she gives me with abandon as I rock my pelvis, stroking her inner walls, and sending lightning bolts across my skin at the same time.

"I love you so, so much, Lilly Darling," I growl in her ear, hitting that sweet spot just inside her, if her pussy flutters are anything to go by. "You make me a better man. You complete me, make me whole, and I'm." Thrust. "Never." Thrust. "Letting." Thrust. "You." Thrust. "Go."

Her cries grow louder, until her nails dig into the backs of my hands where I'm still holding her down, and her cunt ripples around my dick. I can feel the heat pooling in my own core, racing up my spine as I head towards the pinnacle of my release.

"Kai, oh shit, Kai!" she yells, and warm liquid coats me as she comes, her pussy clamping down hard until I'm fighting for every thrust, grunting with the effort to push through.

My movements become frenzied, our hips snapping together with loud, wet sounds as I move faster, impaling her over and over again. With an almost agonised roar, I climax, shooting my seed deep inside her with one final, hard thrust. Stars flash behind my closed eyes, my breaths panting and my whole body alight as I bask in the glow of her. Of us.

Releasing her hands, my own run through her hair as I hold her close to me and find her soft lips with my own. I kiss her deeply, our bodies joined in the most primal way.

A knock sounds on the door.

"Time to get up. I can't hold Loki back for much longer," Ash tells us, his amused voice clear through the partly opened door. "And you'll be late for class."

I smile against her lips.

"What?" she asks, her own lips curving in a smile as I pull back slightly, but not out of her. Not yet.

"It's about time Loki had to listen to someone else fuck you, while he stands there with a raging boner," I chuckle, and she laughs, her pussy clenching around me, turning my laugh into a groan. "Don't laugh, darling. Otherwise we will never leave this bed."

"Sorry," she murmurs softly, a wicked gleam in her eyes.

"No, you're not."

"Not even a little bit," she replies, trying and failing not to laugh again.

Naughty minx.

I give her a smirk, her own eyes widening as she feels me growing inside her, my hips thrusting slowly once more.

We are definitely late for class.

LILLY

I'm bone-weary as I walk with Kai and Loki back to our dorm at the end of the day. I crack what must be my hundredth yawn, both guys chuckling.

"Come on, Pretty Girl," Loki says, pulling me closer and wrapping his arm around my shoulders. "Let's get you back, and I'll run you a bubble bath, while Kai makes you some ramen."

My stomach growls, much to both boys' amusement, as Kai unlocks our door, only to come to a standstill just inside.

"Dude!" Loki hisses, pulling us to a stop just shy of bumping into Kai's back. "What the fuck?"

Kai steps aside, and my blood runs cold, then boiling hot at the beaming face of Julian Cuntish Vanderbilt, standing with Ash and Jax by our dining table.

"Ah, is that Lilly I see with you boys?" Julian enquires, just like the perfect father-in-law. His eyelid twitches as he takes note of Loki's arm slug around my shoulder, but his smile doesn't falter. "Come give your papa-to-be a hug." He spreads his arms out wide, a challenge on his face as he looks at me.

Adrenaline rushes through me, chasing away any tiredness as I step out from Loki's embrace, and walk towards him. After what he did to Jax's mum and the audio message, I can't afford to antagonise the man. But I hate him with every fibre of my being. He quickly wraps his arms around me, pulling me inappropriately close when I step up to him. I hear him take a deep inhale - *did he just fucking sniff me? Gross!*

I catch Ash's gaze, which is full of suppressed rage, his cheeks flushed, as Julian whispers into my ear, holding onto me for far too long.

"You didn't heed my warning, darling. About staying away from the other boys. And now you must all learn your lesson, naughty children." He chuckles, like he is a doting father and just doing his job.

Finally, he lets go, taking a step back, but still with that fucking Cheshire cat grin on his face. *God, I want to smack it off.* I feel sick, a mixture of adrenaline, nerves, and revulsion churning my stomach until my hands shake. Ash steps up next to me, his hand coming around my waist and pulling me into his warm body. I heave a sigh as I snuggle into him, giving no fucks what Julian thinks. Ash plants a kiss on my hair, near my ear.

"You okay, Princess?" he asks, his deep voice laced with concern. I nod.

"Yeah," I whisper, turning my head so that I'm no longer staring into the eyes of *that* man. My blood boils again at the thought of what he's done over the past week or so. Just as my tight muscles relax into Ash, Julian speaks again, obliterating any calm I possessed.

"I hear congratulations are in order, son?"

Both Ash and I snap our heads up, going utterly still as we stare at Julian. I smell vanilla and Kai's wooded scent as I feel their warmth at my back, seeing Jax come up to Ash's other side.

"How far along are you, Lilly, *Darling*?" I shudder at the way he says my last name, like I belong to him.

"Sixteen weeks," Ash replies, my tongue unable to move as panic flutters at the edges of my vision. I feel a hand brush my back, my own coming up to my stomach, in an instinctive act of protection.

"Wonderful!" Julian calls. His smile grows wider, sending shivers over my skin, the hairs at my nape standing on end. It gets a hard edge to it, cutting like a knife. "Although, I do hope that it is yours, boy. I won't tolerate a bastard in the family."

My breath stutters in my chest, my stomach dropping at his words.

"It is," Ash says, standing a little taller, straighter. I look at him to see that he has transformed into the Ice Knight, something he does whenever Julian is around.

"Well, we can always get a paternity test when the baby is born, so not to worry," Julian informs us, like it's a foregone conclusion. Ash's hand tightens on my waist, reassuring me enough that I can take a deep inhale.

A knock sounds at the door, my brows dropping.

"Ah, that'll be Erica. Let her in, Loki," Julian says in a cheery voice.

Loki does as he's bid, and I turn to see a young woman with short buzzed hair walk in, pulling a small suitcase along behind her.

"Mr. Vanderbilt," she greets Julian, a small forced smile on her face. It's almost like she doesn't like him. *Interesting.*

"Erica. So pleased that you could make it on such short notice," Julian replies, stepping around us to air kiss her cheek. She shivers, but he doesn't seem to notice. Then he turns to me. "Erica will be your wedding planner, my dear."

My eyes go wide.

"My...wedding planner?" I question, my hands dropping from my stomach and finding Ash's hand waiting, our fingers intertwining.

"Of course." Julian is back to beaming again. "With your wonderful news, we'll need to speed things up so that you're married to Asher before you start to show fully." He chuckles again like the doting father that he is not. "And with your uncle not giving his permission for your nuptials to go ahead, I think May twenty-first would be a good date. Don't you?"

"But that's..." I trail off.

"Your birthday, yes. What a lovely way to spend the day," he says, his gaze open and oh so sincere. "It doesn't give us a great deal of time for planning, just over eight weeks, and to send invites, etcetera, but I'm sure with Erica's help, we'll manage."

I stare at him, unmoving and in shock. Ash's grip tightens, his fingers rubbing over my knuckles in a soothing gesture.

I'm getting married on my nineteenth birthday. *Shit.*

"Well, I shall leave you to it. Whatever she wants, Erica. No expense spared," he says, pausing beside me to drop a kiss on my cheek. His lips linger for a fraction of a second too long, his fingertips brushing my stomach. "Just think, you could have made me a father again instead of a grandpa," he whispers in my ear, so quietly that I know the guys don't hear.

Bile rises in my throat as he steps away, tears springing into my eyes as I stare straight ahead. I don't move as he leaves, my grip tight on Ash's hand. The door shuts with a loud bang, breaking me from the trance that Julian left me in.

"Excuse me," I rush out, bolting to the bathroom and slamming the door behind me as I throw myself down on my knees, just managing to get my head over the toilet bowl in time, as vomit spills from my lips.

Gentle hands hold my hair back as I retch and cough, a cool cloth placed on my forehead and a glass of water pressed into my hand when I sit back on my heels, my eyes closed.

"What did he say to you, Princess?" Ash asks, stroking my hair back from my sweaty face.

I look into his face, his grey eyes swirling with concern. It takes me a couple of tries before the words will come.

"That he could have been the f-father of my baby, instead of its grandpa," I tell him in a trembling voice, tears spilling from my eyes.

A curse sounds from my left, and I turn my head in time to see Loki punch the mirror, shattering it, shards of glass flying across the room.

"That fucking perverted cunt!" Loki roars, his chest heaving. I leap up, feeling a wave of dizziness that I ignore as I rush towards him, my shoes crunching over the glass.

"Hey, it's okay, my love," I tell him softly, taking his now bleeding hand in mine and tutting.

"None of this is fucking okay, Pretty Girl," he whispers back, placing his forehead against my own. "None of it."

"It will be soon, brother," Ash says, his tone serious as he walks towards us, placing a hand on Loki's shoulder. "They will hurt for what they have done to us, and we'll be the ones watching them bleed. Before the baby is born."

The boys exchange an intense look, Loki nodding as they seal the vow between them.

My eyes drift down to Loki's bleeding hand, watching the blood drip onto the shards of glass at our feet, and a shiver runs through me. There will be more bloodshed before this is over.

I just wonder how much of it will be ours.

CHAPTER TWENTY-SEVEN

LILLY

The meeting with Erica wasn't that bad. In fact, it was actually kind of fun, once I got into the swing of it. After all, what girl doesn't dream of planning her wedding to one of the loves of her life?

Ash basically lets me decide everything, not batting an eyelid when I say that I'd like it outside, with the mountains as our backdrop and a party in the woods afterwards. And he just smirked when Erica asked about what colour theme we'd like, telling her that it would be rainbow themed before I'd even opened my mouth.

Could I love him any more?

We managed to get most of the details down, from the flowers, to the food and music, and she left, telling me that she'd made an appointment with the wedding dress shop in town for me this Saturday.

Two days' time.

My head spins with how fast things are moving, how much my life is changing in such a short space of time.

Friday morning rolls around, and as we leave the dorm, there's something in the air. I can't pinpoint it exactly. It's a feeling of foreboding that sticks to me like tar, leaving my heart rate up and my palms sweaty as we walk down the central stairs and into the main hall.

I see Willow rush up to us, her bush baby eyes wider than usual and her face tight. Her gaze briefly flicks to Loki at my side, before coming back to me, sympathy in her eyes.

"Have you seen?" she asks, holding her Academy iPad to her chest.

"Seen what, Willow?" I ask, my throat thick as her mouth turns down. My heart beats painfully in my chest.

"I'm so sorry, Loki," she replies, my brows dropping as she holds out the iPad and starts playing a video.

It takes a moment for my eyes to make sense of what is on the screen, but when they do, they must go as wide as Willow's.

"Is that...*Clarissa?*" I whisper, horrified as I watch a young, naked Loki, underneath an equally naked Clarissa, who's writhing on top of him. The sounds she's making are those of a cheap pornstar, and bile fills my throat when I realise just how young Loki looks. Maybe he's thirteen at the most. *What is wrong with these fucking people?*

I tear my gaze away to look up at him. His jaw is clenched so tightly, I can hear his teeth grinding together, his cheeks mottled, his whole body tight. I reach out to touch his rock solid arm, but he flinches away at the contact, like it burns him. My eyes sting at the rejection, even though I know he doesn't mean it.

"How many are there?" he asks through gritted teeth, not taking his eyes off that damn video.

"Um, I dunno," Willow answers, cringing slightly. "Maybe twenty or so. But I've not watched them."

My heart sinks.

"Loki..." I start, reaching out again, but he takes a step back.

"Just...leave me alone, Lilly," he replies, his hands shaking.

"Leave me the fuck alone." Then he turns and storms back towards our dorm, his body tight and practically vibrating with rage.

Tears spring to my eyes as I watch him go, and I rub my chest with the pain suddenly there.

"Fucking Julian! This has his stench all over it," Ash snarls, watching Loki disappear. "Kai, can you take this shit down?"

"On it," Kai replies, his own iPad already out as he furiously taps at the screen.

"Good," Ash says, turning to look at me. "Go to him, Princess. And you, Kai. He needs you both." He strokes the side of my face, brushing away a stray tear that falls.

"When will it stop, Ash? Why would Julian share this?" I ask, begging him for answers that he probably doesn't have.

"To hurt us, discredit us. Show us that we are nothing compared to him and the board. Take your pick, Princess," he tells me, pulling me into him and surrounding me with his warmth. Kissing me on the top of my head, he lets go, encouraging Kai and I to go back to the dorm. "I'll explain to your teachers, don't worry."

I flash Willow a grateful smile, getting a sympathetic one back. I really must organise some time with her soon. Talk about the world's worst friend.

We hurry to the dorm, Kai finishing his task just as we open the door to devastation. I gaze with bated breath at the mess that lies in front of us. The new things that we'd just bought, replacing the stuff that Kai had broken, are all lying in pieces on the floor. Feathers float around us from the torn sofa cushions, as *Bad Child* by the Tones and I fills the air with its melancholy beats. My heart breaks for this beautiful boy, who only ever wanted love and affection, but instead was given neglect and abuse.

I hear a whimper, and my gaze snaps around to see Loki, sitting on the bottom step of the spiral staircase, his head in his hands. I approach slowly, cautiously, as you would a wounded animal, Kai behind me.

"Loki, my love?" I say softly, my soul hurting as he slowly brings his head up to look at me. His eyes are red, tears glittering on his auburn lashes, the emerald jewels dull and shattered.

"I was fucking thirteen when she came into my room, sent by my asshole father to 'turn me into a man'," he tells me woodenly, not breaking my gaze. My heart feels like it's a lead weight in my chest, falling to the pit of my stomach as he tells me his awful story.

"Oh, Loki," I breathe, unbidden tears falling from my eyes.

"I was young, stupid, and excited by the free pussy. The first time I was shit, it lasted less than three minutes." He gives a hard laugh that cuts me badly. "But she kept coming back, fucking me, letting me fuck her. Teaching me all about a woman's body."

He runs his hands through his hair, and my soul aches for him. He was so young, and yes, he may have enjoyed it physically, but she was still a predator. And his father...I knew something was wrong with that cunttrollop.

"She became possessive. Wouldn't let me see other girls. Driving any away that I brought home. It took me two years to get out from under her thumb. I'd bulked up a bit by then from our training, so I used that to scare her into leaving me alone. It's not something I'm proud of."

I rush to him as he hangs his head. Dropping to my knees in front of him, ignoring the sharp pain, and taking his face in my hands.

"Loki, she deserved everything she got. She was a predator, regardless if your father was the one to start it." I force him to look at me, to see that I'm not disgusted. That I don't love him any less for his past.

"We told you at the time, dude," Kai says, crouching down next to me, placing a hand on Loki's knee. "She's a grade A cunt."

Loki huffs out a laugh, looking from me to Kai.

"Yeah. I just...feel dirty, you know?" he confesses, his voice cracking as moisture fills his eyes. My heart shatters for him. He turns to Kai. "Kai, please."

My brow furrows in confusion as I turn to look at Kai, who's gone stiff.

"You don't need to be punished, Loki. You've done nothing wrong," he tells the other boy gently, his hand tightening on Loki's knee.

"I-I know…I just need…" Loki stutters, and I jump in, unable to bear the broken look in his eyes.

"What do you need, my love?" I ask gently, his gaze coming back to me.

"Pain."

My heart stutters as his emerald eyes bore into me, digging deep, pleading. I lick my bottom lip.

"Please, sir," I say, keeping hold of Loki's gaze, which widens slightly. Kai takes in a sharp inhale, and I know that his nostrils are flared, a raging heat in his eyes, even though I can't see him.

Suddenly, Loki's gaze is ripped away from mine, a fist in his hair, pulling hard enough that he winces as Kai jerks his head to the side.

"You do exactly as I say, understood?" Kai's voice is hard, his arm corded as he holds Loki's head in place.

"Yes, sir," Loki breathes, and my pussy flutters, a shiver cascading over me at his assent. I know some might say it's fucked up, but sex heals us, we heal each other with our touches. Both pleasant and painful.

"Safeword?" Kai asks, not letting go, his eyes roving Loki's face with a banked heat in the amber depths.

"Eggplant," Loki responds, not missing a beat, and a slight smirk tilts his lips upwards. My own lift in response. *Trust Loki.*

Kai's lips twitch, too, before he lowers them to hover just over Loki's, making my breath hitch. Loki's Adam's apple bobs, and he swallows hard, his head still pulled back and held captive by Kai.

"Good," Kai whispers, slamming his lips onto Loki's in a fierce kiss that sends shockwaves to my centre.

They kiss each other hard, Kai clearly dominating as he forces his tongue in Loki's mouth. My core floods with heat, my thighs trying to rub together as I watch them, lips locked and eyes closed. A low growl sounds in Kai's throat, a groan in Loki's, as Kai nips Loki's bottom lip, hard enough that a bead of blood drips down Loki's chin as Kai pulls away.

"You sure?" Kai asks, voice husky, chest heaving. "I'm not holding back anymore, Loki."

"Fuck, yes," Loki whispers, taking hold of Kai's hand, the one not still tangled in his hair, and bringing it to his bulging jeans. "I'm sure."

Kai's breath stutters as his hand makes contact, sliding his palm over Loki's clearly hard length. *Fuck me, it's gotten hot in here.* Loki groans, thrusting his hips into Kai's palm, who smiles and tuts. Kai turns to me, still gripping Loki's hair.

"And you, Lilly? Are you all in?" he asks, a slight look of uncertainty entering both boys' eyes.

"Fuck, yes!" I gasp out, my voice all kinds of husky and breathy after that show. "I'm all about the MM."

Kai looks adorably confused, until Loki whispers something about 'fucking romance tropes'. Shaking his head, Kai finally releases Loki's hair, stroking the side of his face in a tender gesture that has my heart melting. He takes a deep breath, closing his eyes, and when he opens them a moment later, Kai the Dom is back.

"Upstairs, my room, naked," he orders, standing up. "Now."

Loki and I get to our feet, rushing up the stairs and into Kai's room, panting with huge smiles on our faces. Loki grabs me, pulling me in for a blistering kiss as we strip each other in record time. He releases me with a wink, just as Kai walks in, shirtless, wearing only his navy chinos and glasses, his feet bare. We turn to face him.

"Good, pets," he praises, and I notice Loki's dick bobs as my nipples harden at the nickname.

Kai leaves us standing facing him as he walks over to the window, pulling the drapes closed, ensconcing us in darkness. A lamp flickers on, casting its warm glow over the room. Finally, music sounds, *Renegade (Slowed + Reverb)* by Aaryn Shah playing softly in the background, the sensual beat and lyrics thrumming through me.

Kai comes back into view, walking over to the large cupboard and opening it using a small key. After rummaging inside, he turns around, a pair of black padded leather cuffs slung around his neck by a gold chain, and holding a vibrating butt plug in one hand and a black play wand in the other. I can't suppress the smile that draws the corners of my lips up. Kai sees, turning a positively feral grin on me, which makes my smile falter.

"I got you a new toy," he says, voice low and suggestive, caressing my body with his words. "You can use it as you watch us," he tells me, stalking over to me and pressing the buttons, a low buzzing sound filling the room.

He places it against my clit, and I cry out, my knees threatening to buckle as waves of the most intense pleasure I've ever felt hit me with the force of a tsunami. A dark chuckle leaves him as he abruptly takes it away.

"But you aren't allowed to come until I tell you to."

A gasp leaves my lips, my eyes going wide as I look into his merciless face. He arches an eyebrow.

"Y-yes, sir," I reply in a murmur, heart pounding.

"Isn't she such a good girl, Loki?" Kai asks, stroking my face, then handing me the still vibrating wand.

"Yes," Loki replies, and I look at him to see his eyes ablaze with emerald fire.

"Yes, what, Pet?" Kai asks, his tone hard, and my head whips back to him.

"Yes, sir," Loki rasps out, and fuck me, if I don't drip a little at that.

"On the bed, darling," Kai orders, and I immediately obey, my heart pounding as I settle myself against his pillows. "The wand, use it on your clit."

A small whimper leaves my lips as I bring it in between my legs, the vibrations immediately setting all my nerves alight. *Fuck.*

"Face Lilly, Pet. Hands on the bed," Kai's low, slightly strained voice sounds behind Loki. Loki does as ordered, and I bite my lip at the drop of precum that glints on his tip, making his piercing glisten.

Loki swallows hard at the sight of me, spread eagled and pleasuring myself.

"Shit," he whispers, earning a sharp smack on his arse from Kai. Loki hisses, but not just in pain.

"I didn't say you could speak. Do not talk unless spoken to directly," Kai admonishes.

He takes something out of his pocket, and I hear the opening of a cap, followed by the squirt of liquid. Loki goes to turn round, but Kai forces him down further with a hand between his shoulder blades, pressing him into the bed as he seems to push something into Loki.

A deep, slightly pained groan leaves Loki's plush lips, his eyes closing in ecstasy.

"Do you feel the vibrations, Pet?" Kai asks in a husky voice, stroking Loki's arse with his palm.

"Yes, sir," Loki moans out, moving his hips against the bed, clearly seeking some relief. Another crack lands on his other arse cheek, making him groan again.

"Same rule applies to you, Pet. No coming until I say," Kai commands.

I taste copper as I bite my lip again, trying to ignore the climax that wants to tear through me. I hear Kai's dark chuckle, and look up to see his heated gaze on me.

"Do you like your new toy, darling," he asks me with a smug smirk.

"Y-yes, sir," I reply in a strained voice. "Thank you, sir."

His hands clench into fists, clearly liking the gratitude.

"Good. Stand up, Pet," he orders Loki, who obeys with a groan.

His dick is so hard it looks almost painful, and he has to use his arms to help him up. Kai strokes his palm down Loki's arm, making him shiver. When he reaches his wrist, he takes one cuff, buckling it on, then unclasping the chain that secures it to the other. Reaching up to the top corner of his four poster bed, Kai unhooks another chain, fixing it onto Loki's cuff so that Loki's arm is pulled up tight. Kai repeats this process with the other wrist, until Loki is standing with his arms spread wide above his head, his muscles corded. Although I can't see, it looks like he is on his tiptoes.

"Did I say you could stop?" Kai's sharp voice asks, my hand immediately resuming its tortuous task with the wand, electric ripples running through me.

"Sorry, sir," I mumble, shivering as the exquisite pleasure begins again.

I watch as Kai walks back over to the cupboard, taking something from the back. I gasp when he turns round and I see he's holding a beautiful wood handled leather flogger. The handle is carved and made from a stunning honey- coloured wood. Each leather strand that hangs from it is braided, with a small tab of leather on the end.

The song changes to *Sacrifice*, Black Atlass & Jessie Reyez, the beat pulsing through me, adding to the vibrations of the wand, and I groan, panting in order to hold off the pleasure.

Kai smiles at me, a grin full of promise, as he stalks towards Loki. Shadows play across his face as he walks, flickers of the demon inside of him coming to the surface. My gaze flicks to Loki, and my breath hitches as he watches me with hungry eyes.

Kai steps up behind him, taking the flogger and trailing it over Loki's back, then up over his shoulder, and across his chest. I watch enraptured as Loki's eyes flutter closed, a moan falling from his plump lips.

"Do you know what this is, darling?" Kai asks me, his honey gaze suddenly on mine.

"A flogger," I whisper, a small moan sounding in my throat as I hit a particularly sweet spot, my legs trembling.

"Close, it's a cat-o-nine tails. A leather one, and one of Loki's favourites, isn't it, Pet?" *God, I love it when he calls him that.*

"Yes, sir," Loki moans, opening lust filled eyes as he looks at me. I'm so fucking close I can feel the temptation to fall into bliss, my nerves on fire as the wand works its magic.

"Move closer to him, darling," Kai orders, watching as I scoot down the bed so that my toes brush Loki's thighs. "Good girl. I'm going to hit you five times with this, Pet," he tells Loki, caressing his back once more with the cat-o-nine tails. "Then, I'm going to wrap my hand around that hard, aching dick of yours, and jerk you off until I order you to come all over Lilly." Both Loki and I groan at that visual. "Count with me, darling."

Kai takes a step back, and I watch with wide eyes as he lifts his arm up, then brings it sharply down with a flick of his wrist. Loki's body jerks, a low moan escaping his lips when the strikes hit. My breathing speeds up, my pussy pulsing as I work the wand against me.

"One," Kai says.

"One," I breathe, locking eyes with Loki when he opens them and stares at me. There's pain in there, but also relief, pleasure, and lust all rolled into one intense gaze, that's hyper focused on me. His body jerks again, the sound of leather hitting flesh cutting through the air.

"Two."

"Two," I repeat, my voice barely above a pleasure-pained whisper. Lightning shoots across me, originating in my clit. I don't know how much longer I can last without disobeying Kai. Loki's body moves again, sagging a little in his restraints, before jerking again.

"Three."

"Three," I moan, Loki's heated gaze turning me on like nothing else. Another full body twitch as a hit lands.

"Four." Kai's voice is strained now, but I can't look away from Loki to see whether it's due to exertion, or passion.

"Four," I murmur, swirling that damn wand around my clit to try and give myself a breather.

"Back on your clit, darling," Kai commands, and tears sting my eyes as I comply.

It feels so damn good, it's just too much. Loki's whole body swings with Kai's next strike, the chains creaking with the force of it. Loki throws his head back, anguished rapture on his face as more precum leaks from his cock.

"Five," Kai pants, the thunk of the cat-o-nine tails hitting the floor sounding in my chest.

"Five," I repeat, gasping as Kai undoes his chinos, pulling them and his pants down to let his hard dick spring free.

Stepping out of them, he steps up right behind Loki, whose moans echo mine as Kai's hand glides down his sweat slicked chest and abs, wrapping around his hard member in a tight grip. Loki's hips jerk, his head falling back onto Kai's shoulder, and fuck me if that sight isn't burned onto my retinas for all time, my pussy clenching as I watch them.

"Did you like that, Pet?" Kai rasps out, licking the shell of Loki's ear.

"Yes, fuck, yes, sir," Loki breathes, hissing when Kai pumps his hand up and then back down.

"Such a dirty mouth, Pet," Kai chides, moving his hand in a slow and steady rhythm up and down Loki's cock. "Next time I will have to fill it with my cock to keep those naughty words in." Loki and I groan at the same time, the visuals of Kai's words making my empty cunt pulse and flicker. "But today, I'll make do with coming all over your back, as you come all over Lilly."

Again we moan in unison, and I watch Kai's grin turn feral. He starts pumping harder, his other hand clearly gripping his own dick as his arm moves in sync with the one playing with Loki. *Ambidextrous bastard.*

"Look at her, Loki. Look at our darling girl," Kai orders, and Loki tips his head up, hooded eyes meeting my own.

My own hand moves the wand faster, in time with Kai's, and I can feel the burn of my orgasm threatening to consume me, the fingers of my other hand digging into the sheets.

"Please, sir," I cry quietly. "Please, please, please."

Kai's lip hooks up, teeth gritted, sweat beading his brow as he moves both arms faster. Loki bares his own teeth, hissing breaths escaping him as he holds his own climax back.

"Just a little longer," Kai rasps out, his own hips bucking in time with Loki's. He's close. I can see it in the tightness of his jaw.

"I-I can't!" I moan, fire licking my heels as my whole body tries to light up. "Sir, Kai, love, please!"

"Now!" Kai roars, and we all let go, exploding into fragments of ourselves as we climax.

I watch as Loki spills his seed all over me, with such force that some lands in my hair, but I don't give any shits as I burn and burn with my own orgasm, screaming my pleasure. I feel my release pour from me, soaking my hand, my inner thighs, and the bed beneath me. I hear Kai grunt out his own climax, and just manage to open my eyes to see him bite Loki's shoulder as he comes.

Slumping back, I lie there, eyes closed, panting, sweat and cum covered, as I fall back into my own body, which tingles from the top of my head right down to the tips of my toes. My arms are outstretched, the wand still vibrating in my palm, but I couldn't move even if I wanted to.

There's the clink of a chain, then another, and a warm solid weight falls gently on top of me, settling between my spread thighs. Lush lips find mine, Loki's tongue sliding into my mouth as he kisses me with languorous strokes. I manage to kiss him back, gasping into his mouth as his hips start to move, and I feel him getting hard again.

"Loki, no, I can't..." I trail off with a moan, and he slides inside of me, lighting me up once more when he begins to slowly gyrate.

"Blame Kai," he murmurs against my lips. "He forgot to take the butt plug out."

Church by Chase Atlantic begins to play, Mitchel Cave's sensual voice stroking my overheated skin. I shudder as Loki starts working me up again, my body so sensitive that it almost hurts.

"Naughty pets," I hear Kai chuckle, turning my head to the side to see that he's standing next to the bed, his hard dick in his hand, glistening with lube. *What the fuck are these boys eating to keep getting hard like this?!* "Flip her over so she's on top," he commands, and before I know what's happening, Loki rolls us so I'm on top, my knees braced either side of his hips. Somehow, he's still inside me.

I moan low as the new position allows him to go deeper, my pussy twitching and pulsing around his hardness. I feel the bed dip behind me, a hand running down the length of my spine, making my back arch.

"My beautiful darling," Kai coos, his hand moving down until it reaches the place where Loki and I are joined.

A stuttering gasp falls from my lips as his fingers push inside me, hearing Loki groan a curse at the same time.

"Such a good girl, isn't she?" Kai praises, his voice deep and satisfied sounding.

"Such a good girl," Loki rasps out underneath me. My head rests on his shoulder, my nose tucked into his neck, inhaling great lungfuls of his vanilla scent, mixed in with the musk of sex.

"Loki," I moan as his hands pull my arse cheeks apart, opening me up even more. Kai's fingers leave my cunt, to be replaced by the top of his hard dick. "Kai! It won't…"

"Shhhh, darling. You can take both of us in that sweet pussy of yours," he grits out as he slowly pushes forward, one hand gripping my hip.

The stretch burns, tears springing to my eyes as he continues to thrust forward. Neither guy is lacking in the girth department, and it feels as though I'm being stretched to breaking point. I wriggle, my body trying to escape, but Loki holds me firmly, Kai's fingers digging into my soft flesh hard enough to bruise.

"Please, it hurts," I cry, but that's a lie. Yes, it does hurt, but it also feels incredible having both of them inside my cunt, and in amongst the pain is a tendril of pleasure.

"Just a little more, darling, that's it, breathe through it," Kai grits out, grunting as he thrusts one final time, his hips hitting my arse. "Fuck."

My whole body trembles, sweat coating my skin as we lie there, both boys deep inside my pussy.

"Shit, dude! I can feel your metal," Loki groans, his hands flexing on my arse. I shudder at the visual, both guys groaning as my cunt flutters around them. My hands grasp Loki's shoulders, my nails digging in as I adjust to them.

"Play with her clit, Pet," Kai orders, holding still inside me as Loki lets go of one arse cheek, wriggling his hand between us.

I cry out as his fingers make contact with my poor, engorged clit, electric fire racing across my skin when he starts rubbing it. Kai starts moving, making Loki's fingers falter as he starts to withdraw, only to slam back in.

I let out a choked sound as sparks fly through me, biting down on Loki's neck until I taste copper as the pleasure-pain rushes through me. Loki begins to pull out as soon as Kai's deep inside me, incoherent noises sounding in my throat as they find an alternating rhythm, not giving me time to breathe between thrusts.

"You take us so beautifully, Pretty Girl," Loki praises, his voice harsh and rough.

"Tell me what you can feel," I beg, my own voice sounding broken and raspy, shivers taking over my body as they thoroughly use me.

"I can feel your warm wet walls clamping and fluttering around my hard dick," Loki starts, and my inner walls clench at his dirty talk. "I can feel Kai's piercing rubbing against me, and fuck me, Pretty Girl. I get why you scream so much when he's inside you." He lets out a pained chuckle as Kai thrusts harder, eliciting a sharp gasp from my own lips.

"Let's make our darling come, Pet," Kai chokes out, clearly close to release. "Open your eyes, darling."

I do as he orders, watching as his face comes into view when he lowers himself down, his weight pushing me flush onto Loki. My breath hitches when his lips hover over Loki's, a sinful smile on them. His tongue darts out, licking Loki's lower lip before he presses down in a blistering kiss.

Loki pinches my clit hard, and I'm gone. My whole body flushes with fire, followed by electricity, as I come so hard I black out, unable to take a full breath. My whole body shakes uncontrollably, and I scream as I'm consumed by pleasure. The boys pick up speed, thrusting harder and faster as they chase their own releases, climaxing one after the other with deafening roars.

I come back to the world of the non-orgasmic panting, my poor abused pussy already aching and sore. I whimper as Kai pulls out, flopping next to us, his own body covered in a sheen of sweat, his chest heaving. Loki slips out of me at the same time, a moan leaving my lips, but he continues to hold me to him, my body moving up and down with his deep inhales.

"You are incredible, baby. Fucking incredible," he whispers, stroking a shaking hand over my damp hair, kissing my head.

"So incredible, darling," Kai repeats, breathless as he opens his eyes and locks gazes with me. His hand finds mine, our fingers intertwining as we lie there.

Warmth suffuses my whole being at their words and touch, sinking into Loki's body as I bask in the afterglow of our lovemaking, counting my lucky stars as I often do and thanking whatever gods that exist that we found each other.

CHAPTER TWENTY-EIGHT

LILLY

The next morning I wake up in between Loki and Kai, my pussy sore but my heart full.

"Morning, darling," Kai whispers, his amber eyes gazing into mine as he reaches out to stroke down the side of my face.

"Good morning, my love," I beam back at him, feeling Loki stir behind me.

"Morning," Loki echos, his voice gruff and husky as he pulls me close to him. His hand reaches around, stroking my stomach. I feel those flutters again, tickling my insides.

A knock sounds at the door.

"Willow is waiting downstairs, Baby Girl," Jax says, opening the door and finding me nestled in amongst his friends. His lips quirk up in a smile. "Something about a wedding dress appointment?"

"Oh shit!" I exclaim, scrambling to get out from between the boys. "I'd completely forgotten about that!"

Yesterday I'd messaged Willow, asking if she would come with me today to look at wedding dresses. She jumped at the chance, so I rush around Loki's room, where we all stayed last night, grabbing my clothes and getting dressed. I had a bubble bath before bed, so I still feel fairly fresh, and frankly don't have the time to shower now.

"Catch you guys later," I rush over, kissing first Kai, then Loki. "Don't do anything I wouldn't do." I wink at them, both chuckling in response.

I'm only teasing them. We spoke about the new development in their relationship yesterday, and they both decided that they enjoy each other sexually, but would find it weird if I wasn't there too. I did assure them that if they wanted to play without me that was okay, but they just looked at each other, and shrugged, again saying they would rather I was there. I'm not going to complain, it's like having my own male on male porn show with front row seats. *Hot as fuck!*

I kiss Jax when I reach the bottom of the stairs, grabbing my thermos and a homemade granola bar that he holds out for me.

"The car is waiting for you girls," he tells me, Ash being with his parents again this weekend. I hate that he has to keep going there, especially with what I know about and have experienced firsthand with Julian.

"Morning, babe," Willow says, laughing at my no doubt flustered appearance. "I bet those boys kept you so busy with the D that you forgot. Tell me I'm wrong!" she laughs as my face goes red, remembering what happened yesterday.

"Something like that," I chuckle back, grabbing my phone and purse as we head out of the door.

"I need all the deets, like yesterday!" she begs, linking her arm through mine as we exit the front doors to find a limo waiting for us. *Nice touch, Jax.* "My love life is shit, nonexistent at best."

She huffs, and it's my turn to laugh. I know that she's waiting for the right person to lose her V card to, so she isn't actually that desperate to jump into bed with anyone.

I look up as the driver gets out, coming round our side to open the door for us. A blush steals across my cheeks as I meet the blue eyes of Tom, the driver that took Loki and I to the airport and...yeah. Willow gets in, but my steps falter as he continues to stare at me. Not in a creepy way, but there's an intensity to his gaze that makes me pause.

"Hello, Tom," I greet him, and he blinks as if from a daydream. "Can I, uh, help you with something?"

"Apologies, Miss Darling. You just remind me of someone I used to know," he replies, shaking his head and giving me a small smile. "Congratulations on your engagement."

"Uh, thanks," I say, ducking my head as I climb in the car, blinking that strange encounter from my mind.

As we make our way into town, I give her a rundown of what happened after we caught up with Loki, her eyebrows getting higher with each word.

"Fuck me," she sighs, fanning her face. "Talk about hashtag-livingthedream."

I smile, even though my face is hot and I know that I'm blushing redder than a whore in church. She's right, though, I am living the dream.

The car comes to a stop, and I look out the window to see that we're outside a very up-market-looking bridal shop. It also has a quaint feel about it, being in one of the older buildings, so it doesn't feel sterile like some I've seen and expected this to be.

A bell above the door tinkles as we open it, and a woman in her late forties approaches us, a kind smile on her face and a tape measure around her neck.

"Welcome," she greets us, looking incredibly attractive in a grey pencil skirt, white blouse, and a red silk scarf tied around her neck. "You must be Lilly. My name is Jen, and I'll be helping you today."

"Pleased to meet you, Jen," I smile back, butterflies taking flight in my stomach now that I'm here, surrounded by a sea of white and cream lace. "This is my friend and chief bridesmaid Willow." I indicate Willow, who looks in shock back at me.

"I am?" she asks, her wide eyes a little misty.

"Of course, if you want to be, that is?" I ask, a little hesitantly.

"Abso-fucking-lutely!" she squeals, throwing her arms around me. She pulls away after a quick hug, wincing and looking over at Jen. "Sorry, mum always said I have a sailor's mouth."

Jen just laughs, holding her hand out towards a younger girl, who steps forward with a tray. On it sit two flutes of bubbling champagne.

"I've heard worse," she chuckles. "Champagne? Our secret," she says with a wink.

"Oh, um, I can't, because, um, I'm pregnant," I stutter out, her face showing no shock or judgement. A breath of relief whooshes out of me.

"Amelie, something soft for Lilly, please," she asks the younger girl, who smiles, letting Willow take a glass before heading to the back of the shop, disappearing through a door. Jen looks back at me. "So, do you have any ideas of what you'd like?"

"Well, not really, no," I chuckle, feeling another blush steal over my cheeks.

"That's absolutely fine," she says, guiding us towards a rail of dresses. "Let's start here, at the empire line ones, which will be easier for you in your condition."

She starts pulling out the most beautiful dresses I've ever seen. Lace, tulle, sparkling crystals and beads, all in shades of white, cream, and champagne, a few even in light gold and blonde. She tells us that she designs them all, and with the help of a series of seamstresses, sews them in the workroom at the back of the shop.

But gorgeous as they are, none feel quite me.

"I'm sorry," I tell her, sitting down on a plush grey velvet love seat next to Willow. "They're just not..."

"You. I know. And no need to apologise," Jen reassures me with a smile, looking me over and no doubt noticing my rainbow patterned Run and Fly dungarees. Not exactly subtle and elegant. "I wonder... Amelie," she calls, and the younger girl comes out from the back. "Bring the dress you've been working on, please."

"W-what?" Amelie asks, her eyes wide. "Really?"

"Yes, please," Jen replies, smiling kindly at her, and I admit, I like this woman. Amelie turns around, heading out the back.

She returns a few moments later, and I sit up straighter, my heart thudding as I see the spill of colour across her arm. Standing in front of me, she lets the hem drop to the floor, and I gasp, completely lost for words.

It's an empire line, like the others, with an off white beaded lace covering the shoulders, coming down to cover the bust part as well. My eyes travel down the fall of plain soft white chiffon, that starts just under the bust and ends in a train at the back, the hem decorated with a matching beaded, lace pattern as that of the top.

But the thing that makes this particular dress perfection is that it appears to have been dipped into a sunset, the colours bleeding up the skirt, finishing probably around knee height. It starts as a deep indigo at the hem, turning into violet, then purple, magenta, pink, red, orange and finally, a deep yellow.

"I think, by that look, we've found your dress," Jen says softly, and I tear my eyes away, moisture filling them as I look at her. I swallow hard.

"It's perfect," I whisper, my gaze drawn back to it, loving how the colours shift and change tone as the light falls across it.

"Let's try it on then, although, I suggest we leave any alterations until closer to the time to account for your changing shape," she tells me, ushering me into a changing room and hanging the dress on a hook by its wooden hanger.

Stripping quickly, I reach out, feeling the softness of the material before slipping it over my head. It falls around me like a cloud, as I can't tear my gaze away from my reflection in the mirror, even if the dress isn't yet done up.

I look like a bride.

It hits me then, really hits me, that I am getting married. That I'm having another man's baby, the best friend of my groom to be. What a mess. But looking into the mirror, at the bride that I will be, it suddenly feels so real.

"Are you ready, Lilly?" Jen's soft voice calls on the other side of the curtain.

"Yes," I reply, taking a final look at the woman standing in the mirror before me.

Ready as I'll ever be.

After wowing Willow and Jen at the dress shop, both declaring that the dress was perfect and 'the one', Willow and I head to the tea rooms for a late lunch. Luckily, my sickness seems to be abating somewhat, so I'm able to eat a delicious cream tea, with finger sandwiches and mini cakes.

We head back to Highgate, deciding to spend the rest of the weekend watching Netflix and chilling. Kai and Loki join us, Jax appearing some time later, sweaty and delicious looking from a workout. After showering, he joins us, too, lifting me up and sitting back down, then placing me on his lap and pulling one of the blankets over us.

"Hey," I murmur, snuggling into him as he pulls me closer, a low rumble sounding in his chest.

"Hey, Baby Girl," he replies, and I feel his words vibrate against my ear. "Did you find your dress?"

"She found the dress to end all dresses!" Willow exclaims, gesticulating and sending popcorn flying. I chuckle at her antics, so pleased that she's here with us. "It's fucking incredible."

"I'm glad you found something, baby," Jax tells me, a smile clear in his voice even though I can't see his face. "I can't wait to see you in it, even if I'm not the one putting a ring on your finger."

My heart aches, and I sit up, pushing away so that I can look into his beautiful blue eyes. The light of the TV casts them in a kaleidoscope of blues, changing from almost navy to ice. My brows drop, my lips parting as I struggle to find the right words.

"I wish..." I start, taking a deep inhale, then releasing it slowly. "I wish I could marry all of you, officially. A part of me hurts having to marry only Ash. But it also feels so right at the same time, you know?"

He reaches out, cupping my face in his huge palm, and I can't help but nestle into it.

"I know," he rumbles back. "And none of us hold that against you, we know that you'd marry all of us if you could. Sure, I'm jealous as fuck that Ash drew the lucky straw, and I can't wait to get him in the ring to take a little bit of that out on him," he adds, an evil grin pulling up the corners of his lips that makes me worry for Ash a little. "But I'll get over it. We'll get over it, Baby Girl."

I lean in, placing a gentle kiss on his lips, a sigh caressing mine as I pull away again, aware of Willow being here.

"Thank you, my love," I whisper, his nostrils flaring and his grip around me tightening at the nickname. I love all of their reactions when I use it.

He pulls me close again, his hands stroking down my back in a soothing caress that soon has my eyes closing, his heartbeat lulling me to sleep.

JAX

I hold Lilly tightly as her body grows heavy against mine, her breathing evening out as she falls asleep under my touch. I love how she's so comfortable now that she can do that. Trusting me to take care of her when she's at her most vulnerable.

I meant what I told her. I wish to God it was me she was marrying, but as long as I keep getting moments like this, I'll get over it. Especially if I can get Ash in the ring a time or two.

Willow looks over, seeing that Lilly is asleep, and quietly leaves, saying that she'll text Lilly tomorrow.

"How's Enzo?" Loki asks, careful to keep his voice low so as not to disturb Lilly. She stirs slightly, then settles back down when I keep rubbing her back.

"Good. Pleased about his wedding invite," I smile, remembering Enzo's knowing smile as he told me that he and Rosa will be there.

"Jeez, Erica works fast," Loki comments, sounding impressed. He's right to be, Ash and Lilly only gave her the list of invitees yesterday, and already she'd sent the invites by courier.

"How did training go? Did you get the fight moved?" Kai asks, the TV screen reflected in his glasses hiding his eyes.

"I'm almost back to where I was before," I tell them, feeling the ache of my muscles that I've been working hard on lately. "Enzo managed to get it postponed until May seventh, but they wouldn't do any later."

Loki whistles, and I glare at him as Lilly stirs again.

"Fourteen days before the wedding...better than the day before I guess," he comments, giving me one of his shit eating grins that tells me he's about to say something insulting. "At least the bruising will have a chance to heal a little so you don't look like shit in all the photos."

I growl, grabbing a pillow and launching it at his head. He ducks, which just makes me growl again as it flies past him.

"She'll want to come, you know that," Kai says, and I pull the girl in question tighter against me. "We won't be able to stop her."

"Fuck," Loki hisses, and I agree with him. Underground MMA fights are no place for a girl like her, especially not in her condition.

"You'll have to all keep her safe, away from the scum," I tell them, my lips twitching when Loki's jaw clenches and Kai grinds his teeth.

"Of course we will keep her safe," Loki all but snarls at me, Kai giving a sharp nod of agreement. "And if anyone so much as looks at her wrong..."

I know that my grin is as feral as both of theirs, as bloodthirsty. Some things in life are simple, at least that's what I've always thought.

If anyone goes near our girl, they won't see the sunrise.

CHAPTER TWENTY-NINE

LILLY

I wake up smiling, still surrounded by the scent of sweet lemons, the warmth of Jax at my back. I love that I no longer spend a single night alone. Some might find it suffocating, but it brings me a sense of peace to know that one or more of my guys are with me all night, keeping me safe from monsters, both imagined and real.

Heading downstairs, I'm dressed in one of Jax's huge black T-shirts, which falls off one shoulder, and a pair of soft cotton boy shorts with pictures of unicorns all over them. I'm desperate for a wee, apparently this is most definitely a pregnancy thing, but it should start to ease a little now that I'm at the four month mark.

I startle when I see Ash sitting at the table, an espresso sitting in front of him, the faint light of pre-dawn casting its watery glow across his inked torso. He looks up, and I gasp when I see his face. One eye is puffy, there's a cut on his cheek, and his lip is clearly split on the same side.

"Fuck, Ash!" I exclaim, wanting to go to him, but my bladder is legit going to burst if I don't go right now. "Shit, I'm about to piss myself. Don't move."

His deep chuckle cascades over me as I dash to the bathroom, sighing in pleasure as I sit on the loo - *pissing has never felt so bloody good before!* Flushing, I'm worrying the whole time I wash my hands. Hurrying back out, he's still sitting there, so I swing past the freezer, grabbing an ice pack and tea towel to wrap it in, before going over to him.

"Turn," I instruct, his lips twitching at the order. He complies, and I step in between his wide spread legs - *totally justified btw, he definitely needs the extra space, if you know what I mean.* "Dare I ask?"

"Julian surprised me with some extra challenges yesterday," he tells me, wincing as the ice cold wrapped pack alights against his puffy face. "Including about ten ex-Marines." *God, that man is such a ballsack cunt!*

Ash's hands come to my hips, pulling me closer. His fingers tease along my waistline, his palms resting over my now slightly rounded stomach. I seem to have 'popped' in the last couple of days, a small but definite baby bump visible.

"Oh, Ash," I sigh in a soft voice, wishing there was anything else I could say or do to help, but knowing that there isn't.

"Do you know how fucking jealous I am that it's Loki's child you're carrying, and not mine?" he asks me, rubbing my stomach. The baby kicks, but Ash doesn't react so obviously can't feel it yet.

"W-what?" I stammer, the subject change throwing me as I continue to hold the ice pack to his face.

"I've always been an asshole, Lilly. Possessive and controlling," he growls, hooking my knickers in his fingers, and drawing them down my thighs. My breath catches as his intentions become clear. He needs the distraction of my body, and I am helpless to deny him.

He lets my knickers drop to the ground, taking hold of the hem of my - Jax's - T-shirt, and lifting it over my head as he stands up. The ice pack drops to the floor with a heavy thud as it falls from my hand.

He takes a minute, studying my naked body in the dim light, his eyes caressing me, causing my nipples to peak and my breathing to quicken. An inked hand reaches out, tracing my curves, leaving a fire in its wake. He reaches the apex of my thighs, which I feel more than see with my stomach now in the way.

"Open," he commands, looking at his hand as I obey, shifting my thighs so that they are parted.

I cry out at his first touch, moisture leaking out of me as he traces a finger up and down my slit, swirling my opening and clit. I'm so responsive to these guys, and they know my body so well that it doesn't take much to bring me to the brink. He stops, leaving me panting and desperate for more.

"Turn around, hands on the table, Princess."

The cool wood soothes my hot palms as I follow his instructions, waiting. He kicks my legs wider, and a second later I feel his bulbous head pushing against my entrance. A hiss leaves my lips as he enters me, I'm still a little sore from the combination of Kai and Loki on Friday, but it soon turns to a pleasure filled moan when his piercings rub my inner walls. And the fact that his bare skin is inside me, no barriers between us, drives me wild, making me buck against him.

He pauses once he's fully seated inside me, a contented sigh sounding behind me as my nails scrape the wood of the table in pleasure. He starts to move, slowly at first, tingles racing up my spine as he gets faster, bringing me to the edge once more with his dick this time. I can feel the burn of an orgasm begin, my inner muscles fluttering around Ash's cock, begging him to keep going. Only he slows down and pauses before I can fall over into exquisite bliss.

"I'm so fucking close, Ash. Please," I pant through gritted teeth.

He reaches around, fingertips stroking over my slightly swollen stomach from behind in a loving caress.

"Next time, it'll be my fucking baby in your womb. Won't it, Princess?"

"W-what?" I question, my head spinning once more with his words. He starts leisurely pumping his dick in and out of me, quivers racing through my core, but not enough to allow me to climax. *He's fucking denying me my pleasure, the wankmonster.*

"The next baby to grow inside you will be mine, understand, Princess?" he asks, his tone condescending as fuck, as he continues teasing me with his slow strokes.

"Fuck off, Ash! It's my body, and I'll decide *if* I have another baby, and *who* the father will be," I inform him, all kinds of pissed off, and attempting to straighten up, having had enough of his jealousy.

But his hands on my hips tighten, holding me in place with a mocking laugh that should piss me off more than it does. *Jesus, I'm so fucking messed up that even his cruel laugh makes my pussy flutter.*

"That's where you're wrong, *fiancée*. This body." He squeezes my hips tighter, eliciting a squeak of protest from my lips. *Okay, it's part raw fucking pleasure too.* "This pussy." He punctuates here with a sharp thrust, and a deep groan sounds in my throat. "All of you belongs to me. I may be gracious and share with the others. But don't mistake my kindness for anything other than that." He's growling by the end of his speech and has completely stopped thrusting inside me, holding just the tip in my entrance. "So I'll tell you again. The next baby you carry, *Princess*, will. Be. Mine." He thrusts hard in between each word, reinforcing his point physically.

I'm mewling underneath him, unable to move as he holds me in a bruising grip. He's building me up to a crescendo, my orgasm fluttering at the edges of my vision. Just as the wave is about to crest, he pauses, again with just his tip inside me.

"Ash!" I scream, clawing at the table, giving no shits about scratching it to buggery as I'm beyond frustrated.

"Well?" he asks breathlessly, and I just know that he has one perfect arrogant jet black brow raised. I also know that the twatterdick won't let me come until I agree to his alpha bullshit.

"Fine! Yes!" I shout in response.

"Yes, what?" The git asks back, his tone smug.

"The next baby I have will be yours!" I screech. "Are you fucking happy now?!"

"Ecstatic," he replies, in a somewhat droll tone.

Then he thrusts so hard and fast that if he wasn't holding onto me, I would be flat on my stomach on the table. I cry out as he lets his inner animal take over and fucks me like a demon, snarling and snapping like a wild beast, the sound of his hips hitting against me, loud in the quiet.

I soon see fucking stars, screaming out his name as my whole body tightens, then liquifies with my release. He gives one final, punishing thrust, as if he's trying to impregnate me right now, finding his own climax with a deafening roar.

"Good girl," he says, voice breathy as he pats my arse like a fucking dog.

I'd snap like one, too, you know, if I hadn't just been fucked to within an inch of my life. So I just huff as he pulls out, feeling some of his cum slide out of me. He notices, a growl of what sounds like approval leaving his throat, then I feel his fingers push it back inside my abused pussy, as if he can't bear for any of his essence to leave my body.

And I know that maybe I should take him to task over his alpha bullshit. That it's a product of the time he's spent with Julian recently, that he's been moulded by Julian to crave ultimate control. It's a part of who Ash is, and I love all of him, the good and the bad, the beautiful and the ugly. It's the reason that I heave myself up onto shaky legs, turning to face him and wrapping my arms around his sweat slicked chest.

It's the reason why I kiss the side of his neck, and whisper gently in his ear.

"The next baby can be yours, my love."

His whole body shakes, his arms banding around me in a steel like grip as he buries his face into my hair, inhaling deeply and pulling me so close that it's difficult to know where I finish and he begins.

The others come down just as I step out of the shower, each placing a kiss on my damp head as I pass them on my way back upstairs to get dressed. Deciding to go with comfy, it is Sunday after all, I throw on some loose wine red harems and a new mustard yellow T-shirt that has a picture of a vintage rainbow with 'Bookish Vibes' in seventies bubble font on the front.

I pause as I catch a glimpse of myself in the mirror, turning to the side to admire my little bump. My hands come to cup my stomach, in a move that I'm sure so many women have made before me.

"You're such a MILF, Pretty Girl," Loki drawls from the doorway, and I chuckle as he walks towards me, wrapping his arms around me from behind.

He places his hands on top of mine, our fingers interlacing as we hold my stomach. I watch in the mirror as numerous emotions flit across his features, his gaze on our hands.

"I'm scared, Loki," I confess in a whisper, his eyes coming up to meet mine. "Not of giving birth really, but, shit. We're just kids, and with everything going on with Black Knight..."

His arms tighten around me.

"I swear to you, Lilly, I will never let anything happen to you. Or our child," he vows, his emerald eyes almost glowing with his conviction. "And as for the other thing, yes, we're young. And I'd be lying if I said I wasn't scared. But I know that you will make an incredible mother, you're able to love the four of us assholes." A choked laugh escapes me as tears fill my eyes. "And there are five of us, five people to love the shit out of this baby. That's all it really needs. Our love."

He pulls me closer as tears drip down my face. I'm so sad for him, for this beautiful boy who was missing the one thing he really needed growing up.

"You know, you're kind of wise sometimes, Loki," I tell him, sniffling. He turns me in his arms, wiping my face with his sleeve.

"Not just a pretty face," he tells me, winking. "Kai said we need to start carrying around tissues, you cry so often at the moment," he chuckles, causing more tears to fall even as I huff a laugh.

"Fucking hormones," I reply, making him laugh.

"Come on, baby mama." He takes me by the hand, and we start to walk out of the room. "Let's get you something to eat. Kai is making some bacon, eggs, and pancakes."

After eating a delicious breakfast/brunch, we decide to all go for a walk, as it's a gorgeous spring day. Heading out of the dorm, we make our way downstairs only to see the whole place littered with white pieces of paper.

I get a sinking feeling in my stomach, a shiver coming over my skin despite the sun streaming in through the huge windows. Highgate is nothing if not spotlessly clean, so this must be purposeful. Although, I'm still surprised that the admin staff haven't cleaned it up yet.

Loki bends down to pick up one of the papers, his face going pale as his eyes flit back and forth reading what's on the page.

"Ash..." he says in a tight voice, looking up with a haunted look in his eyes.

He hands the page to Ash while Kai and Jax reach down to grab their own copies.

"Fuck!" Jax snarls, just as Ash crumples the page in his fist, a flush creeping over his cheeks.

"What?" I ask, my heart pounding as I look at their faces, full of anger and devastation. "What is it? Tell me, please."

Kai hands me his copy, his eyes so sad behind his glasses that moisture stings my own. Looking down, my throat goes dry, my breath stilling as I read what's on the page in front of me.

It's a letter, addressed to Ash in a messy scrawl. The paper shakes the more I read, tears falling down my cheeks as Luc's final words swim before me.

Dear Ash,

I can't fight you and dad anymore. I don't want to, and I don't want what he's offering. I just want peace, so I'm taking myself out of the game. The crown is all yours.

Luc

"Oh, Ash," I gasp, looking up at him and remembering that day in front of the chapel, the beautiful voices of Pentatonix behind us as he told me about finding Luc in his room on the last day before summer, dead and covered in blood.

Anger floods my system, overriding the grief, as I realise that this is yet another of Julian's punishments. "How could he do this?!" I exclaim, my jaw tight. "You're his son, for fuck's sake! And so was Luc!" I'm so cross, my blood boils, scaling my veins and tinting my vision.

"Hey," Ash turns to me, letting the paper drop to the floor and taking mine out of my hand. "Don't get so worked up, Princess. It's not good for the baby." He takes my shaking hands in his, prising the paper out of my grip and dropping that too.

Pulling me into him, I'm engulfed by his spicy ginger scent, which calms me instantly. Wrapping my arms around him, I hold on tightly as the angry tears subside. Looking up, I see his jaw is still clenched, but his steel eyes are full of concern for me, and my heart hurts.

"I'm sorry, Ash. I'm such an arsehole for flipping out and then making you comfort me, when it should be the other way round."

He gives me a tight, almost vicious smile, with an edge of resignation to it. It sends a shiver down my spine, and I'm glad that I'm not the one he's pissed at.

"I'm used to this kind of shit, Princess. It's not the first time he's used Luc's suicide against me. And you're not an *asshole*." He gives me one of his trademark smirks, clearly making the point that I'm saying the word wrong. *Twatwaffle*. "Kai, organise a clean up crew to come in and deal with this mess. I want these gone stat."

"On it," Kai responds, his iPad in hand as he starts tapping away at the screen.

"Let's go for that walk, shall we?" Ash asks, letting me go, but tucking my hand into his arm like an old fashioned gentleman taking his lover out for a walk. You know, the lover who's pregnant with his best friend's baby, whilst his father forces an arranged marriage on the couple, not knowing that his grandchild will not be of his blood. *God, I'm living in a Mills and Boon novel!*

Despite the rocky start to our day, I soon settle with the gentle exercise, taking deep soothing breaths of fresh air as we make our way through the forest, leaving Highgate, Julian, and all the shit behind us.

We come to a break in the trees, a beautiful meadow full of delicate spring wildflowers spread out before us. I let the sun warm my face, closing my eyes as I feel its rays caress my skin.

My pocket vibrates with an incoming message, and sighing, I take it out, to see that it's from Julian.

Julian Cuntish Vanderbilt: Just a lesson for the Princess left x

Just like that, all the warmth leeches from my body, and I'm no longer able to feel the rays of the sun, even though there isn't a cloud in the sky.

"What is it, Princess?" Ash asks, brows furrowed, and I shiver at the nickname, hating that Julian just used it. I turn the screen to face him, and a curse falls from his lips as he reads the message.

"When will it stop, Ash?" I ask, my voice thick, suddenly so weary I lean heavily on him as my knees feel weak beneath me.

"When one of them dies," he tells me, a vicious gleam in his grey eyes. "And the others are rotting in jail."

I should feel revulsion.

I should feel horror.

But I don't.

I only feel a sick sense of relief at the idea of being free from the blackness that is Black Knight Corporation. Of finally being free from Julian's oppressive presence.

What sort of person have I become?

CHAPTER THIRTY

LILLY

The next week goes by pretty quietly, Erica popping over on Wednesday after classes finish, to talk table settings and finalise the menu. I have never really agreed with the idea of forcing people to sit with complete strangers, so we decide to forgo the traditional wedding seating plan, letting people choose to sit where they like.

Sheer multi coloured sari tablecloths over white ones will cover the tables, bunches of rainbow-coloured flowers in ceramic jugs sitting in the centre, along with glass jars full of fairy lights. The marquee will be lined in colourful transparent fabric, making it appear like a rainbow tent, with swags of more flowers and fairy lights decorating the edges.

We decide to have a menu that represents both Ash and I; loaded hot dogs, pulled pork, as well as British cheeses with oat crackers, and a play on boiled eggs with soldiers for dessert. The guys looked at me with confused faces when I spoke about it, until I explained that for breakfast we'd often have soft boiled eggs, the yolks still running, with buttery toast cut into slices to dip into them.

There will of course be a rainbow sponge wedding cake, covered in fluffy buttercream as well as a donut cake, each tier being a different flavour of a very well known American donut brand.

She tells me that she'll organise tasters of everything, and we set a date of next Wednesday at some place in town to try all the food and make sure it's what we want. She lets me know that almost everyone who has received an invitation via email, we thought that this would be quicker than trying to post, especially to England, has accepted, and excitement runs through me at the idea of seeing Lexi, Ryan and Mr. Grey again so soon.

Friday rolls around and I find myself once again tired but less exhausted than I was last week. Willow informs me that it's because I'm now in the 'glowing' phase of pregnancy where I look radiant, no longer need to pee all the damn time, and generally will find things a little easier. I must admit that I don't feel sick all the time, although I have banned Kai from preparing any fish dishes in the kitchen, as the smell turns my stomach.

I'm walking back to the dorms with said bush baby fairy–totally a thing–when I remembered something that I wanted her advice on.

"If someone wanted to, say, get revenge on a predatory cougar, what, theoretically, would be the best way to go about achieving it?" I bat my eyelashes at her, causing a throaty laugh to erupt from her lips.

"Hmmmm," she murmurs, a serious look coming over her face. "One could, in theory, leak video footage of said cougar to the police, reporting the abuse," she answers, an excited gleam coming into her eyes. "Oooohhh! Could you also discredit her with Julian somehow? Like, make out that she's disloyal to Black Knight?"

I pause, my head tilted to the side as I think on her suggestion.

"It would be funny to see her carted away in cuffs," I muse, liking the idea. "And you're definitely onto something with casting her in a black light with Julian..."

"Lilly," she says, interrupting my internal plotting. I look at her, pausing when she lays a hand on my arm. "I know that there's more going on here, with Julian and Black Knight, than you can tell me, and that's okay. Just know that I will help you however I can. My brother...he has connections and I will use them."

My eyes soften as I gaze at her, my hand resting on top of hers and squeezing gently.

"You are an awesome person, Willow Anderson, and one of my favourites."

But then a fissure of worry runs through me, and I bite my bottom lip. "But how would Loki feel? To be exposed so publically?"

"You could ask," she replies as we resume walking. "It probably should be him who makes the final call after all."

She's right. It definitely should be his decision. He was the one that suffered the abuse. I just hope he goes for it, as I can't help feeling that it's the closure he needs to finally see that it wasn't his fault. That she was a predator, and he an innocent.

"I'll ask now," I tell her, reaching my door and turning to face her. "Wish me luck."

"Good luck you bad bitch," she says, darting in to kiss my cheek. "I'll catch you tomorrow?"

"Abso-fucking-lutely!" I respond, chuckling as she gives me a dorky as fuck wave, before walking off down the hall to her own room.

Miraculously, she managed to snag a room all to herself, all of the dorms being full after my arrival. She claims that palms were greased, which doesn't surprise me in the least given this place, and the way money seems to talk.

Taking a deep breath to still the butterflies suddenly fluttering in my stomach, I put my key in the lock and open the heavy wooden door. Pausing in the doorway, I take a moment to admire the guys. My loves. The other parts of my soul.

Kai's in the kitchen, preparing something that makes my mouth water and my stomach grumble, as *Nothin but a Monster* by Ari Hicks plays softly in the background. Jax and Loki are sitting on one sofa, Ash on another, all clutching gaming handsets, and playing what looks like a pretty violent game if the blood and gore on the screen are anything to go by. Loki shouts at the screen as something appears to kill his avatar, Ash's lips lifting in a smirk as Loki swears at him. Jax laughs, the sound deep and low, making my nipples pebble even from here.

"You're a dirty fucking cheat, Ash!" Loki shouts, throwing his controller down in disgust, getting up and finally spotting me as he turns. "Pretty Girl!" he exclaims, leaping over the back of the sofa and rushing towards me.

He wraps me up in a breath stealing hug, like he literally didn't see me just this morning. My arms go round him anyway, inhaling the vanilla scent that smells like home.

"I missed you," he whispers in my ear, nuzzling the side of my neck, goosebumps appearing across my skin where he touches me.

"I missed you too, love," I reply, finding his mouth with my own, and losing myself in his plush lips and soft tongue. My whole body relaxes into him as he kisses me back, all of the tension I didn't know I was holding escaping out of me with a sigh.

Reluctantly, I pull away, looking into his eyes. My lower lip slips under my teeth as I try to think of the best way to broach the subject of Clarissa.

"Out with it, baby," Loki tells me, keeping his arms around me as he arches a brow.

"I've been thinking about Clarissa," I blurt out, wincing at my own bluntness. His arms stiffen, feeling like solid marble as they hold me, but he waits for me to continue. "And, uh, how we should deal with her."

His lip twitches on one side, a mischievous glint entering his gaze.

"You planning to seek revenge in my honour, baby?" he teases, some of the tension leaking out of him.

"Yes."

"So fucking hot," he moans, thrusting his hips at me, and I feel his hard length pressed against my rounded stomach.

"Loki!" I chastise, shaking my head. "Focus man!"

"Why don't you two share with the class, Princess?" Ash drawls from the sofa, and I peer round Loki to see him sitting there still, game controller on the coffee table in front of him.

I step away from Loki, taking his hand in mine as I lead him to the others, Kai having sat down as well. I let go of him, placing a kiss on first Kai's, then Jax's lips, then walking over to do the same to Ash. Only, being the Ash-hole that he is, he pulls me into his lap, grasping my face in both hands, and kissing me soundly.

As usual he dominates with his lips and tongue, obliterating everything and everyone else with his touch. My body lights up under his caress, a whimper leaving me as he pulls away with a final peck on my now swollen lips.

"Now, what have you been plotting, Princess?" he asks, sounding cool as a motherfucking cucumber, whilst I'm a hot mess.

I go to get up, but he lets go of my face, encircling me in his arms and pulling me more firmly into his lap. *Guess I'll stay here then.*

"I've been thinking about how we can deal with Clarissa," I tell them, my voice firm and upper lip curling as I say her name. *She doesn't deserve a fucking name, cum guzzling slutbucket.*

Jax growls, but not at me, at the aforementioned slutbucket. Loki stiffens again, and Kai clenches his hands into fists. Ash, unsurprisingly, remains still and unmoving underneath me.

"And what do you propose?" he questions, voice level, letting me know that he's taking what I say seriously. This is what makes him a great leader. He may be an arsehole, but he will still listen to every opinion and suggestion, weighing it and considering it.

"Well, we start by leaking the videos to the police." I watch Loki take a sharp breath, but he doesn't interrupt. "Reporting her for sex with a minor. At the same time, we 'find' evidence of her betrayal of Black Knight Corporation, and share that with Julian, ensuring that she earns his ire, getting the maximum sentence, plus total public humiliation and annihilation."

Jax whistles, Loki's brows raising to his hairline. Kai is nodding, fingers tapping out a rhythm on his thigh as if he's itching to grab his tablet and start typing.

"It'll also have the added benefit of earning Julian and the board's trust, helping to show that you are the good soldiers they've trained you to be, and so can be trusted. That way, they won't see the knife coming when you stab them in the back."

Ash's fingers tighten against my hip, one hand lifting up to my face, grasping my chin and turning me to face him.

"Loki was right, Princess," he whispers seductively, his steel grey eyes boring into mine, banked heat in their depths. "You are so fucking hot when you're plotting revenge."

"So, you like the idea?" I ask, my pulse speeding up as I stare back at him.

"I fucking love it," he tells me, a gleam in his eye and a satisfied smile on his face. "Kai."

Loki doesn't let go of my chin, gazing into my eyes as I hear Kai get up, then sit back down, the gentle tap of his fingers on his tablet sounding soon after.

"I've just transferred several lump sums to her account, under the guise of being from the CEO of Wolfgang Security," he tells us, sounding distracted. My eyebrows raise to my hairline, a chill sweeping over me at the things Kai can do all from an iPad.

"Who?" I ask, still trapped in Ash's stare.

"Our biggest competitor in the security industry," he tells me.

"Also sent some incriminating emails to her from him that I've put in her deleted folder," Kai tells us.

I place my hand on Ash's, silently asking him to release me, which he does. Turning my head, I look at Loki.

"Are you okay with this, Loki?" I ask, looking intently at his reactions to see how he's feeling.

He rubs his hand over his face, drawing his fingers through his auburn locks, my own hand itching to do the same.

"Yeah, I guess. It's about time she paid for what she did," he says, his voice getting stronger as he finishes. Kai stops tapping to place a hand on his knee and squeeze it.

"In that case, Kai, can you send that too please?" I ask, and he looks at me with a cheeky grin which makes my stomach somersault.

"You ordering me around too now, darling?" he questions, his smile getting wider as I blush. He gives me a wink, then looks back down at his tablet, his fingers flying across the screen. Minutes later, he looks back up at me, his look sombre. "Done."

"And now we wait," Ash supplies, trepidation running through me at his words.

Kai sets his tablet aside, getting up.

"Dinner's ready," he announces, heading over to the kitchen and opening the oven.

"I'll help lay the table," Loki says, giving me a small smile, then following Kai over.

Jax stands too, walking over to me and holding out his hand. Grasping it, he helps me up, and we go to take over plates and cutlery to the table, Ash bringing glasses and a jug of iced tea. Loki helps Kai carry Asian baked chicken, veggies, and steaming fragrant rice.

We sit down to eat, as if we hadn't just planned the ruination of someone's life.

Just another day in paradise, I guess.

CHAPTER THIRTY-ONE

LILLY

On Saturday morning we turn on the news to see Clarissa being carted away in cuffs, shoved into the back of a police cruiser, cursing and screaming like a fishwife. I can't help the evil smile that graces my lips at her public humiliation. *Fucking twatwaffle deserved it.* Loki gets a call an hour later asking him to go down to the station to make a statement. After a Facetime briefing with Julian, who rages at the betrayal of the company when the guys tell him about the 'payments', Loki heads into town with Kai, planning - and I quote - 'to bury her pedo ass'.

Classes ramp up a bit the following week, in preparation for more exams apparently, but I'm so used to the workload that I barely notice, spending most of my spare time studying. News of my pregnancy has spread, although everyone assumes that it's Ash's baby, and this is the reason for the rushed wedding.

Things have changed since Julian's 'punishments', there are definite whispers among the students, whereas before, people wouldn't dare to speak about the Knights at all. They still keep their distance, respect and fear mixed on their faces as they gaze at them, but there's an air of sharks circling as we walk through the halls.

Surprisingly, Amber has kept her distance, too, still sneering at every opportunity, but nothing more. She seems to have given up on Loki for the moment, and Julian hasn't pushed the issue either, which makes my skin itch, suspicion crawling down my spine.

With the extra school work and generally feeling tired from being four and a half months pregnant, I almost miss that Jax has started spending most of his time in the gym again.

I catch him heading out one night after dinner, his bag slung over his shoulder.

"Can I join you, Jax?" I ask, halting his movements as he goes to walk out of the dorm.

"Sure, Baby Girl," he rumbles. "I've got your new gloves so we can do some careful practice if you like?" I nod eagerly, and he waits by the door whilst I run upstairs to get changed.

I come down, wearing some maternity leggings, a sports bra, and a tank top. I've just invested in some maternity clothes, finding that even some of my dungarees are becoming a little snug.

We walk in the direction of the school gym, hand in hand, comfortable silence surrounding us.

"How are you, Jax? How's working out now, you know, since getting clean?" I ask softly, glancing at his profile as we walk. God, he is so handsome, with his close beard and blond hair, tied in that man bun.

"I think I'm almost back to where I was," he tells me, a smile on his lips. "I've been training hard, especially with the fight coming up…" His eyes go wide at the same time that mine do, and I pull us to a stop.

"Oh shit!" I exclaim. "Your fight! I'd completely forgotten." A cute as all get out blush steals across his cheeks, and I can't help but beam at him. "When is it?"

"May seventh."

"Oh, that's two weeks before…."

"Yep, it was the most Enzo could manage to get it postponed, otherwise I'd have to forfeit," he informs me, tugging my hand so that we start walking again. We stay silent for a moment, his warm hand in mine as we walk outside, heading round the school to the new state of the art gym and swimming pool building, which was built over Christmas. "I don't suppose I could convince you not to come?" he asks after a beat, and I see him giving me the side eye.

"To the fight? Not a fucking chance!" I laugh, seeing the rueful smile on his face.

"Yeah, that's what I thought," he sighs, gripping my hand tighter for a second. "Just, promise me you'll stay with the guys. These fights...they're not attended by good people, Baby Girl."

"I promise I'll be good," I reply, mostly telling the truth, and he nods his head, releasing a breath.

"Now, come and let me show you how to kick my ass."

I laugh, the sound surrounding us with its lightness.

"Please, we both know that I could have you pinned underneath me any time I choose," I sass back, and the grin he gives me in return is positively feral.

"Is that so, Baby Girl?" he asks, and my heart rate picks up when a decidedly naughty smile tugs his lips upwards. "We'll test that theory later. For now, we train."

"Spoil sport," I grumble, earning a deep chuckle as he leads me into the gym.

It's pretty empty tonight, only two other guys in there who are just finishing up as we walk in. Jax nods to them, leading me to the boxing ring in the centre.

"Now, we're only gonna use the pads, Baby Girl. No contact, just in case. And if you need to stop, just say, okay?" I grumble out an assent as he hands me my new gloves, the ones he bought me for Christmas, with 'Baby Girl' on the wrist straps.

Taking out his phone, he thumbs the screen, and the gym fills with the opening lyrics of *Him & I* by G-Eazy and Halsey. My head bobs with the beat, my lips tugging up as the lyrics flow over me.

We spend the next forty minutes practising boxing moves, until a sheen of sweat covers my body and I'm panting hard.

"I'm done," I gasp out, taking my gloves off and gratefully taking the bottle of water that Jax hands me.

"You did good, Baby Girl," he tells me, not even looking flushed as he stands there in a wifebeater and long shorts. *Fucking cockwomble.*

We leave the ring, and I sit down on the mats to do some stretching, whilst Jax goes over to the punching bags. He doesn't bother with gloves, or even wrapping his hands, as he starts to lay into them with unrestrained violence. My brows begin to dip, my heart pounding as he keeps hitting the bag, his breath hissing out with each strike. I wince as his knuckles split, the red of his blood dripping down his hands as he doesn't even pause, each strike now sounding wet and making the bag swing.

Looking up, his chest heaves with exertion, his face a mask of pain and anger, nostrils flared, teeth bared. I get up, pain lancing my own chest as I walk towards him, knowing that this is no ordinary training session. He's hurting badly.

"Jax, love?" I question softly, keeping back a little, giving him space. The thump of his hits keeps coming, and I bite my lip at how raw his knuckles now look. "Jax! Stop! Please," I beg, my voice choked as I step forward, my hand out.

He looks up at me, eyes wild, sweat dripping down his face.

"It hurts so good, Baby Girl," he rasps out, voice sounding broken. "I need to hurt."

"Oh, love." A sob escapes my throat, and I take another step towards him, and another, until I can place my hand on his quivering bicep.

"I failed them, baby. I failed them all." And my heart breaks as he hangs his head, his shoulders rounding forward in a posture of defeat.

"Failed who, darling?" I ask, my chest tightening. I've been so tied up with everything, that I didn't notice how much he was hurting.

"Mom, Loki, Kai, Ash...you," he replies, his head still hanging.

"What? No, sweetheart, you've not failed us," I try to assure him, but he just shakes his head at me, finally looking up, torment clear in his swirling blue eyes.

"I wasn't there when my mom got beaten up, ending up in the hospital. I couldn't do a damn thing when that bastard Julian was hitting on you. I didn't know that cunt was praying on Loki until afterwards, and Kai...Fuck!" He twirls, punching the bag again so hard that blood splatters his chest. My heart breaks for him. Our protector. "How did I not know, Lilly? How did I not see that he was hurting so bad, for so long?" Anguish is clear in his voice, and he looks at me, begging for answers that I'm not sure I have.

"Oh, love. You were in a hell of your own then. You all were. It wasn't your fault, none of it was your fault."

At my words he drops to his knees, his head in his hands as his shoulders shake, great heaving sobs leaving his body. I don't hesitate, dropping in front of him and wrapping my arms around his huge frame. His own arms band around me, and he buries his head in my chest, pulling me tightly against him. Tears stream down my cheeks as he cries in my arms, falling apart as I hold him.

When will the torment end? When will we be free of the horrors that we've experienced?

We clutch each other, his pain surrounding us like a dark cloud full of stinging insects. Gradually, the smoke lifts, Jax's sobs subsiding until his breathing is somewhat back to normal. He lifts his head, gazing up at me with red rimmed eyes, dried tears on his cheeks matching my own.

"Baby Girl," he croaks out, voice hoarse. "I'm so sorry..."

"Don't you dare apologise for being vulnerable, Jax Griffiths," I tell him sternly. "It's what makes you human, and just makes me love you so much more."

He gives me a smile, letting go of my waist and sitting up on his knees with his hands coming up to cup my face in his bloodied palms.

"I should be the one to apologise. I've been so tied up with everything, the pregnancy, the wedding, and the others. I haven't given you the time you needed, Jax. I'm so sorry." A sob escapes my lips this time, my vision blurring.

"Don't you dare apologise, Lilly Darling," Jax scolds, using my own words against me. "You've had so much happen, in such a short time. And you're the glue that sticks us together, the air that we all breathe. The others needed you more."

"But you needed me, too, and I didn't notice." It's my turn to hang my head, only his grip stops me, forcing my gaze to his.

"You are everything, Lilly Darling," he whispers, pulling back, and he gazes at me with swirling blue eyes, full of fierce love and adoration. "Never doubt that. And you noticed now." I take a deep breath, accepting his words and vowing to myself that I'll keep an eye on my gentle giant.

"There was something that I wanted to ask you," I say, nerves floating in my stomach as I look up at him. It's so silly, given all that we've been through, but I can't help being a little nervous at what I'm about to ask. Even so, I know that it's the right decision.

"Shoot," he tells me, still looking at me like I hung the moon, his blue eyes soft and a little less pain filled.

"So, I was chatting to Lisa the other day, and she, uh, said that she doesn't have to be the one to deliver the baby. So I was wondering if you would?" I say, stumbling over my words a little. He's stock still, blinking, his gaze blue fire. "Jax?"

"You want me to deliver your baby?" he asks softly, his voice holding a note of disbelief. I place my hands on his broad chest, feeling his hot skin through his sweat soaked tank top. His heart pounds hard, like he's just run a marathon.

"I can't think of anyone else I'd rather have, Jax," I tell him, my own voice sincere.

A small gasp leaves me as I see the blue of his eyes turn misted once more. His grip on my face tightens.

"These hands have brought so much death, Baby Girl," he rasps out, and my own breathing becomes painful. "I would be honoured to bring some life into the world for once. Thank you."

A tear escapes my eye, falling down my tear stained cheek as I lean up, too full to say anything, presenting my lips to him. He kisses me tenderly, as if I am the most precious thing in the world to him. As if I am the light to his dark, the good to his bad. The angel to his monster.

I try to heal him a little with my kiss, tell him that it doesn't matter what he's done before, what he might do in order to survive. I love him, flaws, sins and all.

And the room fills with our love as we embrace, chasing away the dark shadows of the past, bathing us in its glow.

I just hope that it's enough. Julian isn't finished yet. My punishment still awaits, and I've the sinking feeling that whatever it will be, will test us to our limits.

CHAPTER THIRTY-TWO

LILLY

Before I know it, the night of Jax's fight is upon us, and I'm standing in front of my, well technically Loki's, mirror. Jax calls himself The Black Knight - *gotta love a theme* - I looked him up, videos of his fights are on YouTube. From what I can tell, he's good, really fucking good, his opponents unable to withstand his methodical attacks for very long. His fights are fast and brutal; he doesn't appear to have ever lost a match and seems to have become a bit of a legend in the underground MMA scene.

I cast my eye over my outfit for tonight, giving myself a smirk in the mirror. I'm soon realising that comfort is key where being pregnant is concerned. So I've opted for sexy loungewear, sporting some MagicStitchWitch leggings, in their red astronomy print, my legs a kaleidoscope of reds, oranges, pinks, and electric blue. On my top half, I'm wearing a white tank top that I had printed especially for the occasion. The internet and express shipping really is amazing. For make-up and hair, I've gone with dark smokey eyes and messy, tumbling brunette waves cascading over my shoulders. As I'm not allowed to wear my beloved heels - *the guys banned them as soon as we discovered I was pregnant, the fuckturds* - I'm wearing a pair of Irregular Choice trainers that Loki bought me as a compromise.

They're not just any trainers, and I may have launched myself at him when I opened the box. They're platform high tops, covered in a crazy busy Care Bear print, with metallic rainbows on the heels, pink faux fur padded collar, and removable Care Bear plushies in front of the laces. *Oh, and they light up, motherfucker!*

A low whistle sounds as the man of the hour walks in, and our eyes meet in the mirror - *that seems to be happening to me a lot recently.* I take Jax in as he stalks towards me, from his black gym shorts, to the all black T-shirt that acts like a second skin, flowing over his muscles, and clinging to every ridge and line.

His lip quirks up as he takes in the design on the front of my tank. It's the Black Knight Corporation logo, only I changed the text to say 'The Black Night', in a font called Beast, which is, well, beast-like. I also included a splash of red in the form of blood splatter across the Knight's helmet that makes up the normal logo.

"You like it?" I ask as he steps up behind me, engulfing me in his lemon drizzle cake scent, his huge arms coming round and pulling me close.

"I fucking love it, Baby Girl," he rumbles, nuzzling his nose into my hairline behind my ear, shivers skittering across my skin as he takes a deep inhale. A growl tumbles from his lips, vibrating through me straight to my core. "I'm gonna need you after the fight, baby. But you'll need to remember your safeword. I won't be in control, so tell me now if that will be too much."

My whole body lights up, my breathing picking up as his words settle inside me, starting a flame in my centre.

"I'm fine with that," I whisper, watching his pupils dilate in the mirror.

"Hard limits?" he asks, watching me back intently. I think for a moment.

"Nothing that might hurt the baby, obviously," I say, and he gives a sharp nod. "And I think no choking, just to be safe. But you can still put your hand round my throat, just not restrict oxygen."

"Time to go, bro!" Loki calls from downstairs, interrupting us.

"Let's go, Baby Girl," Jax murmurs in my ear, taking another deep inhale before stepping back. He takes hold of my hand when I turn round, tugging me downstairs.

"You look hot as fuck, baby mama!" Loki exclaims, his eyes raking over my body. I roll my eyes at him and my apparently new nickname. I still check him out, and he looks mouthwateringly good. He's wearing a black form fitting T-shirt, too, and snug black ripped jeans, tucked into black biker boots, and what looks like a black bandana around his neck.

"You'll need a jacket, Princess. It's cold outside," Ash tells me from behind, and I turn round, my jaw dropping when I catch sight of him.

He's dressed identically to Loki, only his fully inked arms make it look like his sleeves are long, and ink peeps through the rips in his jeans. I've never seen him so casually dressed to go out before, and Her Vagisty practically weeps at the sight. Before I realise what I'm doing, I let go of Jax's hand, stride over to Ash, and grab the back of his neck, slamming my lips against his.

It takes him a second to get over the shock, but soon his arms are pulling me in, and he's kissing me back just as fiercely as I kiss him. It's messy, feral, and glorious. A cough sounds behind us, and I break away, panting and aching for more.

"What the fuck did he do to earn a kiss like that?" Loki whines, and I chuckle, my eyes darting to Ash's red swollen lips that are pulled up into his signature smirk.

"Here you are, darling," Kai's soft melodic voice sounds behind me, and I turn to see him holding out my vintage red and white baseball jacket.

"Thanks, love," I smile back, placing a gentle kiss on his lips and appreciating that his outfit matches the others, with the addition of his black framed glasses.

Putting the jacket on, I walk over to Loki, kissing him on his adorable pouting lips, pulling back before he can deepen it, then doing the same to Jax.

"There you are, everyone has had a kiss."

"Not the fucking same, Pretty Girl," Loki grumbles.

"Come on, grumpy gills," I tease, taking his hand in mine and leading him to the front door of our dorm. "Let's go watch Jax beat the shit out of some poor sap."

It takes about forty minutes to get to the fight location, and I'm surprised to see we're approaching what looks like an old abandoned warehouse in the middle of nowhere.

"What is this place?" I ask as we pull up at the end of a row of cars. There must be over a hundred parked up here.

"This is one of the homes of King of the Streets, an underground fight club," Ash says into the dark interior. He turns to face me from the front passenger seat as Kai puts Jax's truck into park. "Don't fucking wander off. Don't fucking speak to anyone. Understood, Princess?"

I glare at him, feeling a little bratty, but Jax grips my hand tightly next to me.

"Fine," I sigh, earning an eye twitch from my fiancé and a growl from Jax. "I'll be good."

I smell vanilla and cocoa before Loki whispers into my other ear.

"I won't be."

Before I can retort - *although, let's be frank here, what does one say to that?!* - chilled air hits me as he exits the truck, my nipples pebbling under my tank. The other doors open, and Jax keeps hold of my hand, helping me out of the truck. His arm practically vibrates with tension, and I can see him looking around like a predator, evaluating our surroundings.

We enter the building, the low hum of conversation blanketing us, drowned out by the sounds of *Ready or Not* by the Fugees, Ms. Lauryn Hill, Wyclef Jean and Pras. *Got to love a classic fight song!* Harsh floodlights highlight the ring in the centre of the vast space, although ring isn't quite accurate. It's cage-like, in that it's made up of metal fence panels, the kind with metal chain link for sides, so that a cage is created on the bare concrete floor. This is not UFC standard, not by a long shot, and I grip Jax's arm tightly with my free hand as worry floods my system.

As I look around, I notice that most of the people around me have bandana masks covering their lower faces, and a chill shivers down my spine at the eerie sight of so many devils, skulls, and scary clowns that surround me. I look at my guys, seeing them pull up their own bandanas, the lower part of their faces a print of a mediaeval Knight's helmet. Jax is the only one who leaves his face bare.

People take note as we walk towards the ring-cage, and I can see them giving all of us appraising looks. Jax's upper lip curls in a snarl as someone wolf whistles at me, his head whipping in the direction of the sound.

"Save it for the fight," Ash orders, placing a hand on Jax's shoulder, causing my Viking to pause and take a deep breath.

Jax doesn't speak, just resumes walking. I can see the scowl on his face, his eyes distant yet focused at the same time. Like he's not here with us at all, but with his opponent already.

One of the metal fences opens, and Jax leads us into the cage. My breathing quickens as I gaze around at the people surrounding us, fingers gripping the chain link and faces hidden by their masks. A guy comes up to us, his face also hidden, a grinning skull printed over the fabric, colourful ink decorating his arms in full sleeves.

"You ready, Knight?" he asks Jax, and Jax nods, then turns to face me.

His hand leaves mine, coming up to tangle in my hair, pulling my body flush against his. My heart thumps in my chest as he looks deep into my eyes, the blue of his own almost entirely swallowed up by black. Using my hair, he pulls my face to his, his lips dominating mine in a bruising, possessive kiss. I submit, not having any choice or desire to do otherwise, and a moan sounds in my throat as his tongue brushes mine.

A growl leaves him in response, and I swallow it greedily, my skin feeling too tight as his kiss wreaks havoc on me. He starts to pull back, but before he can completely break away, I bite down hard on his lower lip, the copper of his blood filling my mouth. Pulling back, I smirk up at him, then lick my lower lip where his blood started to drip down my chin. He leaves the trail of red to drip into his blond beard, his nostrils flared, and a feral look on his face. His beast is riding him hard tonight for sure.

"You just can't help yourself, can you, Pretty Girl?" Loki asks, stepping up behind me and nuzzling my neck in the same spot Jax did. "Don't worry, brother. I'll keep our girl warm for you," he teases, earning a loud growl from Jax that raises the hair on my arms.

"Seems like you can't either," I respond dryly, letting Loki pull me away and back out of the cage, Kai follows behind us, Ash hanging back for a moment, presumably to give Jax some last minute encouragement.

Jax keeps his gaze on me, until Ash physically grabs his face, obviously telling him to keep his head in the game if the scowl on both guys' faces is any indicator.

A moment later, the colourful inked guy comes back over, and Ash leaves, heading out of the ring alongside another guy. My eyes flit back to Jax to see him squaring off against a mean looking motherfucker. His face is a mess, nose squashed and scars running across it. He's about the same height and build as Jax, so they're clearly well matched.

"Who's he?" I whisper, stepping closer to the chain link fencing, Loki tight to my back but not squashing me. Kai is on my left, and Ash comes up to my right, caging me in a protective semi circle.

"He's known as The Crusher," Ash tells me, the worry courses through my veins when the guy smiles an evil grin at Jax.

"He looks...like a fucking psycho," I say at a loss for a better word to describe the maniac that Jax is about to fight. "And why aren't they wearing gloves?"

"It's an underground bare knuckle fight," Kai answers, his hand brushing mine. "No gloves, no rounds, no rules."

"What?!" I exclaim, watching and feeling sick as Jax and The Crusher step apart, the referee stepping back and signalling for the fight to begin.

The crowd around me goes wild, chanting and shouting, but it's as if I'm under water, hardly hearing them as Jax circles his opponent. The guy tries to kick Jax, but he easily brushes it off, throwing a brutal punch to the man's unprotected face. I wince as blood, and what looks like a tooth, flies across the concrete floor.

"Nice," Ash says beside me, but the madman facing Jax just laughs, then launches himself at my Viking, wrapping his arms round Jax's torso, looking like he's trying to squeeze the life out of him.

"Shake him off, Knight!" Loki shouts angrily as Jax gets pinned to the fence opposite us. Jax punches the guy in the side of the head several times, but Crusher holds fast, even though it looks like blood drips down the side of his face.

The two fighters grapple for what feels like hours, but realistically can only be a minute or two at the most. Jax's muscles strain, trying to get the upper hand, but he can't seem to untangle this crazy motherfucker from round his ribs.

"Looks like our Knight just needs a little more incentive," Loki whispers in my ear, and I startle, not having realised that he'd stepped up so close behind me, his front pressing to my back.

His hand comes round my front, making its way down over my top, shivers dancing over my skin as he lifts my tank and slips his hand under the waistband of my leggings.

"Loki," I grit out, his fingers dipping into my knickers, a husky laugh sounding in my ear as he discovers just how wet I am. In my defence, Ash started it, looking so fucking edible in those ripped jeans, then Jax's kiss added fuel to the fire.

"Looks like watching Jax beat the shit out of that guy is making our girl all hot and bothered," Loki says, loud enough for the other two to hear, and they step closer.

"Loki, what the fuck are you doing?" Ash growls out, tension in his tone. "Fucking exhibitionist."

Loki's fingers slip through my folds, and I moan low, feeling his hardness pressing against my lower back, as he leisurely strokes my clit, lighting me on fire.

"Loki," I groan this time, losing myself to his touch, those clever musician's fingers playing me like a maestro.

"Look at Jax, baby. Watch our boy as I make you come," he murmurs huskily in my ear, and my gaze focuses back on Jax, who's still grappling with his opponent. "Hey, Knight!" Loki leans back slightly and shouts, loud enough to cut through the din of voices around us.

Jax's head darts up, the loss of concentration earning him a sharp jab to the ribs, but he doesn't register it, his eyes taking in where Loki's hand is in between my legs. Loki thrusts two fingers deep inside me, and I can't help but cry out, watching as Jax's nostrils flare and his face fills with rage.

"You've done it now, bro," Kai whispers, amusement in his voice, when with an almighty roar, Jax manages to throw off the other guy, sweeping his foot in a move that sends The Crusher crashing backwards.

Jax is on him in a second, knees either side of the other guy's torso and pounding his head with his fists. Loki matches each strike with a thrust into my dripping pussy, and I gasp and writhe as ripples of pleasure radiate over my skin, building me higher. The crowd are going wild, screaming with bloodlust as Jax whales on his opponent, who can do nothing but try to cover his head with his arms.

Loki's pace picks up, the heel of his hand hitting my clit, and I watch, helpless to fight my impending climax, as the ref walks over and pulls Jax off, raising his arm and declaring him the winner. Loki bites down on my neck just as Jax's wild gaze finds mine, and I explode, my cries lost in the screams and jeers of the crowd.

But Jax sees me, watching with a ravenous hunger as I fall apart on his best friend's fingers. My chest heaves as if it were me in the ring, instead of him, and just as I'm coming down from my high, Jax tears out of the ref's grip, running towards us.

My heart pounds when he leaps at the fence, somehow managing to climb it and drop down beside me, Kai stepping back just in time to avoid being crushed. Loki turns us, pulling his hand out of my knickers, my release glistening on his fingers.

Jax stares at me, chest heaving, ignoring all of the shouts and hollers that sound around us. His gaze flits to Loki's hand as the mischief maker holds it out from behind me. Jax's nostrils flare, scenting the air like a wolf, and he takes a step forward, pressing his sweat soaked chest to mine. He leans down, taking an almighty sniff of Loki's hand, then in a move that shocks me and lights me up all at once, his tongue darts out and licks Loki's fingers, a low rumbling groan sounding in his throat as he cleans them.

My brain short circuits, Her Vagisty screaming *'Hells Yeah!'* as I watch him, his eyes closed and rapturous delight on his face. I can feel Loki's arm trembling, his other hand gripping my waist tightly, obviously affected by Jax's move.

"Maybe next time he'll join us and Kai, huh, Pretty Girl?" he whispers softly in my ear, and I whimper.

Jax's head snaps up at the sound, his pupils so dilated that only a thin ring of electric blue is visible. Loki steps back, leaving my back exposed, but although the warehouse is cold, I burn. I take a step away from Jax, kicking my trainers off and shrugging out of my jacket. I stare into his eyes and watch him like you would a wild animal, trying to anticipate when it'll strike.

He stays still, watching as I take another step back, my flight instincts screaming at me to run.

CHAPTER THIRTY-THREE

LILLY

"Everyone out!" Ash shouts, giving no shits about the grumbling people round us. I don't take my gaze off of Jax, who stands there, completely still apart from the rise and fall of his chest. "Now!" Ash roars, and I feel more than see people scatter for the doors.

Within moments it's just us, and my fingers tingle at the sudden silence. Jax holds my gaze, then takes a slow menacing step forward. I take one back, not taking my eyes off him for a minute. His own eyes widen, sparkling with the chase, as he takes another step towards me, and I back up again, my heart pounding, breathing fast.

We repeat this dance until I round the corner, taking a few steps before bumping into something hard and solid, but warm. Ginger surrounds me, and I feel suddenly lightheaded with relief. It's short lived as Ash leans down, careful not to touch me.

"In the cage, Princess."

I swallow hard, seeing the opening into the cage-ring to my left. Jax growls, and my head whips to face him, seeing that he's almost reached me. So I do what every stupid female lead in horror movies does, backing into the cage, soon finding myself in the middle. Jax enters, the opening shutting with a clang that seals my fate.

Accepting my fate, I close my eyes, my other senses becoming heightened as soon as the darkness engulfs me. I hear Jax stalking towards me, the whisper of his trainers on the concrete loud in the quiet. I feel the tickle of air across my fingertips, smell the tang of blood and sweat in the air. My tongue darts out, and I taste the salt of my own fear on my lips.

The heat from Jax's body caresses my exposed skin as he steps right up to me, and I open my eyes to find his broad sweaty chest in front of me, his T-shirt gone, and his rune-like tattoos on full display. I track my eyes upwards, until I'm looking into his gaze once more, the blue still mostly swallowed up by black.

I tremble as he leans forward, his hand coming up to wrap round my throat, holding my head close and sniffing my hair and neck. Another whimper leaves my lips unbidden as his teeth graze the sensitive flesh where my neck and shoulder meet, and a low rumbling purr comes from him in response.

In a lightning fast move, he lets go of my throat, grabbing the underside of my thighs, and pulls me up so that my legs wrap round his thick waist. He drops to his knees, jarring us, then leans over until I'm lying flat on my back on the concrete, the cool surface making me hiss. Letting go of me, he makes his way down my body, sniffing every so often, his hands tracing my curves, purring as he reaches my rounded stomach. He pauses at the juncture of my thighs, and I cry out as he presses his face down, taking a huge inhale, then rubbing my scent all over his face. Fuck, that shouldn't be so hot, but it really is, liquid pooling in my centre as he marks himself with my musk.

His fingers grip the top of my waistband, pulling my leggings and knickers off and tossing them behind him. Within seconds his face is back at my pussy, eating me out ravenously, like I'm his last damn meal. I get no build up, no easing into it, and am still sensitive from

Loki's attentions earlier, plus wound up from our chase, that my orgasm tears through me almost painfully. Liquid rushes out of me, which Jax greedily laps up, each flick of his tongue making me twitch.

I'm a panting, gasping mess, my entire body tingling, when he sits back on his heels, his huge erection straining under his shorts. He looks at me with a smug satisfaction, his beard full of my release. Leaning forward, he grasps my hips in his large hands, surprising me with his gentleness as he turns me over, bringing my hips up so that I end up on hands and knees, with him kneeling behind me.

A low keening moan leaves my lips as I feel him start to push his way inside me, my arms already shaking from the pleasure that whispers over and through me at his invasion. With a sharp snap of his hips, he bottoms out, a low rumbling purr sounding in his chest, as a cry tears through my lips, his hands rubbing all over my arse.

I feel him lean forward, the neck of my tank going taut before the tearing of fabric sounds in the air. My top falls down my arms, my bra following next, thankfully not torn - *cuntbandit* - a gasp falling from my lips as he rakes his fingernails down my back. The move sends tingles falling all over me, and I push back, feeling him hit my fucking cervix. I swear my eyes roll all the way back.

He grunts, wrapping my hair around a fist and pulling my head back at an angle that leaves my neck exposed. Clearly deciding that he's had enough of taking it slow, he pulls out, his free hand holding me in place by my hip, before slamming back inside me.

I scream with the pleasure-pain that being impaled on Jax's monster cock creates, my whole body shaking and jerking as he fucks me hard and fast. Snarls sound behind me, his grip on my hair and hip tightening, his thrusts wild in their ferocity. My nails try to bury themselves into the concrete, my cries and whimpers filling the room, as my body is assaulted by raw pleasure. I let go completely, submitting totally to his will, and the freedom of letting my instincts take over soon have me reaching an earth shattering climax.

My inner walls slam around Jax's cock so hard that he grunts and snarls louder, forcing his way inside me as my cunt clenches and grips him. Screams leave my throat raw as the orgasm reaches epic proportions, my whole body shaking violently with the force of it. Jax's grip is the only thing keeping me up as he keeps pounding into me, and with one final hard thrust, he comes with a roar, falling forward and biting the same shoulder that Loki did earlier, the sharp pain causing another wave of rapture to hit me.

My arms give way as he twitches above me, his dick still pulsing inside of me. He manages to cushion our fall, rolling us so that I end up half on top of him, my back to his front, my head resting on his enormous bicep and his dick still nestled inside my twitching pussy. We lie that way, panting, our skin covered in sweat, as the high recedes, leaving a feeling of utter euphoria.

"You okay, Baby Girl?" he rumbles out after a while, his voice husky and sending shivers across my skin.

"Yes," I croak out, "I'm amazing."

He chuckles, his hand moving down to cup my stomach. At that moment, the baby decides to do an almighty kick, and Jax freezes behind me.

"Was that?" he asks in wonder, then a delighted laugh sounds behind me as the baby kicks again.

"You can feel it?" I ask, excitement chasing away the lethargy that the incredible sex had left me in.

"Shit, yeah," he replies as another kick lands. "Guys!"

Within seconds, the others are crouched down next to us, looking a little worried.

"Is everything okay? Is the baby okay?" Loki asks, voice panicked, and I can't help the blissed out smile as I grab his hand, placing it over the spot where Jax's was just seconds ago.

Clearly indulging us, the baby gives another kick, and Loki's eyes go wide.

"Fuck, that's our baby."

I can only nod my head, my eyes misting as Loki's glisten, a laugh falling from his lush lips as the baby kicks him again.

"It's got your fighting streak, Jax, that's for sure!" Loki exclaims, making room for Kai, who chuckles when his hand is kicked, too.

"You clever beautiful darling," he murmurs, staring into my eyes with such love, that the mist turns to drops, and one slides down the side of my face, which is still pillowed on Jax's bicep.

"May I?" Ash's low drawl sounds, and Kai moves to one side so that Ash can kneel down and place his hand on my stomach.

For a moment nothing happens, and I hold my breath, begging our unborn child for one more so that he can feel it, too. It's clearly feeling very obliging, or is trying to impress its fathers, as Ash's hand jumps with another kick. His eyes snap up to mine, the steel in them soft.

"Strong, just like its mother," he whispers, and I swallow hard.

"Just like its fathers, too," I reply, another teardrop falling down my cheek.

I shiver as the cold air suddenly hits me, and Ash leans down, placing a gentle, reverent kiss on my lips.

"Come on, Princess. Let's get you home and into a nice hot bath," he says, leaning back, then helping me to my feet.

Loki whips off his T-shirt, pulling it over my head, and I nestle into its warm vanilla smell. Kai fetches, then helps me into my knickers and leggings, and Jax brings me my trainers, helping to slip them onto my feet. I bask in their attention, as they each take care of me, Ash wrapping his arm around me and pulling me close.

We walk out of the warehouse into the night, the stars twinkling behind us and the full moon lighting the way to Jax's truck. Getting in, I'm sandwiched between Ash and Jax, soaking up their warmth, and we start the drive back to Highgate. Back home.

Although, really, we're already home, as home is where the heart is. And mine is sitting around me, cradled in four bodies, in four men, the five of us bound to each other in ways that can never be separated.

CHAPTER THIRTY-FOUR

LILLY

The two weeks after Jax's fight are a complete blur, what with exams - *which hopefully I don't completely fail at!* - wedding planning, and another appointment with Lisa, my midwife. Turns out I'm a teensy bit anaemic, which Kai takes as a personal affront, feeding me steak and green leafy veg until I can't stand the sight of it. Jax gets me some iron infused water, so I start taking that as well.

Luckily, Erica is incredibly good at what she does, organising a taster menu at a hotel in town, getting the marquee sorted and built, as well as contacting the registrar who'll perform the ceremony. She does all this and more effortlessly, which is a huge relief as I haven't a Scooby Doo - clue - what I'm meant to be doing.

She organsied a last minute fitting with the dressmakers, just to ensure that no adjustments need to be made due to my changing shape. A couple of minor alterations later, and it fits me to perfection. The dress hangs in its garment bag in Ash's room, in his woodland mansion, as I've named it. I'm getting ready here, along with

Willow who is my maid of honour and only bridesmaid. She practically cried, throwing herself at me when I asked her, silly fairy.

The boys are staying at Highgate because according to a stupid tradition that no one knows the origin of, they can't be with me, as it's unlucky for the bridegroom to see the bride the night before the wedding.

My hand trails down the garment bag, my stomach turning uncomfortably with nerves as I pace the room. It's late, Willow already in bed and probably snoring away. I worry my lip, unable to settle. My mind races, like a pinball machine, landing on one thought, only to fly to another.

I'm excited for tomorrow, to become Ash's wife is a dream come true. But it also breaks my heart knowing that I can't marry the others, too. It almost feels like a betrayal, even though I know that they don't see it that way. I turn, my back to the open stairway, as I pace to the window.

And all this stuff with Julian, with Black Knight Corp., buzzes at me like a wasp. *How will we take them down? How can I help? What if we fail?*

A noise behind me has me spinning, only to come up short as I see my four Knights, dressed in grey sweatpants and nothing else, standing shoulder to shoulder. It's enough to still my swirling thoughts as my brain short circuits.

"W-what are you doing here?" I ask, a sudden lightness making me feel as though I could float away. Ash steps forward, his tattooed chest looking almost alive in the low lamplight as he walks towards me, stopping in front of me. As always, my heart rate picks up at his nearness.

"We both know that none of us would have gotten any sleep, Princess, if we'd spent the night apart," he murmurs, his voice low and deep, telling me that we won't just be sleeping tonight. At least not straight away.

"We'll be gone by the morning, darling," Kai tells me, stepping forward until he's standing to my left.

"No need to worry about bad luck, Baby Girl," Jax adds, stepping up to my left.

"And anyway," Loki drawls, sauntering towards us until he stands behind me. "We make our own luck in this world, Pretty Girl." My temperature skyrockets at being surrounded by them, being caged in by them. I shiver, my nipples becoming hard points underneath my silk nightdress when a hand trails down my bare arm.

"And the...outfits?" I say, my voice all kinds of breathy as the hand on my other side pushes down the thin strap of the nighty, the other strap quickly following until it pools at my feet in a puddle of rose pink.

"Loki told us that, according to your 'not-gangbang' books, this is lingerie for men," Ash informs me, a slight smirk tilting one side of his lips.

"He would be correct," I breathe, looking down and seeing the clear outline of Ash's, Kai's, and Jax's hard dicks pressed against the soft grey fabric. Not to be forgotten about, Loki pushes his hips against me, proving that he is in a similar state of arousal.

Loki's hands come round my sides, cupping and kneading my breasts, groaning.

"These have definitely gotten bigger," he sighs appreciatively, tweaking my nipples and making me hiss at their sensitivity. "Nipples are more sensitive, too."

Ash bends down, taking one bud in his mouth, sucking and flicking it with his tongue until I'm writhing against Loki. I feel Jax's hand on my left making its way down to the juncture of my thighs, quickly finding the bundle of nerves and circling it.

"So fucking wet for us already," he rumbles out, his finger moving faster until I cry out.

"And so responsive, darling," Kai whispers, his hand dipping below Jax's, two fingers sliding into me with ease.

I gasp as they work in synchronicity, playing my body like experts. Lights dance across my vision, my body going completely rigid as my climax crashes over me. My knees buckle with the force of it, but they hold me up, working me through my shudders and cries, until I'm a glowing thing, floating to the heavens.

"I think she's ready for us, boys," Ash chuckles, and suddenly I'm lifted up, my legs wrapping around a firm waist. I crack my eyes to see that I'm holding onto Jax, my eyebrows squishing together in confusion. *I swear Ash was just in front of me...*

Jax carries me over to the huge bed - *I'm sure it wasn't this big the last time I was here!* - passing me into a set of vanilla scented arms.

"Hey, Pretty Girl," Loki whispers in my ear, pulling my back flush against his front, his hot skin almost scalding me as I realise that he's naked beneath me.

"Hey," I murmur, as he lies down, with me still on top of his body.

"Loki, what..." I start to ask, as he grabs my thighs, bringing them up and over his hips so that I'm opened wide before Jax.

"Shhhh," he hushes, nuzzling my neck as he lets go of one leg, moving his hand so that it feels like he's grasping his hard cock.

"What a sight," Jax purrs, taking a bottle of clear lube that Kai passes him.

He squirts some into his hand, barely warming it up before he coats my pussy making me gasp at the cold, moving to rub some onto my rosebud. He slips a large finger in, and I moan low as he moves it back and forth a few times. I shudder as he pulls the digit out.

"Need a hand, bro?" he cockily asks Loki.

"Thanks, dude." My eyes are wide at this seemingly normal exchange, like Jax is offering Loki to help lift a heavy box, not to help him get his dick into my arsehole.

My eyes go wider still as Jax reaches between my legs, my view cut off by my baby bump. But I hear Loki groan, feeling his tip line up with my puckered hole.

"Loki," I gasp, the sharp sting of his thick pierced cock pushing past the ring of muscle making me squirm.

"That's it, Pretty Girl," he grits out, both hands back on my thighs pulling them apart wider. "Let me in, baby."

My nails dig into his forearms, hard enough to break the skin as he keeps pushing forward until he bottoms out - *pun intended*. Jax looks on with a lust filled gaze, his hand wrapped around his shaft, pumping up and down at the sight.

"Fuuuuck," Loki moans, moving his hips underneath me, pumping himself gently in and out of me.

"You ready, Baby Girl?" Jax asks in a husky whisper, leaning down and capturing my lips in his before I can answer.

He pulls away, taking one of my legs out of Loki's grip, putting my ankle on his shoulder. Loki stops moving when Jax starts to nudge his way inside my dripping pussy.

"Shit!" I cry out as he stretches me. "So full."

"That's it, baby. Take our cocks like a good fucking girl," Loki hisses in my ear, groaning as with a final thrust, Jax's hips make contact.

They start to move, one pulling out as the other pushes in, finding a rhythm that drives me wild, whipping my nerves into a frenzy. I feel the bed dip by my head, and look up to see an upside down Kai, stroking his glinting cock.

"Up on your hands, darling," he orders, and the guys pause to help me balance on Loki's chest. "Good girl. Now open up."

I do as ordered, moaning as Kai slides his thick length into my mouth, not even pausing as he pushes it down my throat.

"Look at that throat bulge," he coos, and Jax rumbles in appreciation, one hand coming up to my neck to encircle and squeeze my throat. Kai hisses, pulling out to allow me to take a breath, before pushing in again, cutting off my airway once more.

Loki and Jax start moving again, and all I can do is relax as they fuck me, waves of pleasure rolling over me.

"My turn," I hear Ash rumble, and I'm tugged off Kai's cock by my hair, his piercings clacking on my teeth. I hear Kai growl, and open my eyes to see Ash pressing the tip of his dick to my lips, painting them with his precum. "Open wide, Princess, and let me fuck that sassy mouth of yours."

I do as he commands, and he fulfils his promise, thrusting hard and fucking the back of my throat with sharp thrusts.

"Shit, dude. You want her to be able to say her vows tomorrow," Jax chuckles, groaning as my pussy tightens around him when he hits my G-spot over and over again.

Ash slows down, his thrusts gentling but still deep. I moan as fingers find my clit, rubbing circles around and over it, sending a fire sweeping through me. My hair is pulled, my lips releasing Ash's cock with a pop as Kai soon pushes his inside. I moan and writhe as the fire spreads, barely noticing Kai's rough moves.

"She's so close," Jax grits out, picking up speed, the sound of his hips snapping against me loud in the room.

Loki follows his pace, and I explode, hearing their grunts as I clench and clamp down around them. Loki is the first to follow me into oblivion, biting down on my neck, sending another orgasm crashing over me. Jax roars his release a second or two afterwards, his hand tightening around my throat and Kai's cock, causing Kai to pour his release down my throat.

He pulls out, Jax loosening his grip and letting go as he pulls out of me, causing Loki to slip out, too. I fall back onto Loki, lying there panting, my heart pounding as bliss coats every fibre of my being.

"My turn, Princess," Ash repeats, pulling me off Loki, my back landing on the cool sheets.

He climbs on top of me, his body flush with mine as he pushes inside my aching cunt. My legs automatically wrap around his hips, pulling him deeper and making us both groan.

"Ash," I whimper, his hands coming up to cup my face, his elbows either side of my head.

"You can come for me, can't you, beautiful?" he coaxes, his hips moving in a slow nerve tingling rhythm.

I vaguely register *Earned It* by The Weekend starting to play, the song bringing back memories of Loki buried inside me, singing, as I was tied to Ash's bed. As if sharing that same memory, Ash chuckles.

"I'll tie you up again soon, Princess," he whispers, bringing his forehead to mine as he starts moving his hips faster. "You were made for us, Lilly Darling. Every atom belongs to the four of us, just as every part of us is yours. You make us greater than the sum of our parts, until we become more than we ever thought possible. You are as vital as the blood that pumps in our veins, as crucial as the air that we breathe. You are our beating heart, and our souls are bound together for all eternity."

Ash may not be able to sing me to orgasm, but he can talk me into one. His words set off a chain reaction inside me, my pussy walls tightening around him as I come with a cry, clinging tightly to him. He thrusts a few more times, prolonging my pleasure, before he succumbs, coming deep inside me with a manly groan.

We stay locked together for several moments, breathing the same air as we hold each other, the high settling into our bones.

"Come, Princess, let's get you cleaned up whilst the guys change the sheets," Ash suggests, and I look around to see the others coming back into the room, shower fresh.

A small sound leaves me as Ash pulls out, then helps me up on shaky legs. He wraps his arm round my waist, walking me to the door, pausing as each of the others place a kiss on my no doubt swollen lips.

After showering, the warm water and Ash's ministrations making me all kinds of sleepy, I walk into the room, holding Ash's hand, to find the others waiting around the enormous bed, wearing boxers.

"Did you get a bigger bed?" I ask Ash, as he leads me to the side, indicating that I climb in.

"I figured that we'd all want to sleep with you sometimes, so it seemed like a good option," he tells me, voice matter of fact and completely unaware of the fact that I've just melted into a puddle of girl goo. "If that's okay with you?"

"It's perfect," I tell him softly, scooting into the middle.

"Shotgun!" Loki hollars, leaping onto the bed on my other side, Ash quickly climbing in beside me.

I giggle as Jax and Kai grumble, but climb in, too, Kai behind Loki and Jax behind Ash.

"I don't want your weapon of mass destruction waking me up, got it?" Ash deadpans, and we all burst into peals of laughter, tears streaming down my cheeks when Jax asks what the fuck he's talking about.

I fall asleep with a smile on my face, nestled in a bed of love, with my unborn child kicking away under two of its fathers' hands.

CHAPTER THIRTY-FIVE

LILLY

I wake up the next morning, my body aching in the best possible way, the scent of my guys lingering in the bed with me. Lying there, I take a moment, the spring sunshine dancing across the ceiling.

I'm getting married today.

The thought fills me with giddy excitement, followed by a rolling feeling in my stomach as nerves settle in. *I wonder how Ash feels?*

"Rise and shine, you gorgeous bride!" Willow calls, stomping into the room and eyeing up the bed. "I'd join you in there, but Ash really needs to work on the soundproofing of this place." Her nose wrinkles even as her eyes twinkle with mirth.

"Oh God," I groan, my cheeks flushing as I hide under the duvet, which doesn't help at all considering it still smells like them.

"Come on, lazy bum!" she responds, way too cheery for this time in the morning as she yanks the covers off me. "The girls are already here to make you into a goddess for your harem."

"Urgh, fine," I grumble, sitting up then realising that I'm completely naked still. "Willow!"

She throws a silk robe at me, cackling evilly as she walks out the door. Putting the robe on, I follow downstairs to find the large sitting room full of people. I pause, taking a deep breath before stepping into the fray.

Erica is the first to approach, an understanding smile on her face.

"How are you doing?" she asks, handing me a glass of juice with ice in it. I take a sip, giving her a grateful smile when I realise that it's tropical, my favourite.

"Terrified," I tell her with a huff of laughter. "Excited."

"As to be expected." She smiles warmly at me, guiding me to the table, one end of which has been set up like a dressing table, complete with a mirror with lights. "Now, Asher made it clear that my ovaries are on the line if you don't eat anything, so eat this up, then we'll get started."

I chuckle, not surprised anymore by Ash's dominating care of me. I do as ordered, finishing my homemade chocolate chip granola bar - *Kai, you legend* - and glass of fresh juice.

"Right, now comes the fun part!" Erica exclaims, leading me to the other end of the table, and sitting me down in front of the mirror. I'm kinda regretting my life choices right now, not having even put any knickers on.

For the next God knows how long, I'm primped, primed, and pampered to within an inch of my life. They even put rainbow colours in my hair to match the hem of the dress, pinning it in a complicated style that leaves the majority tumbling over one shoulder, my long lace edged veil pinned into place. When I look at myself in the mirror after I'm declared 'done', I hardly recognise the beautiful bride sitting before me.

Willow appears in the mirror, looking ethereal after her makeover, her eyes wide as usual.

"You look...wow," she whispers.

"You do, too," I murmur back, and her hand comes to my shoulder, mine coming up to grasp it.

"Dresses, ladies," Erica declares, ushering me out of my seat and up the stairs. "I'll leave you to get your underwear on, just shout when you're ready."

I step inside Ash's room once more, noticing that the bed has been made, a white gift bag sitting on top of it. There's a notecard inside, Ash's elegant scrawl over it.

Wear this for me today, Princess

I smile, taking the ivory silk lace out of the bag, impressed with his choices. Ivory silk and lace briefs, with a matching soft bralette with a low back so it won't be seen underneath my dress. Matching lace-edged thigh high hold ups—the kind that just grip without needing suspenders—complete the set.

There's a flat square box at the bottom, and I open it to find a beautiful lace garter, another note nestled in the lace.

And wear this for the rest of us

Smiling, I put it all on, marvelling at how comfortable it all is, and at how Ash clearly took that into account when buying it.

"Ready," I call out, looking in the full length mirror as Erica and the young dressmaker walk in.

"Excellent, now the dress," Erica claps her hands with glee as the dressmaker helps me into the dress, doing up the buttons that fasten it at the back.

Once secure, Erica brings over my new Irregular Choice heels, a wedding gift from Loki on the understanding that I only wear them for the ceremony, and wear flats for the rest of the day and night. They're the same style as my red sequin Dorothy heels, but are covered in white glitter, with a white bow on the toes.

"You look perfect, Lilly," Erica tells me softly, her eyes a little misted as we gaze at my reflection in the mirror. "Right, time to go."

My fingers tingle as I walk out of the room, my nerve endings firing all at once when I walk down the stairs to see Willow and Ryan waiting.

"Lilly, you look...astonishing," Ryan murmurs gruffly, his voice choked as he gazes at me.

He takes my hand in his huge one, his eyes misty, and I choke out a laugh.

"Don't get me started, my make-up took hours," I tell him, and we laugh. He leans in, pressing a light kiss on my cheek.

"Your mother would be so proud, little one," he whispers, and I blink furiously trying to keep the tears at bay.

"Time to get into the cars," Erica interrupts quietly, effectively dispelling the slight sadness.

Willow steps forward, handing me my bouquet of beautiful rainbow coloured flowers, and keeping hold of my hand, Ryan leads us out of the mansion. An old fashioned white car, with a ribbon wrapped around the flying lady on the front, awaits us, glinting in the sun.

"Where on earth did you get a vintage Rolls?" I exclaim, eyeing up the beautiful vehicle with appreciation.

"Your soon-to-be husband has his ways," Ryan tells me, a smirk of approval on his lips as the driver, who's in a very smart dove grey uniform, opens the door. "You ready?"

I take a deep breath of forest air, our luck holding as the spring sunshine beats down on us, lending its warmth for the day.

"As I'll ever be," I reply, stepping into the car, and towards my future.

ASH

I stand gazing out at the stunning mountain view, beautifully framed by the floral archway. But I don't see a damn thing, waiting for Lilly, my bride, to arrive.

"You okay, bro?" Loki asks, clapping me on the back, his hand squeezing my shoulder. Kai and Jax are showing the final guests to their seats, and have been greeting people as they arrive.

"Why am I so fucking nervous, dude?" I ask, bewildered at the butterflies that have taken flight in my stomach.

"Because you're marrying the girl of our dreams, you fucker," Loki replies, and I know that he's only half joking, his hand tightening a little more on my shoulder.

"Yeah, I know, bro," I reply, turning to look at him, just as the musicians start playing the bride's piece of music.

My heart leaps in my chest as I face the aisle, and the sight that greets me stops my breath, the world pausing as she walks towards me. She looks...transcendent, her beauty surpassing everything in this universe and all the others. Her dress floats around her, hinting at her pregnancy, and I have to suppress a primal growl of satisfaction at her obvious fertility.

The dress is exquisite, and I follow down to the hem, which looks as though she's stepped into the setting sun behind us, bringing it with her. The timing of the ceremony now makes sense at least. She wears a long veil, but her face is free, her hazel stare locked on me when I tear my gaze back up to her radiant face.

I almost fall to my fucking knees at the smile she gives me, unsurety and nerves there but a happiness that I never knew I could inspire.

"I fucking hate you, bro," Loki grumbles in my ear, and I can't blame him. I would hate me, too.

Finally, Lilly is standing beside me, Ryan placing her hand in mine. She gives it a squeeze, a hint of amusement in her eyes as she looks at me.

"Great song choice," she comments, and I smile, wanting to laugh out loud.

I gave her free reign over everything, bar the music for today. And I didn't tell her either, as I wanted to keep it a surprise. The song being played on a baby grand and cello by The Piano Guys is a rendition of *A Thousand Years*, and I chose it after hearing that she went to see the Twilight films at midnight with a group of friends, and squealed when that werewolf took his shirt off. *Fucking amateur.* She laughed at me when I commented that I never understood why Bella had to choose between the two, although personally I was always team Jasper and Alice.

The piece comes to an end, those damn butterflies still flying around inside me.

"Dearly beloved..." The registrar begins, the rest of the ceremony passing by in a blur until suddenly I'm placing a ring, my ring, on her finger, and she's doing the same to me. Her hands don't shake, her words don't falter as she looks me dead in the eye and becomes my wife.

"You may now..." I don't wait for the fucker to continue, cupping her face with my hands and pulling her soft lips to mine.

It's the kiss of a new beginning, all fresh and sweet like the twilight mountain air that surrounds us. I kiss her as if she's the very air I need, the thing that keeps me breathing because she is. And she's so much more, to me, to all of us. She matches me stroke for stroke, her hands on my chest, gripping my morning suit and pulling me closer.

I vaguely register cheers and whoops, mostly coming from Loki behind me, but I'm lost in this woman, my fucking wife, and I don't ever want to be found. Reluctantly, I pull back, grinning when I see that she's just as affected as me, her pupils blown and lips swollen.

"Hello, wife," I murmur, tasting the smile on her lips.

"Hello, husband," she replies, and damn, if my knees don't go a little weak at hearing her call me that.

The registrar interrupts us, reminding me that we need to sign the register and marriage certificate, Loki and Jax following as witnesses. Once that's done, it's time for us to walk down the aisle, her hand tucked into the crook of my arm, man and wife. A delighted peal of laughter rings from her lips, echoing around us as the piano plays a version of *Earned It* by The Weekend. A blush coats her upper chest and cheeks, blooming under her skin, probably remembering what happened the two times she's heard this song.

"Naughty, husband," she teases with a smile as people throw rainbow petal confetti over us. I can't even be annoyed at the petals sticking to me, a shiver running through me at her words. I lean down, close enough to whisper in her ear.

"The next time you call me that, I'll be buried deep inside your sweet cunt, wife."

I watch enraptured as her nostrils flare, the red on her cheeks deepening as she licks her lips.

It's a promise that I intend to keep.

CHAPTER THIRTY-SIX

LILLY

I sit back, stomach pleasantly full after eating our delicious mash up of British and American cuisine. We had scrambled egg and bacon on tiny pancakes, loaded hot dogs and chilli cheese fries, followed by a mango and cream dessert that looked like a boiled egg, and a selection of British cheeses and oatcakes to finish.

Patting my rounded stomach, I hear a deep chuckle either side of me.

"Full, Baby Girl?" Jax asks, his hand quickly dipping to ghost over my stomach in a protective gesture. Like Ash and Kai, Jax wears a light grey tailored morning suit, with a rainbow waistcoat and tie. Loki, my wonderful Knight of mischief, has gone for a full on rainbow suit, the fabric literally striped in rainbow colours. And he looks fucking stunning, as do the others, all tailored perfection and clean lines.

Because of our unconventional seating plan - *aka non-existent* - I'm sitting at a round table with all of my favourite people. Jax is on one side of me - *I dread to think how he won that privilege* - and Ash, my new husband, on the other. I'm not sure I'll ever get used to the fact that I'm now married. I'm now Mrs. Vanderbilt.

Kai is on the other side of Ash, Loki next to Jax. Willow is here with us, chatting to Lex and Ryan, who are also on our table.

I cast a glance over my shoulder and catch Julian's eye, shivering when he gives me a feline smile before turning back to talk to my uncle. Yep, Adrian turned up, and briefly congratulated Ash and I, although the smile didn't reach his eyes as he shook Ash's hand.

The sound of tinkling glass swings my gaze back to Ash, who rises in his seat, standing up and taking everyone in his sweeping steel gaze.

"Ladies and gentlemen, I'd like to start by thanking you for joining Lilly and I on our wedding day," he starts, briefly glancing down at me, a warm smile tugging his lips up. My own mimic him, my cheeks hurting from all of the smiling I've done today, most of which has been at my guys so I'll take the pain. "When Lilly agreed to be my wife, well, it truly was the happiest night of my life." He's staring at me as he says this last part, and my palms sweat, remembering that night at his parents' manor house, and how fraught with tension it was. But he means it, and I realise that really was a happy moment for him, one in a life full of sad moments. "My wife," he pauses, and takes a slight breath, letting me know that he's as affected by these new terms as I am. "My beautiful wife is a fan of Shakespeare, so I'd like to read *Sonnet 116* for her."

He looks back down at me, holding my gaze as he recites.

> "'Let me not to the marriage of true minds
> Admit impediments. Love is not love
> Which alters when it alteration finds,
> Or bends with the remover to remove:
> O, no! it is an ever-fixed mark,
> That looks on tempests and is never shaken;
> It is the star to every wandering bark,
> Whose worth's unknown, although his height be taken.

> Love's not Time's fool, though rosy lips and cheeks
> Within his bending sickle's compass come;
> Love alters not with his brief hours and weeks,
> But bears it out even to the edge of doom.
> If this be error and upon me proved,
> I never writ, nor no man ever loved.'"

I take a gasping breath as he finishes, realising that I'd held it the whole time that he spoke. His image wavers as I blink furiously, trying in vain to stop the tears from leaving my eyes. Cheers erupt around us as he bends down, capturing my lips in a kiss so tender and gentle that a small sob sounds in my throat.

"I love you, Lilly Vanderbilt," he tells me, his lips ghosting across mine as he pulls away so that I taste his words.

"I love you, Asher Vanderbilt," I whisper back, my voice raspy as I try to talk through the lump in my throat.

Another glass rings, and I look to see Ryan standing up, tugging at the neck of his shirt, his face going slightly red.

"I was there when Lilly came into the world, kicking and screaming as Lex passed her into her mother's arms. I was there when she learnt to crawl, then walk - at ten bloody months old mind, which I can tell you was a right nightmare!" He laughs along with us, then holds my gaze. "I was there when she started talking, when she went off to school for the first time, when she experienced a thousand other milestones that a young girl does. And some that she never should have had to." I bite my lip, Ash gripping one hand and Jax the other, his other hand wiping away the tear that escapes. Coughing, Ryan continues. "And now I'm here, standing in front of a beautiful woman, a beautiful wife, and wondering how I got so lucky to have such a wonderful daughter." He swipes his own wet eyes, Lex handing him a tissue whilst a cry-laugh escapes her. "And I couldn't be more proud of the young lady that you've become. We couldn't be more proud. And your mum, well, I just know that wherever she is, she's smiling and jumping around like a loon at how far you've come, at how much you've grown."

Tears track freely down my cheeks as I nod, unable to say a single thing to this man who is a father to me, in all but blood.

"You've found yourself good guys, little one. Good protectors, who'll take care of you for the rest of your life." None of us miss the way that Ryan gives no shits and includes all my Knights, not just Ash, and I couldn't give a flying fuck about the whispers from the other tables. "So, let's raise our glasses in a toast," he continues, a roguish look in his brown eyes as he lifts his champagne flute. "To Lilly and her Knights!" he cries, a shocked giggle escaping my lips as others at our table raise their glasses and make the same toast. The rest of our guests follow suit, a little delayed as no doubt they thought they ought to be toasting the bride and groom, not the bride and grooms. *Ah well, fuck 'em!*

"My turn," Loki leans over to whisper, standing up and coming up next to me, holding his hand out. "Come on, Pretty Girl."

I quirk a brow at him, but let him pull me from my chair and lead me over to the dance floor, a stage set up at one end. There's a band there, a beautiful quirky black haired girl smiling down at me, standing in front of a microphone. I don't notice much else as Loki leaves me standing in front of the stage, pressing a kiss to my cheek, then hops up onto the stage.

He confidently strides over to a high stool, which has an acoustic guitar propped up next to it, and a microphone in front of it. Grabbing the guitar, he sits down, giving me a panty decimating grin.

Then he opens his mouth and starts singing *If We Never Met*, by John K, and Kelsea Ballerini, and I just melt. He holds my gaze as he sings, and there's an intense look in his eyes, like although the song has a fun beat, he wants me to take it seriously. And I do. I take the message he's giving me into my very soul.

At one point, the girl starts singing, and Loki puts his guitar back onto the stand, hops off the stage, and grabs my hand, pulling me towards him and moulding his body to mine as we dance together.

I'd somehow forgotten that this boy can move like he's making love on the dancefloor.

He picks up the lyrics, singing into my ear as he moves his hips against mine in a slow, teasing movement, and my knees go weak, a fire igniting in my core at the memories of the times he's been singing into my ear whilst being inside of me.

All too soon the song finishes, as does his movements, and I'm left pressed up against him, feeling just how affected he is with his heaving chest and hardness pressed against my stomach.

"You may be his wife, Pretty Girl," he rasps into my ear, nuzzling my neck like he just can't help himself. "But you're my soulmate, the mother of my child, and I will love you for my entire goddamn life, and then some."

"I fucking love you, Loki Thorn," I manage to choke out, my voice thick with all the emotions that are swirling inside of me.

A throat clears behind me, and I turn to see Jax standing there, waiting a step behind us. Loki laughs, and I glance back.

"Your other soulmates await," he tells me ruefully, pressing a kiss to the corner of my lip. Before he can pull away, I turn my face, kissing him full on, uncaring of our other guests as I kiss the shit out of him.

It takes a second, but with a groan he returns the embrace, matching my passion with his own. Reluctantly, he pulls away, and looks at me like I am everything in the entire world to him. Stepping away - *luckily he's managed to get himself somewhat under control so that he's not walking around at full mast* - he walks backwards, holding my gaze until I feel a warmth at my back, huge hands alighting on my upper arms.

"May I have this dance, Baby Girl?" Jax's rough voice whispers in my ear, the same ear that Loki murmured into. I shiver with the feel of it, all rough hands and long nights spent wrapped up in each other.

"Yes, always," I reply, turning and letting him hold me in his huge arms. It always feels like coming home whenever Jax holds me, like I'm in a warm room, safely tucked away from the raging storm outside.

The sounds of a country guitar start playing, and when a male voice starts singing, I recognise the song as *Die a Happy Man* by Thomas Rhett.

A happy shiver caresses my skin, and my lips split into a wide grin as Jax leads me into a slow country swing dance. He moves with a grace that only those of us who know him aren't surprised by, and we twirl around the dancefloor, uncaring that we're the only ones dancing.

We lose ourselves in the music and each other, the twist and twirl of the moves, the lead and pull. I know that he chose this song purposefully, telling me how much I mean to him through the lyrics, and the way that he holds me like I'm the most precious thing in the world.

All too soon the song finishes, and once again I'm being held close by one of my Knights.

"You are the greatest thing to have ever happened to me, Baby Girl," he mumbles into my hair, his voice rough with emotion. "And I don't care that you're a Vanderbilt, because you will always be mine as well."

"Jax..." I rasp out, my own throat thick. These boys are determined to make me bawl my eyes out and explode with happiness today.

He pulls back, gazing fiercely into my eyes, his own a swirling blue vortex. Achingly slowly he lowers his face to mine, his lips pausing a hair's breadth above my own, his warm breath teasing me. Tired of waiting, I close the distance, a deep vibrating chuckle erupting in his chest at my brazen move.

Jax's hand comes up to cup underneath my chin, his fingers on one side of my upper throat, his thumb the other. He deepens the kiss with one of his signature growls, the noise heating my core as his tongue decimates mine, leaving me breathless and wanting more.

Before I can do something embarrassing - *like climb him like a fucking spider monkey does a fruit tree* - he pulls away, placing a gentle peck on my lips.

"Two more Knights, baby," he whispers, taking hold of my upper arms and turning me to face away from him.

My head is still spinning from our kiss when honey amber fills my gaze.

"Hello, darling," Kai's melodic voice fills my ears, and even though my cheeks ache with smiling so much today, my kiss-swollen lips lift.

"Hello, my love," I murmur back, and his eyes close in bliss for a brief moment, before opening again. His hand reaches out, his fingers brushing my lips, heat making the amber glow like the setting sun.

The haunting voice of Aaron Smith comes over the speakers, singing *Unconditional*, and tears sting my eyes, knowing the lyrics and knowing that they are perfect for us. For Kai and I.

He holds out his hand, and I place mine in his warm grip, letting him pull me close, taking me in a formal dance hold, waiting a beat, then setting off in a waltz. My heart races as he spins us around the empty dance floor, the lights and colours of the marquee becoming a kaleidoscope as we dance.

The song swells and ebbs, guiding our moves, but Kai stares into my eyes the entire time, captivating me in his gaze as he expertly leads. Everything that has passed between us is there; the immediate connection, the brief doubt, the coming together again and every revelation. Every declaration. Every iota of feeling that exists between Kai and I flows between us, and I can almost see its light, moving between us until it becomes something continuous and everlasting.

My cheeks feel damp when finally, reluctantly, we slow, eventually standing there, still gazing into each other's eyes. His hand lets go of mine, his fingers brushing my tears away.

"You and I are the stuff that dreams are made of, my darling," he tells me, his voice strong yet there's a rasp to it, too. "We are what the stars envy, what the moon longs for, and what the legends of old tell tales of. Our love is more than this world, Lilly. More than a piece of paper with a new surname. And it will remain long after we are gone from the earth."

A choked sob falls from my lips, and I feel them tremble against his as he kisses me with a tenderness that makes the tears fall faster down my cheeks. He worships me with his kiss, his lips parting mine reverently, his tongue caressing the seam until I let him in. His hands cup my cheeks, holding me like the most precious gem as he fills me up with his love, making me taste the truth of his declaration.

My lips chase his when he ends the embrace, placing a tender kiss on my forehead, before taking a step back.

"One Knight left, darling."

Giving him what must be a very watery smile, I turn, my heart leaping and breath catching to see Ash standing behind me. He looks sinfully handsome, the grey of his suit matching his eyes to perfection, tailored to his incredible body beautifully. His ink peeks out at his neck and wrists, tantalising as it hints at what's underneath.

There's a devilish smile on his lush lips as he stalks towards me, all elegant grace with a touch of restrained destruction. He stops just in front of me, our chests just brushing, and I have to tip my head up to look into those grey orbs. *Cuntbucket.*

"Did you enjoy your first dances, Mrs. Vanderbilt?" he questions, his brow arched arrogantly.

"Immensely, husband," I sass back, noticing the glint of possession in his eyes when I call him that. I feel his hand reach around my waist, his palm warming the skin underneath my dress.

"It's about time that the bride and groom had their first dance, don't you think, wife?"

"I dunno," I can't help but tease, loving the flare of annoyance that flashes in his gaze. "You've got a lot to live up to after their performances, don't you think?" I repeat his own question back to him, and his smile turns positively evil.

He gives a small nod, not taking his eyes off me, and a piano starts to play the opening notes of *Young and Beautiful* by Lana Del Ray. My gaze goes wide as the singer starts to sing, and I twist to face the stage, seeing Lana Del Fucking Ray standing there in a beautiful gown, singing into an old fashion microphone as a miniature orchestra plays behind her.

"Shall we?" Ash asks, his voice full of smug amusement, and I face him once more, unable to say anything. "Not like you to be speechless, *wife*."

He pulls my compliant, still shocked body into his, one hand on the back of my waist, the other holding mine in a classical hold, and begins to waltz me around the floor. Years of dancing has my body moving on autopilot as I no doubt gape like a fish.

"T-that's..." I trail off, unable to finish my sentence.

"Lana Del Rey? One of your favourite artists?" he asks, full on smiling now, which doesn't help my short circuited brain. "I know."

"H-how?" I croak out, stealing a glance at the stage as we spin past.

"I have my ways, Princess," he replies, still sounding entirely too pleased with himself. I mean, he should be, so I can't hold it against him really. His face softens. "And I wanted to make today special for you."

"Ash, marrying you is special enough," I assure him, following his lead as he spins us. "You are an amazing man, and I'm proud to be your wife."

The smile he gives me after the words leave my lips would leave the sun in shadow. His hand tightens on my waist, drawing me in closer until our bodies are flush and I can feel his heat warming the front of me.

"Fuck, Lilly. I still can't believe that you're mine, let alone that you are now my wife," he tells me, and the look of slight disbelief on his usually assured face makes my chest tight.

"I still can't believe that you, all of you, are mine," I confess quietly. But he hears me, a fierce intensity entering his gaze.

"Forever, Princess. We will always be yours," he tells me, his deep voice strong and with no hint of hesitation. "We will always love you. Always be by your side, no matter what."

Tears well in my eyes again, and I blink furiously, whilst at the same time feeling a weightlessness in my limbs at his words. The song comes to a close, and Ash brings us to a sweeping stop, dipping me like a fairytale princess and kissing me like Prince Charming would. You know, if that pansy wasn't afraid to use tongue and make his princess all hot and wet for him.

My hands grip his lapels, uncaring if I crease them as I pull him closer, deepening the kiss until he growls and pulls me back upright, abruptly ending the kiss.

"Keep that up, wife, and the guests will get more of a show than they have already," he rumbles out, and I'm sorely tempted to take him up on that offer, but decide to save it for later.

After all, isn't that what a wedding night is for?

CHAPTER THIRTY-SEVEN

LILLY

After that a DJ comes onto the stage, and Julian approaches, all feline grace and wicked intentions.

"A dance with my beautiful new daughter-in-law," he says, but it's not a question, more like a demand.

"Lilly?" Ash asks, and my heart swells, my knees a little weak at the concern in his eyes. He'd refuse his father, for me, and I love him all the more for it.

"It's fine, Ash," I reply with a saccharine smile, and one of his brows lifts. "Can you ask the DJ to play Lilly's request, please?"

"Of course," he assures me, his tone still laced with confusion as he leans down to place a kiss on my cheek. "I hope that you know what you're doing, Princess," he whispers into my ear before pulling away. With one last scolding glance at his father, whose eyes are trained on me, he turns and heads to the stage.

Julian steps closer, pressing his body against mine in a move that makes me shudder, swallowing bile. He pulls me into a hold, one hand just above the swell of my arse, the other gripping my palm.

"Quite a show you've just given your guests, *daughter*," he purrs into my ear, and I clench my teeth when I feel something beginning to harden against my lower stomach. *Fucking hell! He's turned on by calling me daughter!*

The opening bars of an upbeat pop song starts playing, and Julian falters just as a wicked grin spreads my lips. I hear Loki's braying laughter as he recognises *Fuck You* by Lily Allen that's just started playing. You see, I asked the DJ in advance if, when I gave the request, he would play it, as I knew that Julian wouldn't be able to resist being his cuntish self and trying to assert his disgusting dominance over me.

Julian's grip becomes bruising, digging into my soft flesh, but I'm uncaring as I lean away from him so that I can look up into his face.

"What's wrong, Julian? Don't you like the song?"

His face is like granite, all hard lines and cold planes, his eyes silver fire as they try to burn me up. I can't resist poking the bear.

"I've had my lawyers look into Black Knight Corporation, and imagine my surprise to learn that I own more of your company than you do," I tell him, my smile genuine and wide. His nostrils flare, and I have to forcibly relax my jaw when his grip becomes painful.

His jaw clenches, his teeth grinding together as he continues staring into my eyes, our silent battle starting to be noticed.

"Didn't you want to dance? You wouldn't want to let your adoring public down now, would you? Where are they?" I tip my head to the side, looking around as if searching for them. I catch Ash's worried gaze, his brows lowered over grey eyes just as Julian bends to whisper in my ear.

"I see that you learn your lessons slowly, *daughter*." This time he practically spits the word out, and I can't stop flinching, seeing Ash start to head towards us. "Enjoy your honeymoon."

And with that, he drops his grip, turning and striding away from me, shoulders tense. I look after his retreating back, worrying my bottom lip.

"Princess? Are you okay?" Ash asks, suddenly at my side, the others surrounding me in a protective circle. I blink, turning my confused gaze to Ash's.

"He told me that I learn my lessons slowly, then wished me an enjoyable honeymoon," I tell him, watching his forehead crease, his hand coming up to my lower back, resting exactly where Julian's did.

"You don't go anywhere alone tonight, Baby Girl," Jax rumbles, grasping my cold hand in his large, warm one. My eyes lock onto his, the blue churning with worry.

"Hey," I say gently, stepping closer to him and cupping his face with my hand. "He was just being an arsegoblin." I'm rewarded with a quirk of Jax's lips, an almost smile.

"All the same, Pretty Girl," Loki adds, brushing my cheek with his fingers, until I'm lost in emeralds. "Stay with one of us for the rest of the night, yeah?"

I look at Kai.

"I agree, darling. I don't trust him or any of the board," he tells me, taking my other hand in his.

"Ash?" I question, not quite believing that it's as serious as they're making it out to be.

"Better safe than sorry, Princess." His hand rubs the spot that I know will have Julian's bruises, like he knows that his father has hurt me already tonight.

I shrug. "Okay, sure. Now can we just dance?"

I give a little wiggle of my hips, earning relieved smiles from all of them, though there is still a tightness around each of their eyes that causes unease to unfurl in my stomach.

A couple of hours later, I'm sitting with Loki, a pleasant tiredness settling over me as I watch Lex and Ryan on the dance floor, having a great time. Willow is up on stage with the DJ, looking like she might score tonight, and when she glances over to me, I raise my glass of pink lemonade in salute.

Jax is standing with his mother, who insisted on coming today even though he was adamant that she still needed to rest. I can see him hovering, her small hand in his large one, as she smiles and taps her foot to the beat of the song that's currently playing. Kai was called to his uncle's side, something about talking to some new tech developers that Black Knight has an interest in.

"Should we rescue Ash?" Loki murmurs in my ear, his long fingers pushing back the hair from my neck and sending electricity skittering across my skin.

I look over and chuckle to see Ash being hounded by some older couple, apparently some long distance relatives.

"Nah, I need a piss," I tell him, heaving myself to my feet and grateful that I took my heels off some hours ago, replacing them with simple ballet pumps.

"I love it when you talk dirty, baby," Loki groans, laughing when I whack his rainbow covered bicep.

We make our way to the exit of the marquee, posh portaloos having been set up outside and to one side, nestled in the trees and a path lit by strings of bare bulbs in rainbow colours. As we approach the doorway, someone steps up to Loki, and I see that it's his father, Chad.

"A word, son," he says, voice cold, and ignoring me completely.

"Just give me a minute," Loki replies, his voice just as devoid of warmth as his father's.

"Now, boy," Chad hisses, grabbing Loki's arm and halting his steps. Loki glares, his gaze scathing.

"It's okay, Loki. I'll just be a moment," I assure him, unable to wait any longer as the urge to empty my bladder becomes desperate. I hurry off, not able to wait for a reply, and rush to the loos, making it just in the nick of time.

After taking care of business, I wash up and head back outside to find a man, partly in shadow, waiting for me.

"Adrian?" I ask, squinting, then straightening up as the moon emerges from behind a cloud, highlighting his features. His grey suit is tailored to perfection, his black hair littered with more grey than when I saw him back in England.

"Lilly, congratulations," he replies, his voice smooth, and a little detached, his dark eyes locked onto mine. I mean, it has taken him all night to approach me, to congratulate me properly, and a fissure of anger runs through me at how this man, my only blood family, cares less than my chosen family.

"Thank you," I respond tightly, stepping to one side to pass him and head back to the party. He steps with me, and the anger that had been coiling in my stomach turns cold.

"I hate to do this here, today of all days, Lilly. But I've had news. About your mom," he tells me, stopping me dead as ice travels down my spine.

"About mum?" I repeat, taking a step closer to him. My heart races, and my palms sweat as his words sink in. "Have they found who did it?"

Before he answers, something sharp stings my neck, and my hand flies to the spot to bat the bug away. Only my hand doesn't make it all the way there, suddenly feeling too heavy to lift as my knees go weak.

"What the..." I trail off, my lips unable to form the rest of the sentence as my tongue grows heavy in my mouth.

My legs give out, and I hit the forest floor with a thud, unfeeling of the twigs and stones that poke my body. A dark shape leans down, a soft touch brushing my hair from my face, as words caress my ears.

"Enjoy your honeymoon."

I vaguely recall someone else tonight saying those exact words to me, but my brain is sluggish, and I can't seem to make the connection. The sounds of the music from the party fade, the bright lights of the marquee dimming, before everything goes black.

Need to know what happens next? Download Released to find out!

Want to keep up to date with all my news plus a whole load of spicy bonus content with all your favourite characters? Sign up for my newsletter HERE.

AUTHOR NOTE

I know, you're raging at me right now aren't you? I'm sorry, the story goes where it will and I have very little control over it (Honest!).

I can say that all will be settled in the final book. At least I hope that it will...

And one final note. Bound was actually quite difficult for me to write. Chapter Thirteen in particular as I wrote that literally days after my own mother had passed away. It took a lot to go back and reread it to do edits, in fact I couldn't do it for some weeks. But, it was also incredibly cathartic and I actually started writing in a bid to distract myself from my mother's battle with cancer. Now that is finally over, I'm left with something that has become precious to me; writing. So, it's a mixed blessing if ever there was one, but as I'm a firm believer in silver linings I'm taking this to be one of them.

ACKNOWLEDGMENTS

I wouldn't be here, writing all the extra bits for my SECOND FUCKING BOOK (I'm still a bit disbelieving that I have one let alone two books out!), without the help of many simply wonderful people.

My gorgeous alphas and betas who give me incredible feedback, help the story to grow and tell me there is never too much sex. You are all so appreciated and your comments are more precious than gold.

My wonderful editor Polly who literally gives me life with her comments! She makes these books shine and I honestly would be lost without her.

I'd also be totally lost without Julia, my wonderful PA who does so much more than she gets paid for!
 And my lovely Rosebuds and Darlings, my Arc readers and Street Team. You guys don't know how much you do giving me awesome reviews and recommending my books. I love you all!

And of course, my amazing husband who supports me in all that I do, and enjoys the benefits of being married to a steamy romance author (you all know what I'm talking about!). I genuinely wouldn't be where I am today, as a person, craftsperson or author without him.

ABOUT THE AUTHOR

About Rosa

Rosa Lee lives in a sleepy Wiltshire village, surrounded by the beautiful English countryside and the sound of British Army tanks firing in the background (it's worth the noise for the uniformed dads in the local supermarket and doing the school run!).

Rosa loves writing dark and delicious whychoose romance, and has so many ideas trying to burst out that she can often be found making a note of them as soon as one of her three womb monsters wakes her up. She believes in silver linings and fairytale endings...you know, where the villains claim the Princess for their own, tying her up and destroying the world for her.

If you'd like to know more, please check out Rosa's socials or visit
www.rosaleeauthor.com
Rosa's Captivating Roses
Linktree

ALSO BY ROSA LEE

Also by Rosa

HIGHGATE PREPARATORY ACADEMY

A dark whychoose romance

Hunted: A Highgate Preparatory Academy Prequel

Captured: Highgate Preparatory Academy, Book 1

Bound: Highgate Preparatory Academy, Book 2

Released: Highgate Preparatory Academy, Book 3

DEAD SOLDIERS VS TAILORS DUET

A dark whychoose enemies to lovers romance

Addicted to the Pain

Addicted to the Ruin

THE SHADOWMEN

A dark gang & mafia whychoose romance

Kissed by Shadows

Claimed by Shadows

Owned by Shadows

STANDALONES

A dark whychoose Lady and the Tramp(s) retelling

Tainted Saints

A dark whychoose stepbrother Cinderella retelling

Tarnished Embers

A dark whychoose mafia romance Co-written with Mallory Fox

A Night of Revelry and Envy

www.ingramcontent.com/pod-product-compliance
Lightning Source LLC
Chambersburg PA
CBHW030457060825
30593CB00039B/248